"Laughs, danger, and a cast of characters you'll die to hang out with, A Little Too Familiar has everything I want in a romance. Louise is intriguing and passionate, Declan is honorable and undeniably hot, and when you throw in Dammit, the phoenix, you have a recipe for one unputdownable story! Give me book two now!"

~Kristen Simmons, critically-acclaimed author of the *Article 5* series and *The Deceivers*

"A romp of a paranormal romance in the best possible way! Solid world building, a family you'd love to belong to, and a couple you root for the first page. I need the sequel, STAT!"

~Jeanette Battista, best-selling author of the *Moon* Series & *Books of Aerie* series

"Intricate world building, sexy and smart leads who can't live without each other, a diabolical villain you will delight in hating, vengeance pigeons, murder ferrets—all while sneaking in beautiful messages about the family of the heart. What more could you ask of a story?"

~Molly Harper, author of the *Half-Moon Hollow* & *Mystic Bayou* series

"Wildly inventive, thoroughly romantic, and cozily delightful, Lish McBride will leave you head over heels for this world and her characters."

~Gwenda Bond, *New York Times* bestselling author of *The Date from Hell*

"Full of charm, found family, adorable animals and the sweetest alpha ever, A Little Too Familiar is a wonderfully cozy delight. Here's to many more books in this series!"

~Stephanie Burgis, author of *Snowspelled* and *Scales and Sensibility*

"Big laughs and an even bigger heart, A Little Too Familiar gives the high-competence, low-angst romance you need right now."

~Chelsea Mueller, critically acclaimed author of the *Soul Charmer* series and *Prom House*

"Lish McBride's *A Little Too Familiar* is so much fun, but "fun" alone doesn't do this book justice. Lou and Declan's love story is told with warmth and compassion, has an amazing cast of characters, and more heart than any book I've read in a long time. All while making me laugh so hard it hurt. I couldn't ask for more."

~Jaime Lee Moyer

"As both a longtime Lish McBride fangirl and a romance author who has been banging the 'take big swings' drum for a few years now, I cannot express the depth of my glee that Lish has taken a big crack at the genre; her romantic debut is utterly hilarious, warm, romantic, and unlike anything you've read before. A Little Too Familiar is written with a wise and quirky pen, unique but also deeply relatable. A Little Too Familiar is a knock-it-out-of-the-park, magic on every page delight."

~Christina Lauren, *NYT* Bestselling authors of the *Unhoneymooners*

"There was a time when I read a lot of urban fantasy and then I didn't. I moved on, to Romance, mostly. Every once in a while, though, I still want the world-building that Urban Fantasy provides; the rich, immersive world that is *this close* to the world we live in, but with ✳magic.✳ I honestly didn't expect to get that same world-building in a Paranormal Romance, where the nature of the genre means that the characters and relationships must take center stage. Imagine my delighted surprise, then, when I read *A Little Too Familiar* and discovered within its pages the perfect blend of a fully-realized magical world and the emotional satisfaction and Happily Ever After necessary for a good Romance. There are also all of the snark and snappy dialogue and pop culture references that I have come to expect from Lish McBride. Plus food porn and adorable animals and found family and sexy sexytimes. I'm incredibly happy that this is the book that Lish needed to write during the pandemic, because it is exactly the book I needed to read. I'm really looking forward to spending more time in this world and with these characters and seeing all the HEAs to come."

~Billie Bloebaum, Bookseller & founder of Bookstore Romance Day

A

LITTLE TOO

FAMILIAR

by

LISH McBRIDE

Cover design & illustration: Jenny Zemanek
Book design: Vladimir Verano

print: 978-0-9984032-2-9

e-book: 978-0-9984032-3-6

Published in the United States by

Devo-Lish

Contact email: lishmcbride@gmail.com
lishmcbride.com

Please contact the publisher for Library of Congress Catalog Data

To everyone who kept the world spinning over the last few years—especially medical workers, teachers, scientists, delivery people, and food industry folks. You made it possible for me to stay safe and none of you got the respect or support you deserve. Thank you.

CHAPTER ONE

Lou

Mrs. Davis perched rigidly on one of the plastic chairs in the exam room, her large handbag taking up the other seat. The exam room walls were painted a soothing blue color, complemented by idyllic scenes of animals in nature. We'd brought a designer in specifically to make this room the visual equivalent of a cup of chamomile tea. And yet, the client appeared very unsoothed. She actually looked the opposite of soothed, like the faintest nudge would make her crack into several jagged pieces.

I nervously adjusted the little plastic badge that said *apprentice* on it as I tried to decide the best approach.

She held her hands, which were encased in high-heat-resistant gloves, out to me like an offering. I leaned over the exam table to get a better look at a puffball the color of flames nestled in her gloves. Oranges, reds, and a little tuft of yellow over bright obsidian eyes. The baby phoenix chirped at me, the note musical and clear, and my heart totally melted. How cute was he? Answer: *so fucking cute.*

Sometimes, I loved my job.

Other times, well…let's just say I wear scrubs for a reason.

The phoenix shook his fledgling feathers and sparks cascaded down. I spritzed the floor with more water just in case. Birds weren't always my favorite—pigeons, for example, could test anyone's patience. For having brains the size of a walnut, they had an astounding repertoire of dirty jokes. And nosy—you couldn't keep secrets from pigeons. But this little guy? I just wanted to squeeze all his cuteness into a cup and drink it.

Wait. Was that weird? It was probably weird. I needed to spend more time around people.

"Here." She pushed the fledging almost into my hands, even though I wasn't gloved yet.

Surprised, I sidestepped, trying to read her body language. Was she just desperate to hand off the fledgling? I would be the first to admit that I didn't always read humans well. Animals make sense. People...don't.

"I can't live like this." She leaned closer, brushing his feathers against my scrubs. I yelped, jumping back, smacking the fabric with my free hand. The stench of singed cotton filled my nose. Our clinic saw phoenix fledglings so rarely that I hadn't really been prepared when I'd entered the room. I was kicking myself for not grabbing one of our leather aprons. But I'd been so excited to check the little fella in—a baby phoenix!—that I practically sprinted into the room. There was no way Dr. Larsen, or as I called her off the clock, Mama Ami, would miss the singe mark, either.

I had a "your heart is in a good place, but you need to slow down and consider consequences" speech coming my way, which was a classic I'd heard many times before. But come on—*baby phoenix.*

The woman was being careful to keep the sparks from touching her own slacks, which was good, because though I may not know designers or labels, they looked expensive.

I set my spritzer on the exam table, trying to decide how to respond while simultaneously attempting to feel out the situation. You don't just find a baby phoenix in your sink one morning. Phoenix parents were fiercely protective, nurturing their young for the first few months. That was a good thing, because fledglings couldn't control their flames very well. Hence her thick leather gloves and my squirt bottle. If she'd had an adult phoenix, neither would be necessary.

Or if they were bonded, which was where I came in. Or at least, where I wanted to come in, once I was able to finally remove the apprentice badge from my scrubs.

I closed my eyes for a second so I could concentrate on my magic. There was no familiar bond between the client and the fledgling. Maybe something had happened to the parent? It was possible she had found the baby and brought it in, hoping we could bond them quickly. That would be safer for everyone involved.

"I admit he's a little more...." I struggled for a polite euphemism, because I've never really gotten the hang of that sort of thing. But I was *trying.* "Your prospective familiar is a little more temperamental than most, but the trade-offs—"

"I don't want a familiar." She scrunched her nose at the baby phoenix. "I came by him on accident and now I don't know what to do. He almost burnt down my breakfast nook. He eats salamanders—the real ones, the tiny flame lizards? Do you have any idea how hard it is to store food that burns?"

Since it was part of my job, of course I did, but I knew from experience that stressed-out clients don't want to hear "I know." They want to feel heard.

So I made my sympathetic noises. I'm good at sympathetic noises.

It was much easier to make those than lie politely. Animals don't lie. Except for cats. Cats do what they want. But my mentor, Dr. Larsen, was very clear on the topic of cats—respect them for who they are, but don't *be* one.

I needed to think like a golden retriever. Sweet, affectionate, and helpful. The client had an animal she wasn't prepared to care for. It happened, and it was a situation I knew how to solve. Besides, it wouldn't be difficult to rehome the bird, they were highly sought-after. The fledgling chirped, and if it was at all possible, I melted again. Rehoming would need to be done carefully, because it would be hard on the phoenix. Like a lot of avians, they imprinted, and as far as he was concerned, the woman holding him was mama.

I reached out with my magic, making sure to inject soothing warmth into my mental voice. *Hello, little one. What's your name?*

The phoenix perked up, proudly ruffling its baby feathers, making him look like a little fluff-ball of fire. As he got older, he'd shift into a mix of blues and purples, only staying red on the edges. *I am called Dammit.*

I blinked, looking up at the woman, struggling for a second to remember her name. Davis. "Mrs. Davis, did you name the fledgling?"

"It's *Ms.*, and no." She held him over the exam table. "I didn't want either of us to get attached."

Which meant he'd probably picked up his name from her yelling things like, "Damn it, don't roost on the sofa!" I couldn't hold Ms. Davis too accountable for that. If you weren't prepared for a baby phoenix, raising them was difficult. Naming him, though, caused some problems. He would be more attached. Maybe he didn't need to be rehomed. I could feel out the situation, see if she just needed some support to help her keep him.

I dug through the drawer, pulling out a pair of my own heat-resistant gloves, cooing at Dammit. "How did you end up with him?"

Ms. Davis quickly dumped Dammit into my waiting hands. She shifted away, mumbling something as she tugged at the fingers of her gloves, deftly removing them.

"I'm sorry, I didn't catch that." Cradling Dammit, I placed him on the metal scale.

Ms. Davis tucked her gloves into her bag, fussing with it for several seconds before resettling into her chair, her chin held high. "I thought he was a yoni egg."

I frowned, trying to jot down the bird's weight while scooping him up off the scale. He was a little underweight, but nothing worrisome yet. I searched my memory but came up dry—I'd never heard of a yoni. Which wasn't that strange. Lots of creatures out there, and I was still learning. "I'm afraid you lost me."

"They're eggs carved out of semiprecious stones, like jade. You stick them up your"—she dropped her voice, before looking down at her hands clasped in her lap—"you know."

I did *not* know, and I'm sure my face conveyed that. I tried to think of all the places you could stick an egg. It was a short list, and I wasn't sure it was a good one.

I stroked the bird, checking his eyes and beak. Despite being underweight, he looked healthy. His color was good, his eyes bright and alert. I decided to guess. "You stick them in your vagina?" Please let that be it. I mean, adults, do what you want with your bodies, but I personally had no desire to stick an egg up *anything*.

Unless it was a sex thing? Please let it be a sex thing. I was a lot more understanding about sex. The animal kingdom had given me a fairly broad interpretation of "sex," and as long as it was between consenting adults, I was all for it.

"Yes," she said, nodding, and it took me a second to remember she was responding to my vagina question. "It's supposed to strengthen your muscles and help you meditate."

I would find it really difficult to meditate with anything stuck up my vagina, but then I had a hard time meditating, period. "Phoenix eggs aren't cheap."

She shrugged. "I got it off Mage's List. Someone was selling it at decent price, and it was pretty."

There was so much to unpack there. How much were yoni eggs that a phoenix egg seemed cheap by comparison? Or had the seller not realized what they had? Was it listed as used? I really hoped she'd sanitized it, because you didn't want to introduce foreign bacteria into what my roommate Van referred to as "Fort Vajay." Van also sometimes referred to sex as "storming the gates."

Focus. I needed to focus. I was teetering dangerously close to judgmental cat thoughts now, which, while fun, weren't always helpful.

"I can see that. They're very pretty." And I could. Phoenix eggs were gorgeously jewel-toned.

She fidgeted with her hair, smoothing a few wisps that had escaped her ponytail. "I tried using it, but then it got hot. *Really hot.* I have to go to the doctor after this and make sure everything is okay down there." She shook her head. "I'm going to sue the person who put this up as a yoni egg." Ms. Davis grabbed her purse. "Are we done here? My doctor appointment is in thirty minutes and I want to leave time for traffic."

I blinked at her. "You're just going to leave? You know birds bond, right?" I lifted Dammit up. He chirped. *So cute.* "He thinks you're his mother. If you need help learning to care for him, we have some literature—"

Ms. Davis scrunched her nose. "I already told you. I don't want a familiar."

Okay, back to my original plan—rehoming. "I understand. We can help you find a good home for him. With my mentor's help, we can transition the bird over to his new owner in about a week if we really—"

"A week? Absolutely not." She scowled at me.

I looked down at the fledgling in my hands. But he was so *cute.* Dangerous, but cute. "We'd work around your schedule."

She shook her head, already turning away.

"You're not even going to say goodbye?" I lifted Dammit up. Surely she couldn't say no to—

"No, I'm not going to say goodbye! It's a bird!" She threw me another scowl over her shoulder. "It's not like they have real feelings, you know." She waved her hands at me and Dammit. "Bird!" She opened the door, muttering about "weird animal mages." As soon as Dammit saw she was leaving, he got agitated, flapping his tiny wings. My heart broke for the little guy.

I tried to stay calm. I *really* did. As my mentor was always telling me, humans were just as much the patient as the animals. The problem was that humans were absolute *shit* sometimes. Like right now. Animals might eat you for food, but they're not dicks about it. I was out the exam room door before I could stop myself, my hands cradling Dammit.

"Oh yeah? At least birds don't pay gobs of money to stick rocks up their vaginas! I hope he gave you blisters! Big blisters! And they're really uncomfortable!" I'd like to say it wasn't my finest moment, but let's be honest—I'd done worse.

Dammit screeched, and I was immediately filled with shame. My raised voice wasn't helping Dammit's panicked misery, which was evident to me with every feather rustle and squawk. *I'm so sorry, little buddy.*

"Get hexed!" Ms. Davis threw over her shoulder but didn't look back, just left the clinic as fast as her legs could carry her. The waiting room was dead silent, the human patients blinking owlishly at me while dragging their animals closer to them.

Well, shit. Handling the client? C minus. Caring for Dammit? B, at best. Representing the clinic? Fail, fail, fail.

"You're in so much trouble." Lainey clicked open a file on the computer. "In the meantime, I'm going to put her on the 'no return' list." Lainey was an apprentice like me, working under Dr. Larsen to become a fully licensed Switch, which in this case was not a sex thing but referred to an animal mage who specialized in pairing and bonding familiars to their human counterparts.

As part of our apprenticeship, we had to work reception as well as handle technician duties, because Ami Larsen believed that you should understand every aspect of how a clinic works. While Lainey and I were both great with the magic aspect of our jobs, Lainey was actually good with people, and I…shouted at them in reception about vagina blisters.

My shoulders sagged a little, causing Dammit to give me his own sympathetic noises. "Tell me she at least paid."

Lainey's grin was beatific. "She paid the exam cost up front—wanted to streamline her appointment. Our costs are covered." Lainey clicked her way into Ms. Davis's file, her brown eyes lighting up. "And now I'm marking her down for illegal dumping of a protected creature." She waved a hand at an imposing stack of paperwork. "She didn't fill out the forms." Lainey tsked. Lainey was the only person I knew whose "tsk" had ominous tones. Like most animal mages, she was fiercely protective of animals.

She could also wield bureaucracy like a finely honed blade.

Lainey cooed at Dammit, causing the little bird to fluff his feathers at her. A spark went up. She expertly moved her half-empty coffee mug to catch it. "I will bring paperwork down on her so fast, she won't know what hit her." Her voice was sweet as she said it. "I will make it rain. If she ever decides she wants a familiar, she won't get one. Dumping that poor baby bird like that."

She fussed over Dammit some more, making him perk up further. He ruffled his feathers, shifting some of them to flames, casting colored light against Lainey's warm brown skin. She laughed in delight. "How about you duck out and get us both a coffee—give Dr. Larsen some time to cool down before she tears a strip into you."

Dr. Larsen and her husband owned Family Familiar, and you'd think that I, as their somewhat adopted daughter, would get some leeway in these situations. You would be wrong. As far as Mama Ami was concerned, I was just as much her child as the ones she'd actually given birth to, and as such I would represent the family to the best of my ability. Which did not, to my knowledge, include me yelling at a customer about her vagina.

Lainey saved Ms. Davis's file with a few clicks. "Your treat, of course."

"I can't help but notice that I buy you a lot more coffee than you buy me."

She hummed. "Then you also can't help but notice that out of the two of us, you step in it more often."

I wanted to argue, but she was right. I sighed. "I will bring you things. Delicious things. I will shower pastry gifts down upon you. Thank you for having my back."

She nodded, taking her due. "Always."

I quickly pushed my way through the swinging doors that led back to the exam area, keeping an eye out for my boss. I set Dammit down briefly on one of the empty exam tables while I snagged the phoenix carrier off its rung. It was a lot like one you'd see for human children but made for babies who occasionally caught fire.

We had a crate that would work, but Dammit was already feeling vulnerable. He'd fare better if he was closer to me. Once he was safely clipped in, I stroked his head with my finger. *It's going to be okay, little fella.*

He chirped up at me, but it sounded forced. It probably made me a terrible person, but I suddenly wished that Ms. Davis not only had blisters the size of quarters, but that they got infected. I had no problem with someone handing over a creature they couldn't handle. We encouraged it. There's no shame in acknowledging that you weren't the best person to care for another creature. It was obvious that Ms. Davis wasn't a good fit for Dammit, but that didn't mean she had to be cruel.

Swanning off and avoiding her responsibility to Dammit was, in my mind, reprehensible.

Swanning off so that I could briefly avoid my own responsibility, Dammit in tow, probably wasn't much better, but it at least involved coffee. If I kept this up, there was no way Mama Ami was *ever* going to graduate me out of my apprenticeship. The thought made me a little panicky, but I buried it deep, concentrating on the little life cradled to my chest.

CHAPTER TWO

Declan

I zipped up my duffel bag, the dry hiss of the zipper a strangely final sound.

"Is that it, then?" Zoey's voice was scratchy, the skin around her eyes red and puffy, making the blue of her irises almost glow. Zoey had dressed for comfort today. Her jeans were fraying around the cuffs, and the shirt from her favorite comic shop had seen better days. She'd about walked the soles off her Chuck's.

My sister takes after her mother—pale, blonde, waifish, with a spine of steel. I didn't think I'd spent more than a few days apart from Zoey since she was born when I was five. For twenty-three years she'd been in my pocket, and even now I was tempted to take her with me. But she needed to stay. Her business was here, Sid was here, her *life* was here.

And I knew, deep in my heart, that if I wanted to stay part of her life, I needed to leave. At least for now.

Her eyes searched my face and I realized I hadn't answered her question. I nodded, my chest tight. A few boxes, a duffel bag, and a suitcase. My twenty-eight years hadn't amounted to much.

"You sure you don't want to take more? I know you paid for the furniture." Zoey pushed her blond bangs out of her eyes, telling me that she was frustrated with either me or the situation, likely both.

Because I was moving out of the apartment I had been sharing with my girlfriend for the last year. Ex. She was my *ex*-girlfriend. And as the ex-*boyfriend*, I'd decided to move out, because it would be decidedly awkward to share a place with her and not just because I would have to watch her date my little sister.

I made myself shrug. "Nowhere to put it, and honestly, I don't really want it." It was more Sidney's style than mine. She liked modern, sleek stuff, and I hadn't cared enough to argue with her. I hefted up the duffel bag and tossed it onto my small pile. I knew I shouldn't judge my life by my possessions, and I didn't, not really. But they seemed awfully symbolic of the rest of my life. *No job, no woman, no place to live. You have become the cliché of the lone wolf and possible inspiration for a country song.*

What I had left wouldn't even take up the back of my SUV. Then again, I wanted a fresh start. The less stuff, the fresher it would be—I knew that from experience. Keepsakes were there to help you remember, and that's the last thing I wanted right now. Sidney, being Sidney, had cut me a check for the furniture, as well as my part of the deposit for the lease.

"When will you come back?" Zoey sniffed, and I handed her a box of tissues from the coffee table. She blew her nose hard, the delicate skin starting to turn as red as her eyes. I knew how she felt. When I didn't answer right away, Zoey's eyes narrowed. "You are coming back, right?"

I scanned the room for anything I'd missed, my eyes settling on a framed photo of me with my arms around Zoey. I was grinning, holding her up in the air while she waved a piece of paper over my head. That paper was a lease, and the building behind us, Zoey's brewery. She called it ours, but I knew the truth. Without Zoey, the Wulver Craft Brewery wouldn't exist. I lacked Zoey's passion as well as her skills—there were many reasons she was one of the youngest in her field, while I was just backup, filling in wherever I was needed.

And without Sid, the financial and marketing genius of our trio, it wouldn't have stayed afloat. I was the one most comfortable chatting with customers and talking up the beer. That had been easy—despite everything, I still felt a wash of pride over what Zoey and Sid had created. It hurt a little to know that everything would tick along just fine without me, but that was the truth. They loved me, but they didn't need me.

"Your silence is starting to scare me, Dec." Zoey crossed her arms and peered up at me.

"I don't know, Zoey." I caught her panicked look and pulled her into a hug. She fit easily—I'd always been the giant to her tiny dynamo. "It's not like that. I'm not—we're not—" Frustrated at the logjam of words in my throat, I rested my chin on the top of her head and closed my eyes, just holding her for a moment. Then I took a deep, steadying breath and held her out so I could look into her eyes. "It's not a punishment, Zo. You'll always be my sister. Nothing you could ever do would change that."

She looked at her feet, swallowed, and looked up. "Even stealing your girlfriend?"

"You need to stop saying that." I'd told her it wasn't true. You can't steal a person. A person chooses to go. Simple. Painful, but simple. "I'm not taking off in a huff. You and Sidney? I'm not mad, got it?"

Those bright blues bored into my own. "You're not?" She didn't sound convinced. I didn't blame her. Some days, I was barely convinced.

"Look, I'm not going to throw a parade or anything. I'm not going to deny that I'm hurt." Mostly because Zoey wouldn't believe the lie. If I could have gotten away with it, I would have pretended to be happy. Zoey was doing a bang-up job guilting herself to death—I didn't need to add. Because really, it was no one's fault. Or maybe it was everyone's. Whatever it was, we shared it equally, like we'd shared everything else.

"But you and me? We're going to get through this, Zo. I want—" My voice betrayed me and cracked, and I had to take a deep breath and start over. "I want you and Sid to be happy, okay? I really do. It's just to get there, I think we all need a little break from each other. You guys need to build on what you've started, and I need to sort my shit out away from that."

"But we're pack." She looked up into my eyes and I almost caved. I'd never been able to say no to Zoey. The only thing that kept me from agreeing was the knowledge that this was better for all of us. It had been just us for so long. After we'd escaped our father's pack, after our little brother and sister were taken away, we'd become a tiny pack of two.

I butted my forehead against hers. "You're starting your own pack now, you and Sid. I need to get out of the way of that. But I'll always be here for you, you know that, right?"

"Promise?"

I kissed her forehead. "Promise." My heart felt both full and breaking at the same damn time.

She sighed, leaning away and giving her cheek a half-hearted swipe with the cuff of her sleeve. "You can hate me, you know. Not forever or anything, but for a while. I know I would in your spot."

And I had been angry—for about two days. I'd gone into the woods, shifted into my wolf form, and run until my feet were sore. The anger had burned itself out, hot and quick, mostly because the wolf sees things very clearly. Wolves are sensible creatures, and mine explained that I wasn't hurting because I wanted to keep Sidney. I was hurting because it hurts to lose someone. She wasn't my mate, and I needed to let her go.

Knowing that didn't lighten the sting of it, but it helped me determine how I wanted to handle things. I had a choice—choose my pain and wound my sister or choose the path that would help us all get over it. That made it very simple. "You guys didn't do it on purpose. No one decides to fall in love. It just happens."

Zoey rubbed a hand over her sternum. "Intentional or not, it was still a dick move."

I laughed. "Well, you two dicks take care of each other, okay?" I picked up the framed photo of me and Zoey, tucking it into my bag. Just because it hurt right now didn't mean I wouldn't want to look at it later.

"Yeah, well, you better make sure your dick takes care of you, too." She frowned. "I was implying that Trick should take care of you, but wow did that joke sound better in my head."

"Fuck, I hope so." I picked up my duffel.

"It makes me feel a little better, knowing that you're staying with him." Zoey picked up one of my boxes. "Trick will take care of you. He's a good egg."

"I just hope his roommates aren't assholes." I hadn't lived in a house full of people in years.

We walked down the steps from the apartment, making our way to my banged-up SUV in the lot.

"How many people again?"

I hit the fob, unlocking the doors. "In the main house, it's Trick, and then two dudes named Van and Lou. Don't really know much about them. Then downstairs there's a separate mother-in-law daylight basement set up. Van's sister Juliet lives there with her little girl—I forget her name."

"Been a while since you lived with a kid."

I tossed the duffel bag into the back seat. "Won't quite be living with her. Separate entrance. Trick said Juliet brings the kid up sometimes, but you can tell he adores the shit out of her, so I'm not worried about a hellspawn in the basement." Zoey was right—it had been a while since I'd lived with kids, but with my upbringing, I'd been around them all the time. As one of the oldest, I'd had to help out. I hadn't really thought about it, but I'd missed having a few of them around. I opened up the back hatch for Zoey.

"So basically, house full of dudes?" She slid the box in gently.

"Yup." And to be honest, I was looking forward to it. I'd never had any issue with women. Women were awesome. But after this thing with Zoey and Sid? I could use a little break. I'd never been the kind of guy who felt he needed man time or some bullshit, but maybe it would be a good thing?

"So, like a frat house?"

I laughed, slamming the hatch shut before we made our way back up to the apartment. "Can you imagine Trick living in a frat house?"

Zoey pursed her lips, then shook her head. "Nope. Just…nope. Even if Trick didn't give off heavy goth vibes, I've seen him in a Snuggie watching *Star Trek* and drinking hot chocolate. My imagination is pretty good, but picturing Trick in a frat house is a stretch."

We got the last of my stuff out of the apartment and down the stairs to the car.

"But you don't know anything about Van or Lou?"

I shook my head. "Nope."

"Well, based on Trick, it doesn't sound like you're moving into the testosterone jungle."

I shrugged. Maybe not, but I was ready for it. I needed it—a big change.

Once I got everything situated in the SUV, I pulled Zoey in for a final hug.

"Call me when you get to Seattle, okay?"

I gave her another squeeze.

"I mean it, Dec. I know you need a break, but at least let me know you arrived in one piece."

"I promise to check in when I get there, and give you proof of life at least once a week. Okay?" When I caught her eyes, she looked lost. "I'm not going to the moon, Zo. Seattle is what, three, maybe four hours away from Portland? Once things calm down, you can catch the train up." Zoey didn't own a car, but Sid did. I took a deep breath. "Or Sid can drive you up. We'll… we'll figure it out." She was my sister. And while I firmly believed a break would do us both good, it wouldn't be forever. We would both make sure we worked through it.

She fidgeted with the hem of her shirt. "The brewery…."

"If they can't spare you for a few days, I'll come down." I loosened my hold, letting my sister go. "When I'm ready. When we're ready. I… We'll make a day of it."

She brightened. "Okay. Deal." Zoey popped up onto her toes and kissed my cheek. I took the opportunity to draw in the scent of her, mentally wrapping it around myself like a security blanket. Zoey had been home for so long. What would I do without her?

She pulled away. "I'm going to go up so you don't see me getting all smoopy."

I laughed, though it sounded brittle around the edges. "Yes, being smoopy is the enemy. We are wolves. We must be fierce at all times."

She gave me a little push, and I climbed into the SUV, watching Zoey in the rear-view mirror until she was back into my apartment building. I sat in the seat for a moment. It wasn't my apartment building—not anymore. Everything that was mine was in the car. It still hurt, but it also felt good. I was ready. A whole new life awaited me. I turned the key, and the engine rumbled to life. Then I popped the brake and hit the gas.

Seattle, here I come.

CHAPTER THREE

Lou

I walked to Wicked Brews, the closest—and luckily best—potionary in town. Just down the block from Family Familiar, Wicked Brews fit perfectly in Briar Creek, a trendy neighborhood in the north end of Seattle. It was barely still in the city, perching on the edge between a traditionally human district and the place where the magic users lived. Even after a century and a half of being in the open, the Uncanny still made some humans nervous.

The invention of the camera pretty much did us in. Magic users showed up funny in the first photographs. Turns out you can see our auras. Imagine expecting a sepia-tinted photo with stiff-looking people and getting a wash of color instead. Digital cameras don't have the same issue, but I've seen some of the old photos online and they're pretty wild.

I mean, the writing was on the wall, anyway. Humanity was everywhere, the wild places smaller. We simply had fewer places to hide. Some Uncanny blended better with humanity than others. Witches like me, for example. Others, like Dammit, not so much.

I thought it was all for the best, but not everyone agreed. Still, you'd think everyone would be used to it by now.

The bell above the door tinkled as I swung it open, the scent of coffee wafting out into the spring air. I held the door, earning me a smile from the elderly Hind walking through, one hand full of a cardboard tray of drinks, the other clutching the hand of a little Fawn chattering away next to her. From the smear of icing down the front of her pink T-shirt, the Fawn had already had a treat. She was young enough that she still had spots on her deer-like lower half, but my guess was they would fade soon enough. The older Hind smiled indulgently down at her as they clopped into the street. Dammit chirped drowsily from his carrier and the little Fawn glanced back at me. I gave a little wave before ducking into the potionary.

Wicked Brews got a mix of clientele, everything from witches to shifters and human tourists, hoping to get a glimpse of how the other half lived. It was a good neighborhood, the cafe nicely situated in a complex of other small local shops. Bay, my brother, had a shop next door called Ritual Ink, which specialized in magic-infused tattooing and arcane piercing. The block also boasted a small bookshop, a barber, and a few restaurants. Family Familiar sat at the far end, making me feel very at home here.

I was a trifle biased towards Wicked Brews, since my roommate, Vanessa, worked there. But I loved its high open ceilings, the walls painted with warm earth tones, and a big stone fireplace at one end. There were wooden tables and chairs, but also big, overstuffed chairs scattered around for more casual gatherings. On the same wall as the fireplace a set of saloon doors opened and took you into the attached pub, because let's face it, alcohol could be magic when used properly.

When I walked in, Van was stocking one of the glass pastry cases, her gloved hands carefully arranging them on the small silver trays. Inside were an assortment of consumables—many of them actually quite disgusting, but packing a magical wallop worth the horse sweat aftertaste.

Magical edibles came in a lot of varieties, but when it came down to it, they were medicine. You didn't want medicine to look like candy. But Van's bosses had a whimsical bent—the edibles looked like acorns, grass-green bars, or a pressed block of what looked like flower petals. Pretty, but not necessarily delicious. Which was good, because that would be false advertising. The last edible I'd had tasted like grass clippings and talcum powder.

The other case was already full of muffins and scones for people who just wanted a snack. I spotted the cinnamon rolls that had probably given the young Fawn that smear of icing. Dammit chirruped, and I smiled. *No cinnamon rolls for you, little one.*

They kept the tinctures, potions, and other liquid medicinals safely behind the counter under the little framed piece of paper that distinguished Wicked Brews as more than a coffee shop. The license proclaimed that Thea and Emma were accredited and bonded hedge witches and as such were legally allowed to sell the heady and potent potions they brewed.

The potionary was currently experiencing a rare lull between rushes, my roommate Trick the only customer besides myself. Noah, one of the baristas, was behind the counter stocking the milks. I liked Noah—he picked up shifts to work around his classes at Seattle Uncanny University, and besides Van, was one of my favorite baristas at Wicked Brews. I didn't spot the shop's owners, Thea and her wife, Emma, so they were probably in the back crafting their magical wares.

Van and Trick were using this lull to bicker like siblings. Trick sat in his usual place, the set of overstuffed chairs close enough to the espresso machine that Van didn't have to shout at him. I took the empty one across from him, a low, square wooden coffee table between us.

"How could you possibly know if he was a cuddler?" Trick's tight-lipped grin was bemused as he watched Van shove a carafe into place before hitting the switch to start the drip coffee. "Have you gained a new magic power? The ability to assess people's post-sexytimes activities with a single glance?"

"Look, I've become very adept at these things," Van said, blowing her dark bangs out of her eyes. She'd pulled the rest of her hair back into a ponytail. "If I'd stayed, he'd want to spoon. He was a 'stay the night' kind of guy, which would have led to an awkward conversation over half a grapefruit in the morning. Not interested." She shook her head as she filled the milk pitcher, the movement showing off some of the brightly inked tattoos that peeked out of shirt sleeves on her upper arms. "I'm not against cuddling in theory, but it can be difficult for me to sleep with someone wrapped around me like a sticky vine."

"How do you even know what he was going to have for breakfast?" I asked, shifting the carrier strapped to me so I could sit more comfortably. I gasped, pretending to be scandalized. "Did you stop making out long enough to go through his fridge? Dig through his pantry? Paw through his fruit bowl?" I didn't need to ask about the sleep cuddling thing. Van didn't trust easily. You're very vulnerable when you sleep, and the list of people Van would let sleep in her vicinity was short.

Van waved my question off with one hand, the universal gesture for *I just know.*

Trick looked skeptical. "I don't think you can gauge cuddle factor ahead of time. Some people are surprise snugglers. And maybe he was a secret chef and would have made you epic french toast. You love french toast."

Van flipped on the grinder next to the espresso machine, so she had to raise her voice. "He wanted to be my grapefruit spoon!"

Trick made an amused noise before flopping sideways in his chair, his eyes closed, waiting for Van to make his coffee. The upside of working in a potionary that also served coffee—because let's face it, coffee was magic, too—was free coffee. The downside was roommates constantly dropping in to bug you while you made coffee and using that time to dissect your life choices. We did so lovingly, and would butt out if Van expressly told us to do so…which she would never do, because then she couldn't critique *our* life choices. So she was going to hear it regardless, but if she didn't work at Wicked Brews, she would've only had us annoying her at home.

Silence returned as she switched the grinder off and filled the portafilter before tamping down the espresso shot.

I examined Van's expression. She didn't look irritated with Trick, but sometimes even loving bickering could grate. I nudged Trick's foot with mine, mouthing *Be nice.*

Trick gave me a slight nod, clearing his throat. "At least he didn't want to be your soup spoon. That would have made shit weird." Trick settled further into his flop, looking like something the Industrial Goth Fairy dragged into the shop in a fit of whimsy.

If I stepped close to him right now, I would catch the fire and chemical scent he usually had from work. Trick was an elementist, meaning his magic worked with natural elements. Some elementists specialized in water, earth, air, or wood. Trick's element was fire, which he used mostly for metal working and crafting the finest ceremonial daggers I'd ever seen. The high-end ones cost a pretty penny, but Trick took the same time and care creating cheaper, more utilitarian versions as well. Just because you had less money didn't mean you shouldn't have quality.

He was also an amateur circus performer, usually performing for fundraisers and charity. He could juggle fire and do aerial work, and had the nicest abs I'd ever seen outside of a magazine or television. Trick was glib, sarcastic, and wore all black, but he was also the kind of friend that would give you the shirt off his back.

He would just annoy you while he did it.

"Soup spoon," he repeated, dragging it out.

"You heavily implied the grapefruit spoon was weird—how is soup spoon less weird?" Van asked.

"I actually know people who own soup spoons. Do you know anyone who owns a grapefruit spoon?" Trick scoffed. "I think not."

"The nice thing about this discussion is that you're both weird," I said, wrapping my arms around the carrier. "It's why we're friends. Also, you're both getting grapefruit spoons for your birthdays. I just decided."

Van popped the portafilter into place and hit the button, waiting for the shot to pour. Trick liked two ristretto shots, nothing added, in a dainty demitasse cup. It made him feel like a giant, which, since Trick was on the shorter side and slender, wasn't very difficult to do.

I stuck to drip coffee or flavored drinks, as straight espresso made me draw back and hiss like some sort of lizard. Van came around the counter and handed the cup off to Trick, then licked her thumb and brushed it under his eye.

Trick drew back, horrified. "Did you just mama bird me?"

"Your eyeliner was smeared!" Van scowled, but there was no actual heat in it.

"Mama bird is when they chew up food and spit it into your mouth," I said helpfully. I was nothing if not a helper. "So no, she did not just mama bird you."

"Please don't ever do that." Trick sipped his espresso, his eyes closing again, this time in bliss.

"I can't promise you that," Van said, grabbing paper towels and glass cleaner for the display case.

"Why can't you promise?" Trick asked.

Van sprayed the case, quickly wiping away small handprints. "Who knows what horrors tomorrow will bring?"

"Mother hen," I said, still stuck on birds. "I think that's the phrase you were looking for."

"Just once I'd like to see you do your walk of shame in the morning," Trick said, trying in vain to drag us back on topic. "Like either the sex or the person was so amazing that you had to stay." He tipped his cup back, draining it, before holding it out to Van for a refill. "I love you both, and I despair that the dating scene is so abysmal. You deserve better. Little Lou came home early from her last two dates."

"Didn't even make it through the appetizers," I said, brightly enough that Dammit stirred. "To be fair, the second one was kind of my fault. I got into an argument with a pigeon in front of the restaurant. It was basically over after that." Though my date had only heard my half of the argument, he'd been embarrassed by the whole thing. I couldn't entirely blame him, but this was why I had "animal mage" on my FuCupid profile.

"Besides, a walk of shame implies that there is shame involved. Van doesn't have any." I handed his cup back to Van. "And stop calling me little. I'm perfectly proportioned. The rest of humanity is just freakishly tall."

"I have nothing to be ashamed of," Van said, hitting the grinders again, this time turning on both the regular espresso and the decaf. "Sex is a perfectly natural act."

"Birds do it. Bees do it. Even monkeys in the trees do it—trust me, I wrote a paper on it." And I got an A on that paper, thank you very much.

Trick ignored me, instead focusing on Van. "Surely that comment didn't deserve decaf treatment?" Trick asked in only somewhat mock-horror. "Any sex shaming was unintentional. You know that."

Van shook her head. "No, it's a split shot. You get mean somewhere after the third shot, so I've decided this is a good compromise. I do this out of love, not punishment."

"I can go elsewhere," Trick huffed, and we all knew he was bluffing. Trick liked Van's coffee and wouldn't play espresso roulette with another barista.

"You wouldn't dare," Van said, placing Trick's cup on the pick-up counter for him so she could make my coffee. I never ordered and Van never asked, but she somehow always knew what to make me. It wasn't magic—Van just knew me well and was an excellent barista.

"He wouldn't," I confirmed, watching Trick march glumly up to take his coffee. He sighed, but also leaned over the counter to kiss Van on the cheek. "But if he did, that's fine. Then he would be mean somewhere else and not your problem."

Trick drank his espresso without protest, waiting at the counter until mine was done so he could fetch it for me. When he handed me my cup I took a grateful sip—butterscotch latte. I guess Van thought I needed the sweetening today, which I kind of did.

I'm glad I got my coffee when I did, because after that the bell over the door tinkled, and kept on tinkling. The next rush had arrived. Van strode quickly to the swinging door separating the back from the front. "Hey, we need you. The gates of the underworld have opened and coughed up its brethren."

The other barista, Noah, hurried through the doors. "The customers can hear you, you know."

Van returned to the espresso machine, shrugging. Then she brightened at the sight of Jim coming through the doors, turning his broad shoulders to make it into the shop. He also had to duck. Jim was a minotaur, mostly human in appearance, though his head and chest had a lot in common with a highland steer. They were built on bigger lines than humans, and had horns to boot, so ducking through doorways was an old pastime for Jim.

"Sorry, Jim," Van said, taking his reusable cup and giving it a good rinse before she started his drink. "I should have had both doors propped open for you."

Jim handed her a glass container, which Van filled up with his regular order of edibles. She waggled one of the toffee-colored squares, her eyebrows raised. Jim sighed and took it, popping it into his mouth. He winced at the taste, giving his whole body a shake, like a dog after a bath. When the shudder stopped, Jim's fur, horns, and hooved feet were gone. He was still big and bullish in his features, but in a human way.

"That looks so uncomfortable," I said, sipping my coffee and sitting companionably with Trick. Dammit had fallen asleep in the carrier.

Jim looked over at me and smiled. As a favorite regular, Van had adopted him as a friend, which in our group means we shared him now and would cut anyone who looked at him twice. "Hey, Lou. Didn't see you there." He held up his order. "It's not my favorite thing, but I'm on my way to meet with a human client, and I get more work looking this way than not." Jim was a contractor, and having the strength of the minotaur served him well, but I guess it didn't stop people from being prejudiced. I glanced up at the clock, an eyebrow raised. Midmorning was late for Jim to be starting work.

He laughed. "My client this morning was a Sea Hag, and neither of us felt bothered to change." He brought his order over and dropped a kiss on top of my head and then Trick's. He peeked into my carrier. "What you got today?"

Trick and Van were fairly used to me walking around with some critter or another, and so hadn't asked about the carrier yet—which was either a feat of patience or a lack of caffeine. But they both knew that I would show the critter off when I was ready.

"A present for Trick, actually." I whistled at Dammit. "At least, I hope so." The fledgling peeked out sleepily at Trick.

Trick's brown eyes lit up at the sight. "Really?"

"You've been thinking of getting a familiar for work, and this one was almost literally thrown into my lap this morning."

Trick set down his cup and held out his hand, stopping briefly to ask, "May I?"

I unclipped the harness so the front panel eased open. Trick scooped Dammit up with a cooing noise. The bonus of being an elementist that specialized in fire? You can cradle a baby phoenix in your bare hands. The rest of us got to wear giant mitts.

"Does it have a name?" Trick stroked the bird, his face lit up with pure joy.

"He, and currently he is going by the moniker 'Dammit.'"

"Someone dumped him?" Jim asked, smiling down at the little bird but staying back a safe distance. "What kind of person does that?"

"Preaching." I pointed at myself. "Choir." I sipped my coffee. "I'll tell you the whole story tonight. Van will want to hear it. I have to go back to work shortly, and I still need to grab coffee for Lainey." I tugged on Trick's shirt-sleeve. "If you're interested, and he agrees, we can start the bonding soon."

Trick blinked at me in surprise, cradling Dammit in his hands. "Of course I want him. He's perfect. You can do your woo-woo bonding thing with us later if he agrees. I'll think of new names in the interim." He helped me carefully tuck the fledgling back into the carrier.

Once Dammit was secured, I kissed Trick on the temple. "You're the best."

"I know." He looked up at Jim. "You coming by the house tonight? I'm streaming the new episode of *Mated by Fate*..." He raised his eyebrows.

Trick was somewhat obsessed with the dating reality show. I thought it was garbage, but it was really entertaining garbage, so I watched it with him when I was home.

The big minotaur shrugged. "Probably? Depends on how stabby I feel at the end of the day."

"We can accept your stabby and counter it with free beer," Trick said.

"Done." Jim waved at us and left, holding the door open for a herd of customers as he did.

I waited in line to say goodbye to Van, and to pick up some coffee and treats for Lainey and the rest of the staff at the clinic.

The lady in front of me dug in her purse for something. Noah stood patiently behind the till waiting for her, despite the growing line. That was probably why he was on the till. Noah was naturally good with customers, and when he smiled, he got a big dimple in his cheek. Van was less patient, and since they shared tips, it had been decided that it was best to have Noah handling the customers. He straightened his SUU T-shirt as he waited, which had bunched up because of his apron, the soft yellow of his shirt looking good against the deep brown of his skin. If I had worn that shirt, I would look sickly. Some pale people could pull off yellow. I wasn't one of them.

Van tipped her chin at me, her hands full with the milk she was steaming. "Did Trick remind you about the houseguest?"

It took me a minute to remember what she was talking about. The lady in front of me had just pulled a live snake out of her purse and set it on the counter. I watched it slither along the wood countertop. It wasn't poisonous—a garter snake, and not a terribly big one—but I wasn't sure if a snake would count as a health code violation. Noah tracked it with his gaze, but since he didn't reach for it yet, I assumed it was fine. Or maybe he wasn't comfortable grabbing snakes.

"Oh, right." Trick had a friend driving up from Portland to stay with us for awhile—we'd had a house meeting about it. Trick owned the house, and we all had an informal rental agreement with him, so technically he could do as he pleased. Despite that, all big decisions were handled as a team, because though it was Trick's house, we all considered it our home. I liked it because they were good roommates and the house had a cozy, family feel about it. You know, if you actually liked your family. Besides, there was no way any of us could afford our own place.

The customer finally handed Noah a small laminated card.

He stared at it blankly, then handed it to Van.

Van took the card and frowned at it. "What's this?"

"My order," the woman said, laying her hand out on the counter. The snake dutifully slithered up it. "I couldn't remember it all, so I typed it out."

Van stared at it. Then looked at the lady. Then went back to the card. Finally, she handed it back to the customer. "You realize that at 185 degrees, the milk will be burnt, right?"

"I want it to stay warm until I get to work," the woman said, tucking her card away.

Van waved a hand at a small display of insulated mugs. "Our mugs are on sale. If you want, I can make your order and put it in one of those." She grabbed a new container of milk out of the fridge.

The customer shook her head.

Van gave a little shrug that I translated as *it's your milk, and I'll burn it if you want me to.* She kept her smile tight-lipped and didn't say a word as she poured the nonfat and two percent into a metal pitcher in equal measure, before popping in the thermometer, which she never used. Van had been doing this so long, she could go by touch.

Noah popped his dimple at the customer, drawing her attention back to him. "One percent split-shot 185-degree no-foam latte with two packets of Equal." He was very polite, but then, the customer still had a snake wrapped around her arm. Van handed over her coffee and the woman dropped a few coins into the tip jar as she left.

"Did you see the snake?" I whispered to Van as I handed Noah my card to cover my order.

Van tapped the pitcher on the counter before giving it a swirl. "I think I was this close to getting hexed. Thank all the gods for Noah's dimple."

Noah snorted. "You keep relying on it like that and my dimple is going to take its own percentage of the tips."

Van tilted her head. "You know, I think it would be worth it?"

CHAPTER FOUR

Declan

Early afternoon light slanted through my windshield as I parked on the quiet neighborhood street that GPS claimed was my final destination. I'd taken my time driving up, stopping at a state park to shift into my wolf form and run for a while to burn off some energy. The park had been large enough for me to avoid other people—werewolves didn't become mindless, slavering beasts when we shifted, but not every person understood that. I stayed me when I changed, fully in control unless I chose to let the wolf take over, but he wouldn't hurt anyone.

It had felt good to run, and I'd come back to my SUV in good spirits, ready to hit the traffic outside of Tacoma. I'd wanted to be calm, my wolf quiet, when I did.

Two men herded a few small children down the sidewalk of Trick's street, but otherwise the neighborhood was quiet. I sat in my SUV, calling Zoey before I forgot, leaving her a message when she didn't answer telling her that I made it to Seattle okay. I loved my sister, but I felt a little relieved that she hadn't answered. This morning had left me both exhilarated at the idea of my new start and sad because of everything with my sister, so I felt a little wrung out. That done, I got out to stretch and check out my new home.

Trick lived in a gray Craftsman house with white accents and a front porch large enough to have rocking chairs on one side, a porch swing on the other. It was rather domestic and normal looking and not at all what I expected from Trick. It didn't look like it would spit out Gomez and Morticia Addams, for one thing. Maybe he planned on doing the goth transformation slowly as cash allowed. Trick made pretty good money as an elementist, but he wasn't exactly swimming in it.

For a second, I wondered if I'd written down the address wrong. Then I saw the grotesque door knocker and the doormat that said "Go Away" and figured I had the right place after all. I dropped my bag on the mat and was about to knock when the door swung open, revealing Trick and his big shit-eating grin.

"You're here! And you're bearded now, which is exactly what I expect from anyone coming up from Portland, but I'm going to hug you anyway."

I hugged Trick back, instantly enveloped in the smells of clove, coffee, and fire, scents that I enjoyed on their own, but also found comforting because I associated them with Trick. He was also one of the human guys I knew that could hug without doing that awkward back-pat thing. Wolves are very touchy. We hug and comfort with touch, and it's weird to watch humans go out of their way to avoid it. Humans were also pack animals, they just liked to pretend they weren't.

"You smell the same," I said, releasing my friend, feeling better than I had in days. I straightened up, smiling.

"Well, that's not creepy at all." Trick squinted at me. "What do I smell like?"

"Like morning goth—coffee, clove and smoke." In Trick's case, the smoke smell was complex—woodsmoke, but also coal, solvents, and hot steel. "Did you just come from work?"

He held the door wider for me. "Yeah, I knocked off early today so I could be here to welcome you." He cocked his head to the side. "What does evening goth smell like?"

"Coffee, clove, and ennui." I picked up my bag. "The ennui is there in the morning, but it takes all day for the smell to really set in."

"You're seeking revenge because of the beard comment, aren't you?"

"No, I plan on doing that later. When you least expect it." I wiped my feet on the mat and made my way in, leaving my bag in the entryway. "It's not like you don't have the exact same hipsters here as we do in Portland, you just like to make fun of Portland." I toed off my shoes. "It wasn't a big fashion choice, I just didn't feel much like shaving lately." I hadn't felt like doing much at all, really.

"You know, I for one am embracing it?" Trick propped his hands on his hips. "I'm not saying I go for the grizzled prospector look, but I'm all for some well-maintained beardage. It looks good on you." Trick pursed his lips, his face thoughtful. "You know, I take it all back. There's probably someone out there who can really work the grizzled prospector look. I'm going to keep an open mind on it."

I followed him as he led me into the living room. "You're a man of hidden depths."

Trick flipped me off without turning around. "I'm all about depth. And if you turn that into a 'that's what they said' joke, I'll…well, I'll probably laugh, to be honest."

I laughed, feeling light and happy. Being around Trick always made me feel better. He was just one of those people.

"Welcome to my evil lair." Trick waved vaguely at the house around him. I examined my new home and took comfort that while some things do change, they can change for the better. Though Trick's taste was the same, it had matured with him. He still had vintage monster movie posters hanging up in the living room, but he'd framed them instead of stapling them to the wall. A large, deep blue sectional anchored the room, a skull-print throw blanket draped over the back. The bookcases and dining room table were a nice cherry wood, and all together the aesthetic was stylish but comfortable and still one hundred percent Trick.

I waved a hand at a tall metal cage. "New decoration?"

Trick perked up. "I made that today, actually. Lou's bringing home my new familiar." He walked over to it. "I'm going to make another tomorrow for in here—this one's going in my room. Can you help me? It's not heavy, but it's awkward."

While I helped him get it situated in his bedroom, the wolf in me lifted its nose, pulling in scents. There were a lot in the house, and I was trying to parse them all. Many of them were animal scents, which was unusual. Before I could spend too much time on it, we'd moved our tour into the dining area and kitchen.

The kitchen had an open floor plan, with barstools pulled up to one side of the counter, the only thing separating it from the dining space. Several pictures done with finger painting and crayon were stuck on the fridge with magnets.

"This is a real nice place, Trick."

"Surprising, isn't it?

"A little bit."

"You're an asshole, and I missed you." Trick opened the fridge. "Well, the roommates bring my mortgage down nicely, making this place actually plausible financially." He held up a bottle. "Beer? I figured after the last couple of weeks and the drive up, you might want one. Or we have wine. I have a wine cellar, actually."

"By 'wine cellar,' do you mean a shelf full of Boone's Farm in the pantry?" I nodded a *yes* at the beer, noting with some satisfaction that it was a lager from Wulver Craft Brewery, even if the sight of it made my chest ache.

"Please. It's at least two shelves. And don't knock Boone's Farm. I have fond memories of it from my youth." Trick handed me the beer and grabbed a chilled pint glass out of the freezer.

"Fancy," I said, accepting the glass gratefully. The wolf inside me whined, trying to get my attention, but I put it off. It wasn't like we were in danger.

"We aren't total heathens, Dec." Trick grabbed another glass and a beer for himself.

I pulled up a barstool, catching sight of a framed photo on the wall. A little girl—maybe just a little over a year—sat on Santa's lap. It was clear from her flushed face and tear tracks that she'd been crying just seconds before, but now she was smiling tentatively.

Trick stood behind Santa, his arms spread, his face goofy. Three women were in the picture with them—a small woman was bent over and holding her sides, her blond hair obscuring half her face as she laughed her ass off. Next to her stood a taller woman with long dark hair and bangs, her sweater sleeves shoved up, revealing bright tattoos. Her expression mirrored Trick's, totally goofy.

On Santa's other side a short, curvy woman with auburn hair was caught midclap, smiling at the little girl. There was something so inviting about her face—I wasn't sure what it was, exactly. A kind of warmth. All I knew was that seeing her smile made me want to do the same. It was the kind of photo that made you happy even if you didn't know anyone in it—you could practically feel the love radiating from the image. The people in this photo, with the possible exception of the bemused Santa, loved each other.

My gaze went back to the curvy woman. Maybe I could get Trick to introduce us. When I was ready. Definitely not now.

"Ah yes, the infamous Santa photo." Trick leaned on the other side of the counter, his beer in hand. "I'm not sure we're going to do another. We can't top that one." He pursed his lips. "Unless we all dressed as Santa, too. That would be hilarious. I bet I could get Lou and Van on board for that. Not sure if I could get Jules to do it. Maybe a saucy elf, though."

I was still staring at the picture when Trick's words clicked in. Lou. Van. Jules.

Shit.

"These are your roommates, aren't they?" I asked the question though part of me—the part that's a real shithead—already knew the answer and was fucking *cackling* at me.

"Yeah, of course." Trick side-eyed me. "I told you about them."

"You never mentioned they were women."

Trick laughed. "Sure I have. It must have come up." He frowned. "I mean, I can't remember every conversation we've ever had, but it must have been apparent. They all identify with feminine pronouns, except for when Van wants to go by Zool." Trick crossed his arms and stared at the ceiling, thinking. "I can't honestly say I bring up whether or not my roommates have vaginas because that would be weird, but surely other contextual clues made it apparent."

I ran a hand over my face. "I never caught it. Possible I wasn't paying attention." I sucked a deep breath in through my nose. Now that I was really paying attention, the scent trails made it pretty obvious. *Was that what you were trying to tell me?* The wolf's whine turned into a huff. Whatever his point was, I still wasn't getting it.

Trick sipped his beer, his expression concerned. "Why is this a problem? You like women. Probably half of your roommates have been women and your best friend is your sister."

Until my last place, I'd always had roommates. It was difficult to live cheaply without them, and my upbringing hadn't soured me on communal living situations. I had no desire to live with dozens of people ever again, but I was very comfortable with a few roommates.

I didn't feel comfortable right now. "I was expecting men! Their names are Lou and Van, for fuck's sake!" I was yelling at my friend. Why was I yelling? A fine sheen of sweat broke out along my skin. My wolf was panting now, feeding off my stress. Oddly enough, telling myself there was no reason to *be* stressed didn't actually make me feel better.

Okay, deep breath in. Hold it. Count to seven. Let it out. Do it again.

"Yeah, Louise and Vanessa. Are you okay?" His face said that no matter my answer, he knew I wasn't.

I closed my eyes and took a few more deep breaths. Opened my eyes. Drank more of my beer. Manifested a grip on my fucking awful emotions so that rationality could raise its damn head again. "Sorry. I shouldn't have yelled. Of course I don't care." I waved a hand at the picture, intentionally keeping my voice soft. "Your roommates seem awesome." Calm, I needed calm. But my wolf was still whining. Something about the scents... I downed the rest of my beer.

Trick continued to stare at me before understanding dawned. "You were looking forward to living with a house of dudes for once, huh? Soak up the manliness." Trick started laughing uncontrollably, the sound almost coming from his toes. "What kind of manly dudes exactly were you expecting me to live with? Guys who like sportsball and only eat steak and wax poetic about..." Trick hiccupped. "I can't even finish that sentence. I don't know what manly dudes wax poetic about."

"I didn't need to steep in alpha male stereotypes," I muttered. "A little break sounded nice, though."

"Jim's probably coming over later. He follows a lot of masculine cultural norms. He builds stuff and wears flannel. We're going to watch a dating show, but he might also be into sports. There, see?"

I just stared at him. "How did this turn into a discussion about sports?"

Trick held his hands out in a helpless gesture. When I continued to stare at him, Trick gave my arm an awkward pat. "Hey. Don't worry. Van and Lou are the best. You'll see."

I raised my empty beer for a toast. "To the best, then." We clinked glasses, but I had a heavy feeling in my gut. It felt suspiciously like dread.

Which is when I heard the front door click open and shut, and two people talking softly.

Trick grinned. "Speak of the very devils."

Footsteps grew closer until one of the women from the photo stepped in—tall with dark hair, followed by the shorter one, the one that had made me smile. She peeked around her friend, our eyes met, and she gave me a smaller version of her photo smile.

"Declan, that's Van, and hiding behind her is Lou."

"I'm not hiding." Lou's smile widened. "I'm just not shoving my friend out of the way. It's called manners, Trick."

Her gray eyes practically twinkled and I wondered, for the briefest of moments, what someone had to do to make her light up like that. I couldn't look away, even though part of me realized I was being rude by ignoring Van.

I started to smile back, because I couldn't *not* return Lou's smile, when my wolf's whining took on a more plaintive tone.

I took in another deep breath, and a particular blend of scents hit me. People were always a blend—like Trick, who had his own natural smell, but then also the scents that accompanied working with his magic. Right now I smelled coffee, milk, something grassy, and chocolate—Vanessa, maybe? I couldn't tell with them standing so close together. But the other person, possibly Lou, smelled heavily of animal musk. Lots of different scent signatures layered over a brighter note, something that reminded me of sunshine.

And it finally clicked in, everything my wolf had been trying to tell me. Sometimes that happened—my sense of smell was almost as good when I was in human form, but my brain wasn't quite as fast at analyzing that information. But I'd finally caught up.

Animal mage. One of them was an animal mage. Fear shot through me. My pulse skittered, my small smile collapsing in on itself. They were still talking, but I couldn't hear them anymore. Just…noise.

Lou stepped forward, her brow furrowed, her hand outstretched. I lurched backward, my hands tightening instinctively, my beer bottle shattering in the quiet kitchen.

Lou slowly pulled her hand back, glancing at her roommates.

I recognized the look of concern on all their faces, but couldn't do anything about it. My back hit the wall and I realized that I'd kept backing up. I panted, unconsciously mimicking my wolf.

Trick held his hands out, his face carefully blank. "Hey, Dec. You okay?"

"Animal mage." It took me several times to get the words past the restriction in my throat. "Away. Right now. *Now.*"

Trick blinked, his hands dropping.

Van scowled, but Lou—Lou looked hurt.

I didn't care.

I *couldn't.*

Not with panic clawing at my insides. "*Get out!*"

I closed my eyes. I heard two people leave as I slid down the wall until I was sitting on the floor hugging my knees. If I didn't get control of myself, I'd change. This wasn't a situation the wolf would make better.

"Do you need me to go, too?" Trick whispered.

I shook my head. "No. Not you. Them." I sucked in a deep breath. Calm. *Calm.* "You're fine. Just…not her." Lou's hurt face floated up, making me feel like shit, but I couldn't deal with that right now. All I could do was hold myself tight and hope I didn't shatter into a hundred pieces.

That shithead part of me was cackling again. All the places I could have picked, all the roommates Trick could have had, and one of them just had to be an animal mage.

Figures.

CHAPTER FIVE

Lou

Van and I stopped in the living room. The afternoon light slanted in, and I could hear some of the pigeons outside gossiping by our birdfeeder. Out of habit, I started listening to their chatter, only to realize that it wasn't actually my business who my neighbor was sleeping with, so I blocked it out. The kids shouting on the sidewalk made that easy. Outside was loud.

Inside? Absolute fucking silence. Van was frowning hard, pointing at the kitchen, her face clearly saying, *the fuck?*

I shrugged at her. I didn't know what the fuck was going on either, so I was no help beyond making my own *the fuck?* face out of solidarity. A sleepy chirp reminded me that I'd forgot someone fairly important. Dammit was nestled into a metal carrier that I'd left by the door. I spent a few minutes tracking down the cage Trick had texted me about and settling Dammit into his new home. I tried to give Trick and Declan privacy, and thankfully the walls were decently thick.

It wasn't until I was back into the living room that I picked up their voices again. I heard Trick speaking softly, followed by Declan swearing. Despite my worry and hurt, I liked his voice. There was a raspy quality to it that sizzled right up my spine. I might not like what he was saying, but I was on board with the delivery mechanism, I guess.

"Of course," Declan said, and now he was laughing, but it was a painful laugh, reminding me of a wounded animal. "An animal mage. Just fucking perfect."

Van was glaring holes through the door. Declan might be freaking out, but Van was more concerned about how he was making me feel.

For my part, I was oddly paralyzed trying to process what I'd heard. Declan's words were hurtful, yes. Bigotry always hurts. It's a weapon made to flay you open, eviscerating even the hardest shell. Though it manifests as hatred, bigotry was usually rooted in fear. I hadn't heard any hatred in his voice. Panic, yes. Pain. And underneath it, exhaustion. So I was torn between my own hurt—no one likes being yelled at to leave, especially in their own home—and my instinct to heal.

Someone had injured Declan very badly. If I wasn't careful, Van would gleefully harm him some more, and I wasn't quite sure if I could stop her. She reached out for the door and I touched her hand, shaking my head.

Her gaze moved over my face, carefully assessing. She sighed. "At least we're rooming with a hot bigot," Van grumbled, but she also dropped her hand.

Van was right—he was hot. Short brown hair, warm brown eyes—at least at first. Then they'd gone hard, his jaw clenched. His face had suddenly been made up of rigid, uncompromising angles. Except his lips. Those had remained almost decadently soft. I bet they'd feel like velvet.

Not that I wanted to find out. Roommates were always a bad idea romantically, but this roommate specifically would be disastrous.

After a few more minutes, Trick called us back in.

Van went first, barreling through the door, clearly on a mission. I was more hesitant, moving slowly, as if he was an animal I didn't want to spook.

Even leaning against the wall, he was tall, and with his arms crossed, his stance aggressive, he reminded me of a bouncer. My mom really loved the movie *Road House* and though Declan looked nothing like Patrick Swayze, he was giving off heavy Dalton vibes right now. He looked up, his eyes hitting mine again. Despite the weird emotions in the air, my stomach fluttered.

I didn't think he was having the same problem. Right now he was staring at me like I was a question and he wasn't sure he'd like the answer.

I gave him a little finger wave and he blinked, the spell broken.

He glanced around the kitchen, frowning, before rubbing two fingers between his eyebrows, probably trying to push away a headache. "You're both witches, but one of you is an animal mage, aren't you?"

Witches was the catchall term for anyone gifted with magic—animal mages, arcanists, hedgewitches, we all fell under the same umbrella. Even elementists, so technically, Trick was a witch as well.

I raised my hand.

Van crossed her arms, and she was still scowling but she also kept stealing glances at me. Neither of us could quite grasp what was going on. "Is that going to be a problem?"

Instead of answering, the guy started laughing. I mean, leaning-over, gut-busting laughter. We watched, bemused, as he wiped away actual tears. When he could finally gasp for breath, he said, "Nothing. Absolutely nothing."

Van and I exchanged another *the fuck* moment. What the hell was going on? The concern on her face mirrored mine when we looked over at Trick.

Trick had gone completely sheet white. "Oh, Dec. I'm so sorry. Fuck, I'm an asshole. I didn't even think—"

Declan shook his head, shoving the apology away.

Van's glare had become speculative. She looked at me. *Why is Trick apologizing to the hot bigot?*

I shrugged. *I don't know, but I do know Trick, and we're missing something here.*

Trick picked up one of the guy's bags. "I'll show you your room—"

He shook his head, snatching his bag back. "I'll find it. They're going to have questions." Then he headed unerringly back toward the open room.

Van pointed at his retreating form. "How did he know where his room was?"

"How did he know my specialty is animals?" I asked at the same time.

"Sniffed both out, probably." Trick considered his empty beer. "Van, you better go take over for Jules. I'll meet you both down there with a six pack, okay?"

"Yes," Van said. "Because beer and babysitting always go well together."

"The best!" I gave her two thumbs up. She returned them, but with much less enthusiasm.

We reconvened downstairs in Juliet's apartment. Van bobbed her niece on her knee while I picked up toys and discarded clothes. Juliet was a very tidy person. She was also a single mother of an almost two-year-old, worked evenings at the bar—Juliet, not the child—and was in the final stages of getting her license to practice counseling. There was only so much one person could do, and children were filth wizards.

Kids could trash a tidy house in under two seconds, and I felt like Savannah was particularly skilled at this. If creating filth was an Olympic event, she'd be taking home the gold. Everything was sticky and it looked like a clothes hamper had exploded. Savannah had her fist in her mouth, babbling away as she chewed, content on her auntie's lap. I waved one of the socks at her. "You are terrible to your mother." I paused to blow a raspberry on her cheek. "It's a good thing you're cute."

"They're cute so we don't murder and eat them," Van said with a big smile as she made faces at her niece.

Once the clutter was picked up, I sat. It wouldn't make any sense to do any real cleaning until Savannah was unconscious. Otherwise, she'd just trash the place again. But tidying gave me something to do while we waited for Trick, and sitting still right now was beyond me. Even though I *knew* the second Van put Savvy down, all of my work would be undone.

Filth. Wizard.

Trick slipped into the apartment, the promised six pack in hand. Once he'd handed us our drinks, he stashed the rest in the fridge before lowering himself into a chair. We sipped our beers, Van expertly keeping hers out of Savannah's grasping hands, Trick sitting across from us, picking at the label on his, deep in thought.

Van pointed her beer hand at him. "Spill."

Trick flopped back into his chair. "I'm trying to decide how much of this is my story to tell."

"Ooooh," Van said, cooing to her niece as she bounced her knee. "That sounds juicy."

Trick ran a hand over his mouth. "It is, and I'm realizing how much I probably should have talked to you guys first. I owe Declan and both of you huge apologies. I was incredibly thoughtless. So, I'm sorry. I just…I guess I've known him so long and I'm so used to it, I didn't think about it."

"I'm now concerned that our new roommate is a serial killer," I said, jokingly. I mean, Trick would never invite anyone into our home that would actually hurt us. "Are we going to be the topic of a future true crime podcast? Do I need to ask the pigeons to watch him?"

He snorted. "No, no. Nothing like that." He tapped his thumb against his beer. "There's just a lot of stigma against werewolves, especially—" Trick shook his head.

Van snorted. "He's not dangerous, or you wouldn't invite him to live with us."

"We all know what it's like," I said quietly. "To be painted with that particular brush." This morning wasn't the first time I'd had some variation of "weird animal mage" thrown at me. "Why would he care if we're witches?"

I might not be close to any shapeshifters, but I'd never heard of them having a beef with witches.

I glanced over at the row of books on Jules's bookshelf, most of them focused on the Uncanny. Juliet was specializing as a GUNC, which was the unfortunate acronym for a General Uncanny Counselor. GUNCs helped different Uncanny blend and cope with the mundane world. We might have been around for a long time, but we'd remained hidden as human society developed. Some aspects of society weren't created with Uncanny in mind, and though many had adapted, you could still smack into workplace issues. Apartments couldn't legally keep a shapeshifter from renting, but it still happened. It was stressful.

On top of that, there were some issues we faced that humans didn't. Mental blocks with our magic, like shifters who couldn't shift or witches whose spells fizzled. Juliet had told me about one case study where a river nymph was afraid of water. Several of the titles on Juliet's shelf were specifically about shifters. So whatever Declan's issue was, I didn't think it was a shapeshifter/witch thing.

"Normally, he wouldn't care if you were witches, obviously, because we wouldn't be able to be friends if that was an issue." Trick went to set his beer down, eyed Savannah, thought better of it, and set it up on the bookshelf behind him. "But he's had a rough time of it lately, so he came up here already off-kilter." He glanced guilty at me. "And Declan had a really bad experience in the past with a witch—an animal mage."

"How bad?" I asked.

"The worst," Trick said.

"Okay," I said, getting up to recycle my beer bottle.

"Okay?" Van asked. "Just like that?"

"No," I said. "Not just like that. I trust Trick. I trust his judgment. So far, I'm not impressed with Declan, but it sounds like he was put in a bad position and I'm willing to give him another shot."

Savvy wriggled, and Van placed her on the ground, where she immediately went after the blocks I'd neatly stacked. Van sighed. "Well, now I feel bad."

I narrowed my eyes at her. "Van, what did you do?"

Van crossed her arms, guilt virtually scrawled across her face in six-inch neon letters. "I might have already hexed him."

"Van!" I couldn't keep the exasperation out of my tone. "That's not helpful."

If at all possible, she crossed her arms harder, practically hugging herself. "He was mean to you!"

Trick deflated, putting a hand over his eyes. "Van. If anyone should have been hexed, it was probably me."

She dropped her arms. "It was just a small one. Nothing terrible." When she examined our faces, she slouched back into the couch. "I'll apologize. I know it's not helpful, Lou, and if Trick says he has a good reason, I get it, but he still hurt you. Not hexing him would be setting a bad precedent." She pointed a finger at Trick. "As for you, we'll think of your punishment later."

Trick groaned.

"Just a small one!" I patted his cheek. "Now, how about Uncle Trick does story time, while Auntie Van cooks and I find where Juliet hid the vacuum?"

Declan

I stayed in my room as the afternoon shifted into evening. Trick had been using the small space as an office. The bare walls were painted slate gray, the only interruptions being a single window and a closet door. When I peeked in the closet, I found a rod and some empty hangers for clothes, as well a few shelves I could use for pants and things.

The furnishings in the room were meager. There was enough room for a compact desk and chair and one of those futon loveseats that collapsed into a bed and always made me wonder how it was any better than simply sleeping on the floor. The space smelled mostly of Trick, lemon cleaning products, and something musky I couldn't quite place. I tossed my stuff to the side and collapsed onto the rock-hard futon.

I dropped my face into my hands. How had everything gone to shit so quickly? My fresh start had popped like a fucking soap bubble. I realized I was breathing deeply through my nose, trying to catch a hint of Lou's scent. I wanted to pull it into my lungs while at the same time it made me want to run for the hills: the scent of Lou herself intriguing me and my wolf, while the layered traces of many animals, a blend we associated with animal mages, repelling us at the same time.

I was, officially, a fucking mess. I scrubbed a hand over my jaw and got up, putting my things away, wondering at the same time if I should bother. Would Trick's roommates even want me to stay after this? Did I want to stay after this? I mentally went over my bank account. My cushion wouldn't last long if I had to go find my own place, and I didn't know anyone else in Seattle. I thought it over as I put my things away, which didn't take long. If I decided to leave, at least it wouldn't take me long to repack.

I had to get my head straight, only I couldn't seem to sit still. It was like the quiet in my room gave my heart the exact atmosphere it needed to voice its complaints, and it was a loud fucker. I rubbed my chest, the hurt almost physical.

I'd never been a lone wolf before.

Even when I fled my father's pack, I had my siblings with me. Then the Uncanny courts placed the twins with an elementist family. The twins had been a surprise. I didn't know much about the genetics, but shifter genes tended to dominate. Something lined up just right for the twins. That had bothered my dad, and I think he wanted to argue paternity, but thought doing so would not only piss off his wife, Eva, but make him look weak. The old-fashioned term was "cuckold" and there was no way my dad would ever admit to being one.

Didn't really matter, anyway. Anyone who looked at them knew the twins were his. It had never bothered me; as far as I was concerned, they were my siblings as much as Zoey was, but the courts saw things differently—like with like. The twins were shuffled off to an elementist's home, and Zoey and I were sent to live with a shifter family. In a blink, I went from living in a giant pack to just a pack of two.

Everything had been torn away so quickly.

But Zoey and I had held on tight. We'd stumbled through on our own. Then a few years ago, we'd added in Sid, and my heart had felt full. I'd loved Sidney, but I was starting to realize I hadn't been in love with her—a fine, but important, difference.

And once again, in a blink, it had all been torn away.

I realized I was standing in the middle of the room, my hands fisted on my empty duffle bag. There was nothing left to do, and there was no way I could sit in here the rest of the evening. I needed to run. I changed into some sweats, grabbed my wallet and phone, and used my sensitive hearing to sneak out the back door without running into anyone.

I knew from experience that the only way to get that painful voice in my head to shut up was to wear out my body. I'd had practice. So much practice.

I jogged down the sidewalk, heading to a park I'd found on my phone. Since I didn't feel like stripping down in a public park and didn't have a good place to stash my wallet, I stayed in human form. No matter how much I ran, I kept seeing Lou and Van's faces. The fucking hurt and anger there. Hurt and anger that I'd caused.

Hot bigot. I didn't consider myself a bigot. I guess no one ever does, right? But in this case, it wasn't so much bigotry as it was, in the words of a former therapist, an "ingrained trauma response." It wasn't that I hated animal mages, it was that I didn't trust them, and that distrust went deep. Zoey didn't trust them, either. We had good reason not to. That didn't make it fair or right, but fear doesn't really listen to reason.

And I could feel that fear congealing in my gut.

The question was, how much effort did I want to put out here? Did I go back, pack my things, apologize for my meltdown, and move on? Or did I want to take the time to at least somewhat explain what had happened and put forth the energy it would take to live with Lou? I didn't know them, but I knew the kind of people Trick kept in his sphere. I wouldn't have to roll over and show them my throat. A bare-bones explanation would probably get us past it.

I'd have to work every day to regain ground, to get to the point where I didn't feel like bolting every time I saw Lou. With everything else going on, did I want to do that? Did I want to add on to the already overloaded emotional to-do list under "becoming a lone wolf" and "giving my sister much-needed space while I get my head on straight?"

Not only that, but just plain missing my damn sister?

I was sadly used to missing the twins. My siblings and I had what you might call an unorthodox upbringing. I'd found that "unorthodox" was a nice euphemism that covered all manner of sins.

It wasn't uncommon for wolves to live in packs. Sometimes a pack will pool their finances and buy a chunk of land and live there together, like my dad's pack had done. A pack was generally centered around a family, much like wild wolves, but humans were more social than that, and often ended up going beyond a single-family unit.

My father took it several steps further.

I closed my eyes and picked up my pace, my long stride eating up the sidewalk. I wasn't going to go there. I'd moved across the country. I'd changed my name. I kept a low profile. That's the kind of thing you had to do when your father was doing time in an Uncanny certified cellblock in a federal prison for starting his own fucking cult. My father wasn't just famous, he was *infamous*. If you googled "Angus Alan Campbell" you would find article upon article detailing the terrible deeds my father perpetrated.

The shock. The horror.

If you dug deeper, you might even find a video of me standing shell-shocked, reporters shoving microphones and cameras in my face. That was what I remembered—the noise. The overwhelming cacophony of it. I'd grown up away from people, mostly outdoors. The urban setting where I'd been dragged into court was like stepping onto another planet.

So I stood there, Zoey at my side, her hand holding mine in a white-knuckled grip. The twins crying at my feet. The sea of reporters barely being held back. I could still feel Zoey's hand in mine. The moment long and terrible. Then we each picked up one of the twins and turned away. Our lawyer managed to get us away from the din, taking us into the courthouse through a side door. After he was done apologizing, I made him promise that it wouldn't happen again. I didn't care how he managed it—I wasn't dragging my siblings through that crowd. They'd already been through so much.

My chest tightened, panic surfacing like it always did when I thought about those days. My father. My stepmother. But I'd survived this long by picking up some tricks. I had to ground myself in the now. The smell of exhaust. The chill rising in the air, the day already a memory. The hurt on Lou's face. For some reason, that stuck with me the most. The way her hands had clenched. They'd both been angry, but there'd been an air of disappointment around Lou. Like she'd expected better of me and I'd let her down. Which was ridiculous, because she'd just met me. But I couldn't shake the feeling.

I found the entrance to the large, wooded park by Trick's place and cut into it, despite the fact that it was after hours. I ran through the trees, giving myself over to the scents and quiet of the forest. The trees smelled like fresh rain, fir, and pine. Scent trails of humans, squirrels, rats, rabbits, and coyotes crisscrossed the trails. The park had a definite bunny population problem, which made my wolf perk up.

I ran until my mind got as quiet as the woods. When I felt settled enough and the past was reburied in a deep, unmarked mental grave, I pulled up the menu for a Thai place a few blocks from the house. My thumb hovered over the call button.

The scene in the kitchen had been a total catastrophe from every angle. On one hand, Trick should have warned me. Then again, Trick had never seen me react like that, either. I wasn't sure it was anyone's fault, just a convergence of many shitty things at once.

When I was younger, there'd been some state mandated counseling sessions. Our therapist was terrible and spent most of the time hopped up on prescription meds, but occasionally he'd pulled his head out of his ass long enough to say something useful. One of those times, we'd been talking about my stepmom, and the therapist had scratched his head and told me that I could no more paint every witch with the brush of my stepmother than I could compare every pack alpha to my father.

Not all witches were bad. Logically, I knew that. But emotionally? I'd thought that had been clear as well, but apparently it wasn't. I'd worked on my issues—not because the therapist had been right on one point, but because that was what I needed to do for me. I didn't want to break into a fear sweat every time I came in contact with an animal mage.

I also couldn't let today get in the way of my own recovery. I'd worked hard to get past my fear of animal mages. Setbacks happened, but I didn't want that setback to be permanent. And I refused to let my baggage hurt Lou. Or Van. Partially for them, but mostly for me. I wanted to be better. I didn't want what my father and his wife had done to forever dictate my path.

They'd had enough of my life. They didn't get any more.

So what did I want to do here? Lou and Van were Trick's friends. Trick surrounded himself with good people. Ergo, Van and Lou were good people. If I couldn't trust my judgment, I could trust his. Despite how things had gone, I knew Trick had my best interests at heart. And yes, it would be easier, at least emotionally, to find another place to live. But I realized I didn't want that. I could handle this—I wanted to move past this setback.

I hit the call button on my phone. When someone answered, I ordered enough for the whole house, getting a little bit of everything. Food always helped a tough situation, right? That was why people brought casseroles to funerals.

My muscles were loose, and my brain quiet, so I walked to the restaurant, trying to cool down. A bell above the door jingled when I opened it and I was instantly greeted by the smell of peppers, coconut, lime—my stomach grumbled. I waved at the guy behind the podium.

"Pickup for Mackenzie?"

"That's me."

The guy stared at me, a weird look on his face as he handed over several bags of takeout. A few younger employees stood a couple feet behind him and kept *giggling*. I looked down. Pants? Check. Shoes? Check. All parts of me human? Checkity-check. Maybe I was super sweaty? I paid for the food and left, deciding it was just one of life's mysteries that I'd never know.

I came home and found Trick sprawled on the couch, the little girl from the Santa photo plastered to his chest, fast asleep. Van and Lou shared the couch with a big guy who looked human, but definitely wasn't. He smelled like bull, wood, and the green smell I associated with hedgewitch potions. They were all focused on the TV, which showed the opening credits for a dating show.

"Jim," the big dude said, not looking at me. "Nice to meet you. If you value your life, you will speak quietly when the show is actually on." The screen shifted to an aerial view of a huge wilderness lodge that was rustic in a very picturesque and glamorous sort of way. Golden lettering unfurled across the screen, revealing the title *Mated by Fate*.

I held up my bags, making sure to keep my voice low. "I brought food."

Van lifted her nose, sniffing theatrically. "Is that curry? Ooooh, that's curry." She looked up at me and then burst into laughter. Trick followed her gaze and groaned.

Jim squinted at me, shook his head, and nudged Van with the flat of his palm, making her sway in place. "You're evil."

Lou finally turned her head and winced. "Van."

Van flushed pink. "I'm sorry! I mean, it's still funny, but I'm sorry."

I must have looked bewildered, because Lou pointed to a tall, decorative mirror hanging on the wall. I scooted over to it.

And finally, the mystery of the giggling staff at the Thai restaurant was solved. Yes, I was sweaty. That wasn't what had made them laugh. No, it was likely the glitter script waving across my forehead. "'Twatopottamus?' Really?"

Van wheezed in laughter before covering her mouth. Somewhere in there, she managed another "I'm so sorry, but it's so funny..." before she wheezed some more. "I feel really bad."

"I can tell." I turned my head, the script glittering across my forehead as I shifted. Really, it was an impressive hex. Despite the long word, the script was legible, and the gold glitter really set it off. "Very nice work." I took my bags to the kitchen, unloading them onto the kitchen counter.

I heard footsteps and glanced back to see Lou walking in slowly, dragging Van behind her. Lou stopped several feet away, giving me space. She poked Van in the arm.

"I'm very sorry." She managed to look contrite. "We didn't know. I just…" She looked guiltily at Lou. "I'm a little protective over my people."

Van and I stared at each other for a minute before she dropped her gaze.

"I understand." I went back to taking cartons out of bags. "I would do the same for my pack."

Van raised her hands up. "I can take it off, if that's okay?"

I clenched my jaw and nodded. I could do this. She wasn't trying to hurt me. I didn't feel anything, but Van moved into my field of vision, examined my forehead, looking relieved. "It's gone." She stood there awkwardly for a second, shifting her weight, before she went back to the living room to see who needed another beer. Lou moved to my other side, making lots of noise and trying to stay in my sight as she started gathering plates. She was treating me like you would a feral creature. I both appreciated it and wanted to bare my teeth.

"These three I got with tofu, assuming you don't eat meat." I waved a hand at the containers, then opened several drawers until I found the silverware, taking out forks and serving spoons.

"That was very thoughtful," Lou said, setting the plates on the counter. She reached out for me, and then froze, her hand hovering between us. My nostrils flared and she drew her hand back. "Despite her giggling, Van is very sorry. So is Trick."

"I know." I started filling my plate. I had a pretty hearty appetite usually, but I'd shifted earlier and I'd just come back from a run. This plate would be the first of many.

"Declan." Lou paused, as if trying to figure out what she wanted to say. She straightened her shoulders. "This is our home. You understand?"

My stomach sank. I did understand. It was her home and she had a right to feel comfortable in it. Despite my intentions of getting through this, Lou wasn't on board. I nodded, my throat tight.

"Which means anything that makes it easier for you, that makes you feel safer or more at ease here, you just let us know, okay?" She picked up one of the spoons, dishing up a large portion of pad see ew onto her plate. "I know we can all be assholes sometimes, but it's meant to be in a good way." She sighed. "We just sometimes need to be told we're *being* assholes."

My hand tightened on my spoon. When I didn't answer, Lou didn't push, just finished filling her plate, and headed back into the living room.

Her words finally sank in and relief hit my system. She didn't want me to leave. *They* didn't want me to leave. My vision suddenly turned blurry. My hands were full, so I tried to wipe my eyes on my shoulders to limited success.

Jim came in and picked up a plate. He saw me, set it back down, and held out his arms. "Do you need a hug, or is this a spicy food thing?"

I laughed, set down my spoon and plate, and opened my arms. He folded me into a hug that I honestly hadn't realized I'd needed, Jim's size making me feel small and safe, even though I'd just met him. After a minute, I leaned away, and he let me go without comment.

He nodded at my now very full plate. "You eating in here, or joining us for *Mated by Fate*?"

I sucked in a deep breath. Let it out. "Joining you."

Jim quickly dished up a plate from the vegetarian options. "Good timing. It's the first episode of the season."

I followed him out, taking a spot on the floor. I wasn't quite brave enough to sit near Lou, but I felt like eating in the same room was a good step. Repeated exposure would help me relax, right? I watched quietly, though everyone else kept a running commentary, despite Jim's earlier warning.

I'd caught the show a few times before—Zoey loved it, even though she knew it was scripted. The odds of going on TV with thirty strangers and discovering one of them was *actually* your mate seemed pretty low. Finding someone to date? Sure, though that seemed almost as unlikely. But mating? That meant my wolf and I would both have to agree on the person in question. It was a conscious choice, and once the bond was made, only death broke it. It was *literally magic,* and I had a hard time picturing that happening on television.

After my fourth helping, I was finally full, and now without the food as distraction, very aware that I was in the room with an animal mage. I wasn't on edge, exactly, but I was definitely *alert*. I didn't even make it until the end of the episode before I mumbled an excuse and went to my room. By the time I closed my door, I was sweating and a fine tremor shook my hands. Not a huge leap by any means, but I'd taken a baby step in the right direction. And I felt, at least for tonight, like I really could do this.

I could make this my home.

CHAPTER SIX

Declan

I wasn't sure what I'd been expecting with my new living situation, but weasels hadn't even made the list of possibilities. I especially hadn't expected them on my pillow first thing in the morning, like a strange version of hotel pillow mints.

They were staring at me. Solid black beady little eyes staring right into mine.

So I yelled.

To be honest, it was more of a scream. In my defense, I hadn't had coffee yet, and also *weasels*.

There was a thunder of feet and my door swung open.

Lou made it through the door first, still in her pajama shorts and a thin tank top. Her shorts were short, the material soft-looking. Her skin looked soft, too—I shut that thought down immediately. Crushing on Lou would be disastrous. And yet, I couldn't look away. I blinked and realized she was carrying a baseball bat, obviously ready to rumble, and I *hadn't even noticed it*.

Van stood behind her, bleary-eyed. She'd inexplicably brought the half-full french press with her to my room instead of leaving it behind in the kitchen. Trick sauntered up last, peeking over their shoulders, casually sipping his coffee. An adorable fledgling phoenix perched on a thick leather pad strapped to his shoulder, otherwise Trick wasn't wearing a shirt. He nudged his way into the room and I caught sight of the arcane symbols tattooed in blacks and grays decorating the insides of both of his lower arms.

The fledgling squawked at me and I startled. Great.

"What happened?" Lou asked, wide eyes darting around the room.

She looked rumpled. I *liked* rumpled.

"Are you hurt?" She licked her lips, and *fuck*.

This was when it occurred to me that A) I was naked. I had a blanket, yes, but right now it was only covering my knees, so I yanked it up to my waist. As a rule, werewolves were pretty okay with being naked, but I was feeling vulnerable this morning, and it was hard to be brave when you were buck naked. B) The weasels had fled, or perhaps had never been there to begin with. Maybe I'd been hallucinating, or possibly they were a side effect of Van's hex, which seemed unlikely. And C) I was destined to make a terrible impression on Trick's roommates.

"Were you having night terrors?" Van asked gently. "I have a cousin who gets those."

"Weasels?" It came out as a question. I hated that. "Weasels." There. That sounded much more authoritative.

"You mean Kodo and Podo?" Van handed the french press off to Trick before dropping down to the floor level and giving a soft whistle.

"They have names?" I wanted to take the entire carafe and drink straight from the spout. My brain felt fuzzy and useless, and as was beginning to be the way of things, I felt one step behind the conversation in this house.

"Van named them after the ferrets in *Beastmaster*. You don't name your pets?" Lou asked, letting the tip of the bat drop until it touched the floor.

"Pets?" I watched Van crawl around near the base of the futon, making clucking noises with her tongue. Now that I was slightly more awake, I re-categorized the smell, taking it from "weasel" to "ferret." I wasn't as familiar with ferrets, though that seemed like it was about to change. The two ferrets ran out from under the bed on the other side and started hopping all over the floor and each other, chittering away at Van. She whisked them up with ease, cuddling them to her Rat City Roller Girls T-shirt.

"Sorry," Van said. "I didn't realize they came in here." She snuggled them close, frowning. "Now I have to figure out how they managed it." She kissed their heads. "To be fair, they are familiars, so they're a little smarter than the average ferret, which is already pretty smart."

"Why?" I asked. "Ferrets. Why?"

Trick sent me a sympathetic look. "I think we broke you. And so soon, too."

Lou shifted, resting some of her weight on the bat. "We were going to get a cat, because tradition, but Trick is allergic."

Van held the ferrets close, her eyebrows pinched together. "Don't say it like that. Don't make them feel like they're runners-up."

Lou looked very solemnly at me. "What I meant to say was that we'd considered getting a cat, but then realized that everyone has cats and though they're awesome, we wanted a different kind of awesome, so Van got ferrets." She was deadpan with her delivery—it was kind of adorable.

I'd barely been able to sit in a room with Lou yesterday, but right now I couldn't seem to stop looking at her. Was it progress, or was I still half asleep? At least I wasn't freaking out. "Ferrets." I rubbed my face with one hand. "Okay."

"Are you afraid of ferrets?" Trick asked. "Is that why you screamed like a small child?"

Trick was my friend and I loved him and I absolutely was *not* considering picking him up and tossing him out of my room.

Lou and Van watched me carefully, and even in my muzzy state, I knew I had to respond carefully here, lest my living situation devolve further. I didn't want to be a lone wolf living out of my SUV while I found another place to live, and I couldn't go back to Portland.

"I just wasn't expecting them," I said. "On my pillow. Right when I woke up."

They continued to watch me.

"They were…staring very intently." I tucked my blanket closer around me.

One of the ferrets crawled up Van's shoulder and started burying its nose in her hair. "I could see how that would be unsettling."

"At least they didn't go anywhere delicate." Lou held one hand up in front of her in a grabby motion. "Little claws." Her gaze dropped to my lap and she smirked.

I don't blush easily, so I was surprised when I felt the heat creeping up my face. Lou's smirk faltered and she dropped her gaze. I cleared my throat. "Little claws?"

Van patted my head. "Poor buddy. We broke your brain." She held one of the ferrets out to me. "This is Kodo." She held out a second one, and I swear they looked identical. At least their scent signatures were slightly different. "This is Podo. I've made them promise to never go near your delicate bits with their little claws."

The ferrets stared at me, and somehow I didn't trust that promise *at all*. I reached out slowly, petting their heads. "Okay."

Trick snickered as he took another sip of coffee. "Usually it takes us a whole week to break new roommates."

"I've always been a fast learner," I said, staring at them all helplessly.

Lou finally took pity on me and ushered everyone out with her bat. "Come on, team. Let's leave the confused naked man alone and maybe go make another pot of coffee out of pity."

I tried really hard to not look at the way her shorts hugged her ass as she left the room.

I failed.

I spent the next few days applying for jobs and partially avoiding Lou. Which made me feel like a coward. During my introductions to the ferrets, I'd managed to keep my cool. I didn't want to lose ground, so I figured if I didn't see her much, it wasn't courting another episode.

It also gave me time to get used to the animal mage part of her scent. If I could start associating it with home and safety, with friends, that would be a huge step in the right direction. That didn't mean I wasn't passively gathering information about her. I tried to tell myself it was because the more I knew, the less I'd be afraid…but I was worried that it might be more than that. Being attracted to Lou would obviously be complicated. I didn't want complicated.

Either way, by the end of the week, I realized I'd done a fair job memorizing her work schedule and picking up on her habits. For example, I'd realized that Lou had a sweet tooth. Was that why I was currently making cookies with the help of two ferrets?

Maybe. Okay, yes.

I also needed to do something that wasn't focusing on the fact that I'd turned in a lot of applications but hadn't heard a peep. Things weren't dire yet, but I couldn't coast for too long.

I opened one of the kitchen drawers, wondering if anyone would mind if I reorganized the kitchen. It was a little haphazard. Of course, from what I'd seen so far, my roommates didn't spend much time cooking. I wasn't sure if they didn't have time or if they didn't like cooking, but so far the kitchen had mostly been used for takeout. "Okay, I give up. Where are the measuring spoons?"

Kodo hopped along the counter, stopping near one of the drawers. He chittered at me.

"You're handy when you're not scaring me half to death." I swept him off the counter and put him on my shoulder. "But I'm not sure if it's hygienic to have you running around the kitchen counters." I opened the door and found the measuring spoons. Where there was one ferret, there was usually another. Sure enough, Podo was peeking into the mixing bowl. I put him on my other shoulder. He immediately started digging through my hair.

I found an old hand mixer in one of the cabinets, set the oven to preheat, and got to work. One thing I liked about cooking, especially if it was a familiar recipe, was that you could just lose yourself in the motions. The ferrets, for their part, seemed content to watch, occasionally helping me when I needed to find something.

I'd just put the first batch into the oven when Lou walked into the kitchen.

I waited for the panic to hit. When it didn't, my shoulders relaxed a fraction. I still wasn't comfortable, but I wasn't strung tight enough to crack, either.

I glanced at the clock. Lou was home early. She was still in her scrubs, her hair pulled back in a ponytail. The skin under her eyes was bruised, the joy she often radiated dimmed. She collapsed into one of the bar stools across from me.

If I wanted, I could reach out and touch her. My heartbeat ticked up and I wasn't sure if it was from fear or not.

For a second, I considered turning off the oven and hiding in my room. Which felt ridiculous. I took a deep breath, reminding myself that it was just Lou. She'd never done anything terrible to me beyond leaving toast crumbs on the cutting board or singing off-key in the shower.

"Bad day?"

She nodded glumly, resting her chin in her hands.

I scooped the next batch of cookies onto the sheet. "Hot tea bad, hot chocolate bad, or shot of tequila bad?" When she didn't answer right away, I added, "Entire bottle of tequila bad?"

Her smile was small, but it was there. "Tea, I think."

I fetched the kettle off the stove, checked the water level, and added more to it.

"You don't have to make me tea."

I shrugged. "I'm already over here." The ferrets scrambled down my shoulders. I held my arms out like tiny bridges so they could get back onto the counters. They bounced over to Lou, chattering until one was combing through her hair and the other was sticking its nose in her ear. She laughed. "Thanks, you two."

I messed around with the mugs, fished out the chamomile tea bags, and made us both a cup. "Want to talk about it?"

She blew on her mug. "You don't have to do this, you know."

I went back to scooping the rest of the dough. "Too late, the tea is made."

She shook her head. "No, I mean, this." She waved a hand back and forth between us. "Comfort me."

I didn't respond right away, focusing on the cookies like they might at any second tell me the secrets of the universe. Lou was giving me an out. Again. I could take it. Set my timer and … I examined her through my lashes, trying to gauge her expression. Miserable. Lou looked miserable and small.

My wolf chuffed. *Not a threat.* It was like he'd decided, and with that, mentally clicked her over into a sort of safe zone. I watched her and realized that I wasn't afraid. My heartbeat was slow, steady.

I didn't want to leave.

Lou needed comfort, and that—*that* was something I understood. A role I knew how to play. I washed my hands, dried them on a towel, walked around the counter, and as Jim had done a few days ago, held my arms open.

Lou frowned at me for a second, like she was trying to decide if this was a trap or not. The frown intensified until her face crumpled and the smallest, choked sob came out, as if she'd tried to catch it and missed. I didn't think, I just closed her in tight against me.

"I'm so sorry," Lou sobbed, her small fist grabbing my T-shirt.

Kodo made a sad noise, his eyes on mine for a second before he tried to burrow in between us.

"Why?"

Lou snuffled. "I don't know."

I laughed, squeezing her tighter. We stayed like that until my timer went off.

"You're going to burn your cookies."

"I can make new cookies."

She gently pushed me away and hiccupped. "It's okay." She sniffed. "We lost one today."

I checked the cookies, adding a few minutes because they weren't quite done. "Lost one?"

"A familiar." She sniffed again. "Mercury. A terrier mix. His little heart gave out." Tears welled in her eyes again, that sad little sob making another break for it. The next thing I knew, I was wrapped back around her.

"It was my fault."

I rubbed circles on her back with one hand, the other arm holding her tight. Noting absently—and a little guiltily—how much better I felt. For whatever reason, giving comfort to someone else always made me feel better. It was almost a relief, knowing I was doing something to help. "How was it your fault?"

"We do a full work-up before we do any bindings. Heart, lungs, blood work—the magic can be...kind of intense, you know?" She hiccupped again. "Everything came back okay and the owner was pushing and—everything seemed fine. He was young. *Healthy.*"

"No red flags at all?"

She shook her head. "Even my mentor signed off. He seemed *fine*." She started crying just as the timer went off *again*. She nudged me away.

I swapped the cookies out for the next batch, the kitchen now smelling of chocolate and sugar. "Lou, I'm not a mage but...if your mentor didn't catch it, if no one caught it, then how is it your fault?"

"He was in my care!" She slumped into her chair, wrapping her hands around her tea. "I should have known."

The cookies were too hot, but I grabbed a spatula anyway, and quickly moved two to a plate and put it in front of Lou. "Unless you can tell the future, how would you have known?"

She sniffed into her tea. "The file will get sent to an overseer. What if... what if I did something stupid? What if they find a mistake?"

I put a third cookie on her plate. "Do you trust your mentor?"

She blinked. "Of course. She's the best."

"Then what's the worst that could happen?"

She picked up one of the cookies, breaking it in half, the melted chocolate oozing out. "Oh, that's easy. They'll realize I'm terrible at my job, I'll never get my license, and they'll shut our clinic down."

"So no pressure."

She stared morosely at her cookie. "I just feel so bad. I'm worried about my license—I mean, this has always been what I've wanted to do. What will happen if I can't do it? And then I feel *worse*, because I remember that poor little Mercury is—" Her face crumpled again.

I gripped the counter for a second, watching her cry. It hurt to watch. I turned, opening the cabinet where I'd found a few bottles of liquor earlier. No tequila, but we had whiskey. I twisted open the top, pouring a healthy slug into her tea.

She laughed a little, crying at the same time. "That's going to taste terrible."

I shrugged. "Better drink it fast, then." I walked out of the kitchen, heading for the bathroom.

"Where are you going?"

"I'm running you a bath," I said, tossing the words over my shoulder as I walked. "Then you're going straight to bed."

I heard a broken sigh behind me, and I paused halfway through the bathroom door. Which is I why I heard her whisper, "Thanks, Declan."

"You're welcome," I whispered back, sure she wouldn't hear it, but knowing I needed to say it all the same.

CHAPTER SEVEN

Lou

It took the overseer two days to clear me. The relief—that it hadn't totally been my fault—was heady, even if I was still mired in grief. It was really hard, losing a patient. I'd never lost someone I was binding before. The risk was usually minimal, and we had a lot of safeguards in place to make sure it didn't happen.

Still, I made Mama Ami watch over all my bindings that day and double check Dammit's work-up before I felt comfortable starting his binding process.

Between work and the emotional drain of the past two days, I collapsed onto the couch next to Trick, feeling like an empty soda can. The kind someone had already stomped on. Trick held Dammit cradled against him. Van's ferrets were running over the back of the couch, chittering advice at me. I hushed them, because I really didn't need any help second-guessing myself right now.

"What do I do?" Trick held out a treat for Dammit to eat. The fledgling snatched the treat away, which happened to be a lump of charcoal. You could use charcoal briquettes in a pinch, but they can have chemical additives that might upset Dammit's gut. I'd recommended Trick keep his food as natural as he could. If Dammit had still been with his parents, they would be feeding him charred bits of nesting material. The charcoal would do fine, nutritionally, but it was a little sad that he wasn't getting this time with his parents.

I smoothed my scrubs—I'd come straight from work and hadn't bothered to strip and shower yet. Normally, I changed right away. I got peed on a lot at work. Or worse. Today I'd managed to come through relatively unscathed. Besides, I didn't want to put this off any longer. "Concentrate on Dammit. Try to make your intentions clear. He probably won't get words on the first go, but he'll get the basics."

Trick stroked Dammit's chin, cooing at the bird softly.

This was one of the harder aspects of my job, but also the most satisfying. A good familiar was a partnership, a symbiotic balanced pairing. Dammit would be smarter, live longer—not just because someone would be taking care of him and offering security, but because of the magic bond itself. His life would be lengthened, and in return, he would assist Trick in his magic.

When the bond was finished, they'd be able to communicate on a psychic level. Trick would get a helper—an assistant who would aid him with spells, share their intuition and insights, and even their magic when needed. The bond was intimate, but not entirely even. Trick would gain the ability to command his familiar. That was one of the many reasons we took such care pairing a creature with a witch. The witch would be in a position of power and we didn't want them to abuse it.

If they didn't approach it as a sacred bond, no licensed animal mage would bind them. There weren't necessarily a lot of rules in what I did, but the ones we had were important. The witch had to be approved, the health of both examined to make sure they could handle the process, and the familiar always, *always* was an animal.

To bind any Uncanny, whether it be a fawn, a shifter, or a minotaur like Jim, was unthinkable. It would be like taking away a vital part of their humanity. They'd lose *autonomy*. Not that we had to worry much about that last rule. Only a truly evil person would do such a thing.

I closed my eyes, finding the strands of their magic with my mind. In my head, it looked like a tangled ball of brightly colored light. Burning reds, shining blues, rich purples, glittering yellows—fire magic. Everything has a little bit of magic in it. A rock might not be able to access its magic, but it's *there*.

That's why elementists can channel magic from their element, whether it's rock, water, fire, air, whatever. They have an affinity with it. Trick's magic pairs with the magic inherent in fire and he can harness that, making it bend to his will. When he's working, he can manipulate the temperature, keep it burning longer, or channel the heat with absolute precision.

Animal mages can also manipulate that magic, though it's not the same. One, I'm dealing with higher consciousness. While some parts of my magic are innocuous—like being able to talk to animals—I don't reach out and grab an animal's magic without asking. In the case of binding, I get the permission from both the witch and the creature. I make sure the creature understands what's happening. That they'll be gaining a master, albeit a kind one.

Some decide that the trade-off—longer, cushier life and higher intelligence—is worth it. Some would rather stay as they are.

When bonding someone to a familiar, I take strands of their magic and braid them together. It's a weaving, done slowly over time. The first braid is simple—a few strands overlapping each other. Then I build on that, until it's like a tapestry. It takes time and it's exhausting for all involved, but it's worth it.

I worked on Trick and Dammit until my hands started to shake. I was overdoing it, and I knew it. During my training I'd learned that while it was important to push myself, I also needed to recognize my limits. It was a difficult balance, because I didn't want to fail. I wanted to be a Switch more than anything.

But I also didn't want to let my moms down. Mama Ami, because she had put in a lot of time and energy mentoring me. And my own mother because... well, mostly for petty reasons. My mom would love me no matter what I decided to do. But her parents? They'd never quite forgiven their daughter for being born a regular human. My mom couldn't manipulate magic. She was a mechanic, which to me seemed a lot like magic because seriously, what the fuck does a carburetor even do? My mom had tried to explain it many, many times and it always went straight out of my head.

I loved my mom. I was proud of my mom. But her parents saw her as less than useless. Their only child was a dud of a witch. It didn't happen often, but it *did* happen. So there was a very petty part of me that wanted to succeed where my mother couldn't so I could rub it in their faces.

Not that I ever saw them.

I grabbed my glass of water and drained it in greedy gulps. I was tired, thirsty, and so hungry I wanted to unhinge my jaw and tip the contents of the refrigerator into it. I probably should have begged off until tomorrow, but Trick had already had Dammit for a week, and I wanted to cement the bond as soon as possible. But now I was worn down to the bone, and I still had to go to my Mama Ami's for family dinner.

Trick stared at Dammit in what could only be called wonder. "I can feel him!" My friend frowned. "He's happy, but he also seems sad. What am I doing wrong?"

"Nothing," I said, putting my glass in the sink. "He's still recovering from the loss of the woman he imprinted on. He's happy, but still processing, you know? Just keep showing him love and taking good care of him and he'll get there. It might be a good idea to figure out your radius—how far you can go from him before the communication gets spotty. Otherwise, he might panic when he suddenly can't reach you."

I shoved one of Declan's cookies into my mouth. There was no way I would make it to dinner if I didn't. I felt like I could eat wood chips right now, I was so hungry. And Declan was *delicious.*

Cookies! Declan's *cookies* were delicious!

Ugh. I'd been trying really, really hard to not think about our moment in the kitchen. Not only because I'd been miserable but also because Declan had smelled *amazing*. Like cookie dough and something spicy and his arms had been—comforting and something he'd offered as a friend and room-mate.

I needed to keep that in mind. He had enough going on without me developing a serious crush. And if he could do me a solid and stop walking around in pajama pants that hung low on his hips and really just highlighted his...*everything*, that would be great.

What was I doing? Right. Reassuring Trick.

"Remember, Dammit understands what we're doing, and he's agreed to it, but emotions are a whole different business. He needs time to heal." We were out of cookies and my stomach rumbled. We were out of a lot of things. I needed to go grocery shopping. And by groceries, I meant cereal and anything in the "hot pocket" aisle. "Any new name ideas?" Dammit had shot down any suggestions we'd made. Apparently, he was rather attached to Dammit.

"No, but I've been thinking. If the name makes him happy, why change it? He's already had a lot taken away from him." Trick gave Dammit another scratch. "I'm so sorry, little buddy. We'll go play with some fire. Will that make you feel better? Who wants to play with fire? You do!" Dammit chirped, ruffling his fluffy red feathers in excitement. "Yes, you do! Who's the bestest boy?"

I left them to it.

Fifteen minutes later, I was showered, changed, and sitting behind the wheel of my car. I was sitting because my car wouldn't start. Stupid car. I tried the key again in case this time it magically worked. Nothing. Just a few dull clicks. I banged my head against the steering wheel. *I hate everything.*

Someone knocked on my window and I screamed.

Declan blinked back at me, his hands held up in apology. I stared into his eyes while my brain came back online. They were the color of root beer, something I'd never really considered sexy until right this moment. His lips curved up at the edges as if his welcome was uncertain. Since I was white-knuckling the steering wheel, I didn't blame him for thinking that.

He had an exceptionally masculine face, but probably the softest-look-ing mouth I'd ever seen. Like if I could shrink down, that would be where I'd curl up and sleep. I'd make myself at home in that plush place where the edge of his mouth met that little furrow we all had that I always forgot the name of. Which now that I thought about it, was probably a weird thing to think.

I shouldn't stare at his mouth.

I apparently couldn't stop staring at his mouth.

I wondered what it would feel like if he—I quickly packaged that thought up and booted it into space. But I was still staring. The soft mouth was turning down, as were his eyebrows. Declan popped my door open. "Are you okay?"

I was still staring at him, but at least now it was in the eyes and not hyper focused on his lips. "I don't usually startle easily, but today..." I blew out a breath. "Today I'm a mage on the edge, I guess."

"Okay, okay, no need to take it out on your steering wheel." He squatted down, until he was below my eye level. I'd spent enough time with animals to understand exactly what he was doing—making himself small, not exactly submissive, but signaling that he wasn't a threat.

Declan hesitated, then peeled my hands from the steering wheel. He murmured soothing nonsense to me in that gravelly voice of his, and for a second I was tempted to ask him to read to me. A story, a recipe, a freaking grocery list—I just wanted to hear that soothing rumble, and so far, Declan hadn't shown himself to be especially chatty.

In fact, he'd made himself so invisible in our house that if I didn't know better, I would have thought we were being haunted by a sexy ghost.

He rubbed my hands, smoothing his thumbs along the pressure points. "I'm sorry."

I felt my heart rate slow, my breathing normalize, and the whole time we never broke eye contact. Which was hot. Why was that hot? Normally, extended eye contact made me fidget. "It's okay. Probably would have been fine if I wasn't exhausted and hangry. I overdid it today."

Another hesitant quirk of lips, like he found me funny, but only in a reluctant sort of way. "Still, I didn't intend to startle you. I just wanted to ask if you needed help."

His hands still rubbed mine and I couldn't help it, I glanced down. He seemed to notice what he was doing and dropped my hands like they'd suddenly become red-hot chainsaws.

It was possible that he released them in a totally normal way and I was overreacting. It's just...it had felt really nice and I didn't want him to stop. "I think you've done plenty, thanks." When he winced, I closed my eyes and let out a breath, reminding myself that I was a grown-up, which was always kind of the worst, but I needed to act like it anyway. "That came out grouchier than I wanted."

He nodded, standing up and shoving his hands into the pockets of his hooded sweatshirt. "Won't start?"

When I shook my head, he jogged over to his SUV and dug out his jumper cables. Which ended up doing absolutely nothing at all.

Motherfucker. I climbed out and slammed the door, resisting the urge to kick it.

He gathered up the cables and slammed his hood before tossing them into the back of his SUV.

"And now I'm going to have to get it towed to the mechanic and be late for dinner." I pulled out my phone. "And she is going to do some hardcore gloating."

"Your mechanic?" His brows furrowed. "Why would your mechanic gloat?"

"Because my mechanic is also my mother and she told me to bring it in two weeks ago to get it looked at and I didn't." I flipped through my contacts. "She won't say 'I told you so,' but she will laugh hysterically, which is kind of worse."

"Ah." He looked down the street for a second, rocking back on his heels. "I can give you a ride."

I glanced up from my screen to see if he was serious. He looked a little nervous and sweaty, but serious. There was nothing on this planet that made a woman feel more desirable than being able to make an attractive man break into a flop sweat. "I could call a ride or something." I'd be a little late, but I'd get there. My stomach grumbled, telling me it didn't like the idea of being late.

"I wouldn't offer if it was a problem," he said, digging his hands into his pockets.

I chewed on my lip, thinking. If this had been anyone else in our house, I wouldn't think twice. I'd jump in and put off the tow until tomorrow. But Declan…was still sweating, but the determined set of his jaw told me he wanted to do this for me.

I pointed my phone at him. "I should say no, because you're obviously offering under duress, but I'm hungry enough to not care." I waved at him. "Let's go."

CHAPTER EIGHT

Declan

I'd been worried about getting into the car with Lou. We'd been doing well in the house, but in the house, I could leave. It was a little harder leaving a moving vehicle. Not impossible, but not always wise. On top of that, the SUV was a small, enclosed space. She'd be right next to me the entire time. I wouldn't be able to ignore her.

My muscles were tense, my wolf alert as we buckled in and maneuvered the car onto the street. Lou put the address into my phone for me, turning on the GPS. I followed the human-sounding robot voice telling me which way to go, and with each passing second, I relaxed more and more. This was Lou.

Lou won't hurt us. The wolf's tone was amused as it lay down, putting his head on his paws. Calm. Which made me calm. I let out a slow breath, and with it, the last of my tension.

Lou was quiet. She always was around me, like she was trying to calm a feral animal. No quick movements. No loud noises. Trying so hard to gentle the world around her. Even her scent was soothing now.

Lou always smelled a little wild, like all the animals she encountered, as well as an underlying note of cedar and her own natural scent. By now, both my wolf and I associated her with home, just like I'd wanted.

My shoulders hunched up momentarily as I worried that this was part of her process, putting me at ease so she could work her magic. Which I knew was just my paranoia talking, but my paranoia was that loud talker in a restaurant who drowns out everyone else's conversation. *Shut up and eat some breadsticks, paranoia.* Breadsticks were delicious.

My wolf chuffed a laugh.

Lou's stomach rumbled. "Quiet, you." She poked her belly as she grumbled.

I reached over, popping open the glove compartment, which was full of jerky, peanut butter cracker packs, and mixed nuts. "Help yourself."

She perked up, grabbing a pack of crackers. "You know, most people keep paperwork in there. Spare napkins. Even maps sometimes. You've got a tiny convenience store."

"Maps are under your seat. I need food more often than I get lost." But I still kept a map or two around. Every once in a while, I drove some place where I didn't have good service and I liked knowing I had a backup plan.

I watched her eat out of the corner of my eye and something inside me relaxed. Not in a calming way, like earlier, but more like I'd been trying to accomplish something, meet some goal, and I'd suddenly done it. A mix of relief and…satisfaction? What was that about?

She pulled her reusable water bottle out of her bag, unscrewing the lid so she could take a sip. "You're my hero right now."

I couldn't help it, I laughed. "That's all it takes? Crackers and a lift?"

She took another sip, and I realized I was watching her again, so I snapped my attention back to the road.

"You clearly don't know me yet. You had me at crackers. I'm feral—you feed me, I'm yours."

Another wave of satisfaction. I'd think about it later. Right now, I was maxed out, mentally. "Go nuts." I waved one-handed at the glovebox. "I can always use another person in my debt."

She shook her head. "I don't want to totally ruin my appetite. You have no idea what culinary delights await me." She gave a happy sigh and I was abruptly and strangely envious of her family for making her sigh like that.

I wanted that sigh for myself, and I realized that despite repeating to myself that it was a bad idea and far too complicated, I had a crush on my roommate. My off-limits-for-many-good-reasons roommate.

Only, I couldn't seem to think of all those reasons right now.

I cleared my throat. From the way she'd been tiptoeing around me, I knew I could get away without bringing it up, but I didn't want it hovering over us. Getting between us. More than that, knowing I'd hurt her and Van, even though I understood why, didn't make me feel good. "I'm sorry. About the first night." I glanced at her, but her expression didn't tell me much. "I hurt you. And Van."

Lou was frowning at me, her brows pinched.

I rubbed a hand against my forehead. Great, the panic sweat was back. "It's not you. Or her. Anyway, I'm sorry." The silence in the car stretched out until I started to fidget. *Please, fuck, say something soon, otherwise I'm going to open my car door and roll out into traffic.*

She made a sort of frustrated noise, though I wasn't sure what it was aimed at. "Declan, as far as I'm concerned, you have no reason to apologize. It was a bad situation all around." Lou shoved her wrapper into the trash bag between the seats. "Not really anyone's fault."

I glanced at her again. She looked comfortable. Shoulders down. Expression open. Slight smile on her face. Was she honestly over it?

"I just … I hated that I hurt you."

"I know, and I'm sorry that we put you in that position, even if it wasn't intentional." She turned in her seat, angling her face toward mine. "Can we start over?" She stuck out her hand. "Louise. Your new roommate and animal mage."

I took one hand off the wheel, taking her palm in mine. "Declan. Shifter." We shook, and I tried not to think about how nice that small, soft hand felt in mine. I bet she was that soft all over … fuck.

I dropped her hand. "Thank you. For giving me another chance." I stretched my neck, trying to loosen my muscles.

Lou shook her head. "I say terrible things *all the time,* so I try to be understanding when other people do it." She rubbed her hands down her thighs and I tracked the movement. "I think we both feel pretty bad about—oh, yay!" The GPS had announced our exit and now she was actually bouncing in her seat with anticipation.

I grinned at her. "Your mom a good cook, then?"

"Oh, hell no. My mom burns toast. She can fix the toaster, but she can't use it properly. No, Mama Ami, Papa B-jou, Gram Gram, and the aunties will be our culinary saviors." Her brows knit. "Sometimes I wonder if family dinner night started because they were all worried that my mom and I might starve after Mama Ami moved out." She leaned forward. "It's that house there—third on the left."

My original plan to drop her off and give her my number so I could come back and get her was immediately dashed as she catapulted herself out of the SUV and ran to greet the mass of people that flowed out of the house. I could get her number from Trick, but it didn't feel right to drive off without a word. I followed slowly behind her, trying to take in everything at once.

The house wasn't huge—a two-story Victorian in bright purples and yellows—but the amount of people coming through the door gave it a clown car feel. A swarm of small children ran ahead of an older, gray-haired lady with a no-nonsense bob and a huge smile, followed by several Asian men and women and a handful of people that looked like they'd be at home in a modern-day Viking reenactment. Since this area had several pockets of Scandinavian influence, my guess probably wasn't far off.

A pale, statuesque redhead folded Lou into a hug. They looked a lot alike, which made me think she might be Lou's mom.

You never know what someone's family will be like. We have this idea that families are a very set pattern—one mom, one dad, possible siblings, grandparents, but very few seem to actually fit that restrictive mold. I had half siblings, my stepmom, and my father. My family wasn't a great template, but that's not because it broke the mold—it was because my dad and my stepmom were toxic. The only pattern that really mattered—love—Lou's family displayed so casually it was almost humbling. This was a family that loved each other and it was there in every laugh, movement, and gentle chide.

I absently clicked the lock button on my SUV, making it beep. They all turned, their expressions a mix of curiosity and wariness, like I was a lone wolf that had stumbled into another pack. With a start I realized they were kind of right. I was an interloper, danger status unknown, and Lou's family would protect her without thought—it was all in the body language.

I dropped my shoulders and dug my hands in my pockets, trying to look nonthreatening.

The redhead quirked an eyebrow. "And who's this?"

"Mom, this is Declan, my new roommate—"

I cut her off before she could confess about her car and stepped forward, offering my hand. "Pleasure to meet you."

A man came forward, slinging an arm around Lou, giving her a kiss on the cheek. His black hair was longer on top and slicked back, the sides razored almost to the scalp, emphasizing the handsome lines of his face. His skin was light brown except his arms, which were covered in bright tattoos. His arm stayed around Lou and I was surprised by a sudden jolt of jealousy.

I shook it off. Lou wasn't mine. Lou would never be mine. I was lucky we'd reached the point where we could easily be in the same room.

The guy jutted his chin forward. "This the guy Van hexed?"

Lou groaned and pushed him away. "You been talking to Van?"

"I told him." A young woman stepped around them, greeting me with a smile. Juliet, Van's sister, had golden hair that was pulled back into a ponytail and a spray of freckles over delicate features. Her daughter, Savannah, was balanced on her hip. A blue butterfly barrette held back Savannah's brown hair, framing big, dark blue eyes that were definitely judging me.

Lou tickled Savannah's chin. "I didn't know you'd be here."

Savannah hurled herself into the guy's arms. He released Lou, swinging Savannah onto his hip without thinking. "I've been trying to convince Jules to let us watch Savvy for her on dinner nights."

Juliet huffed. "I don't want to impose—"

The guy rolled his eyes. "Yeah, because clearly it's a hardship." He curled Savannah more firmly to his side and she threw her chubby arms around his neck. He held a hand out to me and I shook it, glad he didn't do that weird dominance thing some men do where they tried to crush all the bones in your hand. "I'm Bay, Lou's brother."

Lou's mom shooed them away, stopping to squeeze my shoulder. "Welcome to family dinner night. A bit overwhelming at first, but you'll get used to it. I'm Jory, by the way." She herded me in the door.

"Oh, I wasn't—"

She leaned in close to me. "Do yourself a favor, Declan, and come to dinner."

I was ushered through the house and into the backyard before I could argue. Lou reappeared from somewhere and detached Jory from me.

Lou rolled her eyes, but her grin was good-natured. "Mom, stop." She quickly maneuvered me off to the side and dropped her voice. "You're invited and welcome to stay, of course, but don't let them bully you with their aggressive hospitality." Lou rested her hands on her hips and blew out a breath. "There are at least four more animal mages here and you don't know anyone, so I'd understand if you want to bolt."

I glanced around at the crowd. Someone had set up several large picnic tables, complete with tablecloths, silverware, and mason jars full of wildflowers. Big, brightly colored lanterns were strung from the trees. There were two grills, one manned by a robust, middle-aged blond man grilling salmon. An older woman, her black hair shot through with silver, handled the other one, deftly sliding skewers of pork onto the grill. Everything smelled amazing.

I wanted to stay. I hadn't been to a party like this in a long time. The weather was perfect, the people were friendly, and my mouth was already watering at the scents wafting off the grills. "Can you point them out so I'm not surprised?"

Lou stood on her tiptoes and scanned the crowd, pointing several people out. "Mama Ami of course, her husband at the grill, Papa Bjorn. He's one." She frowned. "Both their daughters, though I only see Astrid…" She brightened. "Oh, there she is, and the taller one next to her is Tova." She motioned to two young women carrying platters of food out to one of the tables. "And one of Mama Ami's sisters, but I'm not sure she's here tonight. If I see her, I'll let you know." She turned back to me. "But if you want to go, I'll make excuses for you. No problem."

I considered the situation for a few moments. I'd been making progress, and this might be a good time to push myself a little. After all, Lou's family seemed so nice, and we were outside, so I wouldn't feel hemmed in with any of the animal mages. Plus, my keys were in my pocket. If I needed to leave, I could. I straightened my shoulders. "I think…I think I want to stay."

Any remaining doubt disappeared as Lou's face lit up. "Great!" She took my hand. "I'll introduce you around. If you need a break, just let me know, okay?" Lou immediately began leading me around, introducing me to so many people they quickly started blurring together. Someone gave me a beer, and every few minutes, I was offered different appetizers to try. The whole time, Lou never left my side.

Basically, it was heaven.

After about a half hour, Lou had to use the bathroom, so she handed me off to her brother. Bay still had Savannah on his hip. I spent a second waving at her before we were joined by a big, heavily tattooed guy holding a tray. He must be another family friend—I'd smelled traces of him around Trick's house.

Bay handed me a fresh beer. "This is Will. He's a piercer at my tattoo shop."

Will was taller than me, blond, and built on sturdy lines. He had an air of affable humor about him that made me like him right away. Colorful tattoos started on his neck, dipped under his shirt—which had a big glittery kitten on it—and continued again down both arms.

Will presented his platter with a flourish. "Have you had lumpia before?"

I shook my head.

He handed me three. "Problem solved."

They looked like small spring rolls, but with a thinner, crispier wrap. Will turned the platter so I could dip it in the sauce and take a bite. The taste of pork, cabbage, green onions, and garlic hit my tongue and it was all I could do to keep my eyes from rolling back in my head in absolute bliss. "Holy shit, that's good."

I ate the other two quickly and ended up licking my fingers like an animal. Turns out I had no shame when it came to lumpia.

Will handed me another before taking the tray over to one of the tables already covered with dishes. The array was varied—I saw what appeared to be pickled herring, sausage that smelled like venison and blueberry, a noodle dish I was told was called pancit, a beet salad, pork skewers—it was a mouth-watering array. I hadn't realized how hungry I was until I saw it.

Lou walked back over to us. She'd taken out her braid and was now trying to wrap her hair into something bun-shaped, her beer bottle shoved awkwardly in her pocket. Every step jostled the bottle, and I wasn't sure, but it seemed to be edging slowly out of her pocket.

Without thinking, I grabbed the bottle, then stood there awkwardly holding it for her.

Once she had her hair out of the way, Lou grinned at me and it felt like a reward. "Thanks." She took her beer back. "Are they playing nice?"

Bay looked affronted. "Of course we were." He splayed a hand on his chest. "I am the embodiment of kindness and...."

Lou grinned around the lip of her beer bottle. "You can't even finish that sentence."

"I can't." He shrugged. "How you doing over there, Declan—you overwhelmed yet?"

I tore my eyes off of Lou's mouth. "A little, but it's...nice." And it was. Their family was the good kind of overwhelming. Everyone was laughing, hugging, talking. The pure joy they all felt together made me want to bounce on my toes. This was a bonded family, and for a moment I felt a longing so deep that I thought I might break in two.

"Yeah," Lou said, "they can be a little much at first." She smiled at me then, and *fuck me*, she lit up when she smiled like that. I gripped my beer tighter, because for a second I was concerned that I was going to drop it. I buried the flash of attraction deep. Roommates and sex were a tricky combo at the best of times, and this wasn't the best of times. This was supposed to be a fresh start. I needed to make good choices.

I corralled my brain back on track. What had we been talking about? Right. I took in the crowd. "A little much can be pretty great."

Lou nodded. "Proof that good things can come out of crap situations." She tipped her nose up. "Obviously, I'm a gift to Bay in every conceivable way. Someone had to keep him in line until Astrid and Tova showed up."

He poked her side and she yelped. "You're such a shit."

A passing aunt playfully tweaked his ear. "Language."

I was curious now, but not sure my questions would be welcomed. "Can I ask?" I waved my bottle back and forth at them. "How this happened? Or is that a terrible question? Feel free to tell me to fuck off."

The same aunt came back, her hands full of plates, but she still managed to tweak my ear, though she was smiling. "Language."

I dipped my head. "Sorry."

"Busted." Bay snickered as Savannah squealed and grabbed a fistful of his shirt; without even looking at her he began to bounce her on his hip, much to her delight.

"You've met my mom." Lou pointed at Jory and then to the woman who had been introduced to me as Mama Ami, a delicate-looking Filipinx woman directing several large people to do her bidding with the swift and absolute authority that a military general would envy. "That's Bay's mom. She was married to an asshole named Gerald."

Bay took over the story. "When she was pregnant with me, she discovered that Gerald had a girlfriend. Mom kicked Gerald out and told him she wanted nothing to do with him. While she was piling his stuff together to burn on the lawn, she found a printout of Jory's ultrasound."

Lou finished off her beer. "Mama Ami decided that while Gerald was a despicable waste of humanity, her baby should know his sibling, so she tracked Jory down." Lou grimaced at this. "My mom was training as a mechanic. She was only nineteen. Mama Ami was almost done with graduate school, but still had at least a year and then her residency or internship time. Both would have to struggle to complete their studies and would need help, only my mom's family…" Lou pursed her lips searching for the right word.

"They suck," Bay said.

I studied Lou out of the corner of my eye to see if Bay's words would upset her, but she just nodded, pointing her beer hand at him. "They do kind of suck."

"Lou's being nice. They're assholes." Bay held Savannah above his head, wiggling the giggling toddler back and forth. When he settled her back down, he jerked his chin at the gathering. "As you've probably figured out, my family picks up strays."

Lou elbowed him and Bay winced.

I smiled around my beer. "I don't consider myself a stray."

Bay repositioned Savannah on his hip. "Sorry, anyway, when our moms met, they decided to pool resources. Help each other. Jory moved into my mom's house. We were raised together in the same house until my mom married my dad."

Lou snagged another beer from someone as they passed. "Papa Bjorn is the best. Honestly, we could have stayed in the house with them, but my mom wanted to give them their space, and we were doing better by then. Of course, she bought a small bungalow next door." Lou pointed at a neighboring house, where I could just make out the roof and a little bit of the siding behind the large fence…that had an open gate that obviously didn't get closed often. It was covered in a clinging vine that had stuck it to the fence.

At this point we were interrupted by Papa Bjorn carrying a wooden slab covered in grilled salmon. He leaned over to kiss Lou on the cheek. "It's good to see you, darling girl."

Lou returned the kiss. "You too, Papa B-jou."

"Salmon is ready. We're about to eat."

"Papa B-jou?" I murmured.

Lou flushed, but I think it was more from the beer and happiness than embarrassment. "I had a hard time saying 'Bjorn' when I was little."

Bjorn grinned. "It was endearing."

Bay's mother, Mama Ami, came up behind Bjorn and gave him a squeeze. "It's about time. I'm starving."

He slowed his movement so Ami could stay connected to his back. "It's not my fault. I left the office on time. Lara and Jen were late. Something about losing one of their prep people."

They left our sphere, moving together to put the salmon on the table, which was for the best because I was about ten seconds away from swiping it from him and eating it right off the board. You'd think I hadn't had a bite in weeks, or that I hadn't been stuffed half full since I got here.

Maybe I didn't realize how hungry I was until I smelled the food. Except now I wondered if I was mistaking one hunger for another. Lou's family surrounded me and for the first time I fully understood how fucking lonely I felt and how starved I was for this. It was like stepping into a sauna after walking for three days through frozen tundra. All around me people were chiding, bickering, laughing, and squabbling and there was so much damned love that I was suddenly ravenous.

Someone passed me with a full plate and my stomach rumbled. Then again, maybe it was the food.

Lou gave my arm a squeeze. "I'll grab us some plates, okay?"

Or maybe I was hungry for something else altogether. I tracked Lou as she dodged family members.

Savannah brought my attention back to the group by slapping my elbow. Without thinking, I reached out and grabbed her hand gently, letting her wrap her chubby fingers around one of mine. I leaned down and pretend to snap at her fingers with my teeth and she giggled. When I looked up, Bay's expression was thoughtful.

"Jules said you've been looking for a job?"

I nodded, but my attention had returned to Savannah. She was giggling like mad now and enjoying the game.

"We need a part-time counter person at the shop," he said slowly, thinking.

"Tattoo shop, right?" I continued to pretend snap at Savannah's fingers. "I don't really know anything about it." I didn't have any tattoos, though I had friends who did.

"You can learn." He grimaced. "But it's only a few opening shifts. Not enough to really pay all the bills. But maybe…you got any cooking experience?"

I was distracted by his question, giving Savannah an opportunity, which she seized—she grabbed my beard and yanked. Maybe it was time for a trim. I carefully extricated her hands. "Nothing professional. My last job was sort of being the social media person and general helper for Wulver Craft Brewery." I straightened but kept hold of Savannah's hands. "I filled in where they needed me, basically." Zoey had always referred to me as her support team, and I felt a sharp, quick pinch in my heart. Savannah pulled her hands from mine. "I've cooked for a lot of people before doing large prep, but nothing in a professional setting."

"How do you mean, 'large prep'?" Bay adjusted his hold on Savannah as she leaned in to grab both of my cheeks and stare into my eyes. She wasn't a wolf, but I'll be damned if she wasn't attempting to show dominance like a baby alpha. Juliet must have her hands *full* with this one.

75

"I grew up in what could kindly be called a commune." I bumped my forehead against Savannah's. *You're not the alpha here yet, baby child.* She huffed at me, smacking my cheek. "We all had to help out. The numbers shifted, but we usually had anywhere from fifteen to twenty families around at a time. I learned how to cook by helping with everything from prepping to serving for one hundred or more people every night. I'm no chef or anything, but I can follow a recipe." I braced myself for questions, but they never came.

Bay shifted Savannah onto his hip so he could grab my arm, yanking me along. "Come on, I've got an idea."

He pulled me away from Lou, and I almost dug my heels in, because I didn't want to leave her. I glanced back at her and she tilted her head, pointing a finger at her chest. Did I need her to come along? My impulse was to say, 'Yes, of course I do.' She wouldn't question it or think any less of me. But I was a grown man and I didn't need to pull her along like a baby blanket.

I *wanted* too, but I didn't *need* to. Except with Lou, the line between the two was quickly eroding, like a sandcastle hit with a strong wave. I shook my head anyway and she poked two fingers at her eyes, then turned her hand toward me in the classic 'I'm watching you' gesture. My shoulders dropped. Even if she wasn't right next to me, Lou would keep an eye on me.

I followed Bay as he wove through the crowd, stopping when he reached two young women—one short, her tan arms covered in tattoos of colorful flowers from her wrist to the strap of her tank top. Her long, straight black hair was up in a messy bun, her eyeliner a perfect cat's eye. The other woman was taller, sinewy, with short purple hair that she'd somehow managed to style like a mini pompadour. I could see a single tattoo on the shoulder facing me: a skull and crossed rolling pins. They both smelled like garlic, spices, and oil mixed with a baseline of their natural scent.

Bay stopped in front of them, and they paused midbicker to coo at Savannah while simultaneously assessing Bay.

"You've got your 'I want something face' on." The tall one reached out to take the toddler from him. Savannah took it in stride, clearly used to being passed from family member to family member.

"Yes, but not for me." Bay waved his now free hands at me. "Declan, this is Lara." He gestured at the short one. "And Jen." He repeated the half-hearted hand wave in the direction of the one with purple hair. "He's Lou's new roommate and Trick's friend. You guys had a prep person quit?"

Jen and Lara took on identical shrewd expressions as they examined me. "You cook?"

"I'm not a chef," I clarified. "But I do have experience prepping for large meals."

"What does that mean?" Lara asked.

I gave them an abbreviated explanation like the one I gave Bay. Their eyes went wide, but again it was Lara who spoke.

"Huh." She tilted her head to take me in again, as if I might have some telltale feature that could have clued her in to my upbringing. Like I should be named Rainbow Waterfall Freehugs and reek of patchouli, or wear clothes I made myself out of cotton my family loomed. None of those things were bad, but they didn't apply to me. The word "commune" carried a lot of cultural baggage. "Cult" even more so.

I don't offer further explanation. People reacted strangely when I told them about my childhood, and I didn't want a pity job out of these two. I also didn't want to be examined like a bug. I already felt somewhat beholden to Bay for leaning so hard on family connections. But I'd had zero progress so far on my own, so why not?

Lara and Jen exchanged a look. Lara shrugged.

"Okay," Jen said. "Can you start tomorrow? We're a bit desperate."

I blinked. "Really? That's it? You don't want to look at a resume or anything?"

Jen snorted. "What part of 'desperate' was unclear?" She softened her sarcasm with a small smile. "Besides, you came here with Lou, and Bay brought you over to us. That goes a long way."

"Consider this week a working interview," Lara said. "You'll get paid, but if it doesn't work out, we split ways, no hard feelings."

"Thank you." Relief rushed through me. Even if they fired me after a week, I at least had *something* coming in and—

Bay was shaking his head. "A week? Not much of a learning curve. What kind of pay are we talking here? You split tips with the staff?"

Jen bristled. "Are you calling us cheap? We don't cheat our employees!"

I opened my mouth to speak, afraid of having the job offer revoked, but Bay was already there.

"Jen, please." He rolled his eyes. "I'm just looking out for my boy here. Calm yourself."

She folded her arms. "You're such an ass." She waved at me. "What should we offer him, then?"

"I want to make sure he gets a living wage. You pay minimum over in your death trap?"

I thought for sure Jen would be pissed, but her eyes lit up. She was *enjoying* this. "Did you just call my food truck a death trap? What about your rat-hole of a shop?"

Bay spluttered.

Again I opened my mouth to jump in, but this time Lara stopped me by putting her hand on my arm. She leaned in close. "Best to let it go. They're competitive as fuck. Don't ruin their fun."

An auntie nearby clicked her tongue. "Language, Lara."

Lara startled. "Sorry." She dropped her voice into a whisper. "It's like they have bat ears sometimes."

"I just don't get why he's arguing at all," I whispered back. "Why would he care?"

Lara slapped me on the back. "Welcome to the family, I guess."

That brought me up short. I was used to taking care of those around me—raising Zoey. Keeping an eye on Sid. But when was the last time anyone had stuck their neck out to make sure I was covered? Trick gave me a roof—but we were old friends. Bay had just met me. I wasn't used to having any sort of safety net, and for a second, I felt slightly unmoored.

Jen grunted. "This will go on all day. I'm stepping in." Jen joined the fray, all three of them ignoring me as they discussed when they needed me and where, because apparently, I'd just agreed to work counter at a tattoo shop and prep for a food truck.

I should probably have said something, since they were bandying about my future, but I just stood there. It felt so weird having someone else fight for me. Good, but weird. So I stood by, my chest strangely tight but in a good way as they negotiated everything from my hours to my pay.

At some point, Savannah swung her arms toward me and Jen handed her off without pausing their negotiation. Savannah sighed, nestling into my chest. I started to rock her, listening as Bay talked about my "best interests," which was surprising since even I didn't know what they were right now, but he apparently had a firm idea as to what they should be. By the time Savannah started snoring, I had a set schedule, decent pay, the possibility of benefits through the shop, and two new jobs.

When all was said and done, Bay reached out to shake their hands but paused, looking slightly sheepish. "All that okay with you?"

"Yes," I said, the words coming out gravelly. Weight lifted off me so fast I felt dizzy with it, and it wasn't only because I had work—I also had the sudden understanding of how lucky I'd been to move in with Trick. I'd thought I was moving to Seattle with only one friend at my back and a place to stay, and suddenly I had so much more. I grinned. "Thanks, really, to all of you."

Bay shrugged, shaking Lara and Jen's hands. "Hey, I'm just helping you get the foot in the door. Whether you keep the job or not, that's on you."

"I'll keep it," I said, firmly. "You won't regret it. None of you will."

Lara patted my arm. "No, but you might after we have you dice ten pounds of onions."

CHAPTER NINE

Lou

Not everyone gets my and Bay's relationship. A lot of siblings, especially born so close together, fight constantly. And I didn't know if it was because we had different mothers, or a large family to give us an endless sea of love and attention, or our own natural personalities—we never had to compete like traditional siblings. Oh, we bickered and antagonized, but it was never serious.

There was just no need for any real fighting. We had an abundance of resources to share. We were close enough in age to be twins, and sometimes we acted like it. I know we didn't share a womb, but it *felt* like we did. The thin layers that separated us before we were born were so close—our mothers wept, laughed, supported, and lived together. They raged together. They were in each other's corner from the moment they met and I think Bay and I came out more than happy to keep that pattern going.

If I fell, Bay picked me up. When he had a bad day, I was there with a stack of action movies, a case of beer, and his favorite pizza—which also happened to be mine, too, and I felt sorry for the people who hadn't accepted hot peppers and pineapple into their lives yet. We did our homework together and learned to drive together. He taught me how to read and I helped him figure out how to double knot his shoelaces.

So if a new friend or prospective beau didn't pass the Bay test? It's "don't pass go and fuck your two hundred dollars" without a second thought.

Still, even I was surprised at how quickly he adopted Declan. A few days after the family dinner I stopped by Ritual Ink. I'd gone to my mom's house to pick up my car, and she asked me to drop something off to Bay since his shop was on my way home. It was my day off, so I swung by Wicked Brews and grabbed a tray of coffees for everyone. I knocked on the glass door, since it was only a quarter to eleven and they weren't open yet.

Will let me in to the front of the shop, which I'd helped make into a comfortable waiting area when Bay first opened. A tan faux-leather couch and matching chairs surrounded a coffee table full of magazines. The walls were painted a light tea green, with either framed custom art by the tattoo artists or the smaller, pre-made flash designs for people that either wanted something small and simple or weren't sure what they wanted yet. The back wall didn't have any frames, but instead boasted a large panther mural.

Once he relocked the door, Will immediately leaned over the coffee tray like it was one of those boxes of chocolates where you had to guess at the flavors. He wiggled his fingers over them, momentarily indecisive, before snagging the tallest to-go cup. "Pikachu, I pick you!" He took a sip and sighed happily.

Will was easily one of my favorite people. He was well over six foot, broad-shouldered, and had tattoos that started on his neck and kept going down. He made a great piercer, because he seemed to naturally generate calming waves. I'd never tested it, but I was pretty sure standing next to Will lowered your blood pressure.

Watching him pierce kids' ears was one of the cutest things I'd ever seen.

"I didn't know you were into Pokémon," I said, leaning into the hug I knew he would offer. Will was a hugger. He was good at it, too. Every single person in my house had stopped in on a bad day just to get a hug from Will. He should start charging.

"I'm not, but it's been on my mind all week ever since this lady came in to test an experimental sex toy." He let me go and took a long sip from his coffee.

I waited. Nope, he was just going to leave it like that. "You're going to need to help me connect the dots between 'Pokémon' and 'experimental sex toy' and why you were involved in the process."

He nodded. Totally normal conversation for Will. "Oh yeah, well, she needed to see if the jewelry we use for genital piercings would be a problem. I guess the ball involves magnets and she was concerned because she didn't know what our body jewelry was made of." He tilted his head and squinted. "I can imagine that it would cause issues if you had iron in delicate areas. Unfortunate tugging and all of that. I told her that none of our jewelry has ferromagnetic properties—our basic jewelry is made of implant grade titanium—but she wanted to see for herself."

Will took another sip. "It looked like a Pokémon ball."

"Ah." I patted Will on the cheek. "Your job is weird."

He grinned at me. "So is yours."

"Touché."

Still smiling, he leaned back his head and yelled, "The coffee fairy is here!"

Ritual Ink wasn't tiny, but it wasn't huge, so Will's yelling was probably unnecessary since no one had turned on the music yet. Once you were past the waiting area, Bay's tattoo shop opened up, revealing six tattooing stations, each partitioned off with portable folding screens in case people needed privacy.

There was also a piercing room, where Will worked. Next to that was the dirty room, which shared a wall with the aptly named clean room. The dirty room had a little window so people could pass through the scrubbed and packed gear into the clean room. Once it was in the clean room, they would autoclave the packs of tools or jewelry they used in the shop, like piercing needles. We had a similar setup at Family Familiar.

In the back there was a little break room where the artists went to eat or sketch out tattoos for appointments. Not all the artists at Ritual Ink could do what Bay did. They were talented, creating works of art out of ink and skin, but they weren't magic. The tattoos Bay could do were different, down to the special set of inks he used.

Bay specialized in sigil work—using arcane symbols, runes, and so on to create an effect. Need to write your dissertation, but can't focus? Trying to get a promotion and need a dash of luck? My brother can help you. He'll craft a tattoo to suit your needs, sealing it in your blood for extra kick. If someone needed something smaller, more basic, Bay had a series of temporary tattoos he could use…as long as you were okay with saliva. I mean, something had to kindle the magic, and the list of bodily fluids he could use for that was short.

Once the magic had been used up, the design disappeared. It was precise work, more art than science, and expensive as hell.

Nicki, one of the other artists, came over and squeezed my arm. "I could kiss you. How did you know I had the tireds?" Her normally neatly styled black hair was slicked back under a hat, and her eyes had dark circles under them.

"Busy night?"

She rubbed her eye with the heel of her hand. "Super busy. Did a fundraiser for the pet shelter last night. So many adorable pet portraits! Next time I'll be smart and arrange my schedule so I can at least come in late the next day."

I handed her the large drip coffee. "Sounds wise."

She took the cup with a hopeful expression on her face. "Black like my heart?"

"But warm like your love for me," I said. "Did you raise a lot of money?"

Nicki lit up. "Six grand! Plus a lot of donated food and other supplies. We're totally going to do it again." She grabbed the soy latte from me. "I'll give this to Bay and let him know you're here. He has his headphones on and I don't think he heard Will's bellow."

I thanked her and headed over to reception. Declan was scowling at the computer screen, and I could hear the faint strains of music coming out of his earbuds. Since he was so focused, I took a few minutes to drink him in. Declan's shoulders bunched under his shirt as he hunched closer to the screen, the material clinging to him like a second skin. His usually soft mouth was pinched, his jaw tight, and his brow furrowed. Whatever highlighted mess he was looking at didn't make him happy. Add in the bruising under his eyes and you had someone that was tired, stressed, and frustrated.

The instinct to wrap my arms around him and bury my face into the back of his neck was strong. I bet he smelled delicious. I bet he *tasted* delicious—

Aaaannnd I wasn't going there. I handed him the last drink, which was actually chamomile tea. "It's not poison, I promise."

He blinked up at me in surprise, but didn't startle or tense up. Victory! We'd been making good progress in being comfortable around each other. "Thank you. I wasn't concerned about poison." He sniffed it and smiled before frowning back at the screen. "Not your style," he said absently. "If you wanted to murder me, you'd come at me directly to make sure I knew it was you. Sneaky isn't your way."

"It concerns me that you've apparently put this much thought into it." I'd been joking, but considering our rocky start, had he put *actual* thought into it? "Just to be clear, you know I was kidding, right? I have not now or in the past had any sort of murder plans involving you."

That earned me a small smile. "I wasn't quite that paranoid, but thank you for making sure."

"Okay, good." I tossed the drink holder into the recycling and leaned my hip against the desk. "Now, want to tell me what the computer has done to anger you?"

Declan huffed and sat back, running his hands through his hair. I spent a moment indulging myself by watching what the movements did to his muscles.

I set my own coffee down and put my hands on my cheeks, hoping that would cool them off before he noticed. Luckily, he was still staring at the screen.

"Whoever did this before was either terrible or didn't understand the scheduling program. I've had to straighten out several double bookings."

I winced. Bay had spent a long time developing his client base and was sometimes booked out anywhere from six months to a year ahead. Double booking left a lot of angry clients.

"You're right to make that face."

Declan hadn't looked over at me, which meant he had to be watching me out of the corner of his eye. Did that mean he'd caught me staring at him? My cheeks were practically on fire now. Damn.

Declan tapped his fingers along the desktop. "Your brother's been working long days to fit everyone in, and he's exhausted. It's going to take him another week or so to catch up. And apparently they never scheduled any sort of break in for Will. He works open to close some days and he's booked solid. When's he supposed to eat? No one wants a piercer with low blood sugar."

Will would bust his ass, too. A good chunk of his pay came through tips and commissions. He wouldn't take a break if he had a client.

"So, trial by fire, eh?" I grinned at him.

He finally shifted to face me, returning my smile just as Bay waltzed in and collapsed onto Declan's back. I was a little jealous of how quickly they'd bonded. I had to remind myself that Bay's magic wasn't like mine and hadn't hurt Declan. Someone with my kind of magic had. I refused to take Declan's wariness personally, because this wasn't about me.

"I'm going to marry him. Your boy is good."

I wanted to argue that he wasn't my boy—but he wasn't *not* my boy, either. Which made no sense, so I just sipped my coffee.

"It's too soon," Declan said, absently patting Bay's hand. "What will people think?"

"That you married me for my dick, which is a totally valid reason." Bay sighed and got up, coming over to greet me with a hug. "Did you know your boy here is a social media whiz?" Bay was practically glowing, he was so happy, which I completely understood. Bay *hated* social media but had to use Instagram at the very least for the shop. People liked to show off their new tattoos, and if they tagged the shop, he could get more referrals.

Declan snorted. "You would think anyone was a social media whiz if it meant you didn't have to do it. It's not that hard. There are programs where you can integrate everything and handle it from one spot, scheduling posts and—"

Bay put a hand over Declan's mouth. "Shhhh, don't ruin the magic."

Declan knocked his hand away, but looked amused. "I'm just capitalizing on the work everyone has already put in." He took a sip of his tea. "Things like Nicki doing the fundraiser for the pet shelter, or Will doing that safe piercing video for Seattle Children's Hospital."

I remembered that video. The hospital had reached out for a local piercer to make a short, informational video about good piercing practices for parents—like what to look for in a piercer as well as after-care tips. It played in the waiting room at the hospital, advising parents on how to get their children's ears pierced in a safe and sanitary fashion.

Will had been a little uncomfortable on camera and kept doing this weird hand motion where he rolled his wrists and then held his palms out, like he was presenting an invisible something. *The whole video.* It was cute, but the teasing had been relentless, especially from Van. We'd eventually called a truce, though sometimes Van would stand behind Will and make the hand motion and I'd have to excuse myself to go laugh in another room.

"It's not magic," Declan said. "It's just image. You have a lot of repeat clients, but some of the other artists aren't as established yet. It's also a good way to let people know about guest artists. We post this stuff and people get that the artists here are welcoming, compassionate, and talented." Declan rubbed his face. "As soon as I untangle your scheduling mess."

I wanted to reach out and touch him—a hug, a shoulder pat, something. Animals found touch reassuring, comforting, and I'd picked up that habit. Humans, despite needing touch just as much, often shied away. Most shifters treated touch like animals did—as a comfort, but I wasn't sure about Declan. We were still being oh-so-careful around each other. We had a tentative friendship building, and I wasn't sure if a casual touch would be welcomed or not, so I kept my hand fisted at my side.

Bay noticed my hesitation and threw me a confused look. Declan wasn't looking at us, so I shrugged and mouthed, "I don't know."

Bay glared at me, crossing his arms. He mouthed the words "You're making it weird." I set down my coffee to mimic him. We glared at each other until Bay threw up his arms, muttered something about getting his transfer ready for his first appointment, and wandered off.

I hated to admit that my brother had a point, albeit a silent one. Declan and I weren't going to bridge our gap by me holding back or pretending to be someone other than myself, and I was affectionate with my friends. I'm a hugger. I'm not saying I shouldn't take his trauma into account—if he didn't like me being physically close to him, I could take note and adjust until he changed his mind.

I just needed to pay attention to his reaction—people tell you a lot with body language. But I couldn't keep putting up distance—we lived together and I was casually demonstrative with my other roommates, and he would notice that sooner or later if he hadn't already and might wonder why I was different with him. If I was shunning him. I didn't want that doubt in his mind.

Declan was visibly stressed. His shoulders were bunched beneath his thin T-shirt, his jaw tight. If this were Trick, Van, or Juliet, I would comfort them. He was a new friend, but he was still my friend.

I took a deep breath and laid a hand on Declan's back. His muscles tensed slightly beneath my hand, reminding me of interactions with feral or abused creatures. He wasn't rejecting my touch, but he wasn't sure if I was going to wield it in kindness or harm. It wasn't a reaction most people were born with—it was taught. I felt a sudden burst of rage at the person who'd made Declan learn that response. To make a shifter wary of a simple hand on their back went against their entire nature.

I took a deep breath, releasing my tension and doing my best to radiate calm. If he were a patient, I would have added magic to my touch, using my power to calm his emotional state. Taking his pain into myself and offering a sliver of my own peace in return. Sort of like an emotional transfusion.

Declan wouldn't take kindly to that. He'd see it as an invasion. Instead, I kept myself relaxed and rubbed my hand in gentle circles between his shoulders. "It will be okay. Bay knows you stepped into a mess." My lips tilted up.

Declan looked at me, his body relaxing slowly by degrees. His eyes held such relief when he finally slouched into my touch. Yup, I definitely wanted to murder the person who'd hurt him. Which made Bay right—Declan was my boy, whether that meant friend or more, and I would do what I could protect him. Simple as that.

Something must have showed on my face because Declan's eyes narrowed. The muscles under my hand stiffened back up. "What are you doing?"

I paused, but kept my hand on his back. "Not magic. I promise."

His gaze was heavy on mine, trying to assess if I was being truthful. He gave a slight nod before turning back to the screen. "Your brother took a chance hiring me. I don't want to let him down." His hands hovered over the keyboard. "I don't want to let any of them down."

Now, that was a feeling I completely understood. I gave his shoulder a final pat. "You'll be fine. Bay knows you're still learning." I checked the time on the wall clock. I was due back at the house to watch Savannah so Juliet could get some studying done. I waved at everyone on my way out, smiling at Declan when he waved back. We may have had a rocky start, but we were on the right track. I just knew it.

Declan

Sometimes I was reminded how different shifters were from humans. It made it difficult to interpret their actions. The look on Lou's face when she rubbed my back had been fierce. There had been a very clear *I am alpha and you are mine to protect* vibe going. Except she wasn't a shifter or my alpha—she wasn't even my pack.

Was she?

I held the cooling paper cup in my hand. She *had* brought me tea. Lou knew I liked chamomile. She'd specifically ordered that with me in mind. But humans did stuff like that all the time, friendly gestures that weren't meant to be a big deal. If she'd been another shifter, it would have different meaning.

The pack alpha made sure everyone was fed. Even my dad got that one right.

It wasn't the same with humans. I was probably overthinking or making too much of it, but I couldn't ignore that it had taken one offhand gesture and a back pat to practically undo me at the seams. Was I so desperate for affection that the barest crumbs brought me to my knees, or did the gesture mean more?

I rubbed my face, suddenly very tired. I didn't have the mental capacity right now to untangle our interaction. Despite hopping between the two jobs and the learning curve at both as well as daily runs, I wasn't sleeping. My nightmares were back, and it didn't take someone like Juliet to tell me why. Living with an animal mage was dredging up a lot of things for me.

I closed my eyes for a second, breathing in my chamomile tea. Unfortunately, I also got in a good whiff of Lou as well, which sort of negated the calming effect of the tea. Her scent was more…exciting. It was her day off, so the animal scents were muted, bringing out the usually buried traces of cedar and sandalwood from her soap and shampoo, along with her own natural base note.

The first part—the animal part—no longer made the wolf in me put his hackles up and growl, which was a relief.

If wolves could roll their eyes, mine would do so. *Lou isn't Eva. Lou wouldn't hurt you. Lou would never muzzle the wolf.*

Lou wasn't my stepmother. My wolf had picked that up much faster than me. Now that we'd *both* come to terms with that part of Lou's scent, though, we were left to focus on the rest of it. And my wolf? Well, he liked the rest of it a lot. Lou smelled good. *Really* good. And because of my bang-up idea of trying to reassociate Lou's scent with something comforting and safe, Lou now smelled like home.

Which would still be okay if I wasn't attracted to her and if I didn't think dating a roommate would be too complicated right now.

But I was. And I did.

And it wasn't helping me untangle this schedule. The nightmares keeping me from sleep weren't helping, either. Maybe I'd stop by Wicked Brews on my way home to see if they had any magical concoctions that would help.

It was well into the evening by the time I left Wicked Brews, purchase in hand, and made my way back to the house. I had to be at the kitchen Jen and Lara rented for prep work early so I could put in a few hours for them before my shift at the tattoo shop. The food truck didn't do breakfast, thankfully, but I still had to be there at six to help prep for lunch. Then straight from there to the tattoo shop by eleven, which was when they opened.

I desperately needed a good night's sleep. Food prep involved using a lot of sharp things like knives and I wanted to keep all of my fingers where they belonged. My phone vibrated in my pocket and I checked the screen. Zoey's name flashed and my thumb hovered over it, trying to decide if I should accept or decline. I hadn't talked to her except for the odd text or two to tell her I was okay.

My chest ached and I rubbed a hand over my sternum. I missed Zoey. There was a big hole in me she used to fill and I felt like any day now I was going to fall into it and not come out. But I was still a mess, and I was also driving— she would give me shit for talking and driving, and I hated speakerphone.

I declined the call, even though I disliked doing it. I'd call her back when I got home.

It didn't escape my notice that I didn't miss Sid nearly as much. I really hadn't loved her the way I thought I had. That probably meant a good amount of my hurt was wounded pride more than anything. Which didn't exactly make me feel any better.

I got home, set my sleep draughts on the counter, and opened the fridge, thinking to grab a quick bite before calling Zoey back. With how unstable I'd been, it wasn't a good idea to add hungry on top of that. Hungry people got hangry. Hungry werewolves—well, no one wanted to deal with a hungry werewolf.

The fridge didn't have much in it besides the groceries I'd purchased yesterday. Last night for dinner Lou had used the last of the milk to eat a bowl of cereal, and she'd looked ready to pass out into it. At least she'd eaten something. She didn't always. She had a hectic schedule—all my roommates did—and they didn't seem to have time for cooking, sometimes skipping meals all together.

I didn't like that.

Lou needed to eat. It wasn't that much more effort to cook for four as it was to cook for one. I frowned. Juliet didn't eat enough, either. She was great about taking care of Savannah, but not so good at remembering to do the same for herself.

So make that five.

I put water on to boil, salting it heavily to get it ready for the pasta. Then I cut up peppers, onions, cherry tomatoes, and some of the vegetarian sausage I found in the fridge. It wouldn't taste the same to me, but if I put in meat, Lou couldn't eat it.

If I made Lou dinner, she'd have at least one good meal today. I scowled at the faux sausage and reordered my thoughts. If I made *everyone* dinner, they'd have at least one good meal today. Yes. Better. That felt right.

I threw it all in a pan with some olive oil and cooked it while the pasta boiled. Once that was going, I put together a green salad, adding in lots of different veggies for color, whisking together a quick vinaigrette when I was done, though I kept that separate. That finished, I drained the pasta and tossed it with the sausage mix. Juliet came in to the kitchen then, a sleepy Savannah on her hip.

She looked about ready to collapse. I didn't know how she managed to juggle a kid, school, and work without the help of a partner. Mothers were tough as shit.

"Hey, I was just—" She paused and took in a deep breath. "Wow, that smells good."

I took Savannah from her and guided her into a chair before she could protest. Then I snagged a plate, put a healthy serving of pasta onto it with my free hand, topping it with freshly grated parmesan. I handed her a fork and put the plate in front of her as she blinked in surprise. Savannah leaned against my shoulder in that trusting way truly loved children seemed to master, and hummed, running one hand through my close-cropped beard. I swayed with her as I put some salad into a bowl for Juliet and set it next to her plate.

She held a fork in one hand, her mouth and eyes full. I thought for a second she was going to cry.

I didn't want to see Juliet cry over dinner. It would break my fucking heart. "Just take a moment to eat," I told her gently. "It's just food. We're fine."

I made myself a plate and joined her, eating in silence as Savannah continued to hum, though I could tell she was falling asleep. She'd stopped petting my cheek, her fingers tangled in my hair. The front door opened and closed and a second later, Lou and Trick came in to the kitchen. Trick had come straight from work, the tang of fire, metal and chemicals strong on him. Dammit snoozed in the carrier strapped to Trick's chest.

Lou looked like she was ready to pass out on her feet. From what Trick had told me, she'd been bonding him and the phoenix on her off time, wanting to connect him to the bird quickly. A fast visual assessment told me that Lou was overextending herself. She looked pale, the skin under her eyes bruised. For a second, I debated skipping the food so I could pick her up and tuck her into bed instead. She needed sleep.

Of course, if I tried to tuck her into bed, she'd rightfully freak out and tell me to fuck off. Especially because, for a split second in my mind, I considered what it would be like to crawl into bed after her.

Curl around her warm body.

Smooth my hand up her hip and…

Let's just say I'd been considering a lot lately, and right now it was as bad of an idea as it usually was. Fuck, it was worse, because I was standing here holding Juliet's kid while serving dinner.

There were times when a public boner wasn't a big deal but now wasn't one of them.

Food first. Deal with everything else later. At this point I'd back-burnered so many issues, my internal stove was going to catch fire and burn the place down.

I got up and practically shoved Lou into a waiting chair.

Trick took one sniff and settled in happily across from her. "Oh, good. I was hoping you still liked to cook."

I brought them some food, making sure Lou's serving was on the hearty side. She needed the calories. She ate half of it before she seemed to come back to herself, frowning at the plate. "This is really good. Thanks, Declan. You don't have to feed us."

I returned to my bowl at the table. Eating with one hand, rubbing Savannah's back between bites. "It's not a big deal."

Lou eyed me, her face grave, and my heart gave a little skip. Probably from fear. That was a thing, right? Or some other unspecified sort of arrhythmia. I could google it later.

"It is a big deal," Lou said, jabbing her fork at me. "You know how I feel about people feeding me." She took another bite and sighed in contentment.

I really wanted to hear that sigh in another context.

I *really* needed to stop considering.

"Is this going to be an all the time thing?" Trick asked. "Please let it be an all the time thing."

Juliet stared at her empty plate. "I think I'm going to cry because the food is gone. I need more sleep."

"Declan, don't let him bully you into cooking for us all the time." Lou shoveled another bite into her mouth. "When I make pasta, it's never this good." Her eyes narrowed. "Why is this so good?"

"It's fresh pasta," I said, taking a bite of salad. "Store bought, though. I usually make my own, but I didn't have time." I frowned at my plate. I should have made time—

"I know that look," Trick said. "And no, I don't own a pasta whatever it is you need to make pasta. You don't need to do everything from scratch." He pointed his fork at Lou. "I'm not going to bully him, but I will offer him a break on rent if he cooks for us on the regular." Trick batted his eyes at me. "I just want a handsome man to feed me. Is that too much to ask?"

I laughed, which had been his aim.

Still, I thought about what he said as I ate. The thing is, I truly did enjoy cooking. Not as a job, really, though it was fine for now. But there was something about feeding friends and family that I loved. Knowing that I made something that comforted and nourished. Sure, my roommates were all adults and could care for themselves…in theory. They didn't seem to be doing the best job of it, but I could understand why.

It wasn't my job. They weren't my pack.

Still, it wouldn't hurt to think about easy breakfast options. If I went to the store before my shift…

CHAPTER TEN

Lou

I opened the fridge, surprised to see a paper bag with my name written on it. It sat next to other paper bags with my roommates' names on them, all lined up like little ducklings. The rest of the fridge was full. And *not* full of takeout boxes, but actual ingredients for meals.

Someone had also scrubbed out the fridge. The little blob of barbecue sauce that had hardened into the shape of Florida was gone from the bottom shelf.

This couldn't be right. Since I hadn't had my coffee yet, maybe my exhaustion was making me hallucinate?

I closed the fridge. Opened it. The clean, stocked fridge stared back at me.

Trick came in, sleepy-eyed but dressed, a drowsing Dammit strapped to his chest.

"Did someone steal our fridge and replace it with someone else's fridge?" I asked. There was a vegetable I couldn't identify. I poked it.

"Huh?" Trick rubbed at his eyes. "Why are you poking the kohlrabi? What has it ever done to you?"

"What hasn't it done?" He'd asked a silly question, I was giving him a silly answer. I took the bag with my name on it and peeked inside. A sandwich, carrot and celery sticks with peanut butter, cheese, apple slices, and a small container of pistachios. There was also a note. *Sorry, it was the best I could do on short notice.* I recognized the scrawl as Declan's. My roommate had packed me a lunch. What was happening right now?

I held up the bag. "What is this?"

Trick stared at my bag, then grinned and opened the fridge, damn near clapping his hands in glee when he saw one for him. "This is great! I knew he had it in him."

I set my bag down and pinched the bridge of my nose. "Trick, please remember that I haven't had coffee yet and explain. No, actually, never mind. Let's go get coffee." I turned and walked to the door, grabbing Trick's keys for him as well as my own.

Trick grabbed our lunches and ran after me.

I wouldn't let Trick talk to me until we got to Wicked Brews, ordered from an entirely too chipper Noah, and had our coffees in hand, which was our standard operating procedure. Then I waved at him. "Proceed."

"This is good, Lou." Trick resettled Dammit's carrier on his chest.

I waited, but he didn't feel the need to elaborate. "You don't think it's weird that our new roommate made us sack lunches and also apologized because they apparently didn't meet his rigorous standards?"

Trick sipped his espresso, tilting his head to the side to look at me. "What do you know about wolf shifter pack structures?"

"Not as much as Juliet," I said, taking a sip of my own latte. Look, I know there's a stereotype of Seattle people and coffee but screw you, coffee is delicious, okay? "I'll need help connecting the dots. Please remember that the caffeine hasn't hit my system yet, so use small words."

"But you know about real wolves, right? Like in the wild?" Dammit chirped softly and Trick started running a finger over the top of the tiny bird's skull.

I waffled my hand back and forth. I knew a little, though not as much as I did about dogs, which weren't the same thing at all. "They usually travel in family packs centered around the male and female alpha pair—the parents."

Trick finished his espresso and set it down. "Werewolves are similar. I've always thought Declan might be an alpha, but he's got a lot of baggage in that area." Trick looked sadly at his empty cup.

"Noah's been trained by Van—he'll only give you a split shot," I reminded him. "Werewolf alphas—there's something about food, right? Pack feeding order or something?"

He sighed. "When people hear the word 'alpha,' they picture those dudes that use it to mean pushy and aggressive. King of the hill type stuff. Werewolves—it's not like that. Yes, they protect their pack, but they also care for it. For most shifters, that means they're nosy as fuck. Are you eating okay? Warm? Healthy? How is your boyfriend treating you? Are you happy?" He shook his head. "A truly engaged shifter alpha is worse than—" He struggled for a comparison, probably because he wasn't awake yet either.

"Worse than a whole flock of pigeons." I narrowed my eyes over my cup. Freaking pigeons.

Trick paused, his hand hovering over Dammit. "Sure, we'll go with that."

I looked at my lunch with new eyes. "So you think Declan feeding us is a good thing? I mean, I'm not one to look a gift horse in the mouth if said gift horse is also into catering, but I don't think he should feel obligated to take care of us. I'm an adult. I can make my lunch." I never did, but I *could*.

Trick shrugged. "Fight it if you want, but it's a cultural thing wrapped up in a biological imperative."

"I will fight this all the way to the courts!" I shouted, slapping the table. Yup, the caffeine had finally kicked in.

The next few days, it only escalated. It went from sack lunches to reusable lunch totes with our names *embroidered on the side*. I could now find a homemade breakfast and dinner in the fridge or freezer with reheating instructions. Declan framed raised planting boxes in the yard, bought starters and planted them.

Apparently, it was too late in the year for seeds.

He dusted. He did my laundry and *folded it*. Van complained about cold feet one morning and now we all had matching slippers, again with our names on them. I was almost certain he wasn't embroidering them himself, but I wouldn't swear on it. A small decorative basket filled with tampons, pads, and condoms appeared in the bathroom for us and our guests. The period products were also all natural and compostable, because of course they were.

You couldn't fight it, so we all pooled our various food budgets and left them in Declan's room. Van told the ferrets that if Declan tried to hide the money back in our rooms, they should snitch on him immediately. Trick gave him a break on rent. Other than that, all we could do was just stand by and watch the carnage that was Declan's alpha nesting behavior.

"I don't understand why you find this so upsetting." My mom was *laughing at me*.

"It's not upsetting. I'm not upset." I totally was. "Flustered! That's the word. I find this flustering." I moved the phone to my other ear as I closed down the reception area. This afternoon had been slow, and Mama Ami had sent Lainey home early, so I had the front desk to myself. Everyone else had left except me and Mama Ami. Trick was meeting us to work on binding him to Dammit.

The weaving got more complex the further we got into the process, so Mama Ami would oversee my work. Since I was her apprentice, I was her responsibility. Any big screw-up on my part would reflect poorly on her. If it was big enough, her license could be suspended. That didn't happen often, but the idea left me cold.

My mom scoffed. "Hot man wants to cook for me? That's the dream. You're living the dream."

"He sewed and stuffed sachets with cedar and put them in our closets and drawers to keep away moths. We don't even get moths like that in Seattle." I sniffed my shirt. "Now everything smells like cedar."

"You like cedar," my mom pointed out reasonably, damn her. "You wear cedar deodorant. My car always smells like trees after you borrow it."

I grumbled a reply. She was right. The cedar wasn't the problem. It was Declan. All of my clothes, our towels, my *sheets* smelled like Declan. That was why I was flustered. It was like his scent had drifted into my clothes and I walked around all day surrounded by his pheromones, which couldn't possibly be true. It was really difficult to concentrate on work when I kept smelling my hot roommate. It was giving me *thoughts*.

"Everything smells like my roommate."

"You can smell him over your dryer sheets?" She sounded amused, but at least she'd stopped laughing.

I dropped my shirt. "No. He got rid of the sheets. Bad for the environment. We have these woolen dryer ball thingies now." I smoothed out my scrubs. "Trick has been making a lot of jokes about his woolen balls."

"He cooks, cleans, he's crafty and environmentally conscious. *The dream*." She sighed. "Strike that. If you were also tapping that, then it would be the dream. You're halfway there."

"Mom, ew."

She snickered.

"He's a wolf," I said, fiddling with the hem of my shirt, and only half invested in the conversation now. I swear I could smell him. Would it be weird if I sniffed my shirt again? No one was up here with me. "It makes sense for him to be connected to the earth." I shook my head, clearing it. "Does anyone say that anymore? Tapping that?" I dropped my shirt and flipped the lock closed on the door.

"I do, so yes." There was a scuffling sound as she moved the phone. "I'm a classic. Everything I say is timeless."

"Okay, lady."

My mom was silent for a moment. "Did I screw you up? Because if you're freaking out that someone is *being thoughtful* and *taking care of you*, then I'm pretty sure I screwed you up."

"Mom, no. Absolutely not." This was a constant worry of my mom's, because her parents were elitist shitbirds and my biological dad was a shitbird of another feather. They were officially *worse* than pigeons. At least pigeons were up in your face because they were interested in you. It took my mom a long time to see her own worth, because she'd grown up thinking she was worthless.

She didn't have any magic. It happened sometimes. Didn't mean my mom wasn't amazing. But her parents, they'd taught her that she was trash, and my father had just underlined the message. Sometimes their voices in her head were really loud and she worried she wasn't enough for me. Wasn't a good enough parent. Which was agonizing.

"I'm not freaked out that he's nice." Okay, so I was a *little*. But she didn't need to know that. "I'm just worried we're taking advantage."

"Have you told him this?"

"Yes."

"And you're all chipping in financially?"

"Of course."

"Then trust that he's a grown-ass man and knows his own limits, but if you're worried, keep checking in and making sure it's okay. Maybe contributing more to the household is making him feel like he's more a part of it."

"He doesn't have to make us stuff for us to like him!"

"That wasn't what I meant." A car honked in the background. "I got to go—a client pulled up. Movie night soon?"

"Sure, Mom." We exchanged a quick goodbye and she hung up.

As soon as I was done up front, I went through the double doors into the back. Trick and Dammit were already there. We'd decided this area was safest because it was the least flammable. We also had two fire extinguishers attached to the wall, and I'd brought a small portable one out of the break room just in case.

Mama Ami pulled her chair back and to the side—she was here mostly to observe. Trick sat in a chair directly across from me, our knees almost touching.

Once everyone was settled, I closed my eyes and did my deep-breathing techniques. The antiseptic smell of the clinic filled my nose. I hoped it would overpower Declan's scent and knock it out of my nose for good. But his scent stubbornly stayed, hovering over everything else, making it hard for me to clear my head.

Which was bad. I couldn't do my job with a jumbled brain, so I needed to problem solve. If trying to ignore or replace it wasn't working, I had to change tactics.

What if, instead of fighting it, I settled into it instead? I took another deep breath, this time not fighting Declan's scent at all, but wrapping it around me, like a hug. No, a *cocoon*. I was safe and cared for. I didn't need to worry about anything else except the task at hand.

Suddenly, my mind was clearer than it had been in days. It felt almost like magic, even though there wasn't a lick of magic in it.

I took Trick's hand in mine, settling the other on Dammit's back. We'd already had a few sessions, so we'd progressed past the simpler bit and into the more complicated phases. If you've ever looked at a detailed tapestry, you will understand what I was talking about. I wasn't singling out the threads of their magic and making simple braids anymore, but doing a complex weaving, wefting the strands together in an intricate pattern invisible to the naked eye.

That didn't mean I could do whatever I wanted. The magic had a pattern, and when you trained to do this kind of binding, you learned to see it.

The already blended strands between Trick and Dammit were blinding in their brightness. I'd always thought fire magic was particularly pretty. A handful of cozy warm reds and oranges alongside blues and vibrant purples. I shifted through them, grasping strands and weaving them together. I'm not sure how long I worked, I was so focused on the pattern. This was why animal mages that were new to this didn't do it alone—it was easy to lose track of how long you worked, how much energy you expended.

Most patients couldn't stop you. Both Trick and Dammit were deep in my magic, mesmerized by the flow and hum of it. Even if they were paying attention, they wouldn't know where the line was—the subtle demarcation between "using a lot of power" and "too much."

Everyone had a different limit, and a newbie could easily blow past it, overdo it, and drain themselves until they lost consciousness if they weren't careful. If you somehow made it past that point and stayed conscious, you could overextend to the point where your heart failed.

I found a good stopping point for Trick and Dammit and let their magic go. It took me a second to open my eyes, which felt gritty, my mouth thick. Mama Ami had a glass of orange juice in front of me and some hangover cure—mostly a collection of B vitamins and willow bark. When you went overboard on magic, it was a bit like waking up from a three-day bender on fruity cocktails—a slight sugar crash, headache, and the shakes.

"You're cutting it too fine," Mama Ami said. "One more minute and I would have stepped in. There's no rush, darling girl."

I dutifully chugged my orange juice and tossed the pills back. "He's suffered trauma. And with his early age and lack of control, the sooner they're bonded, the better."

Once he was bonded with Trick, he'd be able to lend some of his control over fire to Dammit, making the fledgling less likely to set random things ablaze. It would also be easier for Trick to step in to the role that Dammit's parents would usually occupy, showing him how to harness his own magic. All of that was necessary and helpful, but even more than that? I wanted to heal all that loss for Dammit—give him back a parent. Give him back his family, even if it looked different now.

Mama Ami took my empty glass, her face sympathetic but implacable. "There's always something, Loulou." She stood and took the glass to the break room, filled it with water, and came back. "Creatures and humans rarely come with a past full of sunshine and rainbows. That doesn't change how we do our job. You're no good to them if you collapse. Work hard, yes, but also smart. Give them time to adjust, too. The bonding of a familiar is no small thing."

"I know." I probably sounded like a huffy teenager. Bay's mom might as well have been my own, and sometimes it was hard not to fall into old roles.

"You have a good heart," she said, shoving her chair back into one of the exam rooms. We got up and followed suit. "That's a wonderful thing, but don't let it get you into trouble." She shooed us with her hands. "Now get going. Bjorn has dinner waiting for me." She fished her keys out of her pockets. "You both should come over. We'll feed you. Unless Declan is cooking tonight?"

My family wasn't happy until everyone was fed. That was a fact. I was about to agree when Trick's phone chimed. He glanced at it and grinned. "We'll have to raincheck on that, Dr. Larsen. We do have dinner waiting for us, and apparently we're *late.*"

Trick showed me a text that had so many grumpy face emojis. "How can he be mad at us for being late if he didn't give us a time?" Maybe I was being an ungrateful jerk, but magic depletion always made me surly.

Trick wasn't upset at all. He was practically doing a jig, which was a sight. Black clothes, boots, eyeliner, fitted black jacket, a baby carrier on his chest, and a grin fit to split his face.

"I thought goths were supposed to be full of darkness," I groused.

"I contain multitudes," Trick said, tapping away on his phone. "This is good news, Lou. He's definitely making us his pack." He scowled at his screen. "Damn it." His phoenix chirped happily at him. "No, not you. My phone just died."

Mama Ami shoved us out the door. "Declan cooked for you? Excellent. He's a good boy. Next time bring him with you to dinner—we'll feed him." She turned to lock the door behind us, but continued to look at me over her shoulder. "He's much better than the last boy you dated."

"You liked Zach fine until he broke up with me." Mostly because he felt I was too focused on my apprenticeship and didn't pay enough attention to him.

Mama Ami sniffed. "Not true. I always thought he was smug. Always *smirking.* Rarely said thank you, and he never came to family dinner."

It was true. He found my family gatherings to be "chaotic" and "overwhelming."

She hit the button on her key fob, making her car chirp. "See, Declan is already better. You hold on to that one."

I threw my hands up in the air. "We're not dating. He's not mine to keep a hold of. He's just a mother hen."

She dipped her chin sharply. "Then he's Trick's?" She patted his shoulder. "Good for you. He looks strong—nice shoulders."

Trick laughed. "He's not my type. We're just friends."

Mama Ami eyed us both carefully, her gaze landing on me. "I see."

I didn't like the evil glint in her eye. "No." I put my hands up. "Absolutely not. He's my roommate. No matchmaking."

She patted my cheek, giving the other one a kiss. "Okay, dear. Whatever you say."

I didn't believe her easy capitulation for a second. "I mean it. No sitting him next to me at meals, setting us up on dates, and no 'subtle hints' about what a catch I am. I love you, but you're about as subtle as a party cruise ship covered in fairy lights."

"Okay, okay." Mama Ami turned to her car, waving goodbye. "Perfectly good man right under both your noses, and do you take advantage? No." Her voice carried easily over the small parking lot. "Fine. I'm going to go home to *my* wonderful husband, because *I* know a good catch when I see one, and I made sure to put a ring on it."

"Is it weird that I now sort of want to propose to Declan out of guilt?" Trick asked.

"No," I said, digging out my own keys. "My family is just really good at getting you to do what they think is best. It's their super power."

Declan

Despite how long my day had been, I had energy. I should be exhausted. This morning started early with prep work at the kitchen space Lara and Jen rented for their food truck. Then home for a quick shower because I'd reeked of onions, garlic, vinegar, and lemon. Delicious in food, but not on a person. After that, I was at the tattoo shop for six hours. To save time, I'd had our groceries delivered to the house. It may be a time saver, but honestly, I hated not being able to assess the ingredients myself.

Once home, I'd put away the groceries, deciding that I would do research tomorrow about local CSAs. You know you're an adult when you get giddy over fresh produce straight from a local farm. Then I cooked dinner, taking Savannah from Juliet so she could eat using both her hands.

I'd bought a highchair yesterday for the upstairs and today I'd set it up so Savannah could try her hands at the homemade mac and cheese I'd made. They'd started coming upstairs for dinner more and more, so it seemed like we needed one. Van insisted on paying me back for it, because she said she should have thought of it first as the official auntie. Even if she didn't, it was worth it to watch Savannah eat. She had tried shoving fistfuls of it into her mouth, which hadn't worked very well. She'd ended up wearing most of it, but had really enjoyed smearing it on her face.

Van had eaten with Juliet before disappearing downstairs to put her niece to bed so Juliet could catch up on some things. I glanced at the clock, frowning. An hour had ticked by while I was busy.

Trick and Lou were late. They weren't usually late.

I checked my phone. Nothing. I sent a text. When Trick didn't immediately respond, I decided to dust and then vacuumed the living room. I couldn't just sit there and rest until I knew they were home and safe.

Once I was done, I checked my phone again. Still nothing. Were they too busy to send a text? Maybe Trick's phone was dead. Or broken. He could have broken it in a wreck on the way home. They might be tangled up in the wreckage right now and—

Maybe I should clean the bathroom. Because standing here and creating doomsday scenarios in my head wasn't helpful.

I peeked into the bathroom. It was still clean. You could probably perform surgery on the bathroom tile right now, not that you'd want to. I sat in one of the chairs and picked up a book, but couldn't concentrate. Kodo and Podo climbed up on my shoulders and started cleaning my hair. I think they were trying to comfort me.

I set the book down and gently dislodged the ferrets.

I should go for a run. I got up and reached for the doorknob, but I couldn't make myself turn it. Not until I knew where everyone was and that they were safe.

By the time I heard Trick's boots clumping up the stairs, I was two seconds away from chewing on the furniture. Metaphorically. Technically, I could shift and chew on the coffee table, but I had *manners*. Besides, I'd just waxed it yesterday and didn't want a mouthful of beeswax and lemon.

They walked through the door, Trick chattering away, Lou looking like something the cat had not just dragged in, but probably played with for a while first. She looked half-dead and it made the anxiety and worry I'd been barely managing surge forward.

"I texted," I said, my arms folded, the words coming out as a growl. My shoulders were bunched, and I'm sure I was scowling, but I couldn't help it.

"I got it," Trick said, shaking his phone at me.

"Did something happen to your fingers so you couldn't text back? Were you trapped under something large and heavy? Out of range? Kidnapped by pirates?" Even before Trick's eyebrows shot up I knew I was being a dick, but I couldn't seem to stop.

"Phone died." As if to illustrate his point, Trick walked over and plugged it into his charger.

"Did Lou's phone also die?" I scowled at her. The bruising under her eyes was a deep purple.

"I didn't know his text didn't send," Lou said, hanging up her jacket. "And besides, how were we supposed to know when dinner was? You didn't tell us a specific time."

It was a perfectly reasonable response. If it had been on paper, I would have torn it into bits and eaten it. "It's Thursday. You're both home by half past six on Thursdays. It's almost eight." There was a rush of relief now that they were home, now that I could see they were safe. But they'd given the wolf too much time to pace and now I was a wreck of frustration, worry, and jangled nerves.

And Lou looks half dead on her feet, he growled at me, which only raised my hackles more.

"We can't conform to a schedule if we don't know there's a schedule." Lou stopped about an inch from me.

My blood pressure spiked, the anger melding with the scent and heat of her to drive me mad. "I've made dinner every night since last week. What would be different about today?" The words came out a low-level growl.

"No one asked you to do that!" Lou threw her hands out. "Just like we didn't ask you to polish the furniture or scrub the toilet or mow the lawn!"

"All of those things needed to be done!" There was no low-level now, just straight-up growling. I leaned in to her space and she leaned right back at me, her eyes flashing. Why was that so sexy? What was wrong with me? I had to stop my hands from reaching for her, from grabbing her hips and tucking her into me—to make sure that she was really safe. My hands shook, so I stuffed them under my arms.

"I, for one, am not complaining," Trick said, opening the metal cage in the living room that he'd built for Dammit. Once the bird was old enough, he'd roam the house, but for now it wasn't safe. "Do not screw this up, Lou. I like having dinner made for me." Trick paused. Sniffed. "Be still my heart, did you make mac and cheese?"

My shoulders dropped a little. "Yes."

"The baked kind? With the crumbs on top?" Trick wasn't waiting for an answer, but was already walking into the kitchen.

"Of course. I'm not a monster." I glared at Lou. I was about to get in her face more when I heard the microwave door open. "Trick, wait. You're going to heat it up all wrong and ruin it." I dropped my arms and stalked into the kitchen.

"Do you hear yourself?" Lou said, following me. "He's a grown man. He can use a microwave without supervision."

I turned to argue with her some more but stopped when I saw her under the brighter light of the kitchen. Her skin was almost paper white, the fingers pushing her hair back had a fine tremor to them. She swayed a little when she stopped. Lou was about two seconds from collapsing.

"Stop arguing." I grabbed her shoulders and pushed her into a chair. When she started to protest, I dipped down until I was at her eye level. "Stop it. This is getting to be a habit between us." I put my wrist on her forehead. She wasn't feverish, but her skin was clammy. I checked her eyes.

"What are you doing?" She batted my hand away. "I'm fine. Just a little overextended."

"You're dead on your feet," I said, standing. I grabbed a bowl, scooped a large helping of mac and cheese into it, adding a splash of milk before putting it into the microwave. I preferred to reheat it in the oven, but Lou needed food now.

"Sorry about my phone, Dec." Trick brought me a beer, setting it next to me before he settled in and drank his own. He squinted at Lou. "You really don't look good."

The microwave dinged. I pulled out the bowl, stirred it, and checked the temp before placing it in front of her. Once that was done, I warmed up a bowl for Trick.

"I'm perfectly capable of taking care of myself," Lou mumbled, but as she was arguing she also shoveled food into her mouth, so I didn't debate her. She could yell at me as much as she wanted as long as she was eating. She reminded me of a feral cat, growling at you while they ate the food you put out for them.

"No one is saying you aren't," Trick said calmly. "But this is how we work, Lou. Leaning on each other for support. It's how your family functions, right?"

"Yeah, but he's not family," Lou grumbled into her food dish, hunched over it in exhaustion. I could tell the exact moment she realized what she said. She straightened, her eyes going wide as she looked at me. "Declan."

My chest seized, and I turned away. I kept my gaze very focused on Trick's bowl as it spun around. The silence in the kitchen was suffocating. I could almost feel the pressure of it as it grew. The microwave dinged and broke it. Trick sighed. Lou swore. I stirred the bowl and handed it off.

"She didn't mean—" he started, his brown eyes pleading with me. I squeezed his shoulder, grabbing my beer with my free hand.

"No, she's right. I'm not family."

And they weren't mine. Not my pack, not my problem. I didn't have one anymore, did I? No place to land when shit went south. I'd even made Zoey off limits right now. I could go back to her, sure. But it wouldn't be the same. She had Sid now. They had each other. Their own pack.

And I…I had nothing.

The wolf inside me skittered about, his claws slicing me up from the inside out. He didn't like me walking away. He wanted me to fix it—wanted this pack, and I just couldn't do it. It hurt too much. "I'll be in my room."

"Declan," Lou pleaded from behind me.

I stalked off, ignoring Trick and Lou as they argued and Lou tried again to call me back. The thing was, she wasn't wrong. They weren't mine, and it didn't matter how hard I tried to make us into a unit, that wouldn't change.

After I closed my door and flipped the lock, I downed my beer in one long swallow. Had I even eaten? I couldn't remember. Everything was swirling in my head—the exhaustion, all of the change. I stared at my sad little room and it suddenly didn't look like much. A place to lay my head, but not much else.

What was a wolf without a pack? I desperately needed an anchor and I didn't have one.

I rubbed a hand over my jaw. One thing at a time. Sleep first. Until I got some solid rest, nothing else would help. My fear and worry had drained away, leaving my limbs feeling heavy as I stripped out of my clothes. I was the kind of tired you felt in your bones, in your soul. If this was what it took to get some real sleep, I wasn't sure it was worth it.

Someone knocked softly at the door. "Declan?" Lou's voice, heavy with apology. Another knock. "Dec?"

I didn't answer her, but burrowed down into my pillow, dragging the comforter over my head. There was a squeak—the ferrets had been curled up under my blanket. I drew them up close and they resettled by my chest. They seemed to like my room, or maybe I was still a novelty to them. Ferrets were curious. It was nice to have them curled close. I couldn't manage people right now, but the ferrets made me feel slightly less alone.

And I couldn't deny that I was alone. I felt bad ignoring Lou, but how could I answer her? There was no way I would be able to keep how I felt out of my voice. I'd been reaching for something I wanted without admitting it to myself. Reaching for pack, for family, for Lou. There was a crushing feeling that came with wanting something so bad, grasping for it, and discovering you couldn't have it. Was it evident to Trick, to Lou, what had happened? Did they know?

If they didn't already know, she would know the second I answered her. I hadn't felt this vulnerable to another person in a long time. I couldn't take it. So I pretended to be asleep and didn't answer. I felt shitty doing it, but I couldn't bring myself to expose even one more bit of myself.

"I—" Lou let out a heavy breath. "Thanks for dinner." Then the soft pads of her feet as she moved away from the door. Part of me, even in my state, wanted to follow her. Wanted to crawl out from my burrow, go to her room, and curl around her. To be both protector and comforted at the same time. But that wasn't my right—she wasn't my pack.

She wasn't mine.

I turned over, pulling at the blankets, causing the ferrets to grumble at me. I was so tired but couldn't sleep. After ten minutes of this, I got up, went over to my dresser, and found my bag from Wicked Brews. I chewed one of the edible sleep aids I'd bought, the flavor of green things and bitter roots flooding my mouth. The chews didn't taste good, but the sleeping draughts were worse because you woke up with an aftertaste that lingered.

The chews would help, and though I didn't like the vulnerability of handing myself over to such a deep sleep without someone to watch my back, there wasn't any other option. I was desperate.

As I sat back on my futon, my phone buzzed from its spot on the floor. I picked it up, blinking at the light of the screen, trying to fight the pull of the magic putting me to sleep. It was from Zoey. While I'd been fighting with Lou, I'd missed several messages telling me to call her. She'd texted three times in twenty minutes, which wasn't like Zoey. She was calling now.

I hit the Accept button. "Zoey?"

Zoey sobbed into the phone. "Declan. Oh gods."

A chill went up my spine. "Zoey? Are you okay? Is it Sid? What's happened?"

"I got a call—from Ryder."

Jack Ryder was the head of the foster pack that had taken us in all those years ago. He also acted as an intermediary should anyone from our old lives need to find us. Like the twins. Or the police.

Zoey was crying so hard it took her a second to get all the words out. "Declan, they're out. Oh gods, they got out. It's not on the news yet. Police… police wanted the pack to give us a heads up. Told them"—her breath hitched—"told them I'd call you."

Fear lanced through me. Only two people we knew could install that level of fear in my sister. Someone had let our dad and stepmom out of prison. Ryder would have asked Zoey to pass along the information. One less phone call—one less chance of them exposing us. Warning us, but being as safe as they could.

We'd changed our names. We'd moved. Would that be enough? I wasn't sure. And right now, there was nothing I could do. The sleep potion was hitting me strong—It was like trying to fight a deep undertow in the ocean. I was amazed I was still conscious.

"Zoey," I slurred.

She made a broken noise, her voice frantic. "Are you okay? Are they already there?"

"I'm okay," I managed. "Sleeping. Sleeping eat." Eat? That wasn't right. "Chew. Safe."

She whined over the phone, her sound pure wolf.

"Stay safe. Mmokay. Morning. Call morning." I had to fight to get that much out. My eyelids were already fluttering. I dropped my phone onto the futon, collapsing back, scattering the ferrets. All I could think about was my baby sister, how scared she must be, but at least she wasn't alone. She had Sid. Sid was scrappy. She'd watch over Zoey.

Who was going to watch over me?

Sleep dragged me down before I could think of an answer.

CHAPTER ELEVEN

Lou

It had taken me a while to go to sleep. Guilt was real crappy that way. The moment I'd realized what I'd said, I wanted to take it back. It was hurtful and it wasn't really true. My mouth tends to disconnect from my brain when I'm tired, and the look on Declan's face when I'd said it? It was like I'd sharpened my words into a blade and stabbed him right in the heart.

I'm not saying it was okay for Declan to be so pushy, but Trick had not-so-gently reminded me that we weren't just dealing with normal behavior here, but the deeply ingrained pack behavior our roommate was born with. So yes, boundaries had to be set and Declan and I needed to sit down and chat about what we both wanted, *blah blah blah*, but I'd also been a jackass about it. Hungry and tired may have been part of the explanation, but it wasn't much of an excuse.

Eventually exhaustion won and I crashed hard, drifting dreamlessly for a while. I'd been dreaming one of those weird mashed-up surreal dreams where I was in a supermarket in my pajamas and I'd left my list at home and a gorilla kept taking things out of my cart. I tried to explain to the gorilla that his behavior wasn't cool, but I wasn't getting anywhere because the gorilla only spoke German. I had resorted to a spontaneous attempt at interpretive dance when someone called for me over the loudspeaker.

I followed the sound, leaving my cart to the gorilla and walking out of the store and into a forest. It was nighttime, but there was enough light to see—a fat, silver moon dangled in the sky, casting the forest in gilded magic. The scent of evergreen trees was sharp in my nose, along with the ozone scent of an impending snow. My breath came out in puffed clouds and I wrapped my arms around myself to keep warm, annoyed that my dream self couldn't manifest a jacket. This wasn't pajamas and slipper weather by any stretch.

My dreams also weren't usually quite this sharp in detail. It was like I was actually there. I looked up at the moon again, at the silvered tops of the trees. This was a pretty far cry from the gorilla in the supermarket. Had I been pulled into someone else's dream? Could I even do that?

Deep in the forest I heard an anguished howl, interrupting my internal debate. The howl sang through my bones and struck my heart, snapping it clean in two. That howl made me weep, my breath hitching in a sob. I couldn't ignore that sound.

I broke into a run. Arms pumping, my heart racing—I was running so fast, jumping over downed logs and across a stream, that I lost my slippers. The cold ground bit at my feet as I charged through the trees, not daring to look at all the cuts and scrapes I was getting as I ran. It didn't matter—I had to get to that howl.

Hours, days, or indeterminate minutes later, I found a small clearing. A wolf cried in the center, its foot caught in a trap. He'd dug at the trap, chewing at his own leg, leaving it a bloody ruin. On the wind, I could hear the hunters coming. Too far to hear footsteps, but I could hear the occasional shout of a high, demanding voice, answered by a chorus of lower responses.

Loud, greedy voices that contained no mercy for the wolf.

He caught sight of me and stopped, his ears popping forward. I held my hands out flat, moving toward him as slow as I dared, trying to ride that fine line between freeing him quickly and not spooking him.

"It's okay," I said. "I'm a friend. Please let me help?"

The wolf sat on his haunches, trapped leg splaying awkwardly to the side, panting away his terror, but letting me approach. Once I was close enough, I could see the trap wasn't an ordinary creation of cruel steel. It was magic, formed out of a malicious type of claiming spell. The trap said *This is mine—my property, and no one else can have it.* It wasn't random chance— someone had set out to trap *this* wolf. To expend so much power, so much work, they must have wanted him badly. Yet the trap kept the wolf vulnerable, leaving him open to other predators or deprivation.

The spell was a creation of pure selfishness.

I reached for the trap and the wolf growled low.

I paused, licking my lips, breathing away my fear. The wolf would smell it, and it would make everything worse. That wouldn't be good for anybody. I looked him in the eyes. He was a beautiful example of a gray wolf—white belly, silver back, his face mask dipping to a dark gray. He had eyes like a winter chill, beautiful and brilliant.

I reached out and touched his muzzle, using my magic to make him understand my words. "You're going to have to trust me. I can undo this, I promise." The sounds of the hunters grew louder—they were so much closer already. The wolf's ears flicked and he stopped growling.

I felt his acceptance, like the brush of warm fur in my mind. He would let me mess with the trap while he kept an eye out for the hunting party.

They were already so close. Given an hour or two, I would have been able to dismantle the trap. I could easily see how it could be done, but I didn't have that time. My pulse pounded in my ears. I wouldn't fail this wolf. I could figure this out.

I quickly examined the trap again. As spells went, it was formidable. Someone had put a lot of time into it. It writhed with the feeling of an old, deep hatred. I had a hard time looking at it, and I hadn't even touched it yet. How long had the spell been biting into the wolf? I shuddered at the thought.

Okay, focus. I didn't actually need to break the trap, did I? I just needed to get the wolf out of it. The trap had jaws, jagged teeth holding on to the wolf's flesh. A trap meant to cause as much pain as possible. But it also left a few small gaps where the metal tooth met the trap itself, like little valleys between mountains.

I dropped down onto the ground in a sitting position, crossing my legs and holding my hands out above the steel jaws. I closed my eyes, calling to my own magic. My strands were wild—the earthy browns, greens, reds, and golds of tree leaves, tangled in with sky blue and glowing silver. I'd have to be careful to keep it separate from the wolf's magic, which was all metallic grays, silvers, velvety blacks, and bold amber.

The wolf tried to push its own magic at me, trying to help, but I shoved it neatly back.

I grabbed a few silver strands of my own magic, carefully plucking out the ones I wanted and sliding them between the trap and the wolf's leg. I pushed the strands down, as many as I could fit into the trap, curling them around the wolf's leg. Once they were in place, I sent a pulse of power, widening the strands.

Nothing happened.

I did it again. And again, growing frantic, less careful. Power, I just needed power.

I was sweating now, my pulse in my mouth. This had to work. It had to—there! Just the slightest movement and a creak as I managed to block some of the pressure from the trap. Triumph filled me. It could work!

The bays of hunting dogs reached me, closer now.

Panic slammed through me as I worked frantically, grabbing whatever magic was close at hand, not even looking at the individual strands, just shoving them in as quickly as they came. The pressure was easing from his leg, transferring to me as I widened the gap, the strands of magic now as thick as my fist. It hurt, holding it open. I wanted desperately to let my magic go, releasing those strands, but if I did that, the trap would snap back into place.

Sweat dripped from my hairline and my jaw ached from clenching it shut. My magic slowly eased the trap open, widening the gap just enough. I strained to keep it that way, the magic pushing back, making my whole body want to crumple up like a soda can. I waited until the wolf pulled his leg free, hobbling slightly to the side. He couldn't go far—my magic still encased his leg, some of the strands caught in the awful trap.

I needed to pull out, but the trap's magic was almost sticky—did it have a taste of me now and wanted more, or did it think I was the wolf? I struggled to yank my magic free. The pressure hurt, like someone had put a vise on my temples and was slowly squeezing it together. I cut a strand and the wolf yelped. I'd hurt him somehow, and I didn't have time to figure it out.

Okay, no cutting. I needed a big push and a yank, but I wasn't sure I had the strength.

In the distance, the hunters blew a horn, the sound slicing through the night. I wasn't sure how far away—sound bounced strangely in this forest, but they were definitely much closer. Too close. Behind me the wolf whined.

"I know, buddy," I said through gritted teeth. "I'm doing my best."

I felt him sniff the back of my neck and chuff, the hot air making me shiver. My teeth were chattering in the cold, my muscles getting so frozen and stiff that I was shaking nonstop. The wolf leaned on me then, sharing his warmth and magic. I grabbed at it without thinking, using the tether to shove myself free of the trap. There was a sharp *snap* as the metal clanged close, and we both rolled back from the force we'd exerted.

For a second, we rolled as one, all arms, legs, and fur. Then we slammed into the base of a tree, the shock making me gasp awake.

The forest was gone.

It took me a moment to get my bearings and shake out the cobwebs the dream had left behind. For a few seconds, I felt like I could still hear the hunters. But that quickly faded, leaving behind the whining of the wolf.

I was on the floor of the hall bathroom, my cheek against the cold tile. My muscles screamed as I raised myself up and peered into the clawfoot tub. Inside was a wolf, his leg bloodied, his tongue curled as he panted in fear. Panic-silvered eyes met mine, right before the foreign weight of a separate mind settled into my head.

Declan. I was staring at Declan. Magic still bound us, the fat, knotted rope I'd made while trying to bust us free. I patted his head awkwardly for about two seconds before my eyes rolled back in my head and I passed out, sending him the only two words I could seem to manage.

Well, shit.

Declan

I tried to scramble out of the tub, but my claws weren't getting good traction. Blood splattered the porcelain sides, the wound from my dream slowly closing. My heart sped along at a rapid tattoo, the quick staccato beat of a woodpecker on dead wood. I was hurt. Lou was hurt. She'd freed me and trapped me. She was safe and not safe—we weren't safe—and I didn't know what to do. The wolf brain wasn't set up for the kinds of emotional variables that human brains manufacture. He growled that I was making it too complicated. Now that we were out of the forest, he was settling down, but I wasn't.

I needed help. We needed help.

Pack.

I clawed hard, scratching the finish on the tub. We didn't have a pack.

But the wolf disagreed. We did have a pack and they were *right there.* I wasn't listening, so for the first time in a long time, the wolf shoved me out of the way and took control.

We tipped back our head and howled, alerting my pack.

The thud of running feet, quickly followed by Trick and Van pounding on the door, their voices getting louder when they couldn't get in. Had Lou locked us in? They argued, and then Trick started speaking through the door, his tones soft and soothing while Van's footsteps retreated.

Despite the situation, we started to calm. Trick would help us. We trusted him. The wolf insisted he was pack, and the wolf was in charge. I reminded him of what happened earlier in the kitchen. He nipped at me, snapping his teeth, like I was a pup to be chastised. I could argue all I wanted, but the wolf said they were pack. I was too tired to keep fighting him, and even I recognized that we needed help.

We rested our chin on the edge of the tub and waited. Van's footsteps returned, followed by the metallic rattle as the key slid into the lock, and then the door flew open and smacked Lou in the arm.

There was yelling then and Van got too close to Lou and we growled. Trick said something sharp to us and the wolf stopped, the growl turning into a whimper. The wolf was worried about Lou.

I was confused. *She trapped us.*

The wolf chuffed. *No. We trapped her.*

That … didn't make any sense. *I need to turn back.*

Tired.

He was right. We were maxed out. The only thing keeping me awake now was adrenaline and the wolf's desire to watch over Lou while she was vulnerable.

I'm okay now.

At my assurance, the wolf cautiously retreated, putting me back in control, even if we were too exhausted to shift back. I scrambled to the far edge of the tub, as close to Lou as I could get.

Van checked Lou's pulse, her face pinched with worry. "Her pulse is steady. We need to get her to the hospital." She tried to pick up Lou and I growled again. She froze, and even if I hadn't been able to smell her spike of fear, I could see it in the rapid beating of the pulse in her throat.

Trick was looking at me funny, his head tipped. "Declan, we're here to help. Understand? We won't hurt Lou."

He was right. Now that I was a little more clear-headed, I understood that Van and Trick wouldn't hurt her. They were pack. I could drop my hackles.

"I don't think you can get through to him right now, and it doesn't matter. We need to go to the hospital."

But Trick had been watching me carefully, paying attention to my body language. "It's okay, he's calming down. But I think if we drag her off to the hospital, he won't like it. Let's wait."

"Wait!? Trick, Lou is unconscious and—"

"Her pulse is steady. She's breathing fine." Trick pulled out his phone. "I'm not saying we won't go, just let me talk to Mama Ami first."

Van's face pinched with worry. "Okay."

Trick hit a few buttons and held his phone to his ear. "Dr. Larsen, this is Trick. Sorry to wake you, but we have a situation here." I tried to listen as he gave her the details, but it was like my brain was skipping. I kept missing bits. Usually, I wasn't like this when I changed. I kept my full mental faculties. This wasn't normal. I wasn't normal, but at least I could understand what they were saying now.

Trick put his phone down on the floor. "She's on her way." He looked at me. "Hey, Declan, buddy, you think you could change back?" When I whined in response, he sighed. "That's what I thought." They both decided it was best if I stayed in the tub, but Trick brought me a bowl of water and a chunk of raw lamb that I'd left in the fridge. I attacked both gratefully.

A short time later, Mama Ami came into the bathroom, a pink and purple tacklebox in her hand, and shooed Trick and Van into the hallway to give her room. I was tempted to scoot away from her—she was an animal mage. But I also didn't want to leave Lou….

Mama Ami didn't give me much time to panic. She started talking to me and my wolf at the same time, her magic making her message clear to both of us. *I'm not going to hurt you or Lou. I won't touch you with my hands or my magic without your permission, but I do need to assess my daughter. Understand?*

I relaxed, setting my chin on the lip of the tub so I could watch.

Good. Then she ignored me, turning her attention to Lou. Mama Ami made a quick assessment before digging into the plastic tacklebox she'd brought with her. She took something out, glancing at me. "Sorry about this." Then she crushed a packet of smelling salts under Lou's nose. The sharp smell of ammonia hit me and I pawed at my snout, realizing as I did that my scampering around the tub had left it—and me—smeared with blood.

Lou jolted awake, her lungs heaving.

Mama Ami called Van back in. "Hold her up. I need her sitting." As soon as Lou was vertical, Mama Ami cracked open a brown bottle of something that smelled sweet and lemony. She held it up to Lou's lips. "Drink." When Lou just blinked at her, Mama Ami waved at Trick. "Tip her head back and hold her mouth open."

Trick complied, keeping Lou steady while Mama Ami poured the concoction down Lou's throat. Mama Ami would pause occasionally, letting Lou swallow. When the brown bottle was half-empty, color started returning to Lou's cheeks. Her eyes seemed more aware, and she actively helped drink the rest of the bottle.

When it was finally empty, Lou grimacing at the taste, Mama Ami thunked the bottle on the bathroom tile. "What happened?"

Lou told her about the woods, the trap, the hunters. Her words slurred a little. At the end of her story, Mama Ami turned her gaze on me.

She looked worried. *And what do you have to say?*

I showed her some quick images—I didn't have to words to articulate what I—what the wolf—had done to get us out of the trap.

I see. But she didn't look relieved. If anything, her concern had deepened. "Oh, Loulou." She shook her head. "You are in so much trouble."

When I whined, Mama Ami took a second to go over what I'd showed her. Lou's magic. My magic. The wolf had done something when Lou was working, adding our magic to hers. When she'd been struggling, we'd handed her a tether. She took it and—I wasn't entirely sure I understood what had actually happened, but Mama Ami made sure I understood the outcome as gently as she could.

Bound. We were *bound.*

Fear shot through me only to hit something and dissolve. Just like that, the fear was gone. Wait, it didn't hit something—it hit *someone.* Lou was in my head. I could feel her there, just at the edges.

It wasn't a terrible feeling, but weird and uncomfortable, not unlike stepping into new boots, the leather at first too tight and stiff. Would our bond loosen and grow comfortable? Would we be bound long enough for that to happen? Would she try to keep me like this, like Eva had? I started to pant again.

Lou clambered to the tub, resting her chin on it not far from me. "Hey. We'll fix this. I promise, Declan. Just calm down. I won't hurt you."

Her words were soothing and I could tell she believed them, but she couldn't see Mama Ami's face. She tried to hide it, but wolves were a heck of a lot better at reading body language than humans. Dr. Larsen was worried, and I didn't think any of this would be half as easy as Lou thought.

"First things first, we need to get you out of that tub." Lou grimaced. "And we're going to need your help, because you're too big to drag out of there."

She was right. An average male gray wolf in the wild can be anywhere from sixty-five to one hundred and eighty pounds. I'm a little bigger than that, hitting around the two hundred mark. I'm not a small wolf.

Eventually, Lou convinced me that it was okay for Van and Trick to hoist me out of the tub. Dr. Larsen didn't want me jumping out on my injured leg. Shifters healed faster than natural wolves, but I was tired, freaked out, and couldn't shift, so the gash in my leg was still a problem, albeit a much smaller one.

Van and Trick grunted and cursed, but got me out in one piece. Trick looking forlornly at his black pajamas, now totally covered in white and gray hair. The blood wasn't as visible.

I shed when I'm nervous.

Van didn't seem to even notice the state of her pajamas.

Lou held my leg as Dr. Larsen cleaned and bandaged the wound, keeping it covered until my body could catch up to what it needed to do. Then she employed Trick and Van using wet washcloths and towels to clean the rest of me as best they could. The ferrets tried to help as well, crawling all over me to get the spots Van and Trick missed. It wasn't great, but no way was I getting a bath right now.

Once that was done, she ushered us out into living room. "I want to see both of you in the morning." Her arms were crossed over her chest and her face set in no-nonsense lines. "You need sleep." She frowned at me. "You need to change back." When I whined, she held up a hand. "Not now. In the morning."

Lou shivered, swaying where she stood. "What's going to happen to us?"

Trick frowned at her. "What do you mean?" He looked between her and Mama Ami. "We're missing something, aren't we?"

"Familiar." Lou's teeth chattered a little over the word. "I made Declan my familiar."

Trick's eyes went wide. "Oh fuck."

All the blood left Van's face. "Oh, Lou. That's—"

"Forbidden," Lou chattered.

Mama Ami grabbed a throw blanket from the couch and wrapped her in it. "I need to bring in the tribunal on this."

Lou collapsed onto the couch. "I'm going to lose my license before I even get it. You're going to lose *your* license when they find out. Oh gods." Her head flopped back on the back of the couch. "Shhiiiiiiiiit."

Dr. Larsen clucked her tongue. "Language."

"Sorry, Mama Ami."

"No one is losing anything, not yet." Mama Ami crossed her arms and scowled, like she was daring the entire universe to contradict her.

I could feel the echoes of despair that flowed through Lou. She was devastated. All of her hopes, up in smoke before they'd even caught fire. I should be afraid of her—of this. But it's hard to be afraid of someone when you can know their feelings echo your own. She wasn't gloating that she'd bound me. She was freaking out and worried about her family. I very carefully laid my head on Lou's knee. She rested her hand on the back of my neck, fingers plunging into my fur, like the contact helped make her feel better, too.

"Could we maybe not tell them?" Van asked. "I mean, not right away? Give her some time to fix this?"

Dr. Larsen was already shaking her head. "No. If they find out she tried to hide it, they would revoke her provisional license. The consequences would be much worse. If we go right away and explain..." She stared at us, the fingers on her right hand tapping on her arm like a little wave. "I hope we can explain, anyway. This isn't...usual."

"Well, they won't be able to explain anything if they're half dead on their feet," Trick said, clapping his hands. "Okay, you two, bedtime. Let's go." He came over and helped Lou up.

Dr. Larsen gathered up her stuff. "I'll call the tribunal tonight, Lou, and text the info."

"What about work?" Lou mumbled as Trick slipped his arm under her shoulders.

"I'm going to rearrange both of our schedules tomorrow. You'll be on hiatus until the tribunal clears you, anyway." She kissed Lou's cheek, patting it afterward like she could press the kiss in deeper. "I will be there for your hearing, baby girl. You won't have to do this alone, promise."

Lou squeezed her hand. "Love you, Mama Ami. Sorry to cause such a fu...fuss."

She waved it off. "Excitement keeps us young. Now take your wolf to bed. You both need it. Try not to spend the whole night worrying. All your problems will keep until morning."

Mama Ami smiled at me. *Take care of her, please.* The wolf chuffed and she must have been okay with that response, because she left.

I padded behind Lou as Trick helped her to her room. I'd been in Lou's room before when I dropped off her laundry. A queen-sized bed rested against the wall under the window. She'd shoved her dresser into the closet to make room for a small desk along the other wall. The desk was made of a light wood—or so I guessed from the legs, since the top was covered in papers, books, and empty mugs.

Clothes were mostly in the hamper. A few framed family photos were clustered on the light-green walls along with a corkboard and a few posters. A small bookcase stuffed with paperbacks balanced out the room. It was the kind of messy that said she was more busy than careless, and it smelled like her and the clinic where she worked. Comfortable. Home.

Van's ferrets perched on Lou's pillows, her pajamas hanging from their mouths. They dropped them into her hands and chirped at her.

"I'm already wearing pajamas," Lou said.

"Yeah, but they're covered in blood and wolf hair," Van said, snatching both the ferrets up and hugging them to her. "This is like a fucked-up version of Cinderella. Stop dressing my roommate."

Lou wasn't as messy as Van and Trick, but at some point, I'd managed to smear her with blood, right at her midsection. I whined.

"It's okay. It'll wash." She frowned at me. "Not sure what to do with you, though. Too late for a bath." She touched my fur, her fingers gentle. "They got a lot of it off. The rest is dry at least."

"I'm going to go get changed." Van kissed Lou's temple. "Everything is going to be okay."

Trick did the same and they both went to leave. Trick held the door open, staring at me.

I sat on the floor and stared back.

Trick shrugged and shut the door.

Lou stood by her bed, her pajamas dangling from her fingers. "I don't think Mama Ami meant it literally. Just that we both needed to go to bed. You don't have to stay in here if you don't want."

I didn't answer, but the bond we shared told her loud and clear that I wasn't going to budge. She might not be taking it literally, but *I* did. She sighed and motioned for me to turn around. I faced the wall.

Lou grumbled as she undressed. "You can turn around now."

She was wearing sleep shorts and a tank top. I very carefully tried to not think about it. I was getting Lou's feelings intermittently—she was tired and her mental walls probably weren't very good right now. In the morning, I might not be able to sense her at all. But right now, the walls were down, and I wasn't quite sure how much she was getting from me. Was it just emotions, or could she get actual thoughts?

The last thing I wanted her to know was that I was imagining taking her shorts off with my teeth. My human teeth, not my wolf ones. This wasn't a creepy Coppertone ad.

Lou flicked off the lights and crawled into her bed. Once she was settled, I planned on lying against the door, so that no one could enter the room without waking me. Before I could even take the first step, I decided to check the bond, see if I could get a gauge on where Lou was at. She was trying to keep it from me, but she was worried. Scared.

I padded over to the bed.

She opened her eyes and watched me for a second, her mouth tipping down. "Declan, you don't need to... I'll be fine. We may be bonded, but—"

I nudged her arm with my nose. When she didn't budge, I did it again.

She sighed, scooting over to give me room. It was a bit of a scramble, but I made it up onto the bed.

"Guess your leg is feeling better, huh?"

I curled up against her side, my head resting on my paws. It wasn't as good as sleeping by the door, but I could see it from where I was, and Lou was between me and the wall, so no one could get to her. She was as safe as I could make her for now.

I listened as her breath evened out. Lou's room had a good window, far enough off that ground that it was unlikely anyone would try crawling into it, even if they could jimmy the latch. The house had good windows, but I could still hear the faint sounds of a city at sleep beyond the glass. Cars went by. Dogs barked. I let my own eyes close. Lou curled in close to me, her warm breath against my fur, her hand buried in so deep that I could feel her fingers on my skin.

Before long, I fell asleep, dreamless and solid, the best rest I'd had in weeks.

CHAPTER TWELVE

Lou

My phone buzzed, rattling along the wooden surface of my desk, telling me I had a text message. I didn't want to move and look at it. My bed was warm, my eyelids heavy. I was wrapped in a perfect cocoon, warm and safe, and all I wanted to do was go back to sleep. My back felt hot and there was a heavy weight wrapped around my stomach. *When had Zach come to bed?*

My eyes snapped open.

Zach had broken up with me over six months ago. Still, I knew the kind of warmth I was wrapped in. A man was in bed with me, curled around me spoon fashion, his arm pulled tight at my waist to keep me close. Whether he was a soup spoon or a grapefruit spoon remained to be seen. I'd have to ask Van, because the spoon thing only made sense to her, anyway.

My tank top had ridden up in the night, and a hand rested warm and possessive against my stomach. I could feel it down to my *toes*. Hot breath huffed against my neck. I had one of those odd thoughts that if I moved a single muscle, I might actually burst into flame.

I reached back with one hand. Hot skin. Hip bone. My fingers clasped it automatically, and I have never in my life been more turned on by a hip bone. Heck of a time to find out I had a weird fetish, though I had the distinct feeling that it wasn't so much about hip bones as it was about this *specific* hip bone.

I should let go. I told my hand to let go.

My hand politely told me to go fuck myself. My hand was an asshole.

I really needed coffee.

His body tensed as he came awake.

I let go of his hip. "Declan?"

He relaxed again, burying his face back into my neck, making me shiver. "Hm?"

120

"Are you naked right now?" I knew the answer, but I asked the question anyway.

He grumbled something and somehow managed to curl around me tighter. Apparently, he had zero problems using me as a teddy bear and thought nothing of sleeping with me completely naked. To hell with soup spoons, Declan was a gods damned *ladle*.

My phone buzzed again. I'd plugged it in before I went to bed last night the first time, and it was all the way over on my desk. Which I could not get to because I was sandwiched between a large, musclebound shapeshifter and the wall.

"Declan." I tapped his head. His hair was soft and thick, like a pelt. My hand, still mad that we'd let go of his hip, buried itself in his hair. He mumbled against my neck, and this time the shiver was joined by goosebumps. It was a good thing he couldn't see my nipples right now, because they were so hard I could probably use them to carve an ice sculpture.

Nothing too elaborate. Maybe a really basic swan.

I hadn't had sex since my last boyfriend and I hadn't had *really good* sex in three years. Waking up like this was one hundred percent not fair to my sad, neglected libido. "Dec, I need my phone. It could be important." A cold wash of reality hit me as I remembered how important that text could be. That text message buzz could be the sad sound of my career ending. Or worse, the sad sound of Mama Ami's career ending.

No, Mama Ami would come out on top. She always did. Her backup plans always had a backup plan. But me? I didn't have a backup dream. What would I do if I couldn't work with familiars? Maybe it wasn't much to most people, but it was my bit of shiny blue ribbon and I wanted it.

Declan eased away from me, rolling out of bed. He put one hand on my shoulder. "Don't move."

I only half listened. I didn't get up, but I definitely twisted enough so that I could watch him, and I had no regrets. Declan padded soundlessly across the hardwood floors, completely, gloriously naked. He'd pulled off his bandage, a faint scar the only evidence he'd been injured.

His back … I wanted to lick his back. Broad shoulders, smooth, shifting muscle, tapering down to an ass that should have its own Instagram following. That ass was an influencer.

He picked up my phone, carrying it back over to me as I tried very, very hard to not look down.

It was impossible.

I looked.

Truth time—I was actually leery of well-endowed guys. My personal experience was that bigger guys were usually crappy in bed. They thought that since they had the inches, they didn't have to work for it. Not that I wouldn't be willing to give Declan the benefit of the doubt, because *hoo boy*.

He smirked, smug but not cruel. I wanted to be mad, but let's face it, he'd earned the right to look smug.

Belatedly, I slammed the door on those thoughts. Though I bound people to familiars all the time, I wasn't used to sharing that bond myself, and certainly not with another person. If I wasn't careful, I'd overshare. By the expression on his face, Declan knew exactly what I'd been thinking. *Uuuugggh.*

He put the phone in my hand and I just stared at it like I'd never seen a phone before as he crawled back into bed behind me, curling up like he'd never left. His arm went back around my waist, his breath returned to the back of my neck as he pressed his face to my skin. I shivered and felt his answering smile.

Okay, then.

I checked my messages. They were, indeed, important.

We had to meet with the tribunal at noon. It was ten thirty. I'd slept for more than ten hours. I was a poor sleeper, usually waking up several times in the night. Considering what I'd been through the night before, I felt pretty good. Which was weird, because between the back-to-back magical output, passing out, and the emotional roller coaster of maybe ruining two careers at once, I should feel like hot roadkill.

In fact, I felt better than I had in months. I'd been working a lot, trying to get as much as I could out of my apprenticeship and prove myself. Mama Ami wouldn't pass me if she didn't think I was ready, it didn't matter if she'd helped raise me or not. In fact, she was harder on me than most, because she had high expectations for her children. I hadn't been sleeping well, working too much, and until Declan, I hadn't been the best at making sure I ate well. I'd gotten into the habit of burning my candle at both ends in college and I hadn't slowed down like I needed to.

I'd been exhausted and hadn't even really realized it. But now? I felt like I'd spent a week sleeping and eating good food. Like I'd had a relaxing massage and then hydrated like they tell you too, which I always forgot to do.

The heat from Declan made me drowsy, despite all the rest I'd had. I didn't want to get up, though I should. Considering everything Declan had been through, I didn't think he was thinking clearly. To be fair, I wasn't sure I was thinking clearly, either. While I'd been pretty happy with managing a comforting back pat at the tattoo shop the other day, this seemed like a mighty big jump.

We didn't know each other enough to cuddle, and certainly not well enough to cuddle naked. Or mostly naked in my case. The shorts the ferrets had brought me barely covered my butt. Which was currently tucked into Declan's lap. Our current position had to be an after-effect of the bond.

I could admit that I would be fine cuddling with Declan naked because...well, he was hot and I was apparently shallow. But he seemed way more comfortable with me than he usually would have if magic hadn't intruded, which meant that me staying here and soaking in the warmth of him was taking advantage. It was like making out with your super drunk friend when you were stone cold sober. Which was sort of unfair, because *hot naked guy*. I mean, I couldn't even objectify him in my mind, because he might see it.

Being an adult was hard.

I tried to turn so I could talk to him, but he held me in place with his arm and a low, rumbling growl. Which just made me mad, something I was grateful for. Anger cleared out my lust-fogged brain.

"Declan, let me go." I kept my voice firm and clear, being careful not to put any real command into it. This was going to be tricky. I wanted him to let me up, but I also didn't want to override his will, because that would make everything so much worse.

His hold softened slightly, but didn't let up. "Five more minutes."

I sighed. "Declan, you only think you want to be here. It's the bond. It's creating intimacy where it doesn't exist." Though my words were gentle, they'd still hurt. I knew this. I wondered if I was his grapefruit spoon—none of my smooth edges cancelling the jagged tip digging into the heart of him.

I realized my hand was back in his hair and I pulled it away, but he butted into it, attempting to keep the contact. I tried again, softer. "As soon as you're fully awake, you'll remember that my magic makes you uncomfortable. I don't want to add to your anger or resentment. I'm not actually your teddy bear, remember?"

Declan's laugh was a short, pained sound. "I remember. It's just..." His arms tightened. "Please?"

He buried his face in the back of my neck and I got a sudden rush of emotion from him before he put up his mental walls and closed the link off. Declan was a lone wolf and he wasn't meant to be. Even if the link was creating a false sense of closeness, he still wanted it. For five minutes he wanted connection. Comforting.

And he wanted it from me.

I couldn't deny him that. I didn't know much about Declan's past, but I could feel that he'd gone through a lot. Mine had been idyllic in comparison. Maybe it was wrong, but I couldn't say no to him.

"You can have ten." I set the timer on my phone.

He sighed, his muscles relaxing. I put my hand over his arm and settled in. If comforting him was wrong, then I would just be wrong.

Declan

When I woke up, all that was left of my wound was a pinkish scar. Which was great, but hardly registered. I couldn't quite wrap my head around how amazing Lou had felt in my arms.

I'd been right. She was soft everywhere.

Well, I wasn't sure about *everywhere*, but I wanted to find out. Test my hypothesis until it was theory. You know, for science.

I didn't want to get up, because once I did, I'd have to deal with everything that happened yesterday. Given a choice between harsh, cold reality and a warm, cozy bed, my arms wrapped around sweet curves and silky skin and it was no contest.

But we had to face the day. I quickly showered and shaved, throwing on a button-up shirt, slacks, and a tie Zoey had bought me that she said brought out my eyes. I needed a little of my sister close this morning. My hand stilled knotting my tie. Shit. *Zoey.*

I scrambled for my phone, which I'd left in my room last night. Two missed calls. I glanced at the time—we had to leave in ten minutes. I hastily hit the Call Back button.

Relief hit me when she answered. "Hey, Zo."

"That's all I get?" Zoey screeched and I held the phone away with a wince. My sister wasn't much of a yeller, but when she got really freaked out, she could hit the higher decibels. "You're barely articulate last night, then you don't answer my calls, and now all I get is a 'hey'?" She made her voice gruff and lower on the "hey," doing a terrible impression of me.

I ran a hand through my hair, grabbing on to the back of my neck. "Fuck, Zo. I'm so sorry. It's—been a lot. Last night. I kind of forgot." As I tried to figure out how to coherently sum up my evening, complete silence filled the line. I had to check the screen to see if she was still there. "Zoey?"

"You forgot?" Her voice was soft. "*Dad* is out, that *bitch* is out, and you *forgot*. They're both walking around free as birds right now." She sucked in a breath. "Remember when I was little and got scared?"

Shit. It wasn't an abrupt subject change like it sounded. Zoey thought I was compromised. When we were younger, we'd come up with a way to let the other one know if we were alone in our respective heads. I wasn't, but Lou wasn't the person Zoey was afraid of.

"Do you remember, back at the camp—I used to sing to you?" The important part was making our prearranged code sound natural. There was no way to work corny spy-sounding jargon naturally into a conversation. It may be fun to say *The eagle crows at midnight. The cheese walks alone*, but it was clearly code.

"What did you sing?" Zoey asked, her voice deceptively calm. "I remember you singing, but not the song."

Zoey had always been a soft soul, and as a child, that had been really difficult for her. Our circumstances didn't reward a gentle, creative person. It crushed them. I'd had to soothe her a lot, and singing always worked best, even though my actual singing ability wasn't anything to write home about. Zoey's mom had died when Zoey was little, and I didn't remember any of the lullabies she'd sung. I sometimes heard other parents singing them quietly at night, but only snatches, not enough to actually learn whole songs.

I'd asked one of the moms to teach me once, only to have my dad's hand clamp down on my shoulder. He dragged me away, making excuses, his fingers digging into my skin. I still wasn't sure why that had made him so angry—with my dad, it was sometimes hard to tell. The littlest things could set him off. I ended up getting extra dish duty for two days until he forgot I was being punished.

I didn't ask about lullabies again.

We weren't allowed to watch TV or listen to the radio. But there had been a beat-up old CD player in the kitchen so the cooks could listen as they worked. Most of the CDs were of bands that were popular before I was born. Zoey had especially liked one song by a band called Sam the Sham and the Pharaohs.

"Hey there, Little Red Riding Hood," I sang softly into the phone, hearing Zoey's voice catch. I kept singing, making my way through the whole verse until Zoey joined me in the hushed howl that began the next verse. I laughed at her *aawoooo*. If I had sung any other song, Zoey would have hung up and thrown her phone away.

She let out a breath. "You scared me."

"I know. I'm sorry." I glanced at my phone. I didn't have time to sum everything up before we had to leave for the tribunal. "Look, I've got something going on. It's...a mess. I promise I'll call you back in a bit and catch you up. Until then, stay safe, okay?"

"Love you, numb nuts."

Something in my chest loosened. "Love you too, short stack." I hung up.

Lou stood in the doorway to my room. She didn't ask about the call, but she tilted her head in question. It was a very wolfy movement, asking without words if I was okay. She'd dressed up too, a cream-colored dress with little foxes on it. Her hair was up, a few pieces falling softly around her face. I think she'd put on a little bit of makeup around her eyes.

She looked beautiful.

"Ready to go?"

"No," She said, "but that doesn't matter."

She was right. It didn't. We had to go anyway.

Despite Lou's other mom assuring us they'd be fair, neither of us were looking forward to the tribunal. Would they see me as the wounded party, and want to punish Lou? Would it be a panel of animal mages? What if they wanted to hush everything up—or worse, what if they liked the idea of getting a shapeshifter of their very own?

Dread filled my gut. It wasn't that those last few were very likely, but what did I know? I had no idea what we were facing. At the very least, Lou was in trouble. I didn't *like* Lou being in trouble. Especially since I had the uneasy feeling that it was more my fault than hers. The wolf had been convinced that we'd trapped Lou, not the other way around. Had I accidentally torpedoed Lou's career?

This morning had been… shit, this morning had been a *gift*. Lou didn't see it that way, I could tell. Didn't want to take advantage. But the weird thing about holding Lou this morning was it hadn't felt like I was holding her. It felt like she'd been holding me. Lou had the biggest, fluffiest fucking heart, like one of those enormous beanbag chairs, but she didn't let just anyone sit on it. But once you were there? She was a fierce little thing.

Having that, even for a moment, had felt like standing in the middle of the fucking *sun*. Maybe it wasn't my sunshine to keep, but basking in hers had felt amazing.

Which made our distance now harder to take. Something had eclipsed the sun and here I was, naked, vulnerable, and shivering in the middle of a field. You know, metaphorically speaking. Literally speaking, I was sitting in a car wearing a damn tie.

I hated ties, even ones that reminded me of my sister. They felt too much like a leash, and the idea of being leashed again made me break into a cold sweat. But I didn't want to show up to the tribunal looking like a scrub, either. That wouldn't do Lou any good.

Lou had closed off her end of the bond. I wasn't getting anything. The silence was thick as we got on the highway in my SUV. Lou wasn't in any headspace to concentrate, and if I'd let her drive, I think we would have ended up in a ditch. To be honest, I wasn't feeling much better, but my hands were steady. Fuck, maybe we should have hitched a ride with someone.

Even though she'd shut down her barriers tight, so I couldn't actually *feel* what she was feeling, I didn't need to—her leg was jiggling a mile a minute and she was chewing on her thumb, a scowl on her face. The thick smell of fear and worry flowed off her. Without thinking I reached over and put my hand on her leg, stilling it.

Touching her made me feel raw, but I didn't take my hand back. Wouldn't unless she told me to. "You'll be okay."

She froze, casting a glance in my direction. "How can you say that?"

I shrugged, suddenly uneasy, my shoulders bunching in a knot. How does one boil down years of experience dealing with misery and terrible situations to let someone understand that you knew what you were talking about, without revealing all of those things? "You're strong. Even if everything implodes today, you won't lose your family. Your friends." Me. "You're a fighter—a comeback kid."

Lou didn't look convinced, but I knew I was right. Lou had a great support system. She was smart. *Strong.* She would make it through whatever they threw at her. I'd be right behind her, not quitting until she was back on top. "Trust me."

To my surprise, Lou relaxed a little. On some level, she trusted me enough to know I meant what I said, even without checking our bond.

I just hoped she didn't notice that I'd said "You'll be okay" and not "We'll be okay." I had no idea how I was going to handle the courtroom experience. It was possible it would be fine. It had been a long time. It was also possible it would be…not fine.

There wasn't anything I could do, so I focused on Lou. She was still too much in her own head. I needed to get her talking to me. "What should we expect from the tribunal?"

Her leg started to jiggle again. I went to settle it for a second time only to realize my hand was still on her leg, right behind her knee. She'd left it there the first time. For some reason that cracked me right open.

I carefully took my hand back. I'm not sure she noticed.

"I don't exactly know. I've never gone before them." She grimaced. "I kind of hoped I wouldn't ever learn first-hand. All I've heard is rumor. Scuttlebutt repeated by anxious students and interns alike." She opened my glovebox, took out two granola bars, and shut it. She handed one to me before she tore into the second one. If Lou was going to be in my truck more, I should stock my snack box with different options. She wouldn't take the jerky.

"Do you know who makes up the council?"

Lou bit into the granola bar and shook her head. "Nope. It's actually a rotating group. Twelve members serve for a period of a year. Their names are then drawn at random for each hearing, so we know we'll get three, but not which three. At the end of their year of service, they won't be able to serve for two years."

She took another small bite. "It's all an attempt to keep favoritism to a minimum and keep things just, but it's not perfect. The three members will need to meet certain requirements—they have to be fully licensed and bonded in their field with at least three years of experience. And by law there must be at least one member who practices the specific magic in question on the panel. If not, they have to bring in a specialist."

"So another animal mage?"

"Yes." She put the wrapper in the garbage bag, but she kept glancing over. "Are you going to be okay?"

I forced a smile, trying to lighten the mood. "Sounds like a party." Dread filled my gut, but I made sure Lou didn't feel any of it.

Lou laughed, but I don't think either of us was fooling the other.

The tribunal wasn't held in Briar Creek, but was instead up north—still in the county, but not in a familiar neighborhood. Lou said the area was less Uncanny and more human. I'd have to take her word for it.

The building was larger than I'd anticipated. It held several mundane civic branches—police, fire, government, and a library, all under the same roof. The Uncanny Tribunal Commission was housed in the same lot, though in a separate building, which didn't surprise me. Humans liked to keep magic close so they could use it and keep an eye on it, but they wouldn't necessarily want to share more than a parking spot with a person who could control fire, like Trick, or someone who could turn into a predator, like me.

Both buildings were new, the stained wood and paint still fresh. Long tinted windows let in light, giving the whole place a sort of Northwest forest lodge look. I parked and got out, walking with Lou until we hit the sidewalk in front of the building.

We both stared at it with trepidation. Now that I was here, I was getting a little shaky. I'd been looking at Seattle as a fresh start. No one except Trick really knew my past, and even he wasn't privy to all of it. If I went before the Tribunal, I might have to share to help keep Lou out of trouble. We'd come a long way since my initial bad impression. I didn't want to look in her eyes now and see pity.

Or horror.

Lou stood next to me, chin up as she took the building in, her hands fisted in her dress, I think to stop herself from reaching for me.

I'd never seen Lou in a dress, and I hated that this awful hearing was the reason. The cream looked good against her skin, somehow bringing out the red in her hair. The skirt flirted with her knees, and for a brief moment, I was envious of fabric. She looked sweet as hell in it and I had a sudden urge to put her back in the car and drive hell for leather away from this horrible place.

Instead I reached out, grabbed her fist, and gently loosened her fingers. Then I laced them with mine. "It's just a building." It was a good reminder for both of us.

"I never said I'm sorry, you know? For saying you weren't family." Lou turned her face up to mine. "I didn't mean it and it's not true." She squeezed my hand. "Are the mages going to be a problem?"

"I don't know. I don't think so." I gave her a soft smile as something occurred to me. "What are they going to do, bind me twice?"

Her face fell. "Declan—"

I pulled her hand up to my mouth, planting a quick kiss on the back of it. "I didn't mean it like that. It's just—what *are* they going to do? I have you now. In a weird way, I'm safe." The idea made me feel better, almost optimistic. I could do this, right?

It was only a building. The courtroom was just a room. I rolled my shoulders. I could do this. After another few seconds, I nudged her with my shoulder, jerking my chin at the building. "It's time."

Lou let out a shuddering breath, then squared her shoulders, her head high. "Let's go."

They made us cool our heels in the waiting room for twenty minutes before we were let into the meeting room. At the front there was a raised dais with a long table. Behind the table hung a large purple banner with the symbol of the UTC on it—a chimera rampant, symbolizing the many forms that magic could take.

Three people sat at the table: An older woman with deep brown skin, her hair pulled back into a bun, sat on the left. Next to her, a gray-haired gentleman with the coldest blue eyes I'd ever seen. He looked like his spine wouldn't bend on its own, he was so stiff, and pale, like an ice king. The last was a young woman, her straight black hair braided back, her tan skin glowing with health. She smiled at us.

A wide aisle separated the dais and a small empty table set up for me and Lou. Behind that table, there were several rows of chairs, most of which were currently full of Lou's friends and family. So far, I was doing okay, and seeing Lou's family helped. We took our seats facing the tribunal.

I turned around in time to see Trick come in. He walked up to the front quickly, giving us both a hug. I'd gotten used to Dammit being with him, so it was weird to see him without the little bird. But it had probably been smart to leave him at home.

"Hey, Van and Jules wanted to be here, but neither of them could get free." He glanced at the judges and grimaced. "Though that's probably a good thing. Anyway, they send their love." He squeezed my shoulder, tipping his head at the back of the room. "I'd better grab a seat. I think they're about to start."

I leaned close to Lou as he made his way to the back. "What did he mean by that?"

Lou's face was impassive, but she was too on edge to keep her shields up and I could feel a mix of loathing, anger, and resignation through our connection. She leaned close to my ear. "The man in the middle is Van and Juliet's father."

My eyebrows winged up. "I thought he was dead?"

Lou frowned at me. "What gave you that idea?"

"Probably because Van told me so. Repeatedly." In the brief time that we'd lived together, Van had probably mentioned her father's unanticipated demise on no less than ten occasions. "I should have guessed it was false after she said he'd died tragically during a dance competition. Lost his footing trying to do the paso doble on the deck of a yacht and fell overboard. Said they'd never found the body, so technically he was considered lost at sea." Come to think of it, Van had told the story with uncharacteristic glee. "I thought she was using humor to cope with her grief."

"I wish he'd get lost at sea," Lou grumbled softly, so only I would hear her.

I examined Van and Jules's father. He wasn't quite sneering, but he was stiff, refusing to look at anyone in the audience, giving the distinct feeling that they were all beneath him. And so were we.

The doors in the back shut and the meeting finally came to order. The Tribunal introduced themselves— Patrice Macklin, water elementist, followed by Elliot Woodridge, master arcanist, and lastly, Prisha Bhatt, animal mage.

After they introduced themselves, Prisha Bhatt addressed the courtroom. "We're here to discuss whether or not Louise Matthews, apprentice switch for Family Familiar under Dr. Amihan Larsen, has broken the law by making a shapeshifter, one Declan Mackenzie, her familiar."

The courtroom didn't sound too shocked—most of the seats were filled with family and friends, but there were a few gasps. Suddenly, it felt like everyone, especially the Tribunal, was staring at us.

At me.

I didn't like it.

It was too much focus, too many eyes on me, suddenly reminding me of other courtrooms, other trials. I wasn't even sure what had triggered the memories—the crappy industrial carpet? The smell of too many clashing perfumes or the sound of Prisha's voice as it echoed through the chamber? It didn't matter—the effect was the same. My heart started to race, and I broke out in a cold sweat. Now it was my turn to jiggle my knee, trying to release the tension like Lou had in the car.

The fun thing about trauma was that sometimes you thought it had gone away, only to hit a little road bump and have it punch you right in the face. But if you'd spent years in therapy, like I had, your training can come back, too. I relaxed my leg. I took slow, even breaths. I couldn't do anything about the sweating, it was an autonomic response. All I could do was try to calm down. But I wasn't doing it fast enough. The Tribunal was openly staring now, making me feel like a bug under a microscope, and that just spiked my anxiety worse.

My leg started jiggling again. I was sucking in breaths like a pissed-off bull.

I heard Lou say something, but I couldn't tell what it was. My brain was processing sound oddly. Anxiety was funny: you could logically understand what was happening and yet be unable to stop yourself from going through the steps anyway.

My nostrils flared and I smelled Lou as our connection slammed open. Suddenly, I felt … calm. My chest loosened. I could breathe normally, and the world snapped back into focus. Not only was I covered in flop-sweat, but I'd also snapped the arms off my chair. I put them on the table. "I'm sorry. I'll pay for that."

"Perhaps we should get one of the guards to fetch an inhibitor collar." Elliot's words were calm, almost detached. "Just in case."

"I hardly think that's necessary," Patrice said, but she looked to Prisha while she said it.

An inhibitor collar was designed to separate the shifter from his animal. It was mostly used on criminals. My father wore one in prison. How badly had I freaked out?

Prisha, the animal mage, moved until she was closer to the table. Her lips were turned down, her brown eyes hard. She was already unhappy with us, and Woodbridge was suggesting collars. Fuck. I'd made things worse.

"I had to ask for permission to use the bond to calm you," Lou said softly, ignoring the tribunal. "I'm so sorry. The calm—it's artificial. I can remove it, if you like. I don't want to override your feelings, but we were concerned—you weren't responding."

"Leave it," I snapped. The Tribunal frowned collectively, and I took another steadying breath. "It's okay, Lou. Thank you. I didn't think—I'd hoped—" I'd hoped that this wouldn't remind me so much of the last time I was dragged into a courtroom. That was the other funny thing about trauma. It was hard to tell sometimes what was going to trigger it. For the first year after my sister and I got out of the cult, we couldn't eat certain foods that reminded us of the place. I still couldn't look at a bowl of Cream of Wheat without getting nauseated.

And sometimes…sometimes you were fine. You forgot for a bit that anything happened to you. Then a little thing like sitting in front of the Tribunal brings it all roaring back.

I held fast to Lou's hand. "I'm sorry. I'm fine."

"No reason to be sorry," Lou said.

I shook my head, because she was wrong. I should have warned her, but I didn't want to. I just…wanted her to keep looking at me and seeing *me* and not the scared kid I used to be.

Prisha's lips were a thin line. She crossed her arms and glared at Lou. "You need to remove the binding, now." She stopped Lou from arguing. "I don't care how or why it happened. We can decide your punishment after we free your wolf. It's clearly affecting him—"

"No." I wiped my sweating palms on my jeans. I'd been thinking about what I'd said earlier to comfort Lou, and as my panic receded, I suddenly really wanted to be Lou's familiar. I just didn't want to explain *why*. "The binding stays."

Prisha's eyes were sad now, and full of the pity I hated oh so much. "Declan, I don't think you understand what's happened. You're being affected by the binding. Your thoughts aren't your own and Lou's emotions are influencing you—"

"No," I said, my tone pure ice. "*You* don't understand."

Prisha blinked at me before glancing back at the tribunal, her worry evident. "Declan—"

I managed to relax enough to unclench my jaw. "If you're already talking punishment, then you've already decided that Lou is guilty. That's not fair or just." When she tried to speak again, I growled. "I know you think you have a handle on the situation, but you don't have the faintest clue. I'm sorry, I'm sure you're educated and very competent in your field, but in this particular case, you don't know shit."

"Declan." Lou said my name softly—a warning? Comfort? I wasn't sure.

"No, listen. Just give me a damn minute." I stared every Tribunal judge in the eye. "You think I don't understand the situation? Lou performed an illegal binding. It's illegal because animal mages are forbidden to bind 'higher' lifeforms as familiars. In Uncanny terms, that means no minotaurs, no shifters, no hinds, and definitely no other humans. It's seen as a form of mental assault." I leaned back in my chair and crossed my arms. "If you want, I can quote the number and article of the law she violated last night." *Please don't make me explain beyond that.*

Again, the Tribunal looked at each other. Patrice, the water elementist, cleared her throat. "You did your homework this morning and looked everything up? That's nice, but knowing the letter of the law and understanding what has actually happened to you is not the same thing."

I laughed and it was not a good sound. "You consider me a victim, but you dismiss my feelings out of hand? Oh, right, because Lou might be controlling me. I could be her little puppet right now." I bared my teeth in a smile.

When a wolf smiles, it's a threat.

I turned to Lou. She wasn't even looking at the tribunal anymore. She was staring at me. No pity, only concern. The tight fist in my chest loosened. I thought about the room full of people behind me. Lou's family, who'd been so kind to me. Offering me work, food, and acceptance. Trick literally taking me in.

People take that for granted, but once you've lost your community, once you know how quickly it can be ripped away, that knowledge never leaves you. You knew how much of a gift it was, how fragile it could be, too. I thought, briefly, about ordering the audience removed from the proceedings. It was my right. But as much as I didn't want their pity, I also didn't want to keep this secret from them.

It wasn't their business, of course, but my past would drive a wedge between us. No matter what, I'd lost my fresh start. But I was suddenly so tired of secrets. Of their hold on me. I rubbed a hand over my face. "I want everyone in this room to sign an NDA saying they won't speak a word of this without my permission. Not to their friends, the media, no one."

Van's father, Elliot Woodridge, finally piped up. "If we can cease the dramatics, and get on with our respective days—"

I slapped my palm flat on the table in front of me. "I know how this works and I know the laws. Sign them. Now. Sign them or I walk."

"If you left the proceedings, a warrant would be issued for noncompliance," Patrice said gently. "That carries a fine and possible jail time."

"I know." This was an official UTC summons, and their word was law. None of that bothered me. The way they were already talking, though, if I left? Lou would lose her license. Maybe Dr. Larsen, too. I didn't want that, but I wouldn't let them railroad her, either. *Here's hoping they don't fight me on this.* "I don't care."

Surprise stamped Prisha's face. "You can't mean that." She glared at Lou. "This is low. Of all of the childish responses. Leave him be and face your consequences."

They thought my response was being controlled by Lou. Great.

Lou paled, but her eyes never left me. I knew she could feel my turmoil and read all of my body language. She knew something was terribly, horribly wrong. She also knew that telling the council to suck it wouldn't count much in her favor. Still, her lips lifted briefly, and she reached out and took my hand. She didn't say anything, but I could hear her emotions loud and clear through our bond, and they were saying, *I got you.*

"I think you should do as Declan says." Lou's voice was firm, and the look she threw the Tribunal was steely. "Now."

It took thirty minutes of grumbling from the Tribunal and various court officers and a lot of paper rustling until the courtroom was handed NDAs to sign. Lou absently rubbed my back, making small circles with her hands. I didn't think she even realized she was doing it. Prisha glared at her, and for a second, Lou took her hand off my back. I glared at Prisha, grabbed Lou's hand, and put it back on me. I needed that comfort right now and the tribunal could fuck right off.

Once everyone had turned their signatures in, Elliot Woodridge, who looked like he'd sucked about an orchard's worth of lemons, spoke. "Now, we've indulged you. May we please get on with this circus? I'm a busy man."

I nodded, my shoulders hunched, my elbows on my knees. I held one of Lou's hands between both of mine and was absently playing with her fingers. When was the last time I'd held someone's hand like this? There must have been times with Sid, but I couldn't remember them. The circumstances were awful, but I was grateful for Lou's small fingers in mine.

I cleared my throat. "My name is Declan Mackenzie. My name has also been Dean Johnson and once upon a very long time ago, it was Dermot Campbell, the oldest son of Angus Campbell."

The room was dead silent for a long moment, and then exploded into noise. I glanced at Lou, searching for pity, but finding none. Instead, she seemed bewildered. It hadn't clicked in yet. I squeezed her hand, giving her a slight smile. "My dad was the leader of the group known as the Moon's Chosen People. Less charitably, we were sometimes called Loonies."

I could see the exact moment when Lou remembered. Her eyes widened and her mouth parted. I knew what came next—pity. Of course, Lou surprised me again. She was good at that. She skipped pity and went right to horror, followed by absolute rage. I had forgotten about the binding for a second, forgotten that she was getting more than just my words.

Lou's beautiful face twisted up in a snarl. "I will fucking kill him. I will track him down and rip off his balls and deep fry them in Lara's food truck." She tried to stand, but I pulled her back down. Then she looked at me, blinked quickly, and burst into tears. I did the only thing I could think of—I pulled her into my arms and let her cry.

CHAPTER THIRTEEN

Lou

I was an asshole.

That was the only possible reason I could think of for my reaction, as it was completely ridiculous that Declan was comforting me.

Juliet once showed us all an article about ring theory, which explained how to comfort someone going through trauma. Basically, the person going through the ordeal is at the center, then close family, then friends, then acquaintances, and so on, going out like the rings on a target.

Let's say your coworker gets cancer. They're the bullseye. You know them, but not well, so you're on the outer edge of the target. You can only pass comfort down to the bullseye, and the people on the inside can only "dump out" their emotional issues to the rings outside themselves. So if your coworker has cancer, you don't complain to their sister about how stressed you are over the illness or how much more work you have to do while they're sick. You can complain to your spouse, who is further outside the circle than you, having only seen your coworker once or twice. But for those inside the circle, you listen, you help, you make a gods-be-damned casserole. You don't *add* by making it about you.

I liked the ring theory. I used it at work when comforting patients.

Declan was at the center of this trauma. I was just his roommate. This wasn't about me, and yet I was sobbing uncontrollably and he was making soothing noises and rocking me as best as he could in the cheap, shitty chair. Yes, I'm sure some of it was runoff from the binding, but not all. I'd followed the case as best I could then—I think I was about nine or ten when it hit the news, but I wasn't quite sure. It wasn't every day something like that happened, but my mom wouldn't let me watch the stories on the news if she could help it. She didn't think it was appropriate for a kid to watch.

I hadn't even been allowed to *watch* it. Declan had *lived it*.

Angus Campbell had perverted the pack system. I remember Mama Ami trying to explain it all to me, but I didn't understand much of it. What I do remember? How angry she was—so mad that she would stop midexplanation, almost chewing on the words. I remember one part very clearly—she said what he did to his pack was unconscionable, and what he'd done to his children was an abomination.

When they arrested him for violating Uncanny Laws, as well as fraud and I think tax evasion, he'd had something like one hundred and fifty people living on his compound out in the middle of nowhere, Alaska. He'd made himself alpha over all of them, something that just didn't happen.

Despite my mom's best efforts, I'd seen some news stories, and kids talked. I remember the pictures—rooms full of bunk beds, wild-looking kids in threadbare clothing, freaked out by the cameras. Adults fighting or cowering in fear at the outsiders they were convinced wanted to do them harm. Shifters in wolf form for so long, they'd almost forgotten they were human.

Declan had to have been a little boy. I couldn't even wrap my head around what he'd been through.

And he was comforting me.

I straightened up, using my palms to brush my face clear. "I'm so sorry."

His smile was brittle. "It's okay. It was a long time ago."

"Declan—"

I don't know what he heard in my voice, but his eyes were suddenly fierce. "Don't do that. Don't pity me."

I took his hand and gave it a brief squeeze. "Okay." What else could I say? I didn't really pity him. I wanted to hug the little boy that had survived Campbell. That wasn't pity, but it didn't matter. What he wanted right now was support, so that's what he would get. I could sort out my own feelings later.

The Tribunal managed to calm everyone down. Prisha and Patrice looked at Declan with a mix of fear, horror, and pity. The pity I got, though I hated it because I could feel how much Declan hated it. I didn't get the fear. The horror was pretty self-explanatory. Elliot Woodbridge was staring at Declan with interest, as if he'd suddenly done a trick Elliot liked. I wanted to bundle Declan up and sweep him out of that room.

"You know I studied your case." Elliot said it like he thought Declan would be pleased. "So fascinating, your father. I even went and interviewed him in prison." His eyes lit up at the memory.

I'd never liked Vanessa's dad. I even hated him at times. This was one of those times. He was the kind of villain you shook your fist at and only referred to by their last name. I narrowed my eyes. *Woodbridge.*

"So much charisma," Woodbridge continued. "Truly fascinating man."

Declan tensed next to me but didn't say anything. Prisha gawked at Woodbridge like he'd sprouted another head.

"It's the joy of being an arcanist," Woodbridge mused. "Gathering knowledge. Studying the very patterns and paths magic takes and learning to bend it all to the mage's will. What your father managed, yes, yes, was terrible, but that doesn't mean it wasn't also extraordinary."

I was certain that my definition of "terrible" was different from Woodbridge's based solely on that statement alone. How dare he act like Declan should be proud. This was why I disliked so many arcanists. They got so involved in the study of magic that they forgot the creatures attached to and affected by it.

"What my father did was repugnant," Declan said flatly. "It goes against every instinct a wolf alpha should have."

Woodbridge sniffed, his eyes growing colder. I sent a thought of caution through our binding. I completely agreed with Declan, but we didn't want to piss off the Tribunal, either.

Woodbridge leaned forward. "You were the oldest boy. I remember now. The rumors—were they true?"

Declan eased back in his chair, throwing one arm over the back of mine, all indifference, but I could feel how tense the muscles in his leg were. I didn't even remember putting my hand there. I lifted my hand only to have Declan push it back onto his thigh with his fingers. I almost took it back off, because it was high up on his thigh, but if it had bothered him, he would have moved it. Certainly didn't bother me. Declan was a stressed shifter and if he needed touch, I would gladly give it to him.

"You'd have to be more specific," Declan said dryly. "There were a lot of rumors."

"About the witch," Woodbridge pressed. "The experiments."

"Animal mage, specifically," Declan corrected.

"The reports said she bound you," Prisha said, her eyes shining with sympathy.

Declan turned his attention to her. "My stepmom was an animal mage and my father's second mate."

"He had more than one mate?" The question slipped out without thinking. Well, everyone was already staring at me. Might as well keep going. "On *Mated by Fate*, they always make a big deal over the mating for life thing werewolves did."

Declan gave me a sad smile. "Technically, he mated for life. My dad was a widower when he bonded with Eva."

"Getting back on topic," Woodbridge said, giving me the stink-eye. "Ms. Bhatt asked if Eva bound you."

"When we were unruly, she took steps." He shrugged, trying to be nonchalant, but I could feel all the turmoil roiling inside him. "My sister and I were often unruly. My other two siblings weren't shifters, so she couldn't bind them."

"She kept you in your animal form for a year." I don't think Prisha even meant to say it. The words just fell out and then she looked shocked at her own admission.

Declan's voice was carefully even. "Three months was the longest."

Three months was an eternity to be kept in his other form. And as a child? I shuddered.

Woodbridge leaned further over the table now. "How old were you?"

"Seven," Declan said. "When it started."

While shifters needed time in their animal form, too much time wasn't good. Long bouts as a child were dangerous. They could forget they were human and not come back. Until the trials, I'd never even heard of a forced change, let alone on a child for that long.

I'd heard other things, too. Campbell had been arranging marriages. Which shifter packs didn't do. Ever. He'd had absolute control over his people's lives.

Woodbridge looked like he had more questions, but Patrice spoke up. "Mr. Mackenzie, in light of all of this, of what you've already been through, why would you ask the council to leave you bound to another animal mage? To compound a traumatic event in your childhood—an illegal one at that. Your stepmother is still in prison for what she did to you and the other shifters."

I suddenly wanted to hug Patrice. Even though she was looking at me like I was a pile of shit someone had left on her porch. She was looking out for Declan's health and asking him an actual on-topic question instead of probing his wounds for her own curiosity.

Woodbridge lit up. "Ah, I see." He turned to Patrice. "You must have missed the news this morning. Angus and Eva Campbell aren't incarcerated any longer."

Declan kept his casual pose, but his hand under the table gripped mine. "That's right. I don't think they know where I am, but I can't be sure. I hope they will be found and caught—quickly. But I don't know how long they'll be loose. I refuse to be under her thumb again."

Understanding dawned. "If you're bound to me, she can't take you."

Prisha was already shaking her head. "That's not exactly true. She could, but it would be more difficult. You can't keep her out unless you're stronger, better trained, or had a really old and stable bond, hopefully all three of those things." Prisha's expression was pretty condescending, but I kept my ruffled feathers to myself. Now was not the time. In her place, I probably wouldn't think much of myself either. What I'd done, albeit accidentally, was horribly unethical.

Prisha folded her hands in front of her. "From what I've read, Eva Campbell was off-the-charts powerful. She has decades of experience and she's bound Declan before. I'm sorry, but I don't think you stand a chance. It would be better if—"

Declan cut her off with a growl. "No. No other mage. It's Lou or nothing. I will *not* be taken again, and Lou…" He licked his lips. "It has to be Lou." He turned toward me. "Please."

I squeezed his hand. "What about Dr. Larsen, she—"

He threw me a pleading look. "No offense to Dr. Larsen, but I trust you. The wolf chose you."

I'd have a hard time saying no to that argument, and I definitely couldn't say no to the expression on his face. "If that's what you want, then that's what we'll do."

His shoulders drooped in relief and he smiled. It was the kind of smile you had to return, so I did.

"But she's green—she hasn't even finished her apprenticeship yet," Woodbridge argued. "There is no way she's even the same caliber as Eva Campbell."

I could see why Van had been telling Declan her dad was lost at sea. I'd been in a room with him for an hour and I was ready to shove him overboard myself. Into heavily chummed, shark-infested waters.

My family behind me started grumbling. I'd forgotten they were in the room. Ha. Best not start talking shit, Woodbridge. The collective force of the Larsen-Matthews crew was mighty.

Declan glared at Woodbridge. "I don't give a shit what caliber you think Lou is. I don't care about her apprenticeship status. I trust her, which I think we can all agree is no small thing, considering. She is loyal, kind, and a fuck of a lot stronger than any of you think." He tapped his chest. "I can feel her magic. No offense, but you have no idea what she's capable of."

I had to blink back tears. Not only did Declan trust me, but he meant every word he'd just uttered.

There was a rustling behind me, and I looked back to see Mama Ami standing. "If I may address the tribunal?"

Woodbridge looked like he wanted to deny her, but couldn't think of a valid reason why. Patrice appeared intrigued, but Prisha obviously knew Mama Ami, because she was smiling at her. I mean, it's hard not to smile at Mama Ami. She was amazing.

Prisha's smile faltered a little when she caught the icy demeanor on Mama Ami's face. Ha! You poked the bear now, lady. Behind her I could see my mom, Jory, smirking. She winked at me. My mom would always be there to fight my battles at my side, but she also knew that her words right now wouldn't matter. Mama Ami's would. No one could argue her credentials or knowledge.

Prisha cleared her throat. "Of course. The Tribunal acknowledges Dr. Larsen, animal mage and Louise Matthews's current mentor."

Mama Ami took a few moments to go over the details from last night—who'd called her, what she'd seen when she got there, and so on. She held her chin high. "I'm the one that brought this to the Tribunal's attention. Aside from Ms. Bhatt, I'm the only person in this room who fully understands how damaging and wrong this kind of binding is. It's not just illegal, it's immoral."

My stomach plummeted for a second. Mama Ami believed in consequences, and if she thought the right course of action was to throw me to the Tribunal as offering, she would. But she was also wise and fair. Which meant if she truly thought that was the best course of action, it was.

She cleared her throat to quiet the sudden murmuring of the crowd. "That being said, sometimes exceptions need to be made. Like most animal mages, I studied Eva Campbell's crimes extensively. Yes, she is strong, but I believe that Louise has already ousted her once."

I blinked at her, surprised. *I did what now?* I glanced at Declan.

"The trap," he murmured. "It felt like her magic."

I was so glad I hadn't known that in the dream. I still would have tried to save Declan of course, but knowing who I was going up against, how *strong* she was, might have made me doubt myself.

Mama Ami explained what we'd told her about the dream. The Tribunal interrupted a few times, asking us clarifying questions, but mostly they just listened. "Louise heard a hunt—I don't think Eva Campbell knows where Declan is yet. However, she bound him as a child. They have a connection. I think she was reaching out into his dream state, calling to him."

"The trap was made for his wolf," I said.

"That's what I believe, yes," Mama Ami said, nodding. "They were using it to hunt Declan down." Her tones were crisp, and though Woodbridge opened his mouth to say something, she plowed ahead. "Declan hasn't been sleeping well and had to take a sleep aid from Wicked Brews. Because of that, he was especially vulnerable last night. Under the sleep aid, he couldn't rouse himself. His wolf did the only thing he could—he called out to Louise. He instinctively knew she'd help." She motioned toward me. "Explain the tether."

I took a few seconds to describe—with Declan's help—the tether of power the wolf had handed me. That intrigued them and Prisha's expression changed from angry to thoughtful. As soon as I was done, the room was silent for a moment.

Mama Ami turned her attention to me. "Did the hunting party in the dream find you?"

I shook my head. "No. I broke the trap and we got away before that."

Mama Ami smiled triumphantly. I'd made her proud. Yay, me.

"You busted her trap. You busted Eva Campbell's trap." She looked at the Tribunal. "Do you think her so green and weak now?"

"I think you consider her your daughter and you're biased," Woodbridge said. I wanted to punch him in his smug face so bad.

"She *is* my daughter," Mama Ami said. "Which means I hold her to the *highest* standard. Yes, she has much to learn, but she will fight tooth and claw before she hands anyone over to the likes of Eva Campbell. Declan may not have given her express permission to bind him, but his wolf *did*."

She stared every single Tribunal member in the eye. "His wolf trusted her, and so does Declan. So do I. I'll monitor and guide them. I will help them strengthen the bond, so if the Campbells find him, they are as ready as they can be." She put her hand over her heart. "I will also help them dissolve the bond as soon as Eva and Angus are back in jail."

She stared down the Tribunal again. I've been on the receiving end of that stare. It's terrifying. "It's the best option for everyone involved. Before we leave, Ms. Bhatt can examine the binding herself and talk to Declan to make sure Louise isn't forcing this choice on him."

Prisha pursed her lips and considered me and Declan. "I would also want to do surprise spot checks to make sure it stayed that way."

Woodbridge looked torn. On one hand, he didn't like me and wanted to give me the boot. On the other hand, if the Tribunal had to keep tabs on us, he would get a small chance to study Declan.

Greed won out. "Fine, but I want her suspended until this is done. I don't want her in your clinic, Dr. Larsen. She shouldn't be allowed to work on other familiars until she is completely cleared."

I started to argue, but Mama Ami cut me off. "She won't do familiar work, but she will still work in the clinic. She has bills to pay, just like everyone else, Arcanist Woodbridge."

"She should have thought of that before," Woodbridge said, not wanting to budge.

Mama Ami's eyes narrowed. "I will stake my professional reputation on my apprentice, Arcanist Woodbridge. Surely you're not questioning that?"

My stomach dropped. The support was great, but if I messed this up? I didn't want Mama Ami facing serious consequences for me.

Mollified, he waved his hand at her, delight in his eyes. Ugh, suck it, Woodbridge.

Patrice rapped the knuckles of one hand on the table. "I don't like it, but I see the wisdom in it. I'd like to add another condition. While this is going on, Declan should see a counselor. Someone who can help him process what he's going through."

"Agreed," Declan said. "As long as I get a say in who that person is. No court-appointed counselors."

It was by far the best deal we were going to get and much better than I thought we'd do.

Someone banged a gavel, and just like that, the tribunal was over.

We were allowed to go. I got up on unsteady legs and hugged Mama Ami tight. I loved her so much. When I looked over, my mom was hugging Declan. He seemed surprised but pleased. Something occurred to me then. The trial had been years ago. Had anyone been hugging him? Who had been holding his hand? He'd been taking care of us lately, but who had been taking care of him?

Mama Ami let me go, her face stern. "Go home. Rest. I'll see you at dinner."

"Dinner?"

She patted my cheek. "Yes, dinner. You both need a good meal, and your binding needs to be strengthened. I expect you and Declan to be living in each other's pockets as much as possible."

I couldn't help it—I thought back to this morning. Declan gloriously naked and walking around my room. In each other's pockets? "Shit."

Mama Ami glared at me. "Language, daughter. There's no call for such a thing."

All of her children had salty sailor mouths, even her younger daughters, not that I was going to say anything. There was only one response when Mama Ami got that tone. "Sorry, Mama Ami. I'll see you at dinner."

"Good girl."

CHAPTER FOURTEEN

Declan

I let Lou drive. If my wolf was willing to trust her with ourselves, our minds and
magic, then I could trust her with my SUV. That, at least, was replaceable.
Besides, I needed my hands free to call Zoey, and after putting her off and
scaring her, I wanted to be able to concentrate on the conversation. She
picked up on the second ring.

"Hey, Zo. Want to fill me in?"

I listened quietly as my sister talked, her voice still a little shaky. The gist
of her story was that they thought my dad had escaped first—no one knew
how yet. They were still looking into it and the authorities were staying tight-
lipped about the whole thing. An hour after they realized he had disappeared
from his cell, someone had the bright idea to check and make sure Eva was
still in her cell.

She wasn't.

They'd been in different penitentiaries—Angus on the East Coast, Eva
somewhere in the Midwest. The authorities wanted them separate, and they
wanted Angus away from his followers. Because of their abilities, they'd been
held in an Uncanny certified cellblock, something created specifically to hold
anything that fell into the uncanny spectrum.

Zoey made a noise telling me exactly how she felt about that. "Uncanny
certified, my heinie."

"Just say 'ass,' Zoey. Who says heinie?" I slumped in the seat and
watched the buildings go by. "Hell of a flaw in their system, huh?"

"What are we going to do? Are you coming back?"

It was tempting. I wanted to swoop in and take care of Zoey, but… "I
think the Tribunal will freak out if I leave town. Especially since I'd have to
take Lou, and they'd definitely lose their shit over that."

Lou snorted before she flipped on her blinker. "Bhatt would nail me to the wall so fast, and Woodbridge would taxidermy my corpse."

"Why would Lou have to go?"

Oh. Shit. So much had happened on my end, and Zoey didn't know about any of it. I ran a hand over my face. "Funny story about that." I tried to tell Zoey succinctly, but I had to pause so she could shout a little, and she had questions, so there was a lot of back-tracking and jumping around. Eventually, though, she got it.

"You could come up here," I offered.

"The brewery," Zoey said. "I can't abandon my baby for so long."

"Zoey—"

She growled into the phone. "Look, we'll be careful. I promise, but I'm not letting them disrupt my life again! Not when I just got it the way I want it." She huffed. "We both know you're going to be their main target, anyway."

I wanted to argue, but I couldn't. Both Eva and Angus had more of a score to settle with me. After all, it was my fault they were in jail. I didn't love her plan, but I also knew when Zoey was going to dig her heels in, and she had that tone to her voice now. Maybe it was good to keep us separate—better to split their attention than putting both their targets in one place. "Okay, but please—consider taking a vacation. Pack up, take Sid. Distance is a factor, and if you go somewhere that takes a passport, it will be harder for them to follow."

"I'll talk to Sid."

That was the best I was going to get. "Watch your dreams, too, Zo." That trap spell had been nasty. "Everything else going okay?"

Zoey started filling me in about the brewery. She was still talking as we got back to the house, toed off our shoes, and collapsed onto the couch. Lou handed me a beer. By the time I finally hung up, the beer was empty and I was dazed.

"What a day," Lou said, handing me another beer. She curled up on the couch, tucking her feet under her. "We're going to have to sync our schedules. Mama Ami wants us—" She drew her two index fingers together until they were side by side.

"What does that mean, exactly?" I moved my beer back and forth between us. "Like this, or in the same house or what?"

She frowned. "I think more like this? I've never bonded with a person. But we *do* need to bond. So, I guess lots of hanging out." She scrunched up her face. "Hope you didn't want much of a social life, because between our two work schedules…"

I drank some of my beer, thinking. "Staying busy will probably be a good thing." I set my half-empty bottle on the table. "We'll also need to find a counselor and fit that in."

Lou grimaced. "Yeah, about that."

Juliet stared at Lou wide-eyed, her hand paused midswipe as she wiped down the bar top. "You know this is sketchy as hell, right?" She shook her head, leaving the rag so she could take a drink order from one of the waiters. She turned, plucking several bottles off the shelves behind her. "There's no way the Tribunal will sign off on it. I'm your roommate!"

"Your apartment has its own address," I pointed out. "So technically, you're our neighbor."

Juliet laughed as she started assembling a cocktail.

"It's not perfect," Lou admitted. "But I talked about it with Declan— he'd rather talk to someone he trusts. Couldn't you set it up so it's through your mentor? Have her oversee it or something?"

Juliet finished up the cocktails just as the waiter returned, whisking them away on her tray. She went back to wiping down the counter with efficient movements. "I do have to do two to three thousand hours of supervised work in my field. Which means yes, if I did work with you, everything will be overseen by my mentor." Juliet filled up two pint glasses with water and set them in front of us. "If you're really set on this, I can talk to her."

"Please. I know you, which will make it a little easier for me." I was comfortable with Juliet, and I didn't feel like plunking down with a random counselor. I spun my coaster, watching it fall on the bar top. "Do you think the tribunal would make a big fuss over it? You knowing me? Conflict of interest or something?"

Juliet held a finger up, telling us to wait as she poured shots for one guy and a glass of red wine for another. "I don't know, honestly. The ethics… aren't great, and I lack experience. But if that's what you want, I can talk to

Dr. Kobayashi-Jones, my mentor. We could write something up and send it to the Tribunal to make sure they give it their stamp of approval." She canted her head to the side, thinking. "I don't think they'd let me counsel you alone. But I could be there, maybe? Work alongside her? That way you would feel comfortable because you know me, but you'd also get a really solid support from someone you know for certain won't take sides or cause any tension between all of us."

She propped her elbows on the bar. "I want you to think about it. I want what's best for both of you, not just what makes you comfortable. Understand?" We both nodded, and she went on. "I'll talk to my mentor and we'll put together a plan for you. We'll present it and you'll meet her. If you're okay with it, then we'll proceed. If not? No problem. I'll happily help you find another transitional therapist. Deal?"

I looked at Lou. She gave me an overenthusiastic thumbs up. I put out my hand to Juliet. "Deal."

Juliet shook it very seriously.

I grinned—it was hard not to grin at Juliet. I really couldn't see how Arcanist Woodbridge had raised her and Van. Juliet was so nice and Van was so...Van.

As if she was reading my mind, Juliet cleared her throat. "So you saw dear old Dad today, huh?"

Lou made a grumpy noise.

"He's, um..." How to describe Arcanist Woodbridge? "Awful. Just awful. How did you and your sister come out of that?"

Juliet lifted a shoulder and dropped it.

"You'll have to see him," Lou said, scrunching her nose. "If you and your mentor agree to this."

"I know." She picked up the rag off the counter and chucked it into the bleach bucket. "It's okay. I can't avoid him forever." The silence that followed said that she very much wanted to. Then someone hollered at Juliet for a refill and she went to the table to take their order.

"How long since she's seen him?"

Lou frowned at her beer and didn't answer.

"I know it's none of my business, but—they don't talk about either of their parents. The only family photos in the house are of them and you and Trick. Do they not want to share those kinds of things—like, keep them private? Or is it something else?" When Lou didn't respond, I turned to her. "You don't have to tell me either way, but you know I'm the last person who's going to judge them for their past."

Lou traced the condensation on her glass. "He hasn't spoken to Vanessa since she dropped out of school, though they barely talked before that. He did his best to drive a wedge between her and Juliet, but it didn't work. They would do anything for each other."

She drew a little curlicue on the glass. "I don't think Van ever had a good relationship with her dad. He's hated her since infancy. Juliet, though, she was Woodbridge's shining star...until she got pregnant." Lou sighed. "The last time Juliet saw her dad was when she showed him the ultrasound. She'd been living at home to save money while going to school."

Lou grimaced and shoved her glass away. "He threw her out, and she moved in with us. Told Juliet he wanted nothing to do with them. He's never met Savannah."

I sipped my beer, rubbing a hand over my heart. I'd held Savannah more than her own grandfather. I would never understand the people who threw their family away. That was different than sheltering yourself from toxic people.

I wasn't going to try to reconcile with my dear old dad anytime soon. He could go fuck himself. But Savannah was a *baby*. What could she have possibly done to deserve that treatment from him? Not that I thought Juliet or Vanessa had done anything to deserve their treatment, either.

What would have happened if Trick, Van, and Lou hadn't taken her in? Juliet had been in school, and Seattle was expensive. No one ever mentioned Savannah's dad, and as far as I knew, he had no involvement. How could Woodbridge toss out Juliet? How could he toss out his granddaughter? "What an asshole."

"Yeah." Lou propped her chin up with her fist. "I've decided he's a proper villain and doesn't deserve a first name anymore. It's just Woodbridge from here on out."

I laughed, choking on my beer. As I wiped my mouth with a bar napkin, I did some quick mental math. "Why did he throw her out? Juliet was an adult. Things happen. Was it the not-married thing?"

Juliet refilled our water glasses. "That was only part of it." Lou opened her mouth to explain, but Juliet waved her off. "It's okay. I don't care if you tell people, especially Declan. I'm certainly not ashamed of Savannah." She pointed at the glasses. "Hydrate, please. I'm not sending you two off drunk to Mama Ami's."

She wouldn't continue until we both dutifully sipped our waters. "It's pretty simple, really. My dad's an important arcanist. The title, the power, it means everything to him. Van and I were supposed to not only live up to his image, but expand it." She took a minute to pull a cloth headband off her wrist and pull her hair back from her face. "He's always been harder on Van. No idea why. But he wouldn't give her an inch. Then we both disappointed him. Van refused to follow in his footsteps, and I got pregnant and changed majors."

"She'd told him she was going to be an arcanist," Lou said, finishing off her water.

Juliet shrugged. "Most of the prerequisites are the same. I was already planning to switch—I just hadn't drummed up the courage to do it yet." She nudged my water glass closer, until I picked it up again. "Getting pregnant just sped up the timeline."

I dutifully sipped more water.

"If I'd stayed in my major, I would've had to see Savannah's father all the time." She leaned against the counter. "He wasn't *my* professor, but he was *a* professor. I never told Dad who Savannah's father was, and I don't plan to *ever* tell him."

A guy dropped off his empty glasses at the bar and Juliet swiped them up, putting them into the dishwasher under the bar top. "I couldn't afford to transfer schools, to avoid her dad completely, but I did what I could. Took online classes for a while. Anything opposite his schedule."

She looked at my face and laughed. "Don't look like that. This is much better, trust me. I'm starting a career I like." She tipped her chin toward the customers. "I have a flexible job that supports me. I have awesome room-mate-neighbors and the best daughter in the world. It didn't feel like it at the time, but my dad throwing me out was the best thing that ever happened to me."

Dinner at the Larsen household was loud in the best possible way, which helped distract me a little from our real purpose of being there—Mama Ami examining our bond. I didn't think she would do anything terrible, but fear doesn't listen to logic. So I was grateful for the distraction the chatter provided.

Bay sat sandwiched between Savannah's highchair and Will. Bay's younger half-sisters, Astrid and Tova, were currently talking away about their classes—Tova was in her first year in university and Astrid was taking early college classes through her high school. Tova was tall and willowy, while Astrid reminded me of a chipmunk with her animated chatter and bright eyes. Papa Bjorn and Mama Ami sat at the end of the table, close enough that he could lean over and kiss her cheek, like he was doing now.

And while they traded good-natured bickering, I sat in awe of the fact that I was seated at the dinner table with a handful of animal mages and—worry over the looming examination aside—I felt *fine*. Better than fine, really. I liked Lou's family a lot. I trusted that they wouldn't hurt me.

The dining room boasted a long wooden table, which told me that more often than not, there were extras for dinner at the Larsen house. Family photos littered the walls, featuring Lou and her mom just as often as Bay and his siblings. You couldn't look at the array of photos and not see that this was a family who loved each other fiercely.

"Oooh, my favorite." Astrid spooned something that appeared to be chicken—but I'd been told was not, in fact, chicken—onto her plate.

Astrid handed me the not-chicken, and I ladled some onto my plate, curious to see what it was like. I poked it with my fork. It looked a lot like chicken. I leaned closer surreptitiously and sniffed. Didn't *smell* like chicken. Did smell delicious, though—like the garlic, green onions, and spices they'd cooked it in. My stomach rumbled.

There were also green beans, a rice dish, and what appeared to be fried tofu. A few other dishes hadn't made it my way yet, so I wasn't sure what they were. I didn't even realize I was putting some of the tofu on Lou's plate until I looked up into her face. Her expression was serious, but she was laughing at me—I could see it in her eyes. I slowly returned the serving spoon to the bowl. "I wanted to make sure you got some of the vegetarian dishes."

"Thank you." Her tone was grave, but her mouth twitched.

I suddenly felt very silly. "All the food on this table is vegetarian, isn't it?"

Lou nodded, but her happy expression made me feel a little less ridiculous. "Except I suspect the tofu involves fish sauce."

"You can tear my fish sauce from my cold, dead hands," Mama Ami said with a snort. "Some exceptions must be made for my own happiness."

"No one is judging you, Mom, geez," Astrid said, rolling her eyes. She frowned. "Where's Mama Jory, anyway? I was going to have her look over my homework. I'm taking a basic automotive class as an elective."

Lou took the plate of tofu from me and handed it over to Will. "Yeah, where is Mom? I was sure she'd be here after the fun of the tribunal."

"Jory had a date. She was going to cancel, but I forbade her from doing so," Mama Ami said, taking a bigger helping of green beans.

"Mom went on a date?" Lou's eyes widened. "She hasn't been out in months." She paused, spoon held in midair. "That I know of, anyway."

"She's busy—work, friends, us. Sometimes it's hard to find time to go out and spend time with someone who more often than not disappoints her." Mama Ami settled her napkin on her lap. "After Gerald, Jory has very high standards. As she should."

Bjorn put one hand on his chest. "I would like to think that your standards were higher, too. After all, you married me."

Mama Ami laughed, her eyes sparkling. "It would certainly be difficult to lower them."

He held out a hand dramatically. "You flatter me so. I can't stand it."

She kissed his cheek. "You're terrible."

"You love me anyway." He winked at the table, causing his children to groan.

"Ew, Dad, Mom, stop it." Astrid pretended to gag. "No one wants to see you guys be cute."

Tova rolled her eyes at her sister. "You should be happy they still like each other. Do you know how many of my friends' parents are divorced?"

"Bayani Larsen, do not give that baby a lime to chew on. It's bad for her teeth." Mama Ami tsked. "I can't reach him. Will, smack his hand for me."

Will dutifully smacked Bay's hand.

"But she likes it!" Bay argued.

"Babies like to chew on all kinds of things," she said. "That doesn't mean you give it to them. Be the adult."

"But it's funny," Bay grumbled, though he took the lime wedge away from Savannah, causing her to pout. Will snickered.

I wanted to tell them how lucky they were. That not every family comes together like they have. Some fracture and nothing will bring them back.

"What about you, Declan?" Tova asked, stabbing a piece of tofu with her fork. "You have any siblings?"

"Three," I said, pushing around some rice on my plate. Suddenly, I wasn't very hungry.

Bay frowned. "Three? I've only heard you mention Zoey."

I nodded, staring at my plate. "I haven't seen the twins in years." It wasn't really breezy dinner conversation, but I kept talking. I never talked about the twins, except with Zoey, and even then, not very often. It hurt too much. And it kept us all safe. When you're hiding, you don't offer extra details about yourself if you can avoid it.

But Lou's family…it would feel good to tell them. They already knew who I was, and it would be nice to talk about the twins. Sometimes it felt like they existed only in my head, because no one around me knew about them, and it hurt. For once, I wanted to talk about them, even if I didn't have a whole lot to say. "I don't know where they live, or what their names are now. I might not even recognize them if I saw them on the street."

Astrid and Tova stared at me, riveted, their eyes wide. The table was quiet except for Savannah, who was noisily chewing on a green bean. Lou ignored her food, her fork hanging loosely in her hand.

"When's the last time you saw them?" Astrid asked gently.

"They were almost three when the courts placed them in a different home." I stopped pushing my food around and set down my fork. "I know they're safe. A few times a year, I send a letter to an intermediary, who passes it on." I hadn't had a letter back in over a year, but I still wrote. "The intermediary would let us know if…if something bad happened." Maybe they hated me. They probably blamed me for our family falling apart. I didn't even know. My chest felt tight.

"That's so sad," Astrid said, her eyes tearing up. She sniffed, and Tova handed her an extra napkin.

I tried to smile at them, but I didn't do a very good job. I'd never had what Lou and her siblings had, and I felt the jealousy seep through my veins. Which wasn't right. It wasn't their fault my family had fractured, and they clearly appreciated each other. But it still tore a wound open I thought long healed. I stared at my food, afraid that if I looked up, they would see everything in my face.

Under the table, Lou took my hand. I felt a tentative mental "knock" along our bond: Lou letting me know she was there if I wanted to drop my mental walls. If I wanted to let her in. I hesitated. The wolf inside me snorted in irritation.

You're so pushy sometimes, I told him.

He sat on his haunches. *Only when you need the nudge.*

Fine. I dropped my mental walls. Lou was there—all warm reassurance and … support. Like the mental version of her hand in mine, letting me know she was by my side.

My wolf settled down, letting out a sigh. The tightness in my chest eased, and I was able to pick up my fork and resume my meal.

Lou didn't let go. She had to eat with her left hand, which I knew wasn't her dominant one. I should have let go and made eating easier for her, but I couldn't.

I needed her hand, so I selfishly squeezed back and held on tight for the rest of the meal.

After dessert, we were ushered into the family room. Tova and Astrid bolted for their rooms, and Will headed to the kitchen with Bjorn to help with the dishes. Bay held a freshly pajama-ed Savannah as he stood by the window, swaying back and forth. When he turned, I could see Savannah's eyes drooping.

Bay's mom, who clucked at me every time I tried to call her anything but Mama Ami, took both our hands, closing her eyes, examining our bond closely. It took everything in me not to fidget. My belly was full, I was exhausted emotionally and even physically, but somehow I was still wound up.

Mama Ami's eyes opened, and she let go of us both. "I'll say this, it's a solid bond, despite everything. Strong." She grinned and relief coursed through me. I felt like we'd passed a test or something.

"A good start. Tomorrow evening, Lou, I want you to strengthen it." Mama Ami settled onto the loveseat across from us. "There are two ways for you two to build up your bond. Close contact—like spending time together—will help build on it naturally. Lou will also have to weave your magic together."

When she saw my perplexed look, she continued. "Your magic, it floats around you, like tiny filaments or threads. A switch, like Lou, takes those threads and braids them together into a complex pattern. Yours to hers, hers to yours, until it's one big weaving."

"Will it hurt?" I tipped my head toward Lou. "Will anything change?"

"It won't hurt." Lou's face scrunched up in thought. "As for things changing…it should be a lot like now, only more so?" She shook her head. "You being a shifter instead of an animal shouldn't change it too much, but there's limited data for obvious reasons."

Bjorn brought Ami a glass of wine and she smiled at him in thanks before taking a sip. "You don't want to give Eva a chance at a foothold. Build that bond." She waggled a finger between us. "I want you two together. Work together, eat together, brush your teeth together. Got it? If she attacks, Lou needs to be there to respond."

"She wasn't next to me when Eva attacked last night," I pointed out.

Mama Ami took another sip of wine, her shoulders loosening. "She also wasn't far. We don't know where Eva is—she might get closer. Her attacks might escalate. It will be easier for Lou to fight her off if you're touching. She at least needs to be able to get to you quickly. We don't want to give Eva a window of time to attack. Close proximity will also grow your bond quickly."

I cleared my throat, because I saw an obvious issue that no one had discussed yet. "What about at night?"

Mama Ami set down her glass of wine and focused all her attention on me. "If you're not comfortable sharing a bed, one of you can sleep on the floor. You can sleep in your wolf form. Find a way to make it work. I don't want to make either of you uncomfortable, but I also don't want to hand Eva an opportunity if we don't have to."

A slow flush crept up Lou's face. I checked our bond, but she'd locked it down tight. If it weren't for her pinked cheeks, I might think she was uncomfortable with the idea of me in her bed.

But I was beginning to think it was the opposite. Did Lou want me there?

It had felt really good to wake up with Lou curled against me. I'd been content. Happy. Lou thought it was the bond making me feel things that weren't there. I knew that wasn't the case. The only change was that it was easier for me to trust her. I could feel her horror at the idea of controlling someone—of misusing our bond.

I hadn't understood it at the time, but Eva had done exactly that—used the bond to control me. I knew what that felt like—heavy, the weighted feeling exhaustion sometimes brought on. And everything felt far away, like you were riding along in your own body but not in control.

I hadn't felt that around Lou. Not once. I was sure of it. Not only was she not Eva, but I wasn't a kid anymore. I was stronger, and I had more fight in me now.

But Lou would need convincing.

"Don't worry about us." I grinned at Lou and if possible, she blushed harder. "We'll figure something out."

CHAPTER FIFTEEN

Lou

It was a good thing I was used to living with people, or Declan's closeness would have posed more of a problem. As it was, we'd come home from dinner and watched another episode of *Mated by Fate* with Trick and Van. Declan sat right next to me, the line of his body flush with mine. I could feel the heat of him. It was distracting. Really distracting. And he was just *sitting* by me.

For his part, Declan seemed perfectly comfortable. As the show progressed, he'd flopped further against me. Trick, apparently, had liked this idea, so he'd flopped against Declan. By the end of the movie both men were cuddled and half-asleep—Trick appeared fully asleep—and had me pushed against the side of the couch.

"It's like you're the last domino and you didn't fall," Van said, snuggling under her throw blanket. Her ferrets were curled up in her lap.

"They're kind of cute," I said, reaching over Declan to pat Trick's head. "When they're not talking or doing anything."

"Less chance that they'll irritate you," Van said. "Can you even breathe?"

"Yes," I said, shifting a little. "But my leg is asleep. I think Declan eats bricks when we're not looking."

"I'm still awake, you know. I can hear every word," Declan said, his voice rough with sleep.

Van scoffed. "You think we wouldn't say any of this to your face?"

"Fair enough," Declan murmured. He blinked lazily at me. "I work early in the morning, so I need to go to bed. I can carry Trick to his room. Can you transfer Dammit?"

The baby phoenix, like Declan and me, was supposed to spend time with his master. I slipped out from under the human pile and put on the special gloves sitting next to Dammit's cage in the living room. The sleepy bird chirped as I scooped him up. When I looked over, Declan had gathered up Trick in a similar fashion, my friend still dead to the world in the shifter's arms.

"Look at him, all tuckered out," Declan said. "He's clearly been up to no good."

Van got up and folded her blanket, laying it on the back of the couch. "A pack of weirdos woke us up in the middle of the night, screaming bloody murder from the bathroom. I hear he was up all night helping them."

I grimaced. "Sorry, Van. Did we even thank you?"

She waved us off. "All in a day's work around here. Good night, you two. I'll shut down the room."

I led the way to Trick's room, listening to Van as she moved around turning off the lights and flipping over the locks. The door to Trick's room was open, so I slipped in quietly to put Dammit in his nighttime cage, settling him in to a nest of adult phoenix feathers. They were one of the few soft materials he could nest in without setting them on fire. When I had clipped the cage shut, I turned to see Declan tucking in Trick. We both tiptoed out and shut off the lights. It felt a little bit like we were the parents of very weird children.

It was strangely intimate to brush my teeth next to Declan. Trick had his own bathroom, so I was used to sharing the space with Van and even Declan, but we didn't usually brush at the same time. Declan and I both shared the bathroom as we went through our various routines. I wasn't sure about him, but I was desperately trying to not think about the rest of the night. But whether I wanted to think about it or not, I couldn't dawdle forever, and eventually we were both in my room.

"I'll sleep on the outside," Declan said, pulling his shirt over his head.

"You don't have to—"

He paused with his shirt in hands. "The closer the better, right?"

"I know, but…" I waved at him. "You could sleep on the floor or something if that makes you feel better. Or I can." In that moment, if I'd owned a tent, I would have been setting it up in the middle of my room. As it was, I'd locked down our bond on my end, because I was afraid of what kind of feedback he might be getting from me. Half-naked Declan was a *lot*. A smattering of hair dusted his chest, and I couldn't keep myself from following a trail of that hair as it disappeared into his jeans.

He cleared his throat and my head snapped back up. *Busted.*

Declan didn't call me out, but his brown eyes were warm when he dipped his head and caught my gaze. "Which would be better for the bond—one of us on the floor, or sleeping how we did last night?"

I could lie. I was so, so tempted to lie, even though I suck at it. But that wouldn't be good for either of us in the end. I sighed. "Like last night."

He folded his shirt and set it on my desk, then went for his jeans.

"Don't you at least have pajamas? Preferably something Victorian that covers you from chin to toes? Some chainmail, maybe?"

He fought a smile. "I can buy some if you like." His hands hesitated at the waist of his jeans. "If it's a problem...."

He was a shifter—he would run hot and wouldn't sleep well in clothing. I knew this—so far, I'd caught him sleeping both naked and in boxers, because that was more comfortable for him. I sighed. "It's no problem."

Down went the jeans.

I was wrong. It was a problem. I rubbed a hand over my eyes and tried not to think about how his boxer briefs left nothing to my imagination. "But for my sake, at least leave your underwear on." Like his boxers were any help. They were the flimsiest of barriers. They were a one hundred percent cotton lie to myself.

"You have a strange look on your face." He nudged me into a bed, like he was herding me.

"I'm not a sheep. Cut that out."

He blushed. "Sorry. I didn't realize—" He ran a hand over his face before propping both hands on his hips, which let me tell you, *really* showed off his chest.

I wasn't going to make it. I would die right here, burned down to cinders. *Tell my mom I loved her.*

He squinted at me. "You got that look on your face again."

The thing about shifters was that their senses were much sharper than ours. Which meant that at any moment, he could scent the room and get that I wanted to climb him like a sexy tree. Were trees sexy? Japanese maples were pretty freaking sexy. Shit, I was tired.

Best confront this now. You know, since I lacked both a tent and chainmail pajamas.

I patted the bed next to me.

"Oh no. Are we going to have a talk?" He sat, but he instantly started to fidget, like he was nervous. "These never go well. Last talk I had, my girlfriend dumped me."

"Yeah, ouch. So this will be less painful, but what it lacks in hurt, it will make up for in awkwardness." I turned so I could look at him. Might as well go for maximum awkwardness. "Here's the thing. I know a lot of people would be thrilled to be in my position."

One of his eyebrows winged up.

I crossed my arms. "Like, 'Oh no, I have to share a bed with a mostly naked sexy man.'" I pitched my voice in a silly manner in the hopes that it would lighten the mood. I had no evidence that it worked. "Except it's a little like someone placing your favorite cookie on a plate in front of you and saying, 'Don't touch it.' Only plot twist—the cookie is poison. If you eat it, you die. But it smells *delicious.*" I frowned. What was I saying? I was babbling, that's what. "Analogies get away from me. People aren't food. Do you get what I'm saying?"

His face was completely blank and serious. "I'm a poison cookie?"

"Yes. No. That's not—" I buried my face in my hands. "I'm screwing this up." I breathed deep, which was a huge mistake because he smelled amazing, before dropping my hands, taking one of his. "You are an excellent cookie. Person. You are a person. But you are a *tempting* person. Only right now, that would not be okay."

"Lou, it's okay. I'm tempted, too."

I dropped his hand and poked his chest. Oooh, that was a mistake, too. I curled my fingers under so I wouldn't do it again. "That's not the point of this conversation and it doesn't matter. I'm only telling you so that we can keep our boundaries straight."

He made a noncommittal humming noise as he captured my hand, his thumb stroking along the back of it. I shivered. "Lou, it's okay."

I couldn't quite bring myself to take back my hand, and irritatingly, my voice came out a little breathy. "No. That's not okay. There's a power imbalance here. With me on top."

A slow, wide grin unfurled on his face.

"Don't say it."

"I don't mind women on top."

I shoved him playfully with the flat of my palm this time. He barely budged, and he didn't lose my other hand in the struggle. I did it again, but the second time was mostly just an excuse to touch his chest, because I apparently have zero restraint. "I said, 'Don't say it.' This isn't funny. The line of consent gets hazy in situations like this, and I don't want to take advantage of you." I looked at him to see if he understood.

He waggled his eyebrows suggestively.

A suspicion occurred. "And you are one hundred percent fucking with me right now."

He threw back his head and laughed. "I am. It's wonderful."

"That's it—get off my bed."

His laugh trailed off in a sigh, and he picked me up to pull me into his lap. I slapped at his hands. "No."

He paused. "Is that an actual no? Because I'm trying for an apology cuddle here."

I leaned into him. "It's not an actual no, I'm just tired and irritated and freaking out."

He wrapped himself around me like a human cocoon, and it felt glorious. "Louise, stop. Listen to me for a second."

"Okay."

"You're so busy trying to do what you think is best that you're not really listening to me and you're ignoring body language." His voice held a gentle chide. "Ignore the bond for a second. We're just two people. What would you think? Am I interested or not?" He traced a line along my jaw with his knuckle. "Because I think I'm being pretty obvious."

He leaned even closer, dropping his voice to a whisper, like he was sharing a secret. "I want you, too."

He offered that so casually, like the line wasn't completely devastating to my willpower. I don't think I'd ever been so easily wrecked by a statement. I licked my lips, nervous, and he traced the movement with his eyes.

"But the bond—" I cleared my throat and tried again. "What you're feeling…."

He chuffed, sounding very like a wolf. "What I'm feeling was there before the bond."

I thought back to his meltdown, his obvious discomfort when he'd first moved in. "That seems unlikely."

He traced light circles on my arm, and I wasn't sure he was aware of doing it. "Afraid of the mage, attracted to the person." His lips quirked when goosebumps broke out on my arm. Okay, he was aware of the circles. He breathed a sigh and tapped a finger gently against my forehead. "Open up, Lou. See for yourself." I must have looked as dubious as I felt, because he smiled. "Just look."

I closed my eyes, breathed deep, and dropped the block I had on the bond.

It was like trying to drink from a storm-swollen river. There was just so *much* at once. I was used to dealing with animals. Not that animals don't have complex inner lives, but it's simply not the same. After a second, it got more manageable, and I was able to sort through his feelings a little easier.

Everything Declan had been saying was there. His attraction to me. His surety that this was okay. That he wasn't a poison cookie. His trust.

And he felt everything I did, too. My confusion. My worry that I'd do something to betray that trust. Not intentionally, but then, we don't always hurt people on purpose. They still end up hurt.

He brushed the hair back from my face. "You're scared."

I was terrified. He'd been through so much and I was worried I'd destroy any headway he'd made. After all, I didn't know what I was doing. I was still an *apprentice*. But right now, by contrast, Declan's emotions, when I sifted through them, were strong and steady. "How can you be so sure? With everything going on, your past, aren't you a little frightened?"

He smiled again, this one tight-lipped, no teeth. "You're my friend, Lou. I have faith—you can do this."

"That sounds like a very nice sentiment for a greeting card, and I'll try to listen to it over the mantra of 'we fucked' that's currently parading through my head." I pulled the blanket over my shoulders. "It's a big parade, too. There's a marching band and full complement of 'we fucked' dancers. Elephants, probably. Maybe some dressage ponies."

Declan considered this. "We're both tired and the last twenty-four hours have been…"

"A lot?"

"Yes, a lot. We don't have to decide everything tonight. We know where we stand. Let's give each other time to adjust." He tucked the blanket tighter around my shoulders. "Would it help if I talked to Juliet's mentor about it?"

"Yes?" It came out like a question, but I guess it *was* a bit of one to me.

"Then we'll leave it there for now." He curled an arm over my hip.

"Just like that?"

"Just like that."

Declan's bone-deep contentment flowed over the bond, and my "we fucked" parade got a little quieter. The band lowered their instruments and the elephant yawned. The dancers stretched and the ponies began to graze. *Take five, everybody. We'll pick up our catastrophizing in the morning.*

"Okay, then." I snuggled down into the pillows. "And Declan?"

"Hm?"

"Since you're on the outside, you have to get back up and turn off the lights."

He grumbled as he got up and flicked off the switch, plunging the room into darkness.

CHAPTER SIXTEEN

Declan

We spent the next three days juggling schedules, working on our bond, and not discussing my poison cookie status. Which was fine. It felt good to get to know Lou in a new way, and I was enjoying what we already had. I could be patient.

Which was good because the scheduling program at the tattoo shop could try anyone's patience. Some glitch in the system had erased our color coding on this week's schedule. I'd straightened out Bay's appointments, but I still needed to do Will's before I left.

Will did two kinds of piercings at the shop. The first were the kind of piercings you could get at any tattoo shop that had a body piercer. The second—and much more expensive and time consuming—was an arcane ceremony. Will had trained for years to learn how to do it and it was much harder to find a licensed practitioner. It also cost a pretty penny.

Arcane piercings took longer, so we needed to make sure we blocked out the time properly. We also color coded them so that Will could check at a glance and prepare for each appointment properly. I'd spent the last hour correcting the mistake before shooting off an email to Bay letting him know what I'd done and why. Hopefully, we could figure out what had happened so it wouldn't do it again.

That done, I turned my attention to closing, going over the evening checklist since I didn't usually close. The counter person scheduled tonight had a doctor's appointment, so we'd switched. By now, the artists were all gone, their stations cleaned and ready for tomorrow. Will wheeled the mop bucket out of the dirty room, singing along to the music blasting through the shop. Lou was curled up on the waiting area couch, reading until I was done.

I'd dropped the deposit in the safe, finished my paperwork, and was just leaving a note for the opening staff when I felt it. The first pass was a faint brush, like someone sweeping past you in the street. My pen froze on the notepad as my whole body stilled.

I waited a minute.

Nothing.

Maybe I'd imagined it? I glanced over at Lou. She'd turned her face up to me, her brows pinched in worry. "Declan?"

A pulse of fear went through me and I broke into a sweat. *No. Nonono-no—not again.* I wouldn't let her take me again. I was panting now, the pencil in my hand snapping in two.

Lou dropped her book, scrambling up from the couch.

"Eva—" That was all I got out before every muscle in my body went rigid. My eyes squeezed shut and I couldn't open them. Magic rippled through me, my fear a pounding rhythm in my veins as I felt a mental shove. Eva was trying to force me to change. Revulsion at the violation welled up, chasing back some of the fear.

Fine tremors shook my body, sweat beading along my hairline. If I changed, it would be easier for her. She'd have more power over the wolf form—she was an animal mage. I would be closer to her sphere of magic. I needed to stay human. So far, I was shoving her back, but I couldn't move or speak, my hold tenuous. We were locked in a mental shoving match.

And I could already feel my grasp slipping.

It's inevitable, the magic whispered, insidious. *You've never resisted us before.*

The magic was right—I'd never kept her out before. Except with Lou. I *needed* Lou. The wolf inside me snarled. He wanted to fight. Take over. Keep her out. The only thing keeping him from jumping forward into control was that he knew I was right. If I went wolf, she won.

Lou touched my arm and I heard her shout for Will. My shirt slipped up and over my head. Warmth at my back. Then the bond between me and Lou snapped fully open.

My head cleared. It was like our bond was an umbrella, and Eva the storm. I wasn't fully protected, but the brunt of her power slid off the silken edges of our bond, falling away from us. The umbrella was shielding us from the worst of the downpour of power, even if we were still caught up in it.

With Lou at my back, I had a little space. Not much. But I could *breathe.* Enough to move my arms until they were pressed into Lou's, which were wrapped around my stomach. I'm not sure how long we stood like that. Just breathing and holding on—not even fighting back. We had no energy for that. We were barely managing as it was. Fighting could wait. Right now, all we had to do was keep Eva from winning long enough to make her retreat.

The wolf bared his teeth. We wouldn't go down easy. Not this time.

Eventually, Eva's mental assault lessened. My breathing slowed, the breaths going deeper. When my vision came back, I was standing stock-still at the reception counter of the shop, my shirt dangling from the office chair in front of me.

Sweat slicked my skin, my muscles trembled from the sustained strain. Lou's shirt was draped over the counter, and she was pressed up against my back like a limpet. Her arms were still wrapped around me, a steady, supportive presence at my back, with my arms over hers. For a moment it struck me how absurd it was for me to lean on someone so tiny for protection.

The wolf snapped its teeth, getting my attention. *Fierce.* He looked on Lou with open admiration.

Will peered at us from a few feet away. "You two okay?"

"I think so," I said, but I didn't move. "We're going to stay like this for a minute, though."

Will nodded. "I closed the blinds. Wasn't sure Lou wanted people passing by to see her half-naked and sweaty-hugging our counter staff."

"My bra is on," Lou mumbled into my back. "How is that any different than a bikini?"

"It doesn't really matter which one you're wearing when Declan's shirt is off and you're stuck to him like a koala, does it?" Will set two juice boxes on the counter. "When you can move, I want you both to drink these."

"You want me to drink apple juice?" I picked one up.

"Blood sugar," Will said, snapping on a pair of gloves. "Once you've finished those, step into my piercing room, please. But make sure you're feeling steady. I don't want anyone passing out."

"Bay says that happens a lot," Lou said into my back. "People passing out."

"He's not lying." Will's voice floated out from the room, along with the sound of drawers opening and him moving around. "Most of the time it's the person watching."

"The things I have mopped up in that room," I whispered to Lou, "would horrify you."

"I work with animals. If you want to play the gross-out game, I'll win." She gave me a squeeze. "Can I let go of you and drink the juice?"

I reluctantly released my hold, handing her the shirt she'd discarded onto the desk. Or I meant to. The material ended up fisted in my hand. I'd sweated while repelling Eva. A lot. Which I'd known, but what I hadn't anticipated was that Lou was wearing a light pink cotton bra. She'd been pressed tight against me. The damp material was now see-through. I could see Lou's nipples and I hadn't been prepared for it. A fierce bolt of lust went through me and rang my bell. Maybe it was the low blood sugar, but I swear for a second I saw *actual stars.*

Lou held a juice box in one hand, the other extended to take her shirt. When I didn't release it, she looked at me, her eyebrows raised. "You okay?'

I'll admit that I whimpered a little.

Lou looked down, saw her bra, and grimaced. "Gross." She peered up at me. "Please tell me you're not turned on by this." She pointed at her bra. "It's like a wet T-shirt contest, but with *sweat*. That's not sexy."

I stepped close, until she was so near me, I could feel the heat of her skin. "Yeah?" My voice had dropped to a growl, but I wasn't angry. "Then tell me." I breathed her in, letting the scent of her soothe me. Her pulse fluttered at the base of her throat. "Tell me you don't want to touch me right now." I leaned back until I could look her in the eye. "Because I'll know if you're lying."

A shuddery breath escaped Lou. "Fine. You win." She snatched my shirt from me. "But we're not talking about this now."

I nodded, stepping back. She was right. Not the time. But we'd need to discuss where we stood again. Soon.

Lou pulled on her shirt with unsteady hands. "What are you doing, Will?"

"Setting up. You and Declan need my services."

"We do?" Lou peeked into the piercing room.

Will's head popped out. "You do." He pointed at the remaining juice box. "Drink. Then we'll talk."

Lou was already going into the room. "What are you thinking?"

"We do a protection ceremony. It won't be foolproof, but it will help."

I considered this while I drank the juice. "Will—"

He pointed a gloved finger at me. "I know that tone. Forget it. I'm not charging either of you. I'll talk to Bay about it tomorrow. The shop can eat the jewelry and supply fee."

"It doesn't feel right," I said, throwing away my juice box. "Taking something for free. Like I'm stealing from you and Bay."

Will scowled at me. I wasn't prepared for it. Will was usually all sunshine, but right now he was pure thunder. "Lou is Bay's *sister* and my friend. She brings me coffee. Sometimes cookies. If you hug her right, she squeaks, and it's delightful." He jerked his chin at me. "You work here, and you're also my friend. I'm not sure if you squeak yet, but I'd like to find out. You're one of us now, whether you like it or not. So you are going to sit down, shut up, and let me help you."

I'd never seen Will without a sense of humor. He carried a general air of happy contentment wherever he went. It was completely absent now. This Will could crack skulls, take names, and not give a single fuck.

"Do you know how long you two were out?" Will asked, leaning close. "Look at the clock, Dec." His face shifted then, relaxing into anguish. "I called Mama Ami. Told her what was going on. Thought I'd see—see if I could help. I couldn't." A muscle in his jaw ticked. "I watched you both struggle, knowing there was nothing I could do to help you, for almost *thirty minutes*."

I looked at the clock. Son of a bitch. He was right.

"I don't care if you're feeling cavalier about the whole thing. I'm *not*." He stepped back, holding an arm out as an invitation to enter his workspace. Very meekly, I did what I was told.

The piercing room was compact and neatly organized, with several labeled drawers full of needle packs and jewelry, all sterilized and ready to go. A cushioned exam table, like the kind you see in the doctor's office, except it had been reupholstered a deep purple, sat in the middle along with a tall metal tray that held everything Will would need. The room was painted a soothing lavender and smelled like antiseptic and incense.

"As long as your only objection is monetary, I don't want to hear it." He waited a second to see if we had any arguments. When we both shook our heads, he continued. "Good. Then let me do my job." He waited for Lou to hop up onto the table. "Pull up your hair, please."

Now that he was doing something, Will's demeanor had shifted away from anger to something steadier, calming himself so that we'd relax in turn. "I'm going to do two surface piercings." He turned his attention to Lou. "That means the piercing is going to sit flat against the skin—in this case, the back of your neck, which will put the stone of the jewelry in contact with the dermis."

He held his hand out flat, parallel to the floor. "Pretend this is your skin. Piercings usually go through the plane, like this." He poked a finger down next to his flat hand, pointing down to the floor. "Surface piercings use a different kind of jewelry, which follow the plane of the skin." He traced a line under his hand. "Understand?"

"Got it." Lou finished putting her hair up into a loose bun while Will prepared the back of her neck. He cleaned the area with alcohol first, then, using a toothpick dipped in gentian violet, he marked four spots on her neck.

"That's where the actual piercing will go." He drew several small symbols, quickly and neatly around the dots, and leaned back, examining his work. "The rest of this is the arcane part—we're using the ceremony to channel the natural properties of the stones in the jewelry. I picked ones that will help specifically with mental assault."

"We'll take any help we can get." I tightened my fingers on Lou's. Through our bond she confirmed my own thoughts—that last attempt had been close. Too close. We needed a leg up.

"The ceremony also helps channel your own abilities—not adding to your power, really, just streamlining what's there. Making it more efficient," Will said absently, checking his work. "I could do the piercings in your lobes instead, but it wouldn't have the same oomph." He snapped off his gloves and stepped on the trash can pedal so he could throw them away. "This placement is closer to your spine and brain, it'll work better."

He nodded at a metal tray with several packs holding needles and jewelry, sanitized and ready to use. "You'll both get four—double jet, fire agate, and tourmaline." Will opened up another drawer which contained different ritual candles, chalk, and incense. He grabbed the incense he wanted and set it into a well-used holder. When he lit it, the smell filled the small room, and I drew it into my lungs, recognizing the scents of myrrh and frankincense.

Once that was done, he had Lou take her shirt back off. His attention on Lou was focused on his work and putting her at ease. Unlike me. Then again, Will was a professional, and he saw a *lot* of nipples. I should know—I booked his appointments. He used a Sharpie to sketch more lines and symbols on Lou's face, neck, chest, and arms, his face drawn in concentration.

Lou didn't seem concerned, but without thinking, I mentally reached out through our bond to check. That earned me a smile—she was fine, though a little nervous. I took her hand, at the same time sending soothing thoughts through the bond. With each interaction, this was becoming easier, almost automatic. Lou let me calm her further, her shoulders loosening a fraction.

Satisfied with his work, Will set the Sharpie down and put on another set of gloves. He grabbed a piercing needle, which was hollow with a sharp tip, and then stood behind her, hands poised. "Okay, Lou, I want you to take a deep breath in." His deep voice was pitched to soothe and calm. "Now let it out through your nose." As he spoke, he pierced her neck where the first set of markings were.

The second the needle passed through the skin and hit blood, magic crackled through the air. Lou breathed in sharply, squeezing my hand, but otherwise didn't react as the magic continued gathering around us like a mist. I could feel it buzzing along my skin—energy with no purpose, called up by Will's ritual.

He deftly inserted the metal bar before screwing the second stone in to cap it. Once that was done, the nebulous magic surrounding us snapped into place, igniting the symbols on Lou's skin until they glowed a bright purple. For a second, I could see the magic tracing her skin, following unknown pathways until every inch of her glowed. The light coalesced, burning bright for an instant before it disappeared with a flash, the Sharpie markings vanishing with it, like they'd never been.

A drop of blood welled at the site of the second piercing and Will gently pressed a piece of gauze against it. "Bit of a bleeder."

I felt a flare of guilt at the sight of that blood. Because of me, Lou's life had been upended, her schedule completely fucked, and now she had to go through this. The piercings were temporary, and the pain wasn't bad, but she had bled for me and I didn't like it.

"Stop it," Lou said. "I'm fine."

I grumbled an apology.

Lou glared at me. "You didn't ask Eva to come after you. This is not your fault." She pointed at her neck with her free hand. "I didn't tell Will 'no' because he's right, this will help. I chose to take that help, just like I chose to stay bonded to you until this is over." When I didn't seem convinced, she sighed. "Check the bond. I'm not trying to make you feel better." She made a face. "I mean, I am, but by telling the truth."

When I checked, everything was as Lou said—her resolve to be there for me, her exhaustion from battling Eva earlier, and relief that we were okay. The only anger she had was aimed firmly at Eva. Nothing at me. I leaned in and kissed her on the temple. "Thank you."

She flushed. "Of course."

Will went through the ritual once more, until Lou had two sets of stones resting on the back of her neck, the bars hidden under the skin. Will checked them, a look of satisfaction on his face. "That should slow her down." He took off his gloves and tossed them in the garbage, waving Lou off the chair. "Okay, Dec, your turn."

I jumped up and took Lou's spot on the chair. Will toweled off any of the excess sweat left on my chest, and then went through the whole piercing process again. I held Lou's hand, letting her calm me the way I'd done for her. My skin heated as the magic gathered, flaring as the light grew brighter, but it wasn't uncomfortable. Will capped the jewelry, and I sucked in a breath as the magic snapped into place.

Lou beamed at me. "See? No big deal, Dec. I'm fine. We're fine."

I nodded, but it was a big deal. What Lou had already done for me was *huge*. She'd put her future in jeopardy, let me barge into her life, and now this. No, Lou wasn't fine. She was *amazing*. I kept my eyes on her as Will put in the second piercing, and I felt my heart lurch.

I might just be a little bit in love with Lou.

The wolf inside me sneezed, the magic tickling his nose. Then he sat, his tongue lolling out—he was laughing at me. *The signs were everywhere. You are a poor hunter.*

I am not. There are few insults greater to a wolf, and here he was, casually tossing that comment my way. Only his posture and expression let me know he was teasing. Still. *I'm an excellent hunter.*

If she were a rabbit, you would have starved by now.

My wolf was a smug bastard when he was right.

CHAPTER SEVENTEEN

Declan

The Tribunal approved Juliet and her mentor, Dr. Kobayashi-Jones. After a little
schedule juggling, we were able to meet them at the park the next afternoon.
Juliet thought—correctly—that movement and outside time would make
me feel more at ease. She picked the park I'd been running in. It had several
playgrounds, lots of forest to walk through, and a definite bunny problem.
One sat on a patch of grass ahead of us, and it obviously had a death wish. I
was upwind from it. Human form or not, that bunny should have smelled a
predator and bolted. Instead, it sat there munching clover.

"You can't eat that bunny," Juliet said, her face stern.

I stepped closer to the bunny. It still didn't move. I waved at it in disgust.
"Not a twitch."

"Leave it be, children." Dr. Yolanda Kobayashi-Jones laughed, and
it was the kind that simply insisted you join in, and in the twenty minutes
I'd known her, she'd employed it often. She wore a gold dress along with a
chunky purple sweater, had a good handshake, and had a no bullshit rule. I
liked her instantly.

"Why can't I eat it?" I pointed at the little clover-muncher. "Bunny." I
tapped my chest. "Shapeshifter."

"Because I named it." Juliet clasped her hands in front of her, her eyes
wide.

"What did you name it?" the doctor asked.

"Lunch," Juliet said primly.

I laughed, and the bunny finally hopped away. I took a second to check
on Lou—she was helping Bay chase Savannah around the slide. Bay was there
as backup. If Eva attacked again, Lou could rush to me, and Bay would keep
Savannah occupied. She probably wouldn't understand what was happening
if she witnessed an attack—she was too young—but we all wanted to avoid
it if we could.

"Do we need to get closer?" the doctor asked.

I shrugged. "I told her she could sit in on the session but didn't think it was a good idea. She wanted me to be able to speak freely to you." I dug my hands in my pockets. The truth was, I'd rather be chasing Lou around the slide. I just liked being close to her. Instead, I led us onto the wide walking path that wove through the park. "Lou's been adamant about protecting my boundaries, which has the strange effect of making me want to knock them down." In the distance I heard Savannah squeal with laughter. "I'm not usually contrary. I'm a wolf, not a cat."

"It's not strange at all," Dr. Kobayashi-Jones said with a smile. "And not really contrary. Lou is acting in regard to your safety—letting you know that it's important to her. Which makes you feel safe. And if you feel safe, it's natural to relax your guard." She motioned a hand toward Juliet, making the bangles on her wrist chime as they collided. "Much like having Juliet here— someone familiar to you—makes you feel safe, so you're more comfortable talking to me."

"Smooth transition there, Doctor."

She gave me an unrepentant grin. "Yolanda, please. Now, Juliet and I are up to speed as best we can be—I read the tribunal transcripts, and we did some research—but what this all boils down to, for us, is you. So, if you're willing, I'd love you to take a little time and share your background. How did we get here, to this moment, Declan?"

"Everything you say to us is confidential," Juliet reminded me. "And if at any point you want me to leave, let me know. Okay?"

"Okay." I took a deep breath, trying to think of the easiest way to explain everything. "My father, Angus Campbell, started Moon's Chosen People a few years after my mom died. Then he took up with one of the members—a young shifter woman named Daisy—and we got Zoey shortly after I turned five."

"Daisy was his second mate?" Juliet asked.

I shook my head. "No, they never mated. My dad didn't think Daisy was strong enough." I glanced at them both. "The thing you need to under-stand—the mating bond, it's a psychic and emotional bond between two people."

Juliet frowned slightly. "That sounds like the familiar bond."

"But not the same," I said, pausing to let a family pass us by. "In the familiar bond, there's a different dynamic. The mage is in control. The mating bond is a partnership between two people. A balance, negotiated between the partners, but no one controls the other. A bonded pair, they can see inside each other in a way that no one else can." I shrugged. "I don't know how to explain it, only to say that it's very intimate. It made my dad feel vulnerable, and after my mom, he wasn't in a rush to do it again."

"But he did mate with Eva," Yolanda said.

She'd said it like a statement, not a question, but I answered it anyway. "Yes, because Eva was strong, and she could help solidify his hold over the pack."

"He had to know her plans, though." Juliet's words were soft as she tried to work the problem through. "Her interest in binding a shifter as a familiar."

"Yes," I said, and the smile I gave her was a strained one. "But as her mate, she couldn't bind *him*. The two bonds can't coexist like that—the mating bond wouldn't allow it. My father is many things, but at his core, he's a narcissist. He only cared what mating to Eva would bring him." I tipped my face up to the sunshine. "Eva made a good threat. Kept the pack in line."

I herded us back around, aiming for the playground. I didn't want to get too far from Lou. "Still, at least we got the twins." The twins were worth every terrible thing, at least to me. Yolanda's expression was sad, but she perked up a little as Juliet gave me a one-armed hug.

"Okay?" she asked, leaving her arm there.

"Yeah," I said. "Thanks." I was already getting tired of talking, and we weren't even close to end. As quickly as I could, I sketched out the rest of it. The police. The trial. My family and pack, splintering into so many broken pieces. Sidney. Zoey. Finally, my fresh start in Seattle.

After I was done talking, Juliet gave me a squeeze. "I have to say, Declan, considering all you've gone through, and observing you as a roommate, you seem remarkably stable. I think you should be really proud yourself." She dug her hands into her hoodie. The day was on the chilly side, and the large fir trees blocked a great deal of sun. "I'm no expert in survivors of cults, but a lot of them have issues adjusting."

"It's also not my area," Yolanda admitted, "but I agree with Juliet."

"Thanks." The path wound uphill, and I slowed my pace so we could continue talking easily. "I had some lucky breaks. I got to live a little bit as a young werewolf normally does, before my mom died. Then after, my sister Zoey and I got placed with a foster pack family. That pack was healthy, and it helped." They'd probably saved our lives, honestly. They were patient, calm, and supportive. "The twins got placed with another family, people who were more like them—elementists."

My throat tightened. They'd been so little at the time—not quite three. Neither Zoey nor I wanted to be separated from them, but the courts were adamant that it was better for all of us. Though I could kind of understand their reasoning, I didn't agree with it. "When I was eighteen, I talked to their guardian ad litem about getting custody. Of the twins." I kicked a pinecone out of the path.

"They advised against it. The twins likely wouldn't remember us or their upbringing much. They'd settled in. Me taking them would be a disruption." I rubbed a hand over my chest, willing the pain there to go away. It never worked, but I did it anyway. "I wrote to them. They agreed with the guardian." That letter had been like a dagger in my chest. It's not that I didn't understand, but it still hurt.

"That must have been really hard," Juliet said softly.

"It was. I hadn't realized how much I'd hung on to the idea that we'd be back together someday. But I couldn't take them away from a good home. It would have been selfish." I glanced over to the playground, making sure Lou and Savannah were okay. I didn't like either of them out of my sight for long. Bay had Savannah in the air, whooshing her around like an airplane while Lou recorded it on her phone. "The way we were raised, that was one of the worst things, you know? No choice in your own life. No agency. I could have fought, tried to get the twins anyway, but was it my right to do it?"

I rolled my shoulders, trying to loosen them. "I haven't heard from them in a year."

Yolanda examined me, her face concerned. "I can't imagine what you went through. And with Zoey and Sidney, it probably felt like they were leaving you, too. That must have dredged up a lot of past hurts."

We kept walking for a minute as I sorted through my thoughts for a response. She wasn't wrong—it had felt like an echo of the past, my family being taken away again. And yet, it wasn't. "I love my sister. I want her to be happy." I tucked Juliet to my side, needing the comfort. "She has a hard time attaching to people. Dating…" I shook my head. "She's a mess when it comes to dating. Losing my girlfriend sucked. I won't pretend it wasn't painful, but…" I struggled to think of how to say it. "It was sort of tempered by the fact that Sid made Zoey happy in a way I'd never seen."

"How does she do that?" Yolanda asked.

I checked on Lou and Savannah again, relaxing when I saw Lou holding her up so she could touch the monkey bars. "After they told me, I thought back to all the times we hung out. And I watched them interact after the whole mess." I rubbed a hand over my jaw. "It's hard to explain it, but Zoey lights up when Sid's around. They seem…right. I don't know. I think Sid and I had been over for a long time, but neither of us wanted to acknowledge it."

Just the fact that we hadn't had sex in ages, that we hadn't made time for each other to hang out or go on a date, should have been a gigantic red flag. On fire. With klaxons attached. Not that needs don't change, but we'd been very attentive to each other at the beginning, and at some point that had petered out. We'd both been busy, and I'd chalked it up to that. Truth was, we hadn't been interested. I glanced at Juliet. "The longer I'm here in Seattle, the more it seems like something that happened to someone else. It hurt, but I love them, and I want them to be happy, you know?"

Juliet squeezed me with both arms this time. "You're a good person, Declan."

"I try to be," I said. "Sometimes I fail." I looked over at Lou, who was pushing Savannah on the swing. The little girl's face was all smiles as she squealed with each push. "I feel like I've failed Lou with all of this."

Yolanda stopped me. "No. This is not your fault, and it's not hers. All of this rests at Eva's and Angus's door." She checked her watch. "Juliet has put together a few sessions without me—more like check-ins than sessions like this. She's paired them with activities, walks, yoga, and some breathing and meditation." When I didn't argue, she continued, explaining how Juliet would keep her in the loop, and when our next session together would be.

She clasped her hands together when she finished, her smile wide. "I think we've done enough for today." Her smiled dimmed a little as she watched me. "Unless there was something else?"

I could feel my ears get hot as I tried to figure out how I wanted to bring up the last topic. Juliet caught the look on my face and guffawed. For someone so tiny, her laugh was awfully loud.

"The look on your face!"

I grumbled.

She nudged me with her shoulder. "Look, you don't have to say anything in front of me if you don't want to—I can wander over to the playground. I'm here as support. That's it."

"No, stay." I went to rub the back of my neck and stopped at the last second—Will would have a fit if I touched my new piercings. "Mama Ami has been checking the bond. On that end, we're doing well. It's growing stronger, and like I said, we've already blocked Eva a second time." Every day I felt a little bit closer to Lou, my understanding of her slightly clearer, like she was a fuzzy picture coming into focus. "We're both doing our best."

"I'm sure you are," Yolanda said. "But obviously something is bothering you."

I shrugged, digging my hands deep into my pockets. "I feel guilty how much this has changed Lou's life, but other than that, we're coping."

Yolanda waited for me to continue, doling out patient silence with ease.

I was torn on this—should I keep it to myself? Of course, therapy was no use if you weren't open with your therapist. Keeping stuff back only hurt you in the long run. The mess of the last month or two had really highlighted a few things for me. I'd been doing well for a while, but I needed to work on some things. I didn't want my past, my upbringing, my dad and stepmom to have a stranglehold on my future.

I *liked* spending time with Lou. A lot. But we'd need to figure out something soon. This morning I'd woken up with her curled around me, her body flush against mine, my hand possessively on her ass. Her skin had smelled so good, my mouth had actually watered. I'd slid out of bed and took a very cold shower. Which didn't really work, by the way, and besides, cold showers sucked. If I jerked off any more than I already was, I'd strain my wrist.

"We do have a…" I struggled for a few seconds to find the best words. It turned out all the words had left my brain the second I'd started thinking about this morning. "There is a certain…" I threw Juliet and Yolanda a beseeching look. As a therapist, Yolanda would try to make me say the words myself, but maybe if I looked particularly pathetic…

They didn't fall for it.

I gusted out a sigh. "I'm a poison cookie." Which didn't clear anything up at all, so I briefly explained to them Lou's concerns.

They listened carefully, their faces thoughtful.

"I can see why you're both wary," Yolanda said slowly. "And I applaud the fact that you're both communicating so well." Her face turned expectant. "But I assume that's not everything?"

"The problem," I said, holding my hands out almost in supplication. "The problem is I'm having to keep our link locked down tight because I can't stop thinking about her. This morning she was wearing her little booty sleep shorts and tank top while drinking coffee—which should not be a sensual act—and I had to start naming presidents in my head. Last night it was a cat food commercial on repeat because she was sitting next to me. Not doing anything, just *sitting*." I threw my hands up in the air. "I'm disturbed by the fact that I could only remember fifteen presidents and I cannot keep this up."

Juliet smothered a laugh. Yolanda made a reproving noise and Juliet straightened.

I shot her a look. "Are you supposed to be laughing at my pain?"

"As your friend? Yes. Right now? No." Juliet squeezed my hand. "I'm sorry, I really am. I'm not laughing at your situation, but the cat food commercial was funny—" She clicked her mouth shut. "Sorry, Yolanda. Apologies again, Declan."

"How does Louise feel about all of this?" Yolanda asked.

"I'm getting flashes from Lou. Of me." I scrubbed a hand over my face. "I woke up this morning grabbing her ass like I'd fall off the earth if I let go. Lou's concerned that it's runoff from the link."

Yolanda hummed thoughtfully. "Do you think it is? Is there some way you could check?"

"I've been in that spot before—with Eva. I know what mental coercion feels like. This—this isn't it." I took a deep breath. "Lou's afraid I might just be telling her what she wants to hear, or not lying exactly, but tricked by the bond, maybe?" Which, frankly, made my wolf growl. We were *not* being tricked. "She's concerned about me, about losing her license over this—and damaging Dr. Larsen's reputation."

Tension had my muscles tight, my shoulders up around my ears. I dropped them, relaxing my stance. "Coercion can be caught, but only when the animal mage is *actively* doing it." My tone went dry as a bone in the desert. "And frankly, if Lou and I are in a 'poison cookie' situation, I don't exactly want another mage there, you know? Kind of a private moment."

Yolanda and Juliet considered this as we started walking again, staying silent until we passed a couple making out on a wooden bench.

"You could feel it when your stepmom coerced you?" Juliet asked.

"Yeah—I didn't understand what it was at first." I shrugged. "I was a kid. Sometimes it takes a second if there's a lot going on, like when Lou lent me some of her calm in the courtroom. But I *can* tell the difference."

"So the problem is more about Lou's concern and allaying it," Yolanda said, her voice thoughtful. "What if you showed her the difference? Shared what it felt like?"

I nodded slowly. "I could do that."

"The other thing she can do is put you in control of the situation," Yolanda said.

"You mean like tie her up or something?" I felt the tips of my ears getting pink again. I didn't mind talking about sex, but I'd just met Yolanda, Juliet was still new to me, *and* we were talking about a mutual friend for bonus points. I was one square away from an awkwardness bingo.

"That's one way," Juliet said matter-of-factly. "But if you're not into that, just having her let you call the shots until you're both comfortable might help. Alternately, you can discuss beforehand what's okay and what's not—communication will be key." Juliet paused, putting a hand on my arm. "She might still think that any underlying attraction is a byproduct of the link. Ultimately, you and Lou need to discuss it and decide on whether you trust your own judgments or not. No one else can tell you, nor should they."

"Except the Tribunal," I grumbled. "Sleeping with me might endanger Lou's license, right?"

Yolanda stopped me. "I don't know. I don't think there's a specific law against it, but the Tribunal might—if they found out—look poorly on Lou because of it. The only thing you can do is talk it out with Lou. Decide amongst yourselves. But know that your support system is here for you."

We walked in silence for a minute as I mulled that over, heading back toward the playground. I wondered how differently all this would have gone I hadn't needed the bond with Lou to block Eva. I would have had time to get to know her slowly. Take her on a date. Learning each other gradually, to see if we suited. Having the time to decide which role fit better—friend or partner.

Possibly more.

Shapeshifters were picky about mating—we had to find someone that pleased both halves of ourselves. The wolf had to choose and so did I—the bond couldn't just *happen*. It was important, and something we held almost sacred.

One of the fucked-up things my dad did was take control of the pairing process. He couldn't force them to mate, but he matched up shifters in his pack all the same, creating pairings that would benefit him. Would build his empire. Not because they were suited. It was a perversion of our beliefs on a basic level. When the news had broken on our pack, it was a toss-up for what horrified the shifter community more—what they'd done to me, or what had been done creating those pairings.

Some of them had quietly dissolved their marriages after the fact, free to go look for their true mates once it was done. Some… well, they were so far gone on my father's poison that they believed he knew best. It wasn't a recipe for happiness for anyone.

Lou being careful about us was frustrating, but it was kind of… sweet. That she gave a shit. It felt like getting the keys to myself back, in a way. I just needed to figure out how to make Lou understand that this was what I wanted.

She was what I wanted.

We were close to the playground now, Savannah squealing in joy as Bay held her up to bat at the monkey rings. The session had left me drained, but in a good way. Like how I felt after a long run. "You're both pretty good at this."

Yolanda rewarded me with another one of her laughs. "I hope so. Not every session will be fun. We're going to dredge up things that won't be pleasant for you." She offered me her hand and I shook it. "No matter what, though, during our sessions, remember that I'm on your side here. No one else's. Not the Tribunal's, not even Lou's. I'm your emotional battle buddy."

"You have her sword," Juliet said with a grin. "And my ax."

I hugged her to me with one arm. I appreciated a good *Lord of the Rings* reference. "Thanks. To both of you."

I'd never had emotional battle buddies before. Turned out I liked it.

CHAPTER EIGHTEEN

Lou

Declan and I spent a few more days with our heads down, working and ignoring the hormone-bedazzled disco ball elephant in the room. It was a difficult elephant to ignore.

That elephant had some dance moves and I couldn't look away.

I will admit to googling chainmail pajamas today at work. A low moment, for sure. Since I wasn't allowed to work with familiars, I was spending more time up front, doing reception and checking regular clients in. Lainey was really enjoying watching me flounder dealing with humans, and I was having to remind myself more and more to avoid cat thoughts.

Lainey thought it was hilarious, even with her increased workload. I tried to keep my grumblings to myself. In her shoes, I would be laughing, too.

One guy had asked about euthanasia prices for his cat, and when I gave him a quote, he got irritated and said, "A bullet would be cheaper," and then asked why we couldn't just "chuck the bodies out back into the dumpster." I started climbing over the desk so I could assault him with a stapler before Lainey yanked me back down by my scrubs, all while explaining in a sugar-sweet voice that chucking deceased and beloved pets out back would be both a health code violation and a publicity nightmare.

She smiled the entire time while she took my stapler away and somehow managed to calm everyone down.

I regretted not moving faster with that stapler. People were monsters. *Cat. Thoughts.*

Lainey said she didn't mind the additional work, but I still tried to take anything I could off her plate. Declan helped by doing all her filing. He couldn't just sit there through my shift, so he read. Then he filed, swept, washed the windows, and reupholstered the chairs in the breakroom. I didn't know where he got the glue gun, or the rest of the supplies, and Lainey wouldn't let me ruin the mystery by asking.

Lainey had fanned herself watching him work. I googled more chainmail.

If I googled any more, I was going to get carpal tunnel.

All that considered, I wasn't too surprised that I was dreaming of Declan wearing what could generously be called chainmail shorts in my dreams that night. I *was* surprised to be back in the forest.

Declan took in his outfit. "Really?"

"It's been a difficult week," I grumbled. "I'm sorry."

He crossed his arms. "Oh, it's okay. I just want equal objectification."

"Fine." I concentrated until I was wearing a skimpy chainmail top and shorts. "This is both awkward and cold."

Declan grinned. "I'm not cold. At least you got a shirt."

Stupid shapeshifters and their stupid body heat.

In the distance a dog bayed, several other dogs taking up the chorus, the sound splitting the calm night air. My stomach flipped, fear shooting along my nerves. Declan's grin collapsed, his head cocked as he listened.

"Hunters?" I asked.

Declan turned his head away from me, still listening. "Far off, but coming closer."

I did my best to shove my fear aside. It wouldn't help me think—and I needed to think. I absently adjusted my shorts as I considered our situation. They weren't very comfortable. You wouldn't think that chainmail could ride up, but you would be wrong. Which made me realize something. "We're in my dream—not yours."

"What makes you say that?" Declan asked, his head still cocked.

"I changed my clothes." I wasn't one of those people who usually had control over their dreams. Not like this. "What does the wolf think? Does this smell like the forest?"

Declan's nostrils flared as he scented the forest around us. The moonlight gilded his profile, making him look almost like a carving of a wandering god. Eros, perhaps. "Normal forest smells, but I keep catching a hint of something else." He sniffed the air again. "Something…" He dipped his head, his eyes disappearing into shadow. "Eva."

I slipped my hand into his. "I think this is another trap. A spell. Is Eva any good at dream magic?" It wasn't something animal mages were usually skilled at, but anomalies happen. Declan was one thing—he was a shapeshifter and she'd been bonded to him before. I was fully human and a stranger. She shouldn't be able to influence me like this.

He clasped my hand tight, pulling me closer to him. "No, but she could have hired another witch. She prefers to work alone, but she's probably frustrated, so she's trying a different approach. Getting at me by coming through you."

"Yeah, let's not wait around to find out." I wasn't sure how to get us out of the dream, but I definitely didn't want to wait around like sitting ducks. I took a mental snapshot of Declan in his chainmail booty shorts, because if we survived this, I would want to remember how he looked. Just, damn.

He grinned at me, his voice dipping low as he spoke. "I can wear them for you later."

"Get out of my head!"

His low chuckle made my stomach flip again, only this time it wasn't from fear. "I don't need to. You have the worst poker face."

"You're giving me cat thoughts again," I grumbled, deciding to ignore him. Now wasn't the time for this. I concentrated and changed us into jeans, sweatshirts, and running shoes. It was kind of cool—I'd never had control over my dreams before.

Declan opened his mouth to respond, only to snap it shut as the hounds bayed, singing their song of triumph. They'd found our scent. Declan got a better grip on my hand before pulling me along through the woods.

We moved swiftly, cutting through trees and underbrush. Even in his human form, Declan was faster than me. To be honest, I was pretty out of shape. Jogging sucked, and the last time I ran was so I could get to a passing ice cream truck.

Another chorus of howls drifted over the treetops. They were closer. They would catch up to us soon. "What happens if they reach us?"

Declan scanned the woods as he ran, finding us the quickest route. "She'd try to take me from you. We can't even let her catch sight of us."

"She doesn't need to see us to try to tear apart the binding," I huffed. "Just be close."

We came to a river, the water churning into a white froth around a handful of large boulders jutting from the surface. There was no way I could jump to those boulders. They were too far across, and we had no idea how deep the water was or how fast it was going.

Declan came to the same assessment, because he squatted down and motioned for me to get onto his back. "You stopped her last time, so she must have realized that another animal mage is involved. If she can't find me, then she can look for you. She sees you here? She'll know what you look like."

Making me easier to find. I wrapped my arms tight around Declan's neck.

He backed up a few feet, then surged forward, running full speed at the river. He jumped, gracefully landing on the first boulder despite my weight. "I've moved, changed my name, and my legal files are sealed."

He edged back as far as he could on the rock, assessing the jump. I closed my eyes, pressing my face into his neck. If I couldn't see it, he couldn't fall, right? "They're having a hard time locating you," I said, understanding. "But I'm public. If they can track me down, they'll find you." The hounds called out again, the sound faint over the rushing river. "Shit. They'd be able to look me up easily." As an apprentice, I'd had to file paperwork. There were a lot of animal mages, but if they knew what I looked like, it wouldn't take them long.

"It would take her a while, but yeah." Declan's muscles bunched, then once again we were hurtling through the air. He slipped a little when we landed this time, making me cling even tighter to him. "UTC records are confidential, but a good hacker, or a few bribes? She'll find us eventually." We hurtled forward again, this time landing hard as we hit the ground. "Maybe I should keep carrying you."

"I don't think that will work for long." I slid to the ground. "If this is a dream, why am I still out of shape?"

Declan took my hand, once again pulling me through the trees. "Because you expect to be out of shape. It's your dream. Change it."

It *was* my dream. Hope lit through me. Eva had made a mistake. I had power here. I pulled Declan to a stop. "Give me a second."

Declan didn't argue. "What do you need?"

I was momentarily humbled by his faith in me and my abilities. Hopefully, it wasn't misplaced. I'd need a lot of magic for what I had in mind. "Can you loan me some power?"

He nodded. "Just tell me what to do."

"Stay close to me."

Declan let go of my hand and wrapped his arms around me, molding himself to my back. "This good?"

It was *great*. I cleared my throat. "Yes, thank you. Now I want you to close your eyes—it will help you focus on the bond." I closed my own eyes, using my magic to show him our link the way I saw it—our magic, braided tightly together. It was a beautiful thing, each strand glowing bright. "See it?"

"Yeah."

"Okay, watch carefully." I imagined my power flowing slow, like honey, as I sent a pulse down the braid to him. "Understand?"

"I think so." A slow trickle of his magic came back through our connection to me.

"Yes, exactly. Now I need you to turn it up a little—I'll need more than that." The flow increased and I took it, blending his power into mine. If I could control the dream, then I was going to turn the tables on Eva. She wanted to see Declan so bad? I would give her what she wanted. Using the power, I crafted the images of three wolves identical to Declan's wolf shape. I put a little pulse of power in each one for Eva to follow.

As a finishing touch, I gave them Declan's scent. Then I sent them loping off in different directions. Hopefully, it would buy us some time.

Unfortunately, I didn't know how long I could keep it up. I'd have to keep the magic going or they'd disappear, and I wasn't sure how quickly it would drain me. We needed to put some distance between us and Eva in the meantime.

I started jogging, pulling Declan along with me. As I did, I directed a small thread of magic inward, changing the dream version of myself. I wasn't out of breath or plodding—I had lungs full of air and endless energy. I could run for miles, graceful and fast as a gazelle.

We moved quickly then, Declan and I darting through the forest almost as one. Minutes ticked by, trees blurring around us. Occasionally we heard the hounds bay, but they didn't seem to be getting closer.

We burst out into a clearing. I was starting to flag—too much magic out—so I yanked on his hand, getting him to slow down. "Stop, just for a second."

Declan skidding to a halt next to me "Lou, we don't have time—"

I glared at him as I sucked in breaths. "Make time." The moon was brighter here with no trees to filter it, and I could see him clearly. His eyes shone in the light, more wolf than human. "You're starting to shift." Between the fear of capture and his protective instincts, Eva was pushing his wolf to the forefront. We didn't want to give that to her.

"I know." He watched the forest, and I could feel the weight of his worry through our bond.

I squeezed his hand. "I can help."

He watched the woods for another second, then turned his face to me. "What do I need to do?"

The profound amount of trust he was showing right now made my heart squeeze and my throat tighten. "Drop your mental walls." I touched his cheeks with my hands, stepping even closer to him. "We need a strong connection."

I hadn't realized I'd mumbled the last bit out loud until Declan asked, "Like this?" He pulled me against him, his face inches from mine. One arm wrapped around my back, the other cupped my neck, hitting the stones Will had placed there just a few days ago. I felt a spike of heat flow through my spine, the sizzle of protective magic. I immediately moved one of my hands to the back of his neck, completing the circuit. Power flowed through us. I closed my eyes and sifted through our bond, telling the wolf to retreat. That we needed to keep Declan safe.

The wolf agreed, curling up and resting, but kept his ears pricked for danger.

When I opened my own eyes, Declan's face was so close I could feel the heat of his breath on my skin. The soft curve of his lip near enough that all I needed to do was *lean.*

"Hey, Lou?" His voice was a velvet growl, wrapping around me.

"Yeah?" My voice, on the other hand, was shaky and unsure.

He brushed his lips across my cheek. "Do you think you can wake us up? Get us out of here?"

I shivered. "I don't know. I can try."

His lips were so close to my ear now, I could feel the faintest brushes of them against my skin as he spoke, and my nipples tightened. "You should wake us up in about ten seconds."

"Why—" I didn't get to finish my question, because at that moment Declan captured my mouth with his.

The kiss was hot and hungry, his arms tightening around me. My brain completely short-circuited. No thought, just sensations. Cold air against my cheek contrasting to the heated press of his mouth, his hands. The nip of his teeth on my bottom lip. The silken glide of his tongue. My knees actually went weak.

I hadn't thought that was an actual thing until just now.

It was the kind of kiss that would make every single kiss before it fade into the background. Like there could be only one, and this was it.

It was the *Highlander* of kisses.

And I had to end it. *But do you?* Yes, traitorous body, we do. I pulled back, still tangled in him, my lids feeling heavy. "Declan?"

"Hm?" He was nuzzling my neck now and my knees flat out *buckled*. He caught me, and I could feel his chuckle as it vibrated through his chest.

Oh, how I hated to do it, but I put power into my words anyway, making them the mental equivalent of a cold bucket of water. "Wake up!"

CHAPTER NINETEEN

Declan

There are a lot of ways to wake up—slow and gentle, sudden and jarring, confused and groggy. All of them had their pros and cons. I would have liked to say that my current combination—terrified and turned on—was new, but I'd been a teenage boy. Puberty had hit me hard when I was living with the foster pack. From fourteen through nineteen, my every emotion seemed to be tinged with some level of horny. Hungry, sleepy, anxious, it didn't matter. I'd been a walking ball of hormones for *years*.

So while my heart rate was tripping and the sounds of the hounds still rang in my ears, I was aware and comfortable with the fact that I was tangled up in Lou and hard as a damn rock.

One of my hands cradled her head. The other was shoved down the back of her sleep shorts, pressing her against me. She blinked at me, lids heavy, her fingers curled in the hair at the nape of my neck.

I should pull away.

Any second now, Lou would be fully awake and start spouting reasons and excuses as to why this was a bad idea. Her poison cookie defense. If she really wasn't interested in me, I'd back off. I didn't push people into something they weren't ready for or didn't want. But that dream kiss was fresh in my mind, and our bond was wide open. Lou was absolutely, completely interested.

I rolled until I was on top of her and took her mouth again. Slow. Careful. Giving her a chance to push away. And it was perfect. Her body warm, curved, and soft under mine. Her hands traced down my back, legs wrapping around my hips, cradling me to her. The movement tore a sound from me, half groan, half growl. I thrust against her and she arched, her body feeling inexplicably perfect against mine. Her scent alone—which used to trigger a feeling of fear and panic—now drove me half mad with lust.

I deepened the kiss, rocking against her at the same time. Lou whimpered before pulling her mouth from mine. I wanted to howl in frustration, but I didn't chase her.

"Dec," she said.

"Lou," I said, matching her tone. I didn't try to take her mouth again, instead sliding down, nuzzling her tank top until I found her nipple, biting at it gently through the soft cloth. When she moaned, I smiled before sucking at her nipple through the shirt.

Lou swore.

I slipped my hand under her tank top and cupped her other breast, brushing against the stiff peak with my thumb.

"Wait."

I stopped, lifting my face so I could see her in the faint street lights edging around her curtains. I didn't move, though, keeping my hands and body exactly where they were until I had a better understanding of what she wanted.

Because she hadn't moved away from me either.

"Are you ..." She huffed, frustrated. "You're so sure. I can feel it through the bond." She traced my face with her fingers. "How can you be so sure?"

Something in me relaxed—we were finally going to talk about it. "It feels different."

"What does that mean?" Though she still hadn't moved, I could feel her pulling away from me. "I don't want to take advantage—"

I rested my chin on her stomach, smiling at her, though I wasn't sure she could see it. Lou was so worried she was going to hurt me, she was practically cradling me like a baby chick. And it felt *good*, fucking *great*, to be cared for like that.

"I can show you, I think. The difference. But you'll have to help." I reached up and tugged gently at a lock of her hair. It felt like satin between my fingers. "I want this, Lou. If that's all that's holding you back ...."

Her hands fisted in the sheets. "How can I help?"

I slid my hand through her hair, letting it glide over my fingers. I thought I could happily touch Lou, just like this, for the rest of my life. "I need to show you a longer memory, not just an image, but I'm not sure how. Can I do that? Through the bond?"

"Animal familiars can send images from their memory, so I don't see why not. The bond would have to be open." Lou reached out and tentatively pushed one hand through my hair. I leaned in to the comfort. If all she wanted to do was pet me, I'd take it.

"That's it?"

Another soft brush of her fingertips across my temple. "No, then you'd have to concentrate on the memory. It might help to visualize yourself handing it over to me."

"Like a present?"

A faint smile tugged at her lips. "Sure."

"It's going to be a real shitty present."

"You don't have to give it, Declan."

"Yes," I said with a sigh. "I do." I laid a soft kiss on her stomach. "Because I want this, Lou. I want you." I wrapped my arms up around her shoulders and put my cheek on her stomach, closing my eyes. After a few deep breaths—and getting slightly distracted by Lou's scent again—I picked out the memory I needed to show her. Then I imagined me handing it over, wrapped up in a bow.

Lou unwrapped it and we were both plunged into my past.

For a second, the tall grass is Technicolor green, the scents of summer sharp in my nose. Then the memory snaps into place and everything normalizes. I'm standing in the tall grass, holding my sister's hand. I'm supposed to walk her to my father. He's over by the grill with a handful of men—strong alphas from other, smaller packs. They're drinking beer, enjoying the summer weather. Each of the alphas has a boy with them—my age or older—and I don't think too much of it until the wind shifts and I realize that those boys are related to the men they're with.

They're all stealing glances at us, and I don't like the way they're looking at my sister.

I skid to a halt, sweat prickling along my spine, because I suddenly realize why the looks, their scents, are bothering me. I know what this is. My father has gathered prospective bridegrooms for my sister.

My hand tightens in hers. Zoey turns her big eyes up to me, her smile wobbly. She's wearing a white eyelet dress and someone has put a flower crown over her white-blond hair. Even with her bare feet in the dirt, she looks like the angels I've seen in picture books.

And I don't want to take her anywhere near those men.

I'm about to pull her away, though I'm not sure where I would take her, when a familiar weight settles over my mind. It's like going to sleep with your eyes open. My body is no longer mine. No, I'm behind heavy glass, standing next to my wolf. I'm pounding against it and screaming. He howls and yips alongside me.

Eva makes my feet move, and I guide my sister through the tall grass, straight to the grill.

The scene faded, our bond fizzling quiet at the same time, Lou's magic exhausted from the night. We were back in bed now, and I was shaking, the memory rattling me more than even I thought it would.

Lou has felt every moment of it. Without a word I brush away her tears with my thumb.

"That was awful," she chokes out.

"Yes." I was obviously not going to argue with her. It *was* awful. "I think we can both admit that I've effectively killed the mood."

That surprised a laugh out of her.

I levered myself up so I was over her, leaning on my elbows. "I think it's also clear that you have *never* coerced me like that." I nosed along her hairline, letting my mouth drift along her skin. I loved her skin, the hot silk of it. "Lou, I've always wanted your cookie. Even before the bond."

"Maybe we need to let that analogy die," she said, brushing my hair back, her expression serious. "If the Tribunal finds out—if they disapprove, and I'm certain they would—I could lose my career."

"That's a possibility," I murmured, and I hated it. I didn't want Lou to be in that position, to have to make that kind of choice. At the same time, I had never wanted someone the way I wanted Lou. I dropped a kiss on her forehead and sighed. Now that I'd started touching Lou, it would be difficult to stop.

"The problem," Lou said, her voice breathy. "Is that I'm having a hard time caring right now."

I laughed, but it hurt to do it. I was going to have to let Lou go, because I couldn't let her choose me over her career. "Lou—"

"So I guess we'll just have to keep it from the UTC," Lou said. "It's none of their business anyway." Her face scrunched up. "But we'll have to tell Mama Ami and probably your therapist."

There was nothing worse than arguing against getting what you wanted. "Lou, I can't let you risk your career—"

Lou cupped my chin with her hand. "It's my choice, isn't it?"

"Yes, but—"

She shook her head slowly, side to side. "Declan, I love my job. I would hate to lose it." She ran her thumb over my bottom lip and we both shuddered at the contact. "But it's my choice, and I choose this." Another slow brush of her thumb. "Just like I didn't get to make the decision for you, you can't make it for me. You're taking a risk just as much as I am."

She stared into my eyes, her hand reaching up to trace my brow, my cheeks, my chin. She sighed, softening against me.

"So…" My voice was husky even to my ears and I felt Lou shiver. "Are we still at 'wait'?"

Again that slow side to side shake of her head.

My restraint snapped. I captured her mouth, both of us ravenous, like we were making up for years of deprivation. She kissed me back, her hands busy touching, learning my body while I was doing the same to hers. In seconds, she was shoving my boxers down, while I was yanking her tank top up.

"Do you—" she gasped as I nipped at the underside of her breast. "Oh gods, do that again." She grabbed my head as I continued to nibble, keeping to the soft skin of her breasts. "Should we slow down?"

I paused, mouth hovering over her peaked nipple. I breathed on it and she bowed, her short nails digging into my shoulders. "Do you want to slow down?" I leaned down and gave her areola a long, steady lick. Now that I was here with her, that we'd taken this step, I was content. We didn't have to move further tonight. I just didn't want her shoving me away again.

"No," she said, watching me, her pupils wide. "I don't want to slow down. There are condoms in my nightstand drawer."

"I know," I said, moving to the other breast. Couldn't play favorites, could I? "I organized your drawers yesterday, remember?" I sucked her nipple into my mouth.

"*Ohmyfuckinggods*," Lou said, her eyes rolling back. "I forgot." Her voice was breathy. "And why is that so hot? You organizing my drawers?"

"Because it means you know that I'll take care of you." I leaned to the side so I could reach for her condoms, my other hand sliding into her shorts, the only piece of clothing either of us were wearing now. "And that I'm thorough." I slid one finger into her, seeing if she was ready. Not every woman has the same response, but I hadn't found any lube with Lou's condom stash, so I didn't think that was something she struggled with.

My fingers closed on the condom and my other hand built a rhythm, stroking her as my thumb pressed gently back and forth over her clit. I listened to the way Lou breathed, to how she moved, trying to learn how she liked to be touched. She was wet, so wet. I could put the condom on and slide into her now, and it would be good. Amazingly fucking good, but I was going to wait. I wanted to taste her first.

Leaving the condom on the sheets, I slid her shorts down, tossing them behind me. Later, I'd stare. Take my fill. Memorize the way she looked. For now, I was skin-drunk, and couldn't keep my hands, my mouth, off her. I kissed my way back up her legs, gently nipping at her inner thighs, tracing circles on the backs of her knees. Lou opened for me, and I settled in, licking and sucking and learning her body. The *sounds* she made. Nothing in my entire life had sounded sweeter. Nothing.

I hummed my pleasure and she arched, moaning long and loud.

I grinned, leaning back, blowing softly on her overheated flesh. She swore. I traced a finger along her folds, keeping my touch feather-light as I sucked her clit gently into my mouth.

Lou was begging now, yanking at my hair. I stayed stubbornly in place, savoring her, playing with her, taking her to the brink and then backing off again. Her hands dug into my hair like she couldn't decide if she wanted to pull me up or hold me in place. Her impatience lit me up inside.

I grabbed the condom, tearing the package with my teeth before leaning back to roll it on. I took a second to admire Lou, her body flushed and waiting. *Mine.* I leaned down, notching myself at her entrance before pausing to kiss her softly. "Still okay?"

She wrapped her arms around my neck and gave me a gentle kiss. "Declan," she said, her tone grave, "if you don't fuck me this second, I might *actually* die."

"Thank the gods," I said, and thrust into her. *Fuuuuck.* She felt...fuck. I held there, panting. "If you'd said no, I would have cried."

She laughed, pulling me closer, sliding her lips along my neck. "We can't have that."

I laughed back, enjoying the feeling as it meshed with the heavy pleasure of the moment. It felt decadent. Sex with Lou felt serious, but also like play. And it felt good to play, but the heat, the scent, the fucking *feel* of her, changed my attitude quickly. She wasn't laughing now but sighing as she arched beneath me, meeting my rhythm. Her eyes closed, her face tipped back. Beautiful. Lou was fucking beautiful. And I wanted her to look at me the same way I was looking at her.

I stilled, leaning down to bite her lip softly, tugging at it. "Look at me."

Gray eyes met mine. I started to move, pausing as her eyelids fluttered shut again.

She groaned. "Quit stopping."

I gave her another nip on her lower lip before soothing it with my tongue. "Quit closing your eyes."

Lou grabbed my face. "I'm trying, but it feels too good."

I nuzzled her throat, humming against the soft skin, before I shifted to a kneeling position. My hands wrapped around Lou's hips, holding them so only her top half stayed on the mattress. I could see more of her now, her skin flushed in the moonlight. Lou gasped as the angle changed, allowing me to slide in deeper. Heat crept up my spine. Her eyes were wide, her lips parted.

I slid my thumb along her inner thigh, down to the soft thatch of hair, searching for the tiny bundle of nerves that I needed, that she needed. My thumb grazed her clit as we moved, my eyelids heavy as I watched her spine bow, biting her lip to contain the moan that wanted out. I danced my thumb away. Lou growled like a pissed-off kitten. Her eyes were hot on mine as I very slowly brought my thumb up and licked it before returning it to exactly where she wanted. Her breathing stuttered and then she gasped as I changed to harder, deeper thrusts.

Every muscle in her body suddenly locked as she arched against me. My heart thundered as we froze in place, her body grasping mine in waves. Then I thrust again, trying to prolong it, rocking our bodies together, faster, harder, until a white-hot lick of pleasure shot up my spine. I came with a jagged moan, my hands tight on her hips, holding her to me.

I think I forgot how to breathe.

My heart continued pounding in my ears as I collapsed into her arms, my face turned in to her neck. We stayed like that, locked together, her hands stroking my back until our heartbeats slowed. Suddenly feeling bad that I was crushing her, I propped myself up on my elbow. Lou had a soft smile on her face.

Fuck, she was beautiful.

"I didn't just eat the poison cookie," she said, throwing an arm above her head. "I ate the whole pack and now I'm dead."

My heart lurched. Was she already regretting it? I didn't want her to regret it, especially since I was already wondering when we could do it again. "I thought you were letting that analogy die." I licked along her collarbone, sucking gently when I got to the end. "Because I don't want to be poison."

She brushed her fingers over my lips. Then she shoved me onto my back, rolling over until she was on top, but keeping me inside her. She leaned in, her face over mine. "It's okay. It turns out I've built up an immunity."

"Am I your iocane powder?"

She paused, her lips hovering over mine. "Did you just quote *Princess Bride* at me? Naked? In my bed?"

"Yes?" I hated that it came out as a question. "Is that bad?"

"Declan," she said, her hands on my face, her eyes inches from mine. "If you don't fuck me again this second, I really will die."

I laughed, relief hitting my system like a drug. "As you wish." I fisted my hands into her hair and kissed her. "We're going to need to buy more condoms."

"I have like half a box," she breathed. "There's probably five more in there."

"I know," I said, reaching for the drawer. "I'll go to the store tomorrow." Because I planned to go through that box by morning.

CHAPTER TWENTY

Lou

Vanessa sat across from me at our table, both of us drinking coffee. I was trying not to watch Declan outside the window as he did something to our planter boxes. Trying and failing. The way his muscles moved when he worked… I sighed, once again dragging my attention back to the roommate I was having coffee with.

Van stared at me with the hardened eye of a detective trying to crack a difficult case. "Spill."

I sipped my coffee. "You can't take me, copper. I'm innocent, see?"

She slammed both hands on the table dramatically. "Liar!"

I mock-glared at her over my cup. "What do you know?"

She crossed her arms. "I don't reveal my sources."

I set my coffee down. "It was the ferrets, wasn't it?"

Van pursed her lips. "Okay, yes, you woke the ferrets. They told me this morning, first thing. I'm sure you know this, but ferrets have absolutely filthy minds."

"I do know this," I said, getting up to refill my cup. "Why do you think I suggested them for you?"

Van pointed at me. "Sit. I have ways of making you talk."

Will came in to the kitchen then, scratching his stomach, his sweats riding low on his hips. He occasionally crashed at our house if he'd stayed too late—sometimes on our couch, but usually in Vanessa's room—so it wasn't too big of a surprise to see him. He was one of Van's oldest friends, after all.

He grabbed a mug with a large cartoon sun on it that said *"Don't talk to me"* in a bubbly font. "Am I just in time for sexy interrogation role play?"

I put my forehead on the table. "You heard, too?"

"No," he said, doctoring his coffee. "I was referring to Van's method of interrogation, not the topic." He dropped into the seat next to her, eyes bright. "But now I'm intrigued. Did you finally bang our newest employee?" He leaned forward. "As his friend and obvious mentor, I have to ask what your intentions are."

"What?" I blinked at him.

He placed a hand on his chest, affronted. "You have debauched him. Taken his innocence. Ruined him. How will he land a duke? No, he'll have to settle for an industrial upstart, at best. He's lucky he has a dowry." Will shook his head regretfully, sipping his coffee. "Tsk tsk, Louise."

Van put her chin on her fist and leaned so she could look at him. "Are you reading romance novels with your nana again?"

"Never stopped," Will said. "I would have you know that I'm an important part of her book club. I bring the cookies and the saucy commentary." He raised an eyebrow at me. "I can give you a list of Nana's favorite sexy werewolf books. She has excellent taste. You and Declan could read them together." He grinned over the edge of his mug.

"Don't mock," I said.

"He is one hundred percent serious," Van said, eyeing me over her cup. "His nana keeps her reading organized on a spreadsheet. He helps her update it."

"I love my nana," he said. "And book club brings us together."

"I would say that I have a hard time picturing you in a book club with a group of mature women discussing romance novels, but I honestly don't. I can totally see it."

"While I'm currently the only man, book club doesn't discriminate. Anyone is welcome." He shook his head in mock disgust. "Really, Lou. Ageist and sexist."

"I'm sorry," I said. "It's early."

He tilted his head. "It did take a few times for them to get comfortable with me. I brought my cross-stitch to help put them at ease. The discussions are lively, I've learned a shit ton about women and sex, and my nana is happy. It's all win."

"You cross-stitch?" I set down my mug. "How did I not know this?" I glared at him. "You're always here. I follow you on Instagram. We have no secrets, Will!"

"I thought you knew," Van said, sipping her coffee. "His cross-stitch actually has a separate Instagram account."

Will took out his phone, pulled up a photo, and showed me a tea towel with a neat design stitched into it—a teacup with a skull and crossbones. The teacup had the word "poison" on it in bright red thread. "I made that for Nana for Mother's Day."

Vanessa leaned over and kissed his temple. "You are the best of men."

I couldn't be quite sure because he dipped his head to drink his coffee, but I think Will blushed.

"But you are distracting us from the very real topic of Lou knocking boots with our roommate." Van put her mug down and laid her hands flat against the table. "Talk."

"Yes." Will nodded, all seriousness. "You have made the beast with two backs."

"The old lust and thrust," Van added.

"Did the no-pants dance."

"Spelunked the bat cave."

Will's eyes were positively sparkling. "You opened the gates of Mordor."

Vanessa dropped her voice down lower, drawing the words out, like she was a news anchor. "Stormed Fort Vajayjay."

"You're a woman now. Huzzah." Will pretended to throw confetti.

Will was weird in the morning. Scratch that, Will was just weird. "Can we stop saying increasingly disturbing euphemisms?"

"Fine," Van said. "You've had The Sex. How are we feeling about that this morning?"

I was feeling a little sore, a whole lot satisfied, and a bit worried. We hadn't talked about what it meant yet. Did it mean anything? Should it mean anything? Did we even need to talk about it?

"That's a whole lot of thinking over there," Will said. "That's never good."

Van leaned close to him. "The ferrets said he kept her up half the night. Maybe her brain isn't working. I might need to make another pot of coffee."

"I'm going to blister your ferrets' ears," I mumbled.

Will tapped Van's shoulder, mouthing, "How many times?"

She held up three fingers.

Huh. The ferrets had missed one. Well, I wasn't going to correct them.

Will stood up. "Excuse me a second." Then he left the kitchen.

We both watched, quietly, as Will appeared in the picture window in front of us. Declan looked up from his work. Without a word, Will held up a hand and waited until Declan high-fived him. For his part, Declan seemed slightly perplexed. Then Will walked back into the kitchen and sat down. "Sorry, had to be done."

"You're both immature, like children," I said. "Why do I hang out with you again?"

"Because we're immature, like children?" Van asked, taking out her phone.

"And where's my high five?" My tone might have been a little sulky.

Will offered his hand. "Sorry. I'm all about equality."

I reluctantly high-fived him as I watched Van text rapidly. "Now what are you doing?"

"Texting Trick. He won the pool." She shook her head. "I thought for sure you wouldn't last this long." She continued to tap away at her phone. "I'm a little disappointed in you, Louise Matthews."

"You placed bets about when I'd sleep with Declan?"

Van shrugged one shoulder, totally unapologetic. "We're simple creatures and we need simple entertainment. I have to say, I'm in awe of your restraint. The hormones have been so thick in the room between you two lately that I've considered opening windows."

I gave up trying to keep any kind of privacy and explained the poison cookie concept and why I'd thought us sleeping together was probably a Bad Idea. After I explained, I waited for my friends to condemn me or at least lecture me a little.

Van, of course, got caught up on other details. "Wait, it was four times? *Four?* Excuse me." Now it was Will's and my turn to wait as she went out, stared at Declan for a second, hugged him, and then kissed his forehead before patting his back. He looked completely bewildered.

Will ignored her antics, mostly. He tapped his fingers along his empty mug. "You sure you know what you're doing, Lou?"

"I think I've made it abundantly clear that I don't," I said softly.

Will stared at the window for a long moment before turning his gaze back to me. "Look, I'm not saying it was a terrible idea. I'm just also not sure it was a good idea. If it goes bad—you live together. Right now, you have to stay connected 24/7. Your lives are completely emmeshed." He frowned absently for a second, his gaze distant. After a few moments, his focus snapped back into place. "Aren't you scared it could all blow up in your face?"

"I'm terrified," I said honestly. "But…" I looked back out the window. Van was still talking to Declan, her hands all over the place as she told him some sort of story. Declan was laughing, rocking back on his heels, his hands loosely clasped around the handle of a shovel. He looked over at me and smiled. My heart skipped.

I shrugged at Will. "It's Declan." I offered it like it was the only argument that made sense because it was. Watching him now, I knew, *knew* that if I'd been bound to any other shapeshifter, this wouldn't have happened. There was just something about him. I couldn't gather up the words to explain all that to Will, but he seemed to understand anyway.

"Yeah, I get it." Another deep sigh. "Don't think I'm not supportive of you both, I'm just concerned, you know?" Then Will straightened, a haughty expression on his face. "And you best have honorable intentions, or it's pistols at dawn." He tapped the table. "I'll meet you in the study when you're ready so we can discuss terms and wedding contracts."

He stood up and put his mug in the sink with one hand while tapping away at his phone with the other as he headed toward the bathroom to shower.

"I'm calling your nana," I yelled. "And telling her to move your book club away from Regency and Georgian romances. They're giving you ideas!"

He peeked his head out of the doorway. "I already have. Who did you think I was texting?" His phone pinged and he looked at it. "Next one up is a sexy werewolf book. She says good for you and she applauds Declan's stamina."

"I think maybe you and Nana are a little too close!" I shouted. "And stop telling her things about me!"

"No!" Will said, shutting the bathroom door. "I keep no secrets from Nana!"

I grumbled and went to refill my mug before calling out for Vanessa's ferrets. They were going to get a long lecture about boundaries. At least someone in this house would take my wrath.

CHAPTER TWENTY-ONE

Lou

Declan and I didn't get to have a fun "let's dissect last night until all joy has been sucked from its marrow and everyone regrets getting naked in the first place" conversation—as Van liked to call it—right away because we were subjected to our first Tribunal surprise checkup. We only had to deal with two out of the three people from our Tribunal. Unfortunately, one of those two was my very last choice.

Declan came in to the kitchen scowling, followed by Woodridge, master arcanist, major asshole, and Prisha Bhatt, animal mage and dubious supporter.

"Surprise," Declan mumbled at me.

Vanessa froze, her eyes on her father. I racked my brain trying to remember when they'd last seen each other—or even talked. It had been at least a year or two, probably longer.

"Oh no." I made a chopping motion with my hand. "Ms. Bhatt, we agreed to checkups—from you. As the animal mage, that makes sense." I folded my arms to keep from pointing…and possibly poking Woodbridge's eyes out. Repeatedly. You know, on accident.

"There's no reason for Arcanist Woodbridge to be here." Out of the corner of my eye, I saw Declan take out his phone and start typing furiously.

"You agreed to visits by Ms. Bhatt," Woodbridge said. "There was no wording in the contract saying other members of the Tribunal couldn't attend." His smile was cold. I would say reptilian, but I happened to like snakes. Woodbridge, not so much.

I was slightly comforted by the look on Prisha's face, telegraphing that she wasn't too happy with the setup, either. "He's correct. Look, the sooner we do this, the sooner everyone can go about their day."

I was about to say fine and take them to the living room, but Declan cleared his throat, stopping me.

"Our representative will be here shortly. Fifteen minutes, tops." Declan tucked his phone into his pocket. "May I offer you some coffee or tea?"

Declan was such a good host. Why did I think that was so hot?

Woodbridge frowned. "Representative?" He straightened, his chin jutting out aggressively. I'm surprised he didn't tip his nose into the air or refer to us as "peasants." "What are you talking about?"

"Dr. Larsen," Declan said, looking serene as all get out. Only I knew he wasn't because of the link. Inside, he was a mess. "Since her reputation is staked on our binding and Lou's handling of it, she should be here." He bared his teeth. I don't think anyone would have called it a smile. "We can look at the bylaws if you want—"

Woodbridge scoffed. "This is hardly necessary. We're busy people, you know. Unless you're stalling as a cover tactic?"

"You wish," Van muttered. Woodbridge either didn't hear her or pretended not to.

"We will wait for Dr. Larsen," Declan said calmly. "Or you can leave and we can reschedule. Up to you."

Woodbridge's face turned an alarming sort of reddish-purple.

Prisha edged away from him. Didn't want to be in the blast zone, I guess. "That's fine. I would love a tea, thank you."

"Nothing for me," Woodbridge ground out, staring at our kitchen with open disdain. I bet he thought that we'd try to poison him if he drank anything. Ha! Like we'd be so inept as to murder him before witnesses.

I was very tempted to ask Van's ferrets to come in and bite his ankles, though. In my agitation, I must have broadcast my thoughts to them, because they came bounding around the corner, ready to gnaw some serious ankle. Instead, I sent them off for reinforcements.

The ferrets tumbled through the door flap into Vanessa's room. Moments later, the door opened abruptly, and Will came out, shirtless and still slightly damp from the shower, looking like he'd hastily pulled on pants to make it to us faster. Will's normally friendly mien was gone. Instead, he looked like a pissed-off wolverine. A rabid one, at that.

I didn't even know Will could snarl.

Tall, barefoot, muscles and tattoos rippling, Will was actually a little scary. And he was staring at Woodbridge like he was mentally mapping out the best way to take him apart with his bare hands.

Then his sight shifted to Prisha and he smiled, Golden Retriever Will suddenly in full effect. "Hi." Without breaking stride, he reached down and picked up Vanessa. Like hand-to-heart honestly scooped her up in his arms without so much as a by-your-leave. "If you'll excuse us, we're busy. Ritual sacrifices and kinky sex wait for no man." He winked. Then he carried Van off to her room, his face friendly, but I didn't miss the protective way he held my friend.

Declan threw me a look and I returned it with a subtle shake of my head. Will and Van were only friends, but I suspected Will's feelings weren't entirely platonic.

The bedroom door clicked shut, followed by the sound of the flap as the ferrets hopped through it to check on Van. Woodbridge's upper lip curled in contempt. Prisha looked like she wanted to fan herself and had definitely been checking out Will's ass.

I clapped my hands together sharply. "Right! I'll put the kettle on, then, shall I?"

Prisha and I both ended up picking green tea—Declan stuck with his usual chamomile, and Woodbridge continued to steep in his own bitterness. After the most stilted and awkward conversation of my entire life—and that was saying something—Mama Ami arrived and we finally let Prisha check our binding. She reluctantly gave us a positive assessment with a side order of stink-eye for me.

She really didn't like what I'd done. Part of her held out suspicion that I'd somehow engineered this setup, doing it all on purpose to get Declan as my familiar. I tried not to get too grouchy about this, because Prisha was just doing her job. In her place, I'd question my motives, too.

That didn't mean I was completely cowed by her, either. I knew I hadn't done it intentionally and there wasn't anything I could have done differently. Since the bond was currently keeping Declan from falling back into Eva's hands, it was harder and harder to feel guilty about it. Which meant both Prisha and I felt protective of Declan and justified in our actions, resulting in a lot of mutual heavy eye contact as we both channeled our inner felines.

Cat thoughts were so dangerously seductive because they felt good.

"If I set a glass of water by you," Declan whispered, "would you bat it off the table?"

I elbowed him and he laughed.

What really unnerved me was how quiet Woodbridge was. He looked entirely too smug, but hadn't said a peep since our original argument. It was making me uncomfortable. I thought maybe he'd take the chance to look at any of the photos we had up—catch a glimpse of his estranged daughters or his only grandchild. The pictures could have been of strangers for all the notice he paid them.

Once Prisha had seen to Declan, she leaned back in her chair. "What updates do you have for us? Has Eva attacked at all? Anyone tried to make contact?"

"She's attacked twice." Declan caught her up on details of both, though left out some, ah, racier details on the last one. Both of them were interested in hearing about our countermeasures, like the dream magic we'd managed and the piercings Will had given us. Prisha and Woodbridge both checked the protective stones in our jewelry, Prisha making appreciative noises while he gave a disdainful sniff.

"That was a really good idea, the piercings," Prisha said. "You said you used your brother's shop? I'll have to write down the name. I have friends that could use a good arcane piercer—"

Woodbridge cut her off. "Did the recent attack feel stronger than the one at the tattoo establishment?" He'd taken out a small red leather notebook earlier, occasionally making a note in it. Mama Ami glared at Woodbridge as she dug into her purse. She took out a card, which she handed to Prisha. I didn't have to look to know that it was one of Bay's business cards.

Declan frowned. "It's difficult to tell because of the dream state, but it felt about the same."

Woodbridge's pen made no sound as it moved smoothly across the paper. The pen looked elegant and heavy and probably cost more than my car payment. "Which means that with the help of the stones that practitioner"—he sneered slightly at that word, like he couldn't quite bring himself to say "piercer" but wasn't thrilled with labeling him a practitioner, either—"put in, it still felt the same, meaning the attack had been stronger." His eyes lit up as he made notes. "Interesting."

I couldn't tell if Woodbridge's disdain was for Will specifically or arcane piercing in general. I was sure that Will didn't fit any of the criteria Woodbridge had for the kind of man he'd want his daughters to bring home. Then again, he didn't want his daughters to bring anyone home, even themselves, so I'm not sure why it mattered.

I was so busy thinking about it that it took a second for what he'd said to register. "Wait, why is it interesting? How do you know the second attack was stronger?"

"Because both Eva and Campbell are closer, geographically, than they had been," he said the words absently, almost to himself. "It's to be expected that her attempts would be stronger, then, but of course we have so little data on this kind of bonding." He made another note. "Simply fascinating."

"Yes," Prisha said, her voice icy. "Because it's unethical, immoral, and inhumane, which is why we *have* so little data."

Woodbridge ignored her, his pen skimming along the page.

"What do you mean, they're 'closer,'" Declan ground out, all gravel and growl. I grabbed his hand without thinking. Fear coursed through our bond, towing panic in its wake. I scooted closer, until his leg lined up against mine, our shoulders leaning against each other. Feeling me at his side, my scent in his nose, would help. He dipped his head, sucking in a breath.

"Yes," Woodbridge said absently. "I reached out to the police and they've been sharing some information. They've had a few sightings that have been confirmed."

I tried to calm myself, because that's what Declan needed right now, but the sheer callousness of Woodbridge's attitude made me see red. "And you didn't think we needed to know?"

Woodbridge set his pen down. "I'm telling you now."

"Do they know where we are?" Declan asked. "Eva and my father?" His voice was back to normal, but his muscles were tight. He was barely containing himself and I could hardly blame him.

"The police didn't think so." Woodbridge capped his pen neatly. "Not specifically, more of a general direction. They appear to be heading west."

West was in our direction.

Prisha's eyes hardened as she scrutinized her partner. "When did you talk to the police?"

He flipped back through his notebook until he hit the page he needed. "Three days ago."

"And why wasn't *I*, a member of the Tribunal, notified?" She waved a hand at us. "Or the two people this investigation impacts?"

"My office sent a letter."

I could hear Prisha's teeth grinding from where I sat. "You used the mail system at the Tribunal offices?"

"No," Woodbridge pursed his lips, weirdly affronted by her question. "I sent a letter from the university."

"Does that mean you used their internal system or had your assistant walk it to an actual USPS drop?" Prisha asked the question like she both knew the answer and dreaded hearing it.

Woodbridge blinked at her, his head collapsing on his neck like a myopic owl. "The university's, of course. My assistant has better things to do than carry mail to the post office."

"The university," Prisha stated slowly, her tone carefully moderated, "does not have the best reputation when it comes to mail. They might not have even *mailed it yet.*"

Woodbridge waited, his face calm. The *And?* was clearly implied.

"That is important, time-sensitive material that we all needed," Prisha continued in her overly patient tone, obviously surprised that she had to say it. I wasn't. This was the problem with arcanists. They had a sort of ivory tower mentality where the only thing that mattered was research, data, and information. Living things? Didn't matter in the slightest.

Or course, I couldn't rule out spite. From what Van had told me, her father could nurse a grudge with the best of them. But it was also possible that we were just so far beneath his attention that it simply didn't occur to him. At least, not after he got the data *he* wanted and needed.

Prisha annunciated each word carefully, biting them out. "Information you could have emailed. Or, and this would be even better, you could have picked up the damn phone!"

Woodbridge closed his notebook. The *And?* was still implied.

Prisha took a deep, cleansing breath. Her next words were calmer. "If I had known, I would have contacted them immediately to check the binding. I would have warned them to take precautions."

"But that would have changed the outcome," Woodbridge argued, his gray brows divebombing towards his nose. "And skewed the data."

"I'm not a science experiment," Declan said, the growl back but his words clipped and precise nonetheless. His teeth clenched, his eyes turning the ghostly shade of the wolf's. I let go of his hand and wrapped an arm around him, pulling him closer to me in small ways. Prisha and Woodbridge would see what I was doing—Woodbridge would probably make a freaking note in his stupid journal about it—but I didn't care.

I opened our bond. *Do you want me to calm you? Killing a member of our Tribunal is frowned upon. Probably.*

Yes. And *Are you sure? They might let me pass on first offense.*

I'm mostly sure. I chased my words with a shot of calm, taking some of his anger into myself. Not all of it—his emotion was normal, justified, and understandable. I took just enough to keep him in control so he didn't go wolf and rip out Woodbridge's throat. Though it was tempting. Soooo tempting.

Mama Ami cleared her throat, and when she spoke, her words were so sharp I was surprised they didn't slice him to teeny, tiny ribbons. "Next time the police share information pertaining to my apprentice and Declan, you will notify the rest of the Tribunal as well as Lou and Declan and myself *by telephone* immediately."

Woodbridge looked like he wanted to argue, but Mama Ami cut him off. "If you don't, we will petition the Uncanny Tribunal Commission to remove you from the case and replace you with someone who won't endanger their lives." She tapped the coffee table in front of her with her fingernail to make sure she had his full attention. "The only reason I'm not already doing so is because it would take time and I'm not sure we have it." She glanced at Declan, no doubt taking in his tense body language. "I might do it anyway."

Woodbridge's mouth pinched. "Fine."

Declan stood. "If we're done, I need to contact my sister."

Woodbridge perked up.

"No." Declan clenched his fists. "You don't get to talk to her. Eva never bonded her anyway, just me. My sister has had enough of this mess."

"If she was never bonded like you were," Woodbridge argued, "she could give us a better picture of the data." The arcanist was almost vibrating with excitement.

The muscles in Declan's jaw ticked. I took more of his anger, though I had to be careful. Much more and I'd punch Woodbridge myself. He had a very punchable face. Which was probably a cat thought. Ugh, they were so seductive!

"When this is over," Declan said, "I will ask her if she's willing to be interviewed by my counselor, because I trust her. If my sister agrees, and if the counselor feels sharing the information won't cause her further harm, you can read the report. That's the closest you'll get to my sister unless she says otherwise." I could tell from his tone that Zoey agreeing to talk to Woodbridge was as likely as me joining a traveling circus as one of those people who swallowed swords.

I was definitely full of cat thoughts now—of the "evil glee" variety, because I knew Juliet and her mentor would zealously guard Zoey's privacy. Not only because of client confidentiality, but because Juliet knew exactly what kind of man her father was. Since her mentor was the one handling the lion's share of Declan's counseling, if Woodbridge tried to harass or browbeat her into divulging anything, she could simply turn him over to Dr. Kobayashi-Jones.

Woodbridge nodded stiffly, unhappy but unable to argue.

Mama Ami stood. "If that's all?" She phrased it like a question, but everyone understood it as a dismissal.

We said our goodbyes, thanking Prisha and basically ignoring Woodbridge, Mama Ami hanging back with us. Then Declan stared at the two members of the Tribunal until they both gathered their things. It was a very wolfy thing to do, and I appreciated its effectiveness.

"We'll see ourselves out," Woodbridge said.

Declan didn't move, holding me in place, waiting to make sure they both left the house. He wouldn't want them on his territory and wouldn't feel safe until they were gone. In that moment that was very clear—this may be Trick's house, but Declan considered this to be his territory all the same. I squeezed his hand. I didn't think any of us would argue with him.

Once we heard their cars start up and drive away, his shoulders softened. He let go of me and hugged Mama Ami. "Thank you."

"Of course." She hugged him back. "I'm glad you contacted me."

"I know you had to drop everything and this whole mess has upset your schedule—"

Mama Ami waved him off. "It's what family does." The corner of her mouth kicked up. "I'm just glad I'm here to spike Woodbridge's plans and hold him in check. That man—" She shook her head, her lips tight against the profanity she no doubt wanted to heap onto Woodbridge.

I laughed and kissed her cheek. "I love you, Mama Ami. And thank you."

"I love you to, Loulou." She patted my shoulder. "Just keep it up. We'll show them, won't we?"

I walked Mama Ami to her car, leaving Declan to call his sister. When I came back in, he was standing in the middle of the living room, frowning at his phone, waves of concern coming through our link.

"Everything okay?"

"Zoey didn't answer her phone."

I touched his wrist. "Does she usually keep her phone close?"

He shook his head. "No, but she would right now." He tapped his phone, calling her again. With each ring, I felt his tension ratchet higher.

I rubbed small circles between his shoulders, listening as the faint ringing sound stopped and Zoey's voice came over the line, telling us to leave a message. "Is there another way to contact her?"

Declan immediately started scrolling through his contacts. "I can call Sid." He hesitated, thumb hovering over the screen. "I haven't talked to her." There was a wealth of if not sadness, then something similar in his brown eyes.

I kissed him quick and soft. "Want me to call her for you? If you're not ready?"

Declan's arm slid along my waist, tucking me to him. "No, I can do it." His hand dipped under my shirt, his palm hot as it rested on my lower back. "Thank you for offering."

"Want me to stay or go?"

He tucked his face against my neck, breathing deep. "Stay. Please."

"Okay." I pressed my cheek to his chest, holding him, as a river of fear and concern flowed from his end of the bond. I let it crash over me, trying to be quiet and solid, someone steady he could lean against for the moment.

He hit the Dial button, holding the phone to his ear and letting it ring. After a few seconds, a voice came over the line, and I felt Declan relax. "Sid, hey. I—" He had to clear his throat twice to get the words out, and even then they rasped low against my ear. "I tried to call Zoey, but she didn't pick up. I just wanted to make sure everything was all right."

I couldn't quite make out what Sidney said, but Declan relaxed further, so Zoey must be okay. I kept my arms wrapped around him, gently scratching his back through the soft shirt.

He huffed out a sigh. "Can you ask her to leave her ringer on from now on, to save my sanity a bit?" Sid murmured some sort of assent and

Declan cleared his throat again. "How are you? Both of you? Everything okay?"

They talked back and forth for a few minutes, until suddenly the conversation snagged and they both fell silent.

"I should let you go," Declan said, his voice still that deep rasp. "Thanks for picking up. I ... I hope you're both safe and happy. That's ..." He pulled me tighter, resting his cheek against my hair. "That's all I want. Okay? Let Zoey know I love her?"

This time I heard more of Sid's voice, and it sounded wobbly, like she was trying not to cry. "I will. Take care and ... please, Declan. Call again soon, okay?"

He murmured that he would, then he hung up, shoving the phone into his pocket. We stayed as we were for a while, Declan gently rocking me back and forth. The living room windows were open, letting in the city noise around us. Garbage trucks, dogs barking, and one of the neighbors had NPR cranked up, which seemed like a weird thing to blast, but maybe they had hearing issues. Or maybe they liked to rock out to *All Things Considered*.

"You okay?"

Declan didn't respond at first, and when he did, his words were grudging. "I know it's good to talk difficult things out, but it's hard."

"Yes, it is."

He sighed, trying to cuddle me even closer, which I didn't think was possible. "I'm worried about Zoey and Sid."

"Understandable."

"Nothing I could do about it—they're going to handle things as they see fit." Another, bigger sigh. "I'm afraid of Eva, of my dad. Of them finding me, or worse, hurting the people important to me."

"Again, understandable." I didn't ask why it would be worse if other people were hurt, because I understood what he meant. I would rather take on Eva or Angus myself than watch them hurt Declan.

"I *should* be afraid." He leaned back so I could see his face. "And I hate it because it makes me feel helpless. There's nothing I can do."

"It sucks," I said. "And I'm sorry." I ran my fingers along his jawline, just because I could. "And I wish I could say something to make you feel better or do something to help, but I can't." His answering smile was faint, but it was there. "What I can do is offer you a break." I tipped my head to the couch.

"There's a seat right there with our names on it. I think we've both earned a little time out, don't you?"

I spent then next half an hour with my feet up on the coffee table, Declan's head in my lap, his arms wrapped around my middle, as we watched a wildlife documentary. Sitting with him felt easy and comfortable. Touching him made my body hum, like we resonated on the same frequency, and I liked it so much—was getting used to it so fast—that I was already wondering how I would do without it when this whole storm blew past. Or whether I'd have to. We hadn't really talked about what came next.

The narrator finished telling us about sea birds, the screen shifting to panning shots of forest scenes.

"How do you think Van's doing?" Declan asked.

I ran my fingers absently through his hair, enjoying the feel of it as I thought about his question. "She'll probably put on a brave face. Dealing with her dad…she'll have a rough couple of days."

"I'm sorry that I brought her dad here."

I yanked his hair playfully. "Hey, he brought himself here. I thought his kind had to be invited to cross the threshold."

"You're thinking of vampires," Declan said. "Which is a myth."

"Same thing," I said as he nudged my hand with his head so I'd go back to petting him. "I'm glad Will was here. He'll make her feel better, and he won't let her avoid processing it for too long."

"Hmm."

We watched the show for several more minutes before Declan looked up at me. "Why did you choose this show?"

"I don't know—I like nature documentaries." I picked up the remote, holding it out for him. "Did you want to watch something else?"

Declan ignored the remote, turning his attention to the idyllic forest shots moving across the screen. "I was just wondering if I was influencing you though the bond somehow. I'm overdue for a run."

He'd been putting it off in case Eva was getting close. "How's your wolf handling it?"

"He's getting antsy." He trailed off as a bunny hopped across the screen.

"What happens if you don't let the wolf out?"

The bunny was carried off by a hawk and Declan rolled so he could look up at me. "I'll start to get short-tempered. Grouchy. Right now I decide when we shift. If I wait too long, he'll decide."

I brushed the hair away from his face. "Do you want forest? Or does it matter?"

He considered my question, his gaze soft. "I just need nature and you," he said quietly.

I couldn't help it, I blushed.

He smiled then, wide and open, his eyes lighting up, and my breath caught. I liked being the cause of that smile so much I almost asked if we could postpone the run and go back to the bedroom instead. Instead, I shoved him, forcing him to roll of the couch. "Okay, give me ten minutes."

While I got ready, I checked to make sure the place I wanted to take him had cell reception—he wouldn't like being out of touch with Zoey right now—and Declan grabbed a bag to pack us a picnic of sorts. He would be hungry after the shift.

Declan texted my phone number to Zoey and Sid, letting them know he was going for a run and they could call me for emergencies. It was a good idea, so I messaged where we were going to my roommates and Mama Ami. Now was not the time to disappear into the forest and give our loved ones a collective panic attack.

After all that was done, I grabbed a blanket to sit on and we packed everything up into Declan's SUV. I plugged some coordinates into my phone and then we were off. The joy of us going out, on our own, on what could be considered a date, temporarily pushed all of my worries out of my head. I would put it all aside for a little while. Today would just be me, a little sunshine, and my favorite wolf.

CHAPTER TWENTY-TWO

Lou

I took Declan to the beach. When people usually picture a beach, they think of sand, sun, and warm water. Washington beaches aren't like that. First, the water is cold. Super cold. A small percentage of people try to surf in it for reasons that I don't understand, but they wear wetsuits if they're smart.

Second, we have precious little sand. Occasionally, you'll run across a sandy stretch, but for the most part it's rocks, barnacles, and oyster beds. Tons of seaweed and tidal pools. And green, so much green, because we're not the Evergreen State for no reason. Though to be fair, I've always wondered how Eastern Washington felt about that. It's a totally different climate on that side of the mountains, and a lot less green.

It's not necessarily the kind of beach you want to have sexy times on, unless you like barnacles biting into your ass.

We parked Declan's car in the lot, dust billowing around us. I pointed out the trailhead, which was a five-foot break in the trees revealing a compact dirt path. "If you change in the car, you can run a bit through the forest as we head down."

"That means you'll have to carry all of our stuff," Declan said.

"Yes, I'm a very delicate flower and I will die if you make me carry a blanket and our food."

"I wasn't implying anything," Declan said, stripping off his shirt. "It just doesn't seem fair to make you carry everything."

I shrugged, trying to decide whether I should give him privacy as he climbed into the back seat and started taking everything else off or ogle him shamelessly.

Ogling won, because really, *daaaaammmn.*

Now I understood why Declan had tinted windows. "Life isn't fair. Sometimes one person has to carry the load for another. It's called friendship."

Declan leaned forward and kissed me hard on the mouth. "You're a good person. I'll carry everything on the way back."

"Sure," I said. "Because that's when it's lighter. I see how it is."

He threw his shirt at me.

I watched as he slid out of his boxers, now gloriously naked. "Do you need privacy for your shift?"

Declan shook his head. "It's okay if you watch." He dipped his chin, suddenly shy. "If you want."

I rested my head against the seat and waited. I'd never seen someone shapeshift this close before. The process was smoother than you would expect—after all, it's magic. Explaining it was difficult—it reminded me of pouring liquid between two vessels. The wolf flowing into the container that was Declan, but at the same time, Declan flowed to wherever the wolf had been.

Declan shifted quickly, the process finished before I could count to ten, though the amount of magic it contained made the air in the car heavy. When he was done, a gray wolf rested on the back seat, head on his paws, taking deep breaths, the silver hair on his back and sides heaving. Eyes the color of river ice peered out of his dark mask, his gaze weighty as we studied each other.

I closed my eyes, feeling for our bond, making sure it was fully open. This was a time when we needed to be careful and in contact, because the wolf wouldn't be able to shout at me if Eva attacked. It also gave me a minute to collect myself. The experience of watching his shift, of bonding with his wolf like this, felt almost sacred. A gift. Like being granted an intimacy that few others would get. I realized we'd never just sat like this. Just me and the wolf with nothing catastrophic happening.

For the first time, I had a chance to quietly get to know his wolf, and it made my breath catch. I'd always loved wolves. There was just something so captivating about the way they flowed through the world, and Declan's wolf was no exception.

I dropped my mental barriers completely and welcomed this other half of him. The wolf and the human—they're separate and they're not. I don't know how to really explain it. They were more like really close twins that told each other everything, having no secrets, but still having distinctly different personalities. Declan's wolf seemed less playful than he was. Solid and serious, but also calm, like a deep, still lake. His scent filled my nostrils and

I could almost feel his fur as his consciousness rubbed against mine, making me smile.

The wolf stood and shook, sticking his nose behind my ear when he was done. He nudged me suddenly, the sensation making me both jerk away and giggle. "Cut it out."

The wolf sat, playacting at repentance.

I heard someone talking through the window and turned to see a man come out of the trailhead, two young girls following along in his wake. The smaller one, her hair in a messy ponytail, yanked on the hem of his shirt. She whined, holding her arms up, causing the man to laugh and scoop her up.

The wolf watched them, his demeanor shifting abruptly back to a solemn sentinel. I had the sense that if the man did anything to cause that little girl distress, the wolf would step in.

So serious. I stroked the side of his neck tentatively, seeing how he felt about the touch. He nudged my wrist with his nose, asking for more. *Are you worried he will hurt them?* I asked, referring to the man with the little girls.

Someone has to watch, the wolf said back. *To make sure there is no reason worry.* He spoke with such authority.

And you think that's your job?

The man helped his girls into a beat-up sedan, laughing as he set the smaller one in her car seat. The wolf watched, ears perked. *Yes.*

His mind grew distant for a second, and I had the sense he was conferring with Declan. He blinked, head turning to me. *It has always been my job.*

The wolf showed me something then, flashes of images: Declan as a young boy, holding a younger girl, Zoey, I thought, while she shook in fear. Him, a few years older now, walking back and forth and singing to a small, wrinkled infant. Zoey, slightly bigger now, carrying a second baby, her face grave, as she mimicked her older brother in every movement. She looked at him like he'd hung the moon, the stars, and every inch of inky black sky just for her.

The memory skipped forward. Declan holding Zoey's hand, feeling the sweat slick her palm, even if she appeared outwardly calm. She wore a filmy white dress and no shoes. Her light blond hair was down, held back by a crown of flowers. It reminded me of the other memory Declan had given me, the one where Eva took him over, but it wasn't quite the same.

A bigger man stood in front of them and I knew instantly it was Angus. He looked a lot like Declan, but I could see the big differences. Angus held himself differently. Chest puffed out. Chin up. Even standing still, there was an aggressive aura about him, something which telegraphed that this was a powerful man, and he knew it.

Like an Alpha, the wolf whispered. *Strong. Not like us.*

Declan is strong, I argued, showing the wolf. Angus was a sledgehammer. He knocked down those in his way. Declan got back up. Every time. He stretched his hand out, pulling others up, too. If that wasn't strength, I didn't know what else to call it.

The memory moved on: Angus reaching out and shoving Zoey forward until she stumbled in front of a boy and his father. The boy was dressed up, his angular face pale. Flowers in his dark curls. Older than Zoey, I guessed, by at least a few years, but still so young, his face stoic. That was when it clicked—I was seeing a betrothal ceremony. Angus, promising his daughter to another pack.

Zoey tried to step away, but Angus gripped the back of her dress, keeping her in place. There was no escape, not for her.

The memory skipped a handful of months, the days a blur, pausing again on Declan. He was so skinny I could count his ribs, wearing only a pair of too-big shorts, his long hair knotted and wild, stepping through the shadows far back from a dying bonfire. People were singing and dancing, the stars vast and bright overhead.

Magic was so thick on the air, I was surprised I couldn't see it. Somehow, I knew this was the first time Declan had been human in weeks. He stepped carefully through tall grass, eyes on the fire. Eyes on the woman sleeping curled up on a throne of cushions. Curled up like a child, her face soft. The sight of her made Declan pause, fear coursing through his blood like a second heartbeat.

I couldn't see Angus; the memory informed me he was still drunk off the magic, long gone on a hunt in the surrounding woods. I stayed with Declan as he snuck away from the fire, feet placed carefully to keep the grass from rustling too badly. When he got close to the tree line, he bolted, trading stealth for speed.

I didn't know how far he ran, but he was winded and shaking when he got there. Not enough food or sleep, or from the long journey? I wasn't sure. Possibly both. The asphalt rough on his bare feet as he stepped into the thin light of the parking lot. A gas station—one of those *in the middle of nowhere* ones that only have a few pumps and a small store. It also had something I hadn't seen in years—a beat-up payphone.

The sharp scent of urine and less pleasant things assaulted my nose as Declan stepped into the booth, put the phone to his ear, and dialed. He shook from the adrenaline, his heartbeat like a mad thing in his chest. I was so scared for him, this half-feral boy, doing the best he could to protect the people he loved.

Afraid but risking himself anyway.

The memory dissolved and I was back in the SUV, curled up awkwardly in the driver's seat, crying. The wolf whined and licked my face. I laughed, the sound watery, as I dug a tissue out of the glovebox.

You're right. I blew my nose into the tissue. *You had to be serious. You had to watch out for the pups.* Declan had been the adult in his family for a long, long time. I dug my hand into the wolf's ruff, giving him a good scratch. *But not today. Today you can play and I'll watch out for you.* The wolf snorted, like he thought the idea of *me* protecting *him* was hilarious.

But I could also tell that he liked it.

I climbed out of the SUV, let the wolf out, and grabbed our stuff before hitting the lock button. The weather was still a little chilly, and I zipped up my hoodie as I plodded onto the trail. The wolf zipped off into the trees, tearing back and forth through the woods, but not straying too far from the trail. Even though our bond told him I was fine, he still wanted to keep me in sight. I understood why a heck of a lot more now. If I was in sight, he could get to me in time.

He could keep me safe.

When you grow up without something, you tend to overcompensate for the lack as you get older. Grow up poor? You tried to surround yourself with money. Grow up hungry? Become a chef. Grow up in an unstable environment? You want safety and stability. Family, a pack, would mean everything to Declan.

I thought back to our earlier fight—the mac and cheese night where everything had gone so badly so quickly. It made so much sense now. Trick and I had been out of sight, out of touch, even by phone. Late, not responding—his pack out of reach. His protective instinct must have been screaming at him. What an absolute nightmare for my wolf.

My heart lifted as I watched him tear through the woods. I could feel his joy at being outside, the scent of the forest in his nose, the dirt under his paws. It fed my own joy, so that by the time we got down to the beach, I was grinning from ear to ear. The wolf felt lighter now, and though he wasn't completely unburdened by showing me the painful memories, the load had been lessened. I carried part of it for him and that made a difference.

I stepped off the trail onto a short wooden bridge that took me over a swath of marsh grass, then down a few steps to the beach. The water was dazzling today, kicking up sunshine, looking blue-green in the light. In about ten minutes it would probably look gray as clouds moved in. Such was the weather in the Pacific Northwest. But I was wearing layers, we had blankets, and though a sharp breeze was coming off the water, it was still nice to be outside.

I found us a good spot up against a large log—it was basically an entire tree trunk—that was holding back a pile of driftwood. I stretched our blanket out, anchoring it with our bag of food and a few large rocks. It wasn't too windy yet, but I wanted to be careful. Declan was running down the beach, stopping occasionally to smell something or chase a seagull. I could see a few people walking further down the shoreline, but there weren't a lot of people out. It was midweek, school was in session, and spring weather in Western Washington was always shaky. In the summer, it would be packed, especially any of the areas that had sand.

The tide was out, revealing seaweed and tidepools. I found one, pushing aside some of the rocks until little crabs scurried out. Once they were done, I carefully set the rocks back. I walked idly around for a bit, checking out the shallow water and the beach, enjoying the bite of salt in the air. I didn't go far—I'd made a promise to the wolf and I wanted to keep it. I would watch over him as he played.

After a while, I stretched out on the blanket, resting my back against the log. The wolf was chasing seagulls. I could tell through our bond that he was getting hungry. *I don't think those taste very good.*

The wolf snorted at me. I got the clear impression that he was implying that they were more toy than food, but he'd eat one if he was hungry enough. He played for a few more minutes before he trotted over, stopping at the edge of the blanket. I tied his shoelaces together, draping them over his back. Then I rolled his clothes into a tight bundle and handed them to him. He took them in his mouth and trotted off, looking for a hidden spot to change.

A few minutes later, Declan strode out of the woods, picking his way over to me. He flopped onto the blanket.

I dug through the bag, pulling out two metal water bottles and the food Declan had packed. He'd brought hummus and veggies, a thermos full of soup, some sandwiches, cheese, crackers, fruit… I looked up at him as I kept bringing food out.

He shrugged. "I'm hungry after I change."

I found the sandwich that was mine—veggies, cream cheese, and a thick, dark bread—and took a small bite. "Do you want to talk about it? What the wolf showed me?"

Declan took a bite of his own sandwich, the bread barely containing the pile of roast beef and cheese between the slices, as he looked out at the Puget Sound. "It's not something I usually talk about."

"I won't tell anyone," I said. "I hope you know that."

He took another bite. "I'm not worried about that. I just—I hate the way it changes things. People look at you different." He glanced at me, searching for my reaction.

I grabbed an apple slice. "Of course they do. You survived things as a kid I would struggle with as an adult. I can't help if that changes how I look at you. How can I not respect the struggle you went through?"

Declan frowned at his sandwich for a minute before carefully setting it down. He gently grabbed my face and kissed me. It was a lingering kiss, slow and easy. "Thank you."

I blushed. It was a good kiss. "For what?"

"For not pitying me." Declan picked up his sandwich again, taking a large bite. "That's the usual reaction."

I finished my own sandwich. "I mean, I feel like I'm cheating. I can't pity you, because I felt what you went through. I hurt for that little boy, of course I do. I can't imagine what he survived, even after feeling it. You should be very proud of all that you've done."

"It's hard to think of it that way," Declan said. "I mostly rehash my choice, try to figure out why I didn't get us out sooner, things like that."

"I think that's a very human reaction." I grabbed one of the carrots. "What about the last one? When you went to the phone booth?"

Declan didn't answer me at first. He fished a mug out of the bag, pouring the split pea soup into it for me. "No ham, promise. I should have opened this before you finished your sandwich."

"I could have also opened it," I said, waggling my hands at him. "I have these."

That earned me a ghost of a smile as he poured himself the rest of the soup. "The phone call." He stared at his soup. "That was the scariest day of my life. I'd had to wait for days until they were both so occupied they weren't watching me every second. I waited until their full moon ceremony."

"Full moon ceremony?"

He shrugged. "A lot of wolves celebrate the full moon. It doesn't affect us or anything, those are old human myths. It's more…symbolic. I don't know. My father's pack mostly used it as an excuse to party. A big social event. Lot of wolves changing, lots of magic in the air. Eva would make use of it, you know. Experimented with her spells."

He smiled sadly at his mug. "Zoey got ahold of a sleep draught for me and spiked Eva's drink. It broke her hold on me just enough." He sipped the soup carefully. "Things had been getting worse. She was keeping me wolf longer and longer. Angus was becoming more erratic."

Declan turned to me, his usually warm brown eyes stark. "He mostly ignored the twins—they weren't wolf, you know? He didn't care about them as long as no one bothered him. But Zoey? I was worried about Zoey. Angus had plans for us—a pack that he wanted to pair us with when we got older. Cement some ties or some nonsense. He had a nice strapping lad picked out for Zoey." He grimaced at his soup, tipping it back and finishing it. "Time was running out. So, she dosed Eva, I changed, and made a run for it. Everyone was used to me being wolf and under Eva's control, so they weren't watching me as closely as they were Zoey."

"Who did you call?" I'd followed the case a little, but couldn't remember any of this part. "How did you get away?"

Declan grinned at me then, and it was the wolf's grin. "I called 911." He held up a finger. "One phone call. That's all it took, in the end, to topple my father's empire, such as it was." He scratched his chin. His beard was growing out. He'd trim it soon. He always kept it closely cropped to his face. "I suspected they were investigating my father—it would explain his increasing paranoia and evasiveness. How locked down we were in the end."

I put my hand on his and he gripped it. "You must have been so scared."

He nodded, and when he started speaking again, his voice was so quiet I had to lean closer. "I told them everything. After that, to my dad, I was the betrayer. The one that took everything away."

"You did what was right," I said, squeezing his hand.

He shrugged. "That's not how he sees it. Or Eva."

We ate in silence for a few minutes, our minds full. Then I shivered and Declan started packing things up. I tried to argue that I wasn't that cold, but he just shot me a look. I shook the blanket and folded it before handing it to Declan. True to his word, he insisted on carrying our things back up the trail.

I thought about everything that he'd said, everything that I knew about Campbell and Eva. "Why did he pick her as a mate?"

"She was very powerful," Declan said. "He wanted a strong mate, but not necessarily anyone who was actually competition. Eva could rule with him, but the pack would never accept her without him. At the end of the day, she's not a wolf."

"But I'm surprised he picked an animal mage. Wasn't he worried that she would take him over like she did you?" I asked, waiting for Declan as he loaded our stuff into the SUV. He threw me the keys so I could drive. He was tired after the run, and odds were good he'd nap on the way home. I climbed into my seat, closed the door, and buckled up as I talked. "Did he assume she wouldn't try to bind him, or did he think he was strong enough to resist her magic?"

Declan shook his head as he buckled himself in. "No. I mean, don't get me wrong—Angus could be the king of hubris, but he was also a paranoid man. He liked having an animal mage as his partner, but he made sure she couldn't use her magic on him."

"She couldn't put the familiar bond on him?" I said, surprised. "Do you know why?" If Angus had a trick to block Eva, why hadn't Declan mentioned it?

Declan leaned into his seat, his eyes already closing. "Mating bond. It's stronger than the familiar magic, acts as a block. There was no way she could take him as a familiar after that."

"Huh," I said, turning so I could check behind me before I backed up. "Of course, that would mean she had an even tighter hold on him, right? Not that I know much about the mating bond."

Declan smiled, though he kept his eyes shut. "It's a more intimate bond, yes, but the power balance is different."

I thought about that as I pulled back onto the main road. He was right. That was one of the tricky things about binding familiars. The human was, technically, the one in the driving seat. They didn't control the animal per se, but they had power over them. If they were strong enough, they could overwhelm their familiar, or at least influence them until the creature's will twisted in the direction the mage wanted.

That was why taking a shifter like Declan as a familiar was forbidden. If I was powerful enough, I could subvert his will. I could take his choices away, and that wasn't right and it certainly wasn't legal. I didn't think it was an okay thing to do with animals, either, but the laws were less concerned about their rights. From what I knew of Eva, she wasn't the kind of person you wanted having any power over you. "So in the mating bond, it's more like they were equals?"

Declan didn't answer. He was already fast asleep.

CHAPTER TWENTY-THREE

Declan

"How's everything going?" Juliet's voice was muffled. She was currently in downward dog and speaking into her armpit.

I smiled, not that she could see it. "It's been quiet."

Juliet was checking in with me between sessions and suggested we do it over yoga, since we were both stressed, and she thought movement would help us. It was a good idea. I was more relaxed talking while we were outside, moving, than I would have been sitting on a couch in an office somewhere. The afternoon was overcast, but not cold, so we'd decided to go to the park again. We'd picked a flat area where we could both keep an eye on the playground where Lou was playing with Savannah.

I followed Juliet's movements as we straightened. I hadn't done yoga in a while. Not that I minded it, but I didn't usually like the classes. Too many distractions and people who rubbed me the wrong way. I'd tried hot yoga with Sidney once and that had definitely not been for me. But this—this was kind of nice and peaceful. Especially since I could still see Lou and hear Savannah's giggles as they played on the swings.

"Does that bother you? That Eva and Angus have been quiet?" Juliet straightened, twisting into warrior pose.

"Yeah. I don't particularly want to be attacked, but the fact that they haven't tried anything makes me nervous." I held the pose and watched my breathing, keeping it slow and even.

"That's understandable," Juliet said. "It's very stressful, waiting for something bad to happen."

It had been four days since I'd gone on my beach run with Lou. Four quiet days, and I'd loved them, but as each minute ticked past, I got more nervous. "I've been checking in with Zoey. That helps." I moved carefully, mimicking Juliet's movements. "I forgot to tell you. I talked to Sidney the other day."

We moved into the next pose, Juliet twisting to face me. "Really? How did it go? How did you feel about it?"

I told Juliet all about the call until we ended up in corpse pose. I liked corpse pose. It's got a creepy name, but there was something nice about stretching out and just relaxing. To not *do* for a moment. "It wasn't easy, talking to Sidney. It wasn't hard, either." I searched around, trying to figure out how to say what I was feeling. "It was more...weird? Strange. This was someone I saw every day. Someone I cared about, and things are different now. For the better, but still kind of sad? I don't know."

"It's difficult, grieving the relationship and the change in your life, while at the same time being happy for your sister and Sidney. For what it's worth, I'm very proud of you."

"Thank you."

"How are things going with you and Lou?"

"Good. I understand why the Tribunal is concerned and everything, but I feel like Lou is the one really good thing to come out of this. And I'm not just saying that because—" I stumbled a little. The other nice thing about corpse pose is that you were supposed to close your eyes, so Juliet couldn't look at my face. I didn't mind talking about sex, but our situation was a little awkward and it was easier to talk about it if I didn't have to look at her. I was also struggling with how to say it. I have never liked the phrase "being intimate" and "making love" always sounded weird. "Fucking" seemed dismissive, as did "banging."

Words were hard.

Juliet solved the dilemma for me. "Going at it like rabbits?"

I had a sudden image of Lou this morning, hair tousled from sleep, her eyes closed as she rode me slowly. My alarm had gone off early so I could get down to the kitchen space to prep for the food truck. The predawn had etched her face lovingly as her hips ground slowly on mine. The rocking motion had sent her breasts swaying until I leaned up enough to taste them.

I couldn't get enough of Lou's skin. She was made to be savored, and this morning I'd done my best to do so. I'd almost been late to work.

And the sounds she made when I—wait, what were we talking about?

Right. Rabbits.

I filed away the memories of this morning for later. Nothing worse than popping wood in therapy and corpse pose would make it really evident. "I see you've spoken to your sister."

"At length, yes."

I heard her move, so I turned my head and opened my eyes.

Juliet's blue eyes were gleeful. "You can't hide things from the ferrets, Declan. They see all. They hear all. They know all." She grinned. "I'm just glad *I* didn't see all." She pointed a finger at me. "Lock your door. No one wants to walk in on that business." Her expression smoothed out. "Though there's nothing wrong with any of it. Sex is a very natural thing, and as long as you two are keeping communication open and you're doing well, then I'm happy." She scrunched her nose. "I just don't want to walk in on it. That's not something I want to discuss with *my* therapist."

"You see a counselor?"

"A lot of counselors do." Juliet made a snorting noise and sat up. "And besides, you've met my father, right?"

"Repeatedly."

"I'm sorry," Juliet said, getting up and grabbing her water bottle.

I grabbed my own bottle, taking a long swig. "You studied my dad in school. It's not like I'm going to judge you."

She grimaced. "You're right. We are pieces of work, my friend." She clinked her bottle against mine. "Cheers."

I drained the last of my water.

"The thing about where I am now," Juliet said, screwing the top back on, "is knowing that it is possible to heal from a childhood with my father. Move on. Be happy." She nodded down at the park. "I have my daughter. Good friends. A good life. He can't take that from me."

I bent to get Juliet's bag for her, helping her gather up her things, when I felt Lou shout through the bond. I straightened, my head whipping around to the playground.

"What is it?" Juliet asked, coming alert.

"Something's wrong." I tried to pull more information through the bond while I searched frantically for Lou. She sent me another, softer message. I closed my eyes, sucking in a breath to steady my heartbeat as Lou apologized for scaring me. "No one's hurt. Lou was just surprised." I grimaced at Juliet. "Your dad's here."

"You scared me for a second." She put a hand to her chest, trying to calm herself.

"Do you think we summoned him somehow?" I asked.

She laughed at my joke, then frowned down at herself. "Yoga pants, tank top with a baby food stain, and my hair is a mess. Just the way I want to see my dad for the first time since he threw me out."

"You look beautiful," I said, and I meant it. "You don't have to see him, you know. I can run him off, bring Lou and Savannah back up here."

She shook her head. "That, my friend, is the coward's way. I just have to treat him like he's Jareth."

I tilted my head. "The goblin king? From *Labyrinth*?"

She nodded. "There's a line that the girl says in the movie. 'You have no power over me.' That's been my mantra when dealing with my dad for a long time. He has no power over me. Not anymore." She plowed ahead, making her way down the hill.

I followed close behind. "I just really hope he's not dressed as the goblin king," I said. "I can't handle your dad in tights."

We got around to the other side of the playground, Lou coming into view, Savannah nestled in her arms. She never took her eyes off Woodbridge, but sent me a wave of relief through the bond, letting me know she was so glad we were there.

Woodbridge looked at me and Juliet in our sweat-damp workout clothes and his lip curled.

Juliet ignored his expression, plucking her daughter from Lou's arms. "Arcanist Woodbridge, to what do we owe the pleasure?"

"Would you believe he just happened to be in the park?" Lou asked dryly.

"No," Juliet said. "I do not."

Woodbridge wasn't doing anything, but I didn't like him near my pack. I wanted him gone. I would happily pick him up, carry him to the nearest tall building, and toss him out of the highest window. But Juliet had stepped up, it was her fight, and I needed to let her handle it.

If she gave any indication that she wanted my help, I would be ready. We were in the city. Tall buildings abounded. Wouldn't take me long to get to one. I could defenestrate Woodbridge on a dime.

"The park is community space," Woodbridge said. "Should I have ignored you? That wouldn't have been polite." He sniffed. "No need to overreact."

"No need to gaslight, either," Juliet said, her professional voice in place, perfectly modulated. From the look on his face, I was sure Woodbridge had expected her to argue or sputter excuses, but she said nothing. She might as well have held up a sign that said, "We don't give two shits what you think, old man." I wanted to fucking clap.

"So this is the 'counseling' your mentor approved." Woodbridge raised an eyebrow at our workout clothes. "Stretching in a park."

"Sometimes we walk." The words were out of my mouth before I could remind myself that Juliet didn't need me stepping in. Well, I couldn't just leave it at that. "This time it was yoga." I butted my shoulder against Juliet's. "Juliet is an excellent counselor."

A nasty smile lit Woodbridge's face. "Oh, I'm sure you think so. Yoga no doubt highlights her best…attributes."

I couldn't stop the growl that came out of my throat and I didn't want to.

Calm down. Lou's voice in my head was measured, though I could feel her anger at Woodbridge boiling underneath. *Juliet's got this. You're making it harder for her.*

I know, I said apologetically. *He's just such a dick.*

She snorted.

Through all of this, the polite mask on Juliet's face never wavered. "Studies have shown that shifters respond better to counseling if they can move while they talk—even if it's just sitting on an exercise ball and rocking."

"Like hyperactive children," Woodbridge spat out.

"Shifters are physical creatures. While they can, of course, stay idle just like humans, in a heightened emotional state—like discussing problems with a counselor—they manage better when they're allowed movement." Juliet raised one brow, her expression cool. "Why would a patient open up to me if I can't even see to their basic comfort?"

"Seeing to comfort is definitely a specialty of yours." For the first time, Woodbridge looked directly at Savannah when he spoke. "Even if it means crossing professional boundaries."

Juliet's face went white. "What does *that* mean?"

Woodbridge blinked innocently at his daughter. "That you might go above and beyond to help a patient, that's all."

Oh, fuck this guy. I'd been trying so hard to step back and let Juliet handle her father, but my wolf could not deal with Woodbridge verbally attacking my pack. You don't go after pups. I wasn't sure what Woodbridge was going on about, but he'd been implying something about Savannah, that was clear. That was the only thing that could shake Juliet that much.

I growled, stepping forward, forcing Woodbridge to step back. "Arcanist Woodbridge, not another word. Not a peep or a whisper. You will leave." I ducked my face until we were eye to eye. "I don't care if this is a public space or not. While we agreed to surprise inspections, this does not qualify, and Dr. Larsen has already warned you."

"You can't make me leave. I have every right—"

The wolf added his voice to mine, lending me some of his authority so that Woodbridge knew exactly how pissed we both were. "You will leave," I ground out, my voice pure gravel, my eyes fading to the color of the wolf's. "Or we will be petitioning for your removal."

Woodbridge swallowed hard, forgetting himself for a second. Then he straightened, his cheeks red. "You have no grounds, no matter what Dr. Larsen said. None of this is enough to remove me from my rightful place. The bylaws are clear."

"Perhaps," I said, my words a predator's glide through the forest. The wolf wanted to stalk Woodbridge badly. We hunted for words, searching for the ones that would hurt him the most. I grinned when I found them. "But if you keep this up, I won't speak at another meeting. You won't hear about any of my experiences. I will answer all of Mage Bhatt's questions in private and you will get nothing. We may have to let you attend, but we will give you the bare minimum. Which means your research will be *incomplete*."

Woodbridge's face turned an almost purple color, his lips pinched and quivering. For a long, tense moment, we stared at each other.

Without another word, he turned and walked away. The wolf and I watched as he stomped his way through the park, finally stepping into the parking lot.

Lou reached out and touched my arm, and I realized I'd started growling again. I sucked in a steadying breath, letting the tension flow out of me. My pack was safe. The intruder had left.

"Thank you," Juliet said softly. Savannah grabbed my cheeks, yanking on my beard. I really did need to trim it again—it was too easy for her to get a handful. "Good woof." She leaned forward and put her forehead against mine, the deep blue of her eyes less than an inch away. Then she gave a little howl, like a wolf pup. "Awooo?"

I laughed, leaning forward and kissing her nose. "Yes, little one. Awooo." I didn't howl, but said the sounds back to her.

She clapped. "Good woof."

We went home, Juliet and Savannah disappearing downstairs while Lou and I went up. I stepped into the house, greeting the ferrets as they bounded up, Van nowhere to be seen. I walked back to my room, stripping off my shirt as I went. Trick passed me in the hallway, giving me a friendly wolf whistle, which Dammit tried to mimic. Trick laughed, stroking the puff of feathers on the little bird's chest.

"Stop treating me like I'm a piece of meat," I said, pretending to clutch my shirt to my chest in outrage.

"I treat everyone like a piece of meat," Trick said with a grin.

Lou folded her arms with a scowl. "Oh really? Where's my wolf whistle, then?"

Trick touched his chest, his expression pious. "Right here, in my *heart.*"

Lou rolled her eyes. "You're so weird."

He nodded. "But you love me."

She sighed. "But I love you." She kissed his cheek before shooing me down the hall. "You should shower before he does something else weird and distracts you."

I grabbed clean clothes from my drawers and hit the shower, rinsing off the day. I dried and dressed quickly, heading to Lou's room. My phone started to buzz as soon as I opened her door, Zoey's name on the screen. I answered it as I flopped onto Lou's bed. "Hey, Zoey."

"Hey, Dec," Zoe said, sounding a little tired. There was a lot of noise in the background, making me think she was at the brewery. "Got a minute?"

"Sure. What's up?"

I heard a door click and the line got quiet on her end. She'd gone into her office, meaning she wanted privacy. "I got a call from Ryder."

I flipped onto my back. "He give you an update?"

"He was able to send a message to the foster family that's been raising Tamsin and Rory."

The twins. I sat up. "And? How are they?"

She huffed. "They haven't responded yet beyond letting us know that the message was received and they'd pass it on to the twins. Apparently, they've been away at boarding school."

My shoulders hunched and I frowned. "Boarding school?"

"I guess it's not that uncommon for elementists to spend the last two years of high school like that, especially if they're powerful. They likely outstripped the local teacher and had to go somewhere else to continue schooling."

I relaxed again. Everything I'd heard about the foster family made me think the twins were well cared for, but it was difficult to really know on such little information. Zoey had gone quiet, making me realize she wasn't done with her news. "What else?"

"Ryder talked to the detectives on the case—got an update. They've figured out how Dad and Eva got out."

Some of my tension must have leaked into the bond, because Lou slipped into the room, moving quietly when she saw me on the phone. I patted the spot next to me in invitation and she took it, hopping onto the bed and sitting tailor style. I leaned against her, letting her soothe me. I needed to listen to Zoey, and freaking out wouldn't help.

"The UTC dispatched a team of investigators to both prisons," Zoey said. "I guess they spent days examining video footage, looking for trace magic, even screening urine samples of the guards for magical residue."

I snorted. "It do any good?"

I heard the creak of her desk chair over the line, and I had a sudden memory of Zoey sitting at her desk, making her chair swivel as she talked. She couldn't sit still when she was agitated. "The problem was, they were looking for a magical angle, because that was what most Uncanny would have used. Imagine their chagrin when it turned out to be a totally mundane escape."

"How?" I asked, wishing Zoey would cut to the chase.

"They had someone on the inside," Zoey said. "Several someones, really. Guards go through a rigorous screening process, but…"

I could easily finish that sentence. "But it's been years and things got lax and they underestimated the power of Dad and Eva." Lou's hand clasped the back of my neck in reassurance.

"Yup," Zoey said, her voice overly chipper. "They took a look at their history, screened bank accounts for bribes, but it was simpler than that. In Angus's case, he simply won over a few of the guards."

"You don't start your own cult of personality without having some serious charisma," I said flatly.

"Our dad, such a charmer," Zoey said, sarcasm in every syllable. "And in Eva's case, a few of the former cult members slipped in through administration. They got jobs as cleaners or cooks—people who don't come into contact with inmates aren't scrutinized as heavily."

She let out a frustrated breath. "They must have been planning this for ages. Those people worked for over a year before they started to train for other positions, eventually transferring into areas where they would encounter Eva. In the end, they were snuck out of the prison by people on the inside."

My pulse quickened. "If there are people on the inside there, then they likely infiltrated other systems as well." I stared at Lou, knowing that my eyes had faded to wolf.

Lou didn't flinch.

I kept the phone to my ear, but directed my words to Lou. "Call Prisha. Tell her someone has to look at every single person who had access to my information at the UTC, my sister's, the twins'. Anyone who could possibly find out where we moved to or what our new names were."

Lou nodded, pulling out her phone and ducking out of the room, already dialing.

"If they've planned this for years…" Zoey's voice faded to a whisper. "If they've infiltrated UTC's systems…"

"If they knew everything already"—I swallowed, my throat tight—"they'd already be here."

"They'll find something," Zoey said. "Eventually. You know they will."

"I know," I said. My father wouldn't give up. I'd betrayed him. I'd betrayed his pack. He would need to put me in my place. "Maybe he'll only come after me—leave you and the twins alone."

Zoey scoffed. "He'll come after all of us, Declan. Just to hurt us. Just because he can." I started to argue but she cut me off. "I better call Ryder back. Make sure that Rory and Tamsin's foster family really understands that the twins aren't safe, either."

"Okay," I said. "Be careful, Zoey."

"You too, big brother."

CHAPTER TWENTY-FOUR

Lou

Our schedule was killing me. Declan's workday started early with the food truck, then we bounced between the tattoo shop and Family Familiar. Even with my hours reduced and the judicious use of naps, I was exhausted. Declan felt bad, though it wasn't his fault. But he'd insisted we visit Vanessa and grab coffee at Wicked Brews before heading to the vet clinic for a few hours.

Trick had joined us, Dammit roosting on his shoulder. The baby phoenix was especially proud of this. Eventually, he'd be able to ride on Trick's shoulder all the time and get rid of the baby carrier completely. For now, it was short stints on the shoulder, with Trick using his affinity with fire and the bond to help control Dammit's flame.

Pride flared in my chest as I watched them. They had both done the work to make this happen, but they wouldn't be there without me. I did this. I brought two creatures together and created something good.

Trick's eyes narrowed. "McKendrick." The name came out as a fierce whisper. Declan looked confused for a moment, but I knew exactly who to look for. After a quick glance, I saw a tall, blond man get in line for coffee. He was impeccably dressed in a tailored gray suit that set off the blue in his eyes, and he had the cheekbones of a Swedish model.

"He's Trick's nemesis," I whispered to Declan. "His *sexy* nemesis." For his part, Trick just grumbled into his espresso.

Vanessa came over with a muffin, collapsing into a chair. "Break time, also known as the best time." She caught Trick's expression. "McKendrick?"

Trick glowered at her.

Vanessa snorted, peeling back the wrapper on her muffin. "Someday you're going to hate-fuck that man, and I bet it's glorious."

"I would never," Trick said, stroking Dammit's feathers.

She laughed and almost choked on the muffin. "Oh, yes you would." She pointed at McKendrick, who was now at the counter ordering from Noah. "That man is toned, his cheekbones could cut glass, and he reeks of competence."

"It's the last one that will get you," I said, sipping my coffee.

"Stop pointing," Trick ground out. "It's rude."

Vanessa ignored him. "There are a lot of fit men, and pretty men, but competent? Like he could just step in and handle shit?"

"Handle you?" I said, my voice getting a little dreamy. Van and I had both trailed off and were now staring into space.

Declan cleared his throat and I gave his arm an absent pat.

He leaned in close to my ear, his voice soft. "Please tell me I'm competent."

"You're practically the dictionary definition." I realized I'd been petting his arm. Eh, I was okay with it. He had nice arms. He had nice everything, but it was socially acceptable to pet his arm in public, so I was sticking with that.

"The bar is really low," Vanessa said. "But you would clear it even if it wasn't."

Declan gave a little huff and kissed the space behind my ear. I reached up and ran my fingers through the hair at the nape of his neck.

"If you two get any cuter, I'll hit you with this muffin." Van held up her half-eaten snack. "And it's chocolate chip. It's fucking delicious and it would be a travesty to waste it, just like it's a travesty that Trick isn't tapping that."

"I fucking hate all of you," Trick grumbled into his cup.

"You love us," Vanessa said with a grin. "And you shouldn't lie to those that you love. I won't make you admit it to us right now, but you need to at least admit it to yourself. You would hate-fuck that man into a coma of spent lust."

"Coma of Spent Lust would be a pretty good band name," I murmured.

"Or maybe just Spent Lust should be the band name and Coma could be the first album," Declan said, his voice thoughtful.

"You're both wrong," Van said. "Coma should be the band name and then the albums would all be things that *caused* the comas."

The door jingled, and Jim entered, turning his big shoulders to make it through the door. He'd taken his magic for the day, because he looked like a big, auburn-haired guy and not a bull. He saw us and smiled, heading over.

When he got close to us he stopped. Looked at us. Looked at Trick. Tipped his head. "McKendrick?"

"Ha!" Val said, pointing at Jim while turning a look of pure triumph on Trick.

Trick cradled his cup and continued to give us the death glare, mumbling threats under his breath.

"I'd feel bad," I told Trick. "Except you do this to me and Vanessa all the time. I enter into evidence the Great Spoon Debate that we had in this very café."

Trick continued to glower. "I don't like the taste of my own medicine."

"Nobody does," Vanessa said kindly. She turned her focus to me. "Juliet mentioned you running into Dad. What happened? She was kind of upset and glossed over the incident."

I caught her up, telling her everything Woodbridge had said to us. Vanessa set aside the rest of her muffin, her face thoughtful.

Finally, she shook her head as if clearing it. "I don't get it. Ambushing you in the park seems really ham-fisted. My dad is usually sneakier than that." She got up, brushing muffin crumbs off her jeans. "Either he's desperate for information on Declan and Eva, or he's slipping in his dotage."

"I considered finding a tall building to throw him out of," Declan grumbled.

Vanessa bent and kissed his head. "And I love you for it." She checked the clock. "And I better get back to work. You want any coffees for the clinic?"

"Please. Lainey's usual and a cookie?" Lainey kept telling me she didn't mind, but I still felt terrible that we'd accidentally increased her workload. The blatant bribery from us would continue for now.

After we got coffee, we went to the vet clinic. The schedule was completely booked, and a few emergencies had called in, so Lainey was glad to see me. I helped answer phones, put patients into rooms, got their vitals, and checked people out. It was a nice reminder that while I couldn't help with Mama Ami with the familiars, I could still be useful.

Lainey handed me a folder. "You get to check in this one."

I glanced at it. A new patient, an adult cat named— "Oh no," I groaned softly, making sure the patients couldn't hear. "Not a 'Baby.'" Anyone who had ever worked with animals knew how it went: the sweeter the name, the more vicious or evil the animal was likely to be. If given no other data about an animal, I would pick "Cujo" over "Princess Sweetums" any day. "You're evil."

Lainey cackled, totally unrepentant.

After I checked in Baby, then cleaned and bandaged the scratches she gave me, I went into the back to change my scrubs. I can deal with most things, but owners didn't like it when you walked into a room reeking of cat urine. I quickly changed in the bathroom, shoving my dirty set into the laundry by the kennels.

I had a moment before I had to rush back up, so I stopped to pet and soothe some of the patients in recovery. We did surgery in the morning so that we could watch them during the day to make sure they were doing well enough to be sent home later in the afternoon or if they needed to be kept overnight.

I cut through the back room on my way up front and found Declan holding a chow for one of techs. Declan was using his alpha stare to keep the dog calm and still so the tech could draw blood. All of his focus was on the chow, meaning he wouldn't notice me studying him. He really was ridiculously handsome, even though he looked worn out and worried. His eyes held a pinched, shadowed look to them that told me how exhausted he was. My heart squeezed at the sight.

In the short time that he had lived with us, he'd done so much for the house. So much for me. I knew he blamed himself for what I was going through, but it was far outweighed by the good he brought to our cobbled-together little family.

I simply couldn't picture our home without him in it.

That realization hit me hard. There was a very good chance I would come out of this mess banned from bonding familiars. That would hurt.

Not having Declan as part of my family would hurt more.

I'd been worried about what everything would do to Mama Ami, but if I was talking to her right now, I knew exactly what she'd say—ultimately, she was a healer. Healers valued life, and the binding had saved Declan's. From what I'd seen, Eva binding him again would crush him. Mama Ami would tell me to put Declan's life on one side of the scale, and my career on the other. One vastly outweighed the other.

Would it be fair if I lost my career? Of course not. But life wasn't fair. I could find a new job. Declan couldn't find a new life.

The tech was done, stepping away, and Declan loosened his hold on the dog, who immediately licked his face. Declan spluttered and laughed, his joy spilling over into our bond.

Yes, I would miss familiars, but there were lots of other jobs working with animals. I could find something fulfilling, something that made me happy. Having Declan in my life—in any capacity—was worth it.

Declan looked up then, warm brown eyes meeting mine. He grinned and it felt almost physical. Like I'd dipped my toe in a hot bath and that heat flowed through me all the way up to the roots of my hair. I actually blushed.

Just from a smile.

Later that night, I went over to my mom's place to watch a movie. With everything going on, I hadn't been able to spend time with her. Not that we were by ourselves. Declan of course came with me.

My mom was making popcorn on the stove in her small kitchen while I supervised. Neither of us wanted burnt popcorn. As soon as it was done, we'd sit down to watch whatever film she'd picked out. We took turns picking movies and tonight was hers. Tonight we were watching *Clue* because it was one of her favorite movies and she'd discovered that Declan had never seen it.

I peeked into the living room and spotted Declan stretched on the couch, completely sacked out. He had one arm flung over his head, his face turned into the cushions so I only saw the back of his head. His stomach lifted up and down slowly with each breath. He looked so peaceful.

Mom also peeked around the corner to see what I was staring at. She grinned.

"Shut up," I said, giving her arm a playful shove. Not too hard, though—she was cooking, after all.

"What?" She batted her eyelashes at me, her eyes wide. "Did I say anything?"

"You didn't have to." I crossed my arms and leaned against the counter.

She shook her head. "Only you would break the law and get that guy in return. If I did that, I'd end up with a troll. The kind that yells at you to get them a beer while they scratch themselves on your couch."

I rolled my eyes and moved to grab the popcorn bowl out of the cabinet. "Please. You'd toss that guy out on his ear. Your track record hasn't been that bad. You know, besides Dad."

"Your dad was enough," Mom muttered.

"I heard you went on a date recently," I said. "How was it?"

"I don't know. It wasn't a crash and burn, but he wasn't my usual type, and I can't see a future, you know?"

"What do you mean?" I held the bowl until Mom needed it, cradling it to my chest.

She blew a lock of hair away from her face. "He took me to the opera." She mumbled it, so I had to lean in to catch it all.

"He took you to the opera? What an asshole."

She mock glared at me. "And out to a fancy restaurant downtown. There were real linens and candles and no prices on the menu."

"I take that back, he's an absolute monster. I hope you reported him to the neighborhood watch."

Mom swirled the pot, keeping an eye as the kernels started popping. She was silent a moment. "It's a screwed-up reaction, isn't it? A man takes me out on a nice date—he was articulate, charming, kind, and there was no pressure to do anything except enjoy the evening. He knew I'd never been to the opera, so he asked me at intermission if I was enjoying it, making it clear that we could leave if I wasn't." She made a face. "And he meant it."

She quickly poured some of the popcorn into the bowl, putting the lid back in place before any jumped out onto the counter. "I go out on a date with a kind, handsome man, and my first reaction is to run for the hills." She shook her head. "I'm glad Ami found a good partner so you at least have one solid example of what a healthy relationship looks like."

My poor mom. She did her best with what she had and she never felt like it was enough. "Okay, first of all, I'm glad too, but come on, Mom. You've given me plenty of good examples."

She shook her head again. "Not of that." She poured the rest of the popcorn into the bowl and shut off the burner. "I'm not whining, baby. I really am grateful that Ami has a man worthy of her, and that between us we filled out each other's weak spots. She taught you how to make a study schedule. I taught you and Bay how to change a tire and ride a bike. Between us we did good." She poured a little salt into her hand, measuring it before dumping it onto the popcorn. "I just wish this was one of the things I was better at."

I grabbed a beer out of the fridge, handing one to her. "I don't know, I think you still managed to set a good example. You both taught me that I deserved to be loved, to set expectations, and trust my instincts. That counts for something." I fished a bottle opener out of the drawer to open our beers. I left it out in case Declan wanted one. "So were you just not into the guy? Hated the opera? What?"

Mom let out a breath. "No, there's definitely chemistry. I didn't think I would like the opera, but it was actually kind of fun? There were some things I didn't get, but he didn't make me feel stupid for asking questions. We had a great time, actually." She fiddled with the label on her beer. "I told him that for the second date, we're going to a destruction derby."

I thought I knew what the problem was now, but I wanted to make sure. "Did he turn his nose up at that?"

She took a pull of her beer and let out another deep exhale. "No, he said it sounded fun. He's never been."

"Then what's the problem?" I'd guessed, but I wanted her to tell me.

She dug her phone out of her pocket and flicked through several screens until she pulled up a picture and shoved it at me. Someone had taken a photo of them outside the opera house. My mom was gorgeous, of course: Jory looked like one of those women pilots painted on planes in WWII, all pinup curves and curly red hair.

I didn't have her height, and though Mom was two inches shy of six feet, that didn't keep her from wearing heels. She used it as a litmus test—if a man whined about her height, she could toss him into the discard pile. My mom was beautiful in a grease-stained coveralls and work boots. Wearing the gown and heels she had on for the opera? She was a showstopper.

Her date was looking at her like she hung the moon. Without her heels, he would be taller than her, but with them he was an inch shorter. If he cared, it didn't show up in the picture. Tan skin, warm brown eyes, and a sweet smile—he could stop a few shows himself. Even from the photo I could tell that his suit was tailored to him, which meant he had some money. I gave a low whistle. "Good job, Mom. He could cut glass with those cheekbones. What's his name?"

"Luis Velasquez."

I sandwiched her phone between my hands and made my eyes wide. "He practically has my name. It's a sign. Can I have a new papa? Pleeeaaaasse?"

She snatched her phone back from me. "I have clearly made a mistake telling you about him."

I laughed. "Mom, I'm joking. He sounds amazing, he's hot, and you like him. Again I ask, what's the problem?"

Mom grimaced and took another swig of beer.

"Is it that he's obviously a fancy man used to fancy things and that's scaring you off?"

"That's not it." She picked more at the label on her beer. "He's got magic."

Ah. Now things were getting clearer. My mom's parents—I didn't consider them grandparents really, because they had nothing to do with us— were upper-middle class people who had very specific hopes for their only daughter. Since she didn't have magic herself, they'd wanted her to explore other avenues to bring glory to the family name: either a career they could brag about, or a husband.

When my mom didn't do those things, they'd basically disowned her.

Someone like Luis would not only bring up all those old feelings of inadequacy from them, but Mom would also instinctually balk at dating someone who met their qualifications.

"So he's a fancy man used to fancy things, it's scaring the shit out of you, *and* hitting all your hot buttons."

She shoved a handful of popcorn into her mouth to stall, giving herself precious seconds to think while she chewed. "Okay, fine. It's just…he's ed-ucated—he's got an MBA. He's funny, kind, and has plans to take me to the ballet. Not because of how it makes him look, but because he actually *enjoys* going. I watched him during the opera. He loved it."

"So did you."

"Louise, I have grease permanently embedded under my nails. I didn't even know Seattle had an opera house until he took me. How's a guy like that going to stay interested in me?"

That talk was coming straight from my grandparents. They weren't happy that Mom got pregnant young, but they were furious that she chose a trade over a college education. Never mind the fact that trade schools were just a different kind of education, or that my mom was good at it, or that it kept food on our table. Bay was right. My grandparents sucked.

I squeezed her face between my hands until she looked like a squished puffer fish. "Mom, you just channeled Grandma and Grandpa, which means you've earned a fish face."

"You're mean," she said, or at least attempted to say through her fish face.

"I'm not letting you out of fish jail until you say you're as proud of yourself as I am of you, which is a lot."

She batted my hands away. "Cut it out." She sighed. "I don't know what to do."

I snorted. "Don't toss away a good person that you like because your parents suck." I grabbed a handful of popcorn. "Give yourself more time to get to know him and see if *you* like him. You had a good time and he treated you well. Why not take him to the destruction derby? Then bring him to a family dinner. Really test his mettle."

She blinked at me. "Wow, you really *are* mean."

I nodded slowly. "Baptism by fire. If he has a good time at the derby and can withstand the full onslaught of our family, then you know he wants to stick around."

She hugged me. "I love you, baby girl. So mean. So wise." She leaned back and tipped her head to the living room. "You think you're being wise there?"

"I thought you liked Declan?"

My mom let go of me and picked up the popcorn bowl. "I do. I like the way he treats you. It's just been fast, you two getting together, and under lots of stress. Relationships built under those kinds of conditions tend to burn out."

"I know, Mom." And I did. I wasn't stupid, it was just… Declan and I hadn't talked about it. There'd been so much going on. Did he want something long term? Something permanent? I didn't know. But I thought about earlier in the vet clinic, realizing how much I liked him being in my life. What would I do if after this, Declan wanted to move on?

I thought about waking up in the morning alone instead of with him wrapped around me, and I hated it. Hated. It.

I grabbed the beers so Mom could carry the popcorn, my mind spinning. When had I gotten so serious with Declan? When had my feelings leveled up? I had no idea—and I certainly didn't know if he felt the same way.

All I knew was I'd grown used to the packed lunches and all the little things he did to take care of us. Grown accustomed to his laugh, his quiet strength. Yes, everything my mother said was true. That didn't mean my feelings were wrong, either.

I didn't want to let him go. Oh gods, what would I do if he didn't feel the same way?

In the midst of my mild relationship freak out, I'd paused in the doorway. My mother gave me a nudge and we went into the living room. Declan woke up as we sat down, his hair mussed, his eyes still cloudy from sleep. They cleared when he saw me, and he smiled.

I couldn't help but smile back.

We might have moved fast, but how could I not want him in my life after watching how he dealt with adversity? How much he cared for people? How sweet and kind he was? This was a man who would move mountains for the people he cared about, never once thinking about what they would do for him in return.

He wrapped an arm around me and I settled into the embrace, wondering the whole time if anyone in Declan's life had ever moved mountains for him. I didn't think they had. A shame, for sure, but one I was planning on rectifying.

CHAPTER TWENTY-FIVE

Lou

As the days continued to pass without Eva attacking, we both grew more and more tense. It was an awful feeling, waiting for doom to fall. You began to wish it would, just to get it out of the way. We worked, spent time with friends, and spent time together. I began to know Declan's body as well as my own. I'd never had a partner who seemed so happy to explore every inch of me to see what made me lose my mind.

Unfortunately, some of our exploration didn't go unnoticed.

Which was why we were spending the morning of our first day off in over a week replacing the shower door. I felt bad about breaking the door, and I had an interesting bruise on my ass, but I didn't regret the sex. Just thinking about it made my pulse kick up and my nipples tighten.

Declan groaned. "Stop thinking about it, because you're making me think about it, and one of us is going to end up injured. Sex and power tools don't mix."

"Says you. Do you think Trick was mad?" I asked, helping Declan slide the new tempered glass piece into the metal trim at the bottom.

Declan's lips twitched. "I think he was torn between being impressed and irritated." He released the glass once it was in place, and I handed him the new corner piece.

"Fair enough."

A short while later, we finished the door, then Declan cleaned up while I put the drill back into its case. Declan smiled at the neat label with my name on it resting on the bright yellow plastic. "Something sexy about a woman who owns her own tools and knows how to use them."

"And if I didn't?"

He shook his head. "I know this trap. It won't work. I'm well aware that gender has nothing to do with it. It's just like you said—competence is sexy.

But if you didn't know how to use the drill?" He waggled his eyebrows. "Then I'd get to show you."

"If you make a drill sex pun, I'm breaking up with you. I have to hold my boyfriend to *some* standards."

We both froze at the same time. Despite my realization that my feelings for Declan ran pretty deep, I hadn't brought it up with him. I'd chickened out. He hadn't brought it up, either. And here I was accidentally initiating the conversation in an awkward manner. Huzzah, I guess.

He still hadn't said anything. Maybe I should give us an out? "I was kidding?"

"About breaking up with me over a bad joke?" His voice had gone all gravelly again and I shivered. He put the glass cleaner and rag down. "Didn't think you were serious." He put his hands on my hips, and I could feel the heat through my shirt. "That's the first time you've called me that."

I swallowed. Well, might as well barrel forward. We couldn't avoid this conversation forever. "Is that okay? I know we haven't talked about it, but—"

He buried his face in my neck, breathing deep. "More than okay." Declan kissed my neck, setting off a tiny detonation of heat along my skin, and I straightened. He grabbed my chin gently, his gaze hot and heavy. "If it wasn't clear, Lou, this isn't—you're not just a fuck for me, okay?"

"I didn't think that," I said softly. I couldn't look away from him. No one had a right to be this hot. It was unfair.

"Good." He dropped his hands back down to my hips, gripping them hard, but not painfully. "This—you—are a big…you're…" he said, stumbling over the words. He huffed, his eyebrows slamming down. "Important. I—" He growled in frustration.

The next thing I knew, he'd thrown the link wide open and crushed his mouth to mine. He poured a lot into the kiss, and into our bond, showing me what had been hard for him to say. I'd stacked my doubts about how Declan felt, what he wanted, into a tidy pile in the corner of my mind and I'd been ignoring them. He burned that pile to ash in a second, incinerating it with a kiss.

Not only a kiss, but a wave of emotion so strong it made my knees buckle.

Good thing I had him to hold on to.

I wrapped my arms around his neck, pulling him so close that only our clothing separated us. Then I gave back as good as I got, pouring everything I had into the kiss, into our bond, repaying his honesty with my own.

He whimpered, the sound cutting straight to my heart.

I bit at his lower lip and he growled, scooping me up and setting me on the countertop. With a soft sigh, I pulled him close again, wrapping my legs around him. The counter was not quite the right height, so we weren't lined up and I let out a groan of frustration.

Declan's hands were under my shirt then, kneading me through my bra. "Did Trick say no more shower sex, or is all bathroom sex completely verboten?" Declan asked as he nibbled his way down my jaw and onto my neck. His fingers dipped under my bra so he could trace the soft undersides of my breasts while brushing over my nipples with his thumb. At the same time, he gently bit the spot where my shoulder and neck met. Whatever answer I'd been about to utter came out as gibberish.

"You're right," Declan said, acting like I'd given him a real answer. "Best not push it. Especially since we don't know where the ferrets are and they tattle."

He eased back from me and for a moment, I thought he was going to call everything off. I may have actually squeaked in protest, a sound I wasn't proud of but was too far gone to care about. I grabbed his belt, yanked him back, and moved to undo his zipper. In a second, I had him in my hand, caressing the soft heat of him with my fingers.

Declan let out a moan and braced himself against the counter with his palms. I loved the feel of him, but also the knowledge that he was as completely undone by me as I was by him. Still, it wasn't enough. I wanted more.

Now it was Declan's turn to let out an undignified squeak as I let him go and nudged him back. I leaned over, locked the door, and hopped off the counter. I pushed him against the sink, dropping my knees, the thud softened by the thick bathmat.

Making quick work of Declan's belt, I shoved his jeans down around his thighs. I'd never known I had a thing for thighs until I saw Declan's, but they were a work of art. I'd paint them, if I could paint. Sculpting was equally out of the question. Or maybe I'd write an ode to them, except I couldn't write either. Since I couldn't do them justice through art, I did them justice with my tongue and fingernails, his breath stuttering out of him before I even took him in my mouth.

Declan put his hand in my hair, closing a fist around a handful of it close to my scalp. He pulled—not hard, just enough to make me moan around him. He shuddered at the sensation, his breath gusting out of him.

"Fuck, that's—" He groaned again, words dying as I took him deeper, pulling back slowly and circling my tongue around the head. He moaned again, louder this time. I didn't think anyone was home, but Declan could get loud sometimes. I leaned back, using one hand to slide over his shaft as I reached into the lower cabinet and grabbed a washcloth.

Letting him go for a moment, I stood, rolled up the washcloth, and held it in front of his face. "I have a suggestion."

His brows drew together. "I have a wash?"

"You're loud," I said with a laugh. "And we're already on bathroom probation."

His brows lifted as he understood. His grin was wicked as he opened his mouth, letting me place the rolled-up terrycloth between his teeth. He clamped down tight. I kissed his chin, his beard soft. "Try to be quiet." I pulled off my shirt, tossing it aside. Then my bra. "Emphasis on try."

He stared back at me, eyes hot, his jaw clamped, groaning around the washcloth.

Then I went back on my knees and slipped my lips over his cock, taking him as far as I could. What I couldn't fit, I stroked with my hand. Declan threw his head back, his hands in my hair. Every muscle was taut, his body strung tight enough to shatter.

He reached through our bond, pouring affection, desire, and an abundance of *want* into me as I stroked him faster, ratcheting up my own response. I felt like I was ready to bust out of my own skin.

Muffled cursing came from between his clenched teeth. When I looked up at him, he was breathing hard around the washcloth, his eyes tightly shut. He was close. I moved my mouth faster over him, letting my hands drop down to my own waist. I unbuttoned my jeans and pulled the zipper down. Then I slid one hand down to the lacy top of my panties, sliding my fingers beneath them, using the bond to show Declan exactly what I was doing so he knew, even with his eyes closed. Letting him know how good it felt.

My other hand went back to stroking Declan while I stroked myself, my fingers making quick circles. Now when I looked up, I could see Declan watching me, his eyes molten. He grew harder, his jaw almost white from biting down on the washcloth.

I could almost hear his voice as his words slid into my mind. *Let me see you. I need to see you come, sweetheart.*

My fingers moved faster, my own orgasm winding up. I could feel the flush of it, my hollowed cheeks turning pink. I sucked him harder, taking my hand off his cock so I could cup one of my breasts. Declan's eyes followed every movement, his hips bucking as I plucked my nipples into tight points. I didn't think I'd ever been turned on so much in my life. It felt like my entire body was going to burst into flame.

Fuck, Lou, that's—fuck that's good. Declan gripped my hair, making sure he didn't pull too hard. His chest was heaving, his nostrils flaring, his jaw still clamped on that washcloth. *I need you to come.*

I moaned, moving my fingers faster, so close but not quite tipping over. Declan did something then, something with the bond, twisting it until his pleasure flowed with mine, going back and forth between us in a continuous loop.

Now, Lou.

My orgasm slammed through me. I gasped. Declan pulled out of my mouth with a curse, scooping me up and depositing me back onto the countertop so hard, my ass slid into the sink. I yanked the cloth out from between his teeth, and he took my mouth in a deep kiss. His hand closed over his cock, jerking once, twice, before heat painted my stomach as he came. He moaned into my mouth.

For a long moment, our bond was nothing but white-hot bliss. I'd never felt anything like it.

We stayed like that, trembling, the aftershocks shooting through us. After a few minutes, Declan picked up the washcloth and cleaned me up, shifting me into a more comfortable position on the counter, and I let him, because I wasn't sure I could move.

He dropped the washcloth into the laundry hamper. Then he pulled up his pants and buckled his belt, though I have no idea how he was moving so easily. My limbs were made of putty and I couldn't seem to get up the energy to move. I felt like I'd swallowed the sun, all glow and heat.

Declan picked up my shirt and shoved my bra into his back pocket. He gently put my shirt back on, helping me put my arms through the correct holes. Then he scooped me up, unlocked the door, and carried me back to the bedroom.

"What are you doing?" I mumbled as I snuggled closer to his chest.

"We're going to take a nap," he said. "Then I'm going to take my time with you until you're screaming my name." He grinned at me. "Which will be fine, because I brought an extra washcloth."

I hadn't even seen him grab it. "I'm never going to be able to look at a washcloth again without getting hot and bothered," I said as he laid me gently on the bed.

His smile widened, looking entirely too smug. "For our next date we're going to one of those giant bed and bath stores where they have acres and acres of towels."

My eyes widened as he crawled over me. "You wouldn't. You fiend!"

He lowered himself until he was cradled between my legs, his arms wrapping around my shoulders. "Then I'm going to make you watch a bunch of laundry commercials. The ones where they fondle all those big, fluffy towels and sniff them. Or some of those folding videos you can find online."

"You dirty bird," I said, kissing him.

He growled, sucking on my lower lip. *Mine.*

Yours, I said back.

He reached back and grabbed something out of his other back pocket and shoved it into my hand. I didn't have to look to know it was a washcloth.

We'll nap later. He pushed my shirt up and took my nipple in his mouth. I arched against him.

We did nap, eventually, our bodies spent and sweaty and tangled together. Contented, I fell asleep wrapped up in Declan.

Declan

I leaned against the brick wall outside of Ritual Ink, the bright colors of the mural behind me doing their best to lift my mood. I'd just left a voicemail on Zoey's and Sid's phones. No answer on either. I'd talked to Zoey yesterday morning. Not hearing from them for one day didn't automatically spell doom.

But I didn't like it. I *really* didn't like it.

I called the brewery. Neither of them was in, but it was also Zoey's usual day off. I shoved my phone into my pocket with a growl. I would call them again in a bit. Or they would call me. They were fine.

Please let them be fine.

I sighed and straightened, stretching my muscles before making my way to the door. I paused outside, catching the sight of Lou and Bay talking

through the window. Will jumped in on their conversation, talking anima-
tedly with his hands. I was glad to be at work, to be with Lou. If I'd been
home today, it would have been more difficult to distract myself away from
my worry. It was also difficult to be stressed around Will and Bay. Will was a
big, tattooed ball of sunshine, and Bay was entertaining as fuck.

The smell of incense hit my nostrils when I opened the door, woven
through with all of the cleaning chemicals, inks, and a few of my favorite
people. Lou's laugh filtered through the music and I automatically smiled. It
was hard not to when I heard her laugh.

Mine.

Yours.

Did she mean it? And if she did, what did she mean by it? Just for that
moment? For a few weeks? Forever?

Did I want forever? That seemed like such a vast thing to consider. All I
knew was that I was happy where I was. Lou felt like home.

I wrapped my arms around her, pulling her back against my chest.

Will brightened. "Oh, are we cuddling now? Is it cuddle time?" Will
put his arms around us. He squeezed and let out a happy sigh. "I love cuddle
time."

"You have no boundaries," Lou said, patting his shoulder.

"Do you want me to stop cuddling you?" Will asked the question, but
it was apparent that he was sure of the outcome. "That's what I thought," Will
said, his tone smug. "Bay, get in here."

Bay grumbled, but joined in the hug.

"Nicki," Will yelled at the other tattoo artist in the back. "You want in
on cuddle time?"

"You touch me, you die!" Nicki chirped.

"Fair enough," Will said. "I just didn't want you to feel left out!" Will
made a scoffing noise. "No boundaries, indeed."

"I take it back," Lou mumbled. "Now let me breathe."

The other two men backed off, but I stayed attached to Lou. "Your last
appointment seemed pretty happy," I said to Will. "Big tip."

"She should be happy," Will said. "She left here with a four-hundred-
and-fifty-dollar vulva."

Lou made a rolling motion with her hands. "Explain."

"Rose gold jewelry," he clarified. "A gift from her husband. She said that 'her girl was worth it.'"

"Was her girl worth it?" Lou asked curiously.

"It is if she says it is," Will said. "Nothing wrong with treating yourself right." He looked at Bay. "Speaking of treating yourself right, I'm coming with you to dinner, right?"

Bay checked his phone. "I've got a consultation." He tucked his phone away. "So you might want to ride with Lou and I'll catch up when I can."

We agreed to take Will and then I got back to work, finishing up what I needed to do before we had to leave.

At five I clocked out, and Will, Lou, and I left for the Larsens'.

This time, I was greeted like I had always been there, Lou and Bay's family smiling and hugging Will and I just as much as their actual family. After Mama Ami checked our bond over and gave it a thumb's up, I helped set up tables and played with Savannah. It felt good and I took a moment to revel in the feeling that I was somewhere that I belonged. Where I was wanted.

Lou's family was sensory overload in the best way, and it kept me from checking my phone constantly. I still checked a lot. Zoey and Sid didn't call, didn't text. I was getting really worried.

As the evening wound down, Will caught a ride home with someone else, since Bay decided to stay and spend more time with his other sisters. I gave Lou my keys because I was tired and I wanted to try calling Zoey again from the quiet of the car. After I packed our leftovers into the back, I settled down in the passenger seat, my heart and my stomach very full.

Lou buckled her seatbelt and moaned, the sound traveling down my spine. "I'm never eating again."

I grabbed her hand and kissed her knuckles. "Poor thing. Should I take the leftovers back inside?"

"You take that food back and I will not be responsible for my actions," Lou said, checking her mirrors before she pulled into traffic. Lou was a good driver, and I liked watching her as she drove, which she said was "slightly creepy," even though she blushed every time she caught me doing it. I dialed Sid and Zoey again as passing streetlights illuminated Lou's face.

It was still going to voicemail.

Lou reached across, squeezing my thigh. "You okay?"

"Just worried," I said. "I keep reminding myself that there's probably a very good, non-terrifying reason for them not answering, but..."

"But you care about them and you're concerned." Lou slowed the car to a stop as a light shifted from yellow to red. "Would it make you feel better if we had a plan in place?"

"Like what?" I asked, rubbing a hand over my face. I was suddenly so tired, the big dinner, the warm car, and the emotional exhaustion catching up to me. "There's nothing we can do, is there?"

She tapped her fingers along the steering wheel. "How about this—if they haven't called you back by morning, we go down there. Put eyes on them. Let you see that they're okay."

I blinked at her. "You would do that? What about work?"

The light turned green and Lou stepped on the gas pedal. "I think this qualifies as a family emergency. Work would understand. It's only a three-hour drive." She wrinkled her nose. "Unless we hit traffic. We'll probably hit traffic. But it would be worth it, right?"

My throat grew tight. "I can't believe you'd do all that for me."

She shook her head. "Hardly moving mountains for you, Declan. A day off and a short ride isn't much of a hardship."

I settled a hand on her thigh, wishing she wasn't driving so I could kiss her properly. "Feels like mountains to me."

"It's a plan, then," she said, resting her hand briefly on mine. "If we don't hear from them by the time you get done with the food truck prep, we'll go to Portland."

"Thank you," I said, the tightness in my throat spreading to my chest.

"Of course." She pulled onto the onramp for I-5.

I settled into my seat, relaxing now that we had at least a vague plan. The car was quiet, and I was full, warm, and content, which meant that pretty soon my eyes were trying to close. Lou put some music on, and I let the motion of the SUV lull me into a half sleep. I kept one hand outstretched and resting on Lou's thigh. It wasn't a long drive, but touching Lou was soothing. I let myself drift.

I was almost asleep when Eva's mind slammed into mine, like an axe through a log. I screamed in pain, my vision whiting out. I couldn't see. Just pain. Only pain.

Lou. Where was Lou? *I couldn't feel Lou!*

I screamed for her, my heart slamming against my ribs. Fear in every thudding beat, my mouth sour from it.

Something struck the back of my neck and my vision snapped back into place. Lou, her hand firm on my nape, shouting my name. Her other hand trying desperately to control the wheel.

We grazed the guardrail on my side, the metal shrieking and sparking. Lou jerked the wheel. We careened to the left, missing cars by inches. Wheels screeched. Horns blared.

I grabbed the back of Lou's neck, my palm over her piercings, the bond between us flaring back to life and shoving Eva out. The pain in my head receded.

Lou's face was bloodless, her knuckles tight on the wheel. She tried to control the car one-handed, afraid to let me go. Afraid Eva would come back.

Putting herself in danger to keep me safe.

No. *No.* I wouldn't let her.

I yanked her hand off me, shoving it toward the wheel. I could feel her terror through the bond. I was sick with it, my pulse stuttering.

She was so scared. *For me.*

And all I could think about was her.

The car slid as she pulled us back, trying to keep us in a lane. I wasn't sure she could actually see where we were going. Her eyes weren't tracking right.

Traffic was mercifully light at this time of night—but it was still Seattle. There were cars on the road. Too many.

And we were about two seconds away from side-swiping a green Subaru.

Lou wasn't correcting our path.

I grabbed the wheel, turning us away, changing course. We missed the Subaru, our car going into a spin. We'd lost all control, the world through the windows whirling by.

A silver minivan hurtled toward us, a yellow *Baby on Board* placard in the back window. I shouted and Lou hit the brakes. We missed the back bumper of the van as we slid past, metal crashing as we clipped the edge of a guardrail.

We bounced up a hill, our bodies jerked by the force, and I lost my grip on Lou's neck. The SUV tore through the grass—we were slowing, but not enough. A wall of trees loomed in front of us. Panic shot through me.

I yanked on the emergency brake.

Between the brake and the hill, the SUV lost some momentum. It wasn't enough. We crashed into a tree hard enough to make the airbags go off.

For an endless moment I lost sight of Lou. Desperate, I grabbed at the bond. *Please be okay*, I pleaded—possibly out loud, I couldn't tell—as I searched for her through the bond, almost collapsing in relief when I found her. She was there but faint. Too faint.

My airbag deflated, and I batted it aside, the inside of the car thick with dust. I wheezed, still frantically trying to get to Lou. I heard her cough.

I shoved the last of the airbags away and she was suddenly there. Right there. In front of me. Blood trickled from her nose, but she was alive.

I yanked off my seatbelt so I could slide over to her, grasping her face in my hands. She grabbed my wrists.

Relief flooded me. Lou was here. We were alive. We'd made it through.

I brushed blood off her lip with my thumb. "Lou?"

She shook her head, her eyes wide. "My ears. Ringing. All I hear is ringing."

I tightened my hold on her face so she was looking at me again. "Lou, are you okay?"

"No." She blinked owlishly at me. "I'm not okay." Another blink, longer this time. "Bitch tried to take you away." She patted my cheek. "Not fucking happening."

Then her eyes rolled back in her head and she slouched into her seat.

"Lou?" I patted her cheek. "Lou!" No response. Panic flared. I yanked her to me, shouting her name. Her head lolled to the side. I was sobbing her name now, wanting to pull her close, but suddenly afraid I might jostle her. What if she had a brain injury?

What if we'd made it through, only for me to lose her? The thought chilled my veins. Seeing Lou now, like this, ripped out my heart.

It was too much. I couldn't take it.

So the wolf took my place.

CHAPTER TWENTY-SIX

Lou

Someone was banging on my window. I startled awake, wishing I hadn't. Everything hurt. My mouth was thick, tasting of blood. A heavy, chemical smell burned my nostrils as I tried to breathe, causing me to cough.

"Ma'am?"

I blinked at the person through the window. Flashing lights illuminated a short, compact woman in uniform. "Yes?"

"Emergency services—can you get your mate to let us in? We need to get you out of there and they won't let us."

I stared at her a minute before I was able to process what she was saying. Mate? I heard the growl then. Declan's wolf crouched in the passenger seat, his lips curled back in a snarl. Though everything ached, I reached over and dug my fingers into his ruff. He whined, his distress evident, but he kept his eyes on the paramedic.

Even in my state, it was easy to see what was going on. I was injured. Declan's wolf was in protective mode and he didn't know these people. "It's okay. They're here to help," I tried to explain over the bond. I wasn't sure how much got through. I was having a hard time focusing.

I must have passed out again, because next thing I knew, I was in the ambulance, the small woman, Rosa, flashing a light in my eyes. I was on a gurney, the wolf sprawled across my legs. He was panting, agitated. I gripped his fur with one hand, the other hooked up to an IV. Rosa said something to me and I tried to answer, but I'm not sure if I did. The world blurred after that, winking out like a star.

The next thing I knew, I woke up in a hospital room. It was small and blessedly a single. The walls were painted light green, with a strip of chalkboard paint lining the room in the middle, as well as a small whiteboard. The akesoite must have come in while I was unconscious, because the chalkboard strip was already half covered in sigils. Incense burned in the wall sconce, mostly covering up the antiseptic smell found in most hospitals. Three small glass globes filled with herbs hung from the ceiling. The lights were dimmed, the drapes pulled, making me think it was still nighttime.

The wolf slept at my feet, otherwise the room was empty.

The door clicked open, revealing a man in scrubs. Even with his hair cropped close, you could tell there was some curl to it. He brightened when he saw me awake. "Welcome back." He waved at a small whiteboard with a bunch of notes scrawled on it. "My name is Jacob. I'm your nurse tonight. How are you feeling?"

"Okay," I said, surprised that it was mostly true. They must have had me on some solid drugs. "Headache. What happened?"

"You were in a wreck. Your akesoite will give you a better rundown, but the summary is you have a minor concussion and some bruising." He flashed a light in my eyes, because apparently that was the theme for the night.

"I'm going to touch her now," Jacob said, grabbing one of the machines nearby, and it took me a second to realize he wasn't talking to me. He held up the blood pressure cuff. "The machine will make some weird noises, but I promise it won't hurt her."

"Are you talking to Declan?"

He smiled, one of his cheeks dimpling. "That your wolf?"

I tried to nod, but it hurt. "Yeah."

"I've got a mate myself—a coyote." He lifted my arm, fitting it with the cuff. "Sweet as pie until I get hurt. Then he loses all sense." He secured the cuff, throwing the wolf at my feet an amused glance. "I've found it helps if I explain what's going on."

"Declan's not…" I was going to say he wasn't my mate but realized I couldn't. We were bonded, and Declan being my mate would explain that. If I told Jacob the truth, he would be horrified. He would tell his mate. Word would spread through the shifter community. It would be awful for me and Declan, for sure, but it might also get back to Eva.

"Declan's not usually like this," I finished awkwardly. I swallowed and it hurt, so Jacob passed me a plastic cup with a straw in it. "Thanks."

Jacob shook his head, grin still in place. "Wouldn't trade my mate for the world, but sometimes I wish he came with instructions." He hit a button and the machine whirred, the cuff on my arm puffing up.

"He probably wishes the same about you."

Jacob laughed. "True enough."

Jacob finished taking my blood pressure and went about taking my other vitals, explaining what he was doing before each one so the wolf would be at ease. Declan must have been really panicked once I'd lost consciousness. If he had gone completely over to the wolf, then there was no way anyone would have been able to get near me. I was pack and I was injured.

"Can you sit up?"

When I said I could, Jacob helped me ease into a sitting position. "Any other problems besides the headache? Pain, vision issues, anything?"

"Just sore."

He nodded, then pushed down on my shoulders. "Can you raise your shoulders?"

After that, there was a battery of tests which included me smiling, sticking out my tongue, and so on. When he was satisfied, I got to rest and wait for the akesoite.

I'd been resting for about half an hour when Van showed up. She came waltzing into the hospital room, acting like it was no big deal, but I could see the pinched look of worry on her face. The wolf opened his eyes, saw it was Van, and went back to resting mode.

"You look like shit."

"Thanks, Van. I love you, too." I hit the button to incline the bed into a better position. "Not that I'm complaining, but what are you doing here?"

"You listed me as an emergency contact in your phone. That was a fun call to get." She pulled up a folding chair to the side of the bed. "The roommates wanted to descend, but I talked them out of it. I also didn't call your family yet. Didn't want to cause panic until I knew what was going on."

"Thanks," I said. "The akesoite should be in soon. I think they're going to let me go home as long as someone will check on me every hour."

"That always seems so sexy in books." Van took my hand in hers. Her fingers were cold. "But in reality, it's exhausting as shit."

I laughed, then winced. "Ow, don't make me laugh."

"Do you want me to call your family now?"

"Not yet," I said, after I thought about it. "I'll call my mom and Mama Ami on the way home. They can descend on the house and Mama Ami can check the bond." I only had flashes of memory from the crash, but Eva had done something awful and I wanted someone to assess it for damage. "It doesn't make any sense to have them converge on the hospital if I'm just going to be checked out."

"Then we wait," Van said, getting comfortable. "Is there a reason Declan is in his wolf form?"

"I don't know. I kind of assumed he would have shifted back by now." I reached out to the wolf. He didn't raise his head off his paws, but his eyes flicked my way.

I am here until you're out of trouble. Then he closed his eyes again.

I shrugged at Van, which I instantly regretted, because *ow*. "This is protective mode, apparently."

"And you think you're going to be more helpful than human Declan right now?" Van asked the wolf.

One of his ears flicked, but otherwise he didn't move.

Van snorted. "I'm going to take that as a yes."

We were interrupted by a knock on the door. When I told them to come in, the door swung open, revealing a woman of medium height, her black hair pulled back from her face. She wore the hospital akesoite standard—slacks, lab coat, stethoscope, and carrying a tablet. The pocket of the lab coat made a noise when she moved, making me think it was probably full of chalk. In her wake a raccoon toddled in on its hind legs.

"Good to see you awake!" She smiled, tapping her tablet until the screen lit up. "I'm Ake. Luo. This is Kitkat." The raccoon chittered a hello. Ake. Luo pulled up a chair. "How are you feeling?"

I gave her the rundown. She listened as she glanced at my chart, and asked a few questions, making notes on her tablet. When that was done, she took out a black marker, drawing a series of diagnostic symbols on my arm. She handed me a small velvet bag. "Hold this, please." The akesoite held my wrists, muttering a quick incantation. When she was done, the symbols on my arm disappeared, the magic dissolving into my skin.

The raccoon, Kitkat, opened a drawer, pulling out what appeared to be a bamboo cutting board. Kitkat handed it to Ake. Luo. "Thank you." Now that it was closer, I could see that the board was covered in small circles, sigils, and other symbols I didn't recognize. She held it out flat in front of me. "Okay, empty the bag, please."

I dutifully emptied the bag over the board. Several objects fell out—mostly pieces of bone, but also a worn silver coin, an old copper penny, a few river pebbles, and a clamshell the size of my thumbnail. The objects hit the wood, moving smoothly around the board until they found the spot they wanted.

Ake. Luo took a picture of the board with her phone before jotting down a few notes on her tablet. "Well, your diagnostic looks pretty good. Especially for what sounded like a pretty heavy-duty psychic assault." She closed the notebook. "I'm going to send you home with some over-the-counter pain meds for the aches and pains, and an arnica cream for the bruising."

She took the board from me, holding it down so the raccoon could pick up the pieces and put them back into the bag. "I'll also send home an herbal sea salt soak for you. It should help with any nasty residues the assault left behind." She smiled at me. "Do you have any questions?"

I shook my head and, again, regretted it instantly.

The akesoite laughed. "Yeah, I would take it easy for a few days and check in with your usual practitioner for a checkup in about a week."

Ake. Luo gave me and Van a list of symptoms considered dangerous and made sure someone would be checking up on me every hour. We assured her that she didn't have to worry about us taking it lightly. I was very fond of my brain and took head injuries seriously. The akesoite left after that, her adorable raccoon familiar toddling along behind her.

Vanessa had the forethought to bring me a change of clothes, which made me swear my undying love and possibly my firstborn. The clothes I'd been wearing when we crashed had to be thrown away. Miraculously, our cell phones were okay—the paramedics had grabbed them as well as Declan's wallet and my purse for identification purposes.

Declan was probably going to have to get a new car. My head ached and I decided not to think about it. We could deal with all of those things tomorrow. For tonight my only job was to go home and rest.

Vanessa didn't own a car, so she'd borrowed mine, which she'd long had permission to do. I let Declan into the backseat, then climbed in after him.

"You're going to make me a chauffeur?" Van asked, buckling into the driver's seat.

"It's either that or he's going to climb onto my lap in the front seat, which isn't safe."

"Fine," Vanessa said. "But for the rest of the drive, you will only refer to me as Pennyworth. Now call your mom."

I called my mom and Mama Ami to let them know what had happened, managing to keep the calls short only because they hung up so they could meet me at the house.

Both of them were in my front room waiting when I walked in, Declan on my heels. Trick, Will, Bay, and Juliet were all there as well. The baby monitor in Juliet's hand told me that Savannah was still asleep downstairs.

"What horror have I unleashed?" I muttered, right before they all descended on me. After a careful hug, my mom headed off to prepare the first sea salt bath, handing us over to Mama Ami.

My family knows how to take care of the sick, injured, and hurting. There's a mix of coddling and tough love that they manage to weave into a smothering blanket that leaves you both grateful and gasping for air. I loved it.

Mama Ami took one look at the wolf and crossed her arms. "Unless you want to take a sea salt bath like *that*, I recommend you shift back." Somehow the wolf managed to look sheepish. "That's what I thought. Off you two go. Fifteen minutes. We'll make up a schedule while you're in there. When you're done, I'll check your bond." She shooed us off and I shambled to the bathroom with the wolf in tow.

Mom was turning off the tap when we came in. "I prepared it according to the ake's orders. Fresh towels on the toilet." She pointed a finger at me. "Soak and get out. Neither of you are in any condition for anything else."

"Ew, Mom. Thanks." I ushered her out of the bathroom, shutting the door behind her but not locking it, just in case I passed out again. I felt a surge of magic behind me and when I turned back around, Declan had taken the wolf's place.

Physically, Declan seemed fine. Any bruises had already faded, courtesy of his superior healing ability.

But he wouldn't look at me.

"Declan?"

That earned me a brief glance as he herded me to the tub. "Yes?"

"You're not looking at me."

"You need to get in the tub."

I folded my arms. "So do you."

He shook his head. "I'll soak after you. There's no space—"

I wanted to stomp my foot, but it would hurt too much. "What absolute bullshit." I pointed at the steaming water. "Get your ass in that tub now. Please. Then I'll climb in and you'll explain why you're being weird."

For a second, I thought he'd argue. Then Declan sighed, his shoulders drooping. He climbed in the tub.

I quickly stripped my clothes, joining him. The hot water smelled heavily of rosemary and stung where my skin was abraded, but otherwise felt good on my aching muscles. We adjusted ourselves, trying to get comfortable, and I ended up with my back to Declan, nestled against him.

I gave him a few minutes, letting the hot water relax us both. It wasn't long until his arms were around me, his nose buried in my neck. I left our bond alone—I didn't want to keep using it until Mama Ami checked it over thoroughly.

"I thought I was going to lose you." His voice was so soft I wouldn't have heard it if I hadn't been so close.

"You didn't."

"But I could have."

I snorted. "Declan, we could lose each other any second of every day. That's how life works."

"I can't." He heaved a breath against my skin. "I can't lose you."

I folded my arms over his. "You won't." When he didn't answer, I shifted so I could see his face. "You're blaming yourself for this, aren't you?"

He dropped his eyes.

I scowled at him. "Declan…" I frowned. "I don't know your middle name."

"Sinclair," he mumbled. "It was my grandmother's surname."

"Right." I regained my scowl. "Declan Sinclair Mackenzie, this is not your fault." He *still* wouldn't meet my eyes. Oh, that was *it*. I clambered around in the tub, Declan protesting, but I ignored him until I was straddling his hips. I grabbed his face and made him look at me. "Please hear me. You did not hurt me. Eva did."

"But—"

I pressed a kiss to his lips. "No. Put the fault where it lies and let it go."

He traced his fingers down my cheek, my chin, my neck. "Maybe… maybe we should sever the bond."

I stilled. "Why?"

"Then Eva wouldn't go after you again."

Oh, you stupid man. "Declan, if you think that severing the bond will keep me from being at your side, from shielding you from Eva every chance I get, you're high."

He barked a surprised laugh before settling his arms around the small of my back, anchoring me to him. He was looking at me now, his eyes bright, like he couldn't get enough of what he saw. "What did I do to deserve you?"

I ran my fingers over his chest. "Just lucky, I guess."

He smiled, pulling me in to a kiss. "Yes, I am. Very lucky." He let out a long breath. "You scared the shit out of me, Lou."

"Same," I said softly.

He framed my face with his hands. "I love you. I love you so much. I watched you in that hospital bed and that's all I could think about. That I might have lost you, that it was my fault, and I hadn't even told you—" He swallowed hard. "I love you, Lou."

I felt like I'd swallowed several suns, their light burning me from the inside out. Which sounded painful, actually, now that I thought about it. But it wasn't. It felt like joy.

I kissed him then, long and slow. What else could I do? Words didn't seem like enough, though I offered him the only ones I had. "I love you, too."

Declan kissed me back, and it escalated quickly. In two seconds, my arms were wrapped around him, his hands were on my ass, and I was seriously considering another round of verboten bathroom sex. From the feel of things, Declan was thinking about it too, but alas, it was not to be.

Because of course someone knocked on the door. "It's been fifteen minutes," my mom said. "And I'd like to remind you that you were just in a major wreck and both of your mothers are outside. If that's too subtle…"

"It's not!" I yelled. "It's the least subtle!"

Declan rumbled a laugh. "She could have said 'no fucking.'"

"If we don't get out now," I said, reaching for my towel, "that's coming next."

They made up a schedule for who would wake me during the night, but also who would drop food by the house during the next few days. I was not allowed to go to work, which meant neither was Declan. Mama Ami checked over the bond. She couldn't find anything wrong with it, but recommended taking it easy anyway.

Declan tried to call Zoey and Sid. Still no answer. With the wreck, our plan was out the window. There was no way anyone was letting me go anywhere.

"I will call Prisha Bhatt in the morning," Mama Ami said, patting Declan's arm. "She can contact the Portland UTC. Get someone to do a wellness check."

"I know it's not the same as putting eyes on them yourself," I said. "But would that work?"

Declan nodded, putting away his phone. "I just want to know they're okay. I don't care how we do it."

With everything settled, my mom and Mama Ami made their goodbyes after we promised to check in tomorrow morning. Juliet had disappeared sometime during our bath, so we said goodnight to Trick, because he had to work early in the morning. Which just left Vanessa, Bay, and Will, who were staying up to take the first shift.

"We are going to watch terrible movies and then poke you every hour to make sure you're okay," Will informed me.

Bay groaned. "No, for once we're going to watch something good. No giant poorly rendered snakes, sharks in weird places, or zombie anything."

Van, wisely, decided to stay out of the argument, instead rolling her eyes at me.

Will's eyes went wide. "How dare you, sir. How *dare you.*" He threw his shoulders back and lifted his chin. "Those movies bring joy."

"I'm not saying they don't," Bay argued. "I'm just saying tonight I want something with a plot that makes sense."

Will crossed his arms, his fingers tapping on his biceps as he thought. "Fine. *Strictly Ballroom* it is."

"We have watched that movie thirty-seven times," Bay said, flopping onto the couch. He waved his hands at me. "Go to bed, Lou. This is going to take time."

Van curled up on the couch with them and I left them all bickering as I went to bed, Declan's hand in mine.

CHAPTER TWENTY-SEVEN

Declan

My sister didn't call me back or answer my phone. Neither did Sid. The brewery wasn't open yet, but I didn't want to wait. I asked Mama Ami to contact Prisha Bhatt, to see if she could get the Portland UTC to check in on them.

I couldn't sit there waiting, staring at my phone. So I spent the morning after the crash fixing things. I called my insurance, talked to a mechanic, and pampered Lou, who was sore as hell.

I didn't need Juliet or Dr. Yolanda to tell me that I was trying to assuage my guilt. Lou could tell me that the wreck and her injuries weren't my fault, and logically, I understood that. But emotionally? That was coming a little slower. Fuck, I'd been so freaked out I'd almost kept Lou from getting *necessary medical care*. Every time I thought about it, my heart skittered and my palms started to sweat.

That woman had my whole heart. I knew that now. I needed to do what I could to keep her safe. The only thing that had likely saved us from Eva's attack had been the piercings Will had put in. Which meant we couldn't go on like this. I refused to keep putting Lou in danger. But I wasn't sure what I could do, either. Lou wouldn't sever the bond if I was doing it only to keep her safe. That made me feel both cared for and terrified.

The wolf in me was restless, agitated, wanting to claw and bite and chase. Something had come after the woman who was ours, and we needed to protect her. I would leave if I thought that would help, only I didn't know where to go, and even if I did, leaving Lou behind would leave us both vulnerable.

Since I had no good answers, I went and made a second pot of coffee, this one for Bay and Will, who had just gotten up.

"Head forward, Dec," Will said through mouthfuls of cereal. "I want to look at your piercing."

Another wave of guilt crashed through me. I was putting a lot of pressure on new friendships. What if they decided I wasn't worth the effort? I'd just found my pack and—

Will gently pushed my head down with one hand, interrupting my panic spiral. He sighed. "She cracked every single stone, the evil witch." He nudged me into a chair at the table. "You need to sit and calm the fuck down. You're throwing off stress like it's your job."

Bay sat next to Will, sipping his coffee. "Do we need to get my sister in here? Have her put the chill out whammy on you?"

I glared at him. "She needs sleep. If you wake her from her nap, I'll end you."

"You're cute when you're threatening." Bay waved his hand in a circle. "There's a whole badass vibe thing going on."

"It's comments like that," Will said, pointing at him with his spoon, "that make people think we're dating."

Bay looked at him. "I said he was cute, not you."

"I'm aware," Will said, tipping the bowl back to finish the milk. "But you say shit like that about me all the time and then you wonder why people assume we're a couple."

"Nothing wrong with telling another man he's adorable just because you personally aren't into the cock," Bay said. "I'm comfortable in my sexuality." He rested his head in his hand. "Does it bother you?"

"No," Will said. "I think it's nice. Besides, I'm just excited that people think I'm good looking enough to pull you as a boyfriend."

Bay perked up. "Really?"

"Absolutely," Will said, putting his spoon into the now empty bowl. "You're handsome. Clean and fresh. Cuddle-worthy, even."

Bay set down his coffee cup with a thunk. "That is the nicest thing that anyone has ever said to me."

"Do I need to leave?" I asked. "Give you two a moment?"

"No," Will said, getting up to put away his bowl and grab more coffee. "We're good."

"No shame in our love," Bay said, fist-bumping Will. "People should witness its glory."

Will sat a cup of coffee in front of me. "You and Lou need to come into the shop so I can replace your piercings. I assume hers are cracked, too."

I nodded. "Tomorrow? Lou needs to rest."

Will grimaced. "I'd rather not wait. If Eva hits again..."

"She's never hit back-to-back yet," Bay said. "Right?"

"The key part of that sentence is 'yet,'" Lou said, collapsing into the chair next to me with a cup of coffee, her free hand automatically resting on my thigh. My heart filled as I took in the sight of her, but it broke a little, too. She was only sore and a little battered now, but last night I kept waking up in a sweat. I kept hearing her scream in my sleep. She was sound asleep every time I woke up. She hadn't been screaming. It was just me, remembering the wreck.

I had a feeling I'd be reliving that in my nightmares for a long time. "I thought you were going to sleep?"

"I tried to nap. Didn't work. I'm not sure I've ever been this tired." Lou frowned as she carefully rolled her neck. "I thought I'd be more sore, though."

This, at least, was one thing I could be happy about. "It's the bond. You're sharing a little of my healing ability."

"Oooo," Lou said, straightening. "I'm like Wolverine. Quick, let's jump off something and see if I can heal."

"I can make you a cape out of a sheet," Will said. "I'm sure that will help."

My pulse kicked up. "I know you're kidding, but please don't."

Lou sighed. "You never let me have any fun." She sipped her coffee. "We can come in later tonight, Will. I'm supposed to take another bath, and after that I might try to nap again. I'm now allowed to sleep for several hours *in a row*. Just like a real person."

I leaned over and kissed her temple, unable to keep myself from staying in that spot for a minute and breathing her in. I had come so close to losing her.

I must have let some of my feelings boil over, because Lou squeezed my thigh. "I'm okay."

And she was, but for how long?

We took another bath and then I put Lou to bed. I'd wanted to make sure she had a real nap, but we were both restless and I couldn't seem to stop touching her. Reassuring myself that she was okay. I ran my fingers over every inch of skin—claiming every dip and valley. I needed the feel of her in my hands, the taste of her in my mouth. I wanted her scent on my skin.

Lou was equally needy, growing impatient as I mapped her.

Kissing and tasting every inch of someone's body took time, especially since I kept stopping every time she sighed or moaned, concentrating on that spot. It wasn't long until she was pulling at my hair and making threats.

"I swear, Dec, if you don't—"

I cut her off with a kiss, nestling myself over her, enjoying the feel of her body against mine. I grabbed a condom, rolled it on, lost myself in her. Reveled in her. Drunk with the knowledge that she was here, she was safe, and she was mine.

After we were done, Lou fell into a deep sleep nestled in my arms. Lou was not a restful sleeper, tossing and turning half the night. Sometimes it was all I could do to keep my hands on her, but I managed, because sleeping without touching her wasn't an option I was willing to entertain.

For now, her breathing was steady as I ran my hand along the side of her hip. I indulged my love of her curves, touching softly so as not to wake her. Going by the light streaming through the window, it was midafternoon now. Lou would need to get up soon, take her medication. Then we were supposed to text Will. He wasn't working today, so he'd have to meet us at the shop.

I pressed my lips against her temple before slipping out of bed, heading to get a glass of water so Lou could take her medication. Maybe a snack. The entire house was quiet as I padded into the kitchen, making me think no one was home. I grabbed a glass, filling it at the tap, thinking about what Lou might want to eat. What I could bring her to make her wake up with a smile.

I got a little distracted for a second, thinking about several interesting ways I could do that, when I heard a clanging noise, like someone had dropped something. It sounded really close to the house. I froze.

After a second, I turned off the water, waiting and listening.

Silence.

I brought Lou her water, setting it down on her windowsill without waking her. I wanted to crawl back into bed, but I didn't feel comfortable going to sleep before I checked the house. Just in case.

I moved between the rooms, checking windows, locking doors. Everything seemed normal. I heard another noise then—out back by the garbage cans. Not loud, more like a rustling sound. The ferrets. They knew they weren't supposed to go outside, but that didn't mean they wouldn't *go* outside.

I went out the back door, heading to the side of the house where the garbage cans were. One of the cans had been knocked over, some of the recycling spilled on the ground. I picked the mess up quickly, and when I straightened, I realized that one of the kitchen windows was open. Not much. Just a crack, really. An inch, tops. Unease chewed at me.

Had I missed it, or had it been closed before? The frame was up only an inch or so, but both Kodo and Podo were peeking at me through the glass, and it wouldn't take them more than a minute to chew through the screen and wriggle through the gap.

I stepped forward and stopped, catching a scent, something on the shifting breeze that smelled familiar. I lifted my nose, trying to catch it again, but all I got was the reek of garbage and compost.

I was about to go back in the house when something bit into my back. Pain lanced through me, every muscle in my body locking up. I hit the ground, twitching. For endless seconds, my entire existence revolved around the agony.

As quickly as it started, the pain ebbed, but I still couldn't move. It was all I could do to *breathe*.

Boots appeared in my vision. Then a cold prick in my neck.

That's when I placed the smell.

Werewolf.

CHAPTER TWENTY-EIGHT

Lou

The second I woke up, I knew something was wrong. I couldn't feel Declan. Not next to me, and not in my head. He was *gone.*

I panicked, snatching my phone from the bedside table. No calls. I pulled up his number and hit it. It rang. And rang. Voicemail. I tried again. And again.

No answer.

Okay. I took in a deep breath. Panic wouldn't help. I would panic later when everything was fine. For now I would get dressed and search the house.

I was hopping on one leg, trying to pull on my jeans, when Van burst into my room. "Kodo and Podo are gone!"

I stopped, my jeans only half on. "What?"

"They're gone!" She threw her arms out. "I can't feel them. They're not in the house." She crossed her arms, hugging herself. "I should have taken them with me. Now they're out and lost—"

"Declan's gone, too."

Van blinked at me. "What?"

"I can't feel Declan either," I said, pointing at my head, before yanking my jeans on and zipping them up.

"Any chance they decided to run an errand together or something?" Van asked, but I could tell from her tone she already knew the answer.

"Declan wouldn't leave me right now," I told her firmly. "And he wouldn't take the ferrets without letting you know."

Van dug into my drawers, grabbing me a pair of socks and tossing them to me. "What do we do?"

I sat on the bed and pulled on the socks. "When did you last feel the ferrets?"

"At work," Van said, biting her lip. "It's within the radius. I only stopped in for a few hours to cover Noah so he could go to his study group. After, I went to the store to pick up a few things."

Van's familiar bond had a radius of about five miles. Anywhere in that area, she could feel them. So they were at least that far. I had no idea what Declan's and my radius was because we'd never tested it.

I ran a hand over my face. I didn't know what to do.

Van yanked out her phone and started texting.

"Who are you texting?"

"Everyone." She looked up. "Declan's gone. Ferrets are gone. We need a search party. So we're getting the pack together."

That right there was why I loved Van. She just assumed we would all ride to the rescue and she made it happen. "That would be great, but we have no idea where he went."

"True." Van paused, her phone held loosely in her fist as she thought.

I shot up. "The pigeons!" I bolted out of the room, Van at my heels. I snatched my shoes at the door, but didn't bother to put them on. Instead, I ran out the door with them in my hand. I sprinted down to the sidewalk, my hand over my eyes, blocking out the fading afternoon light. Where was a pigeon when you needed one?

Van caught up, her hand holding up half a bagel like it was a holy relic.

"What is that?"

"Bribery."

"I love you." I snatched the bagel from her hand, thrusting it above my head. Tapping my power and sending it out around me, I yelled at every pigeon within shouting distance. *I have half a bagel for the first pigeon who can tell me where my boyfriend went!*

We ended up with fifty pigeons at our feet, not a single one of them helpful.

I got your boyfriend right here! Coo-coo-coo, baby.

Forget him—I'll be your boyfriend, hot stuff.

Take it off!

I glared at the last pigeon. "I will not take it off. But I will turn the hose on you."

Feisty! I like my women with some fight to them.

269

"Pigeons are assholes," I said, glaring at the flock.

"But do they *know* anything," Van asked, her expression tight with worry.

I took out my phone, pulling up a photo of Declan and showing it to the flock. "This is Declan. I need to know what happened to him." I held up the bagel. "If any of you can tell me, these carbs are all yours."

Five minutes later, I was ready to murder every single pigeon on my block. I stood, letting out a breath. "This is useless. Six of them claim he was eaten by cats, eight asked if I had any nude pictures of him, and I'm not telling you what the rest of them said."

Frustration filled me and I wanted to cry. What was I going to do now?'

A car door clanged, and I looked up and saw Trick, Dammit on his shoulder. Trick's face was pale, his eyes wide.

He hustled over to us, scattering some of the less committed pigeons. "Have you heard anything?" He paused, seemingly just noticing the large flock of birds. "Why so many pigeons?"

"I'm trying to get information." I held up the bagel, every beady bird eye following along. "Despite my bounty, they're giving me nothing."

Dammit chirped questioningly at me, so I explained the situation. At first he seemed confused, chirping a question at the pigeons.

Then Dammit understood. The pigeons *knew something*—they had to. They were *pigeons,* the spies of every city. And Dammit adored Declan. Declan was part of his flock.

Part of his flock was missing, possibly hurt, and they had information we needed but *weren't helping.*

Dammit chirped ominously. He pulled his head into his chest, puffing out his body and shaking his feathers. Sparks exploded around him, floating down to the pavement.

The pigeons grew quiet.

"Hey, buddy," Trick said, watching his familiar warily. "You might want to calm down a little…"

Dammit leapt from Trick's shoulder, his fledgling wings spread as he screeched a phoenix hunting cry.

"…or not," Trick said.

Dammit burst into flame, oranges, reds, and blues licking along his wings, his feathers. He dove to the pavement, screeching at the pigeons.

Herding them this way and that, like a pissed-off dragon with a flock of sheep.

Van watched the pigeons scatter, perplexed. "Why don't they fly?"

"They're too scared," I said, watching Dammit swoop down, squawking, chiding, and showering the sidewalk with sparks.

"What is he saying?" Van asked.

"It's not important," Trick said. "Lou, can you wash a bird's mouth out with soap? Is that a thing? Because I have to say, I had no idea the little guy was storing up that much profanity."

Frankly, I was with Dammit, because my patience was gone.

Dammit screeched one last time, long and loud, before landing back on Trick's shoulder pad. He shook himself, settling his feathers.

Before us stood an absolutely quiet, very harassed-looking flock of pigeons. Once more I held up my phone, showing them a photo of Declan. "Who's got information for me?"

Every pigeon began cooing at once.

Thirty minutes later, Will, Bay, and Mama Ami arrived, followed shortly by my mom and a suspiciously large van, so everyone piled in. There were seats left over.

"Buckle up, everyone," my mom yelled from her spot in the driver's seat.

"Mom, why do you have a fifteen-person passenger van?" I picked a seat and buckled up. "Did you steal it?"

"I borrowed it."

I narrowed my eyes at her. "That wasn't a denial."

Someone chuckled, and that's when I noticed that my mom was not alone. A man peered at me from the front passenger seat. I recognized him from Mom's opera photos—Luis Velasquez. "It's a company van."

"Is the company going to mind?" I asked.

He grinned. "It's my company."

"Fair enough." I leaned forward in my seat. "Mom, did you bring a date to the rescue mission?"

"Luis, this is my family. Part of it, anyway. A nice cross-section of the extra for you." She waved a hand in the air. "A sampler, if you will."

Luis leaned further out of the passenger seat and waved at everybody. "Nice to meet you all." He gave us a charming grin, and even from where I was seated, I could tell he was dressed more casually than the photo Mom had showed me.

"Luis, not that you're not a delight and all, but why are you here?" I asked.

He shrugged. "I was with Jory when she got your text. We had plans, but this seems fun, too." His eyes were practically twinkling.

Well, if he thought this was fun, he was going to fit right in. "Welcome, then." I clapped my hands, getting everyone's attention. "Okay, here's what's going on. According to the pigeons, two werewolves tasered Declan and threw him into the back of a van."

"How did they know they were werewolves?" Jory asked.

"They're pigeons, Mom. You can't keep secrets from pigeons." I wiped my palms on my jeans, my hands sweaty. I'd been going on adrenaline so far and it was starting to make me shaky. "The van had lettering on the side—Whittaker Farms. We googled it—it was a small family farm up in Carnation. Doesn't look like they're in business anymore. We don't know for sure that's where they were going, but it's all we got for now. We're at least going to check."

"What if he's not at the farm?" Bay asked.

"Even if he's not, we're hoping he'll be close by. I'd be able to sense him using the bond if we got close." I let out a shaky breath. "If Eva has severed the bond already—because I think we all assume that Angus and Eva are behind Declan's abduction—then we were hoping the ferrets were with him."

I turned to look at Mama Ami. "We need to call the Tribunal," I said. "Right?"

Mama Ami nodded. "And we will—as soon as we leave the city. We want them to know so they can send backup, but we don't want them to stop us."

Mom laughed. "That's the thing I've always loved about you, Ami. You seem so sweet, but it's a ruse, you devil."

"I refuse to let Declan spend more time in Eva's clutches while the UTC argues and mobilizes." Mama Ami shrugged. "Besides, you don't mess with my family." She narrowed her eyes at Luis.

He grinned back at her. Challenge accepted, I guess.

My phone rang before we were out of the city, my screen flashing a number I didn't recognize. I answered it, hoping it was Declan somehow. It wasn't.

"Louise? This is Prisha Bhatt. I've been trying to get ahold of Declan, but he's not answering his phone."

Why was Prisha trying to talk to Declan? So much had gone on that it took me a second to remember that we'd asked her to call the UTC in Portland. "Did you get someone to check in on Zoey and Sid?"

Prisha was silent for a second and I had a sinking feeling that she was unhappy about what she was going to say. "We had someone go to their home address and their work—they're not there. No one has heard from them. They seem to have disappeared."

My heart sank. "Oh no."

"Yes," Prisha said grimly. "From what people at the brewery said, it's very unlike both of them to not show up like this. The UTC in Portland is investigating, but we're worried that the Campbells found them."

At this point, I was fairly sure they had. Which of course I had to tell her. As succinctly as I could, I filled her in on Declan's disappearance and what we'd learned from the pigeons. To no one's surprise at all, she wasn't thrilled with our current choices.

"Turn your car around. I'm calling the authorities. We'll handle it."

I held my phone away from my ear. "I'm sorry," I yelled as Van leaned over to me and started making crackling noises. "I'm going through a tunnel."

"That is absolute bullshit, and you know it!" Prisha yelled back. "Damn it, Louise! You could be sanctioned—"

This time, I made the crackling noises, doing a poor job of mimicking static. "I can't hear you!" I hung up. My phone immediately rang again. It was the same number as before. I silenced it, saving Prisha's number for later. "So what's our plan. Do we have one?"

"It's a little difficult," Bay said, "planning an attack until we know what we're facing."

Everyone started chattering at once, trying to brainstorm ideas, but Bay was right: we had no idea what we were facing. Where was Declan now? What were they doing to him? Was he okay? I hugged myself tight.

"It's okay," Trick said, reaching over so he could give my arm a squeeze. "We'll get there in time. Everything is going to be okay."

"You can't know that." Though I wanted to believe him, anyway. "It's an empty promise." Van squeezed my hand, giving me support.

"Yeah," Will said, handing me a tissue, "but as empty promises go, it's a pretty good one."

CHAPTER TWENTY-NINE

Declan

I woke up in a barn, bound hand and foot, a collar around my neck, the oozing feeling of too much magic used in one place crawling up my skin. Someone had been doing a lot of nasty spell work here. In some magic dense areas—Lou's clinic, for example—I could feel the magic there, but it was like a warm flutter of butterfly wings. Here it crawled along my skin, making me want to scratch until I bled.

All I could do was lie there as my body tried to come back online. I'd made Savannah some homemade Play-Doh last week. She'd laughed as she squished it through her fists. Right now I knew exactly how that Play-Doh felt.

A wave of nausea hit me. From the sedatives or the Taser, I wasn't sure which. I tried closing my eyes and taking slow breaths, but that didn't help, because the barn reeked of dirty straw, rats, and an absolute fuck-ton of were-wolves. It had been a long time, but I recognized some of the scents from my father's old pack.

I was in deep shit.

Pulling up what little energy I had, I tried to shift to wolf and get out of my bonds.

Nothing happened.

I tried again, the wolf inside me yelping.

The collar. Now I really wanted to puke. They'd trussed me up in an inhibitor collar. I wouldn't be able to shift until it was gone. For the first time in my life, I was separated from my wolf. I could hear him, but I couldn't feel him. I broke into a sweat, my stomach heaving.

Lou. I tried reaching for the bond but came up empty. It wasn't gone, but it was like Lou wasn't connected to it. Please let it be because she was too far. That my father's pack took me and let her be. I had to believe that or I would lose it completely.

For now, I was alone in every sense of the word.

Considering how many of my father's wolves I could smell in the barn alone, being by myself wasn't the worst thing. Someone had tossed me on the ground onto a thin layer of dirty straw. Most of the floor was dirt. The barn itself was tall and open, with regularly spaced windows high up letting the moonlight in. There were some stalls in the back still intact, but everything else had been broken down and cleared at some point, leaving a large open space.

In the middle of the dirt floor, paving stones were arranged into a circular fire pit. It was prepped for a fire, wood sticking up above the rim. Most of the magic making my skin crawl was coming from the fire pit. I was willing to bet that if I could see the rim, it would be covered in chalk symbols from whatever spell had been set up.

Besides the moonlight, the only other light source was an old lantern hung up by one of the dilapidated stalls illuminating the wood and paper in the pit. When I thought I could move without vomiting, I arched back and lifted my head off the ground, turning it so I could see what my collar was attached to. A chain went from my neck to one of the pillars supporting the barn roof, each link as large as my fist. I flopped my head back down onto the straw. Well, so far this was going really well.

A shadow moved in the darkness, revealing Kodo and Podo. They were excited, hopping up and down, each coming up to nibble on my hair and beard in greeting. "Holy shit, am I glad to see you guys." The ferrets continued to bounce around, pleased with their cleverness in finding me. "Are you with Van? Lou?" I still couldn't feel the bond, but maybe it had been damaged?

Kodo and Podo chattered apologetically. I couldn't understand them like Van could, but I could listen to their tone. The ferrets were on their own. I remembered seeing them in the window before my attack. Had they stowed away in the van somehow?

The ferrets bounded away from my face, choosing this time to crawl all over me like I was an amusement park. I tried to turn my head and see what they were doing, carefully twisting so I didn't accidentally crush one of them. After a few seconds, I figured it out—one was chewing at the bindings on my hands, the other my feet. "You cunning little bastards. I'm going to get you so many treats." What did Van buy them all the time? Bananas? "Who wants bananas, huh? I will plant you a fucking tree if you help me get out of here."

I felt both of the bindings give just as I heard the unmistakable sounds of footsteps. I hissed a warning at the ferrets, but they had already scampered off, burying themselves in the hay. I turned on my side, making it look like I was still bound while also placing my arms and feet away from the light. If anyone examined me closely, the jig would be up, but hopefully they would just assume all was well.

My stomach dropped as two people entered the barn—the very last people I ever wanted to see again. My dad had aged well, but shifters tended to. He'd put on more muscle since I'd seen him last. Angus had always been tall, with lean muscles on a medium frame. He'd bulked up in prison. His brown hair was short with no sign of gray, his face cleanly shaven.

I looked like my dad and I hated it. The differences were small—the shape of my mouth comes from my mom, as do my ears, which stick out a little. I'm bulkier, or I was before he put on the muscle he had now. Otherwise, we could be photocopies of each other.

Zoey always told me we had different eyes, which I ignored, because they're the exact shape and color as Angus's. It wasn't until she explained that looking into them was different that I understood. When you look into my father's eyes, there's no warmth. No joy. Just an ice-cold dominance that freezes your insides.

Angus stopped a few feet away, his wife, Eva, at his side. Eva was a tiny slip of a thing, her black hair cut short, accentuating her pale skin and big, dark eyes. She looked like an evil Snow White, right down to the blood red of her lips. Putting all the details together, she should have been pretty. But her eyes were like my father's, cold and powerful. The air around her almost crackled with magic.

Angus dropped down to his haunches, reached out and grabbed my hair, drawing my face back and exposing my throat. He examined me critically for a few minutes, making sure to catch my eyes at the end. He sneered, his lip curling back to reveal teeth. "You think you can challenge me now, pup?" When I didn't answer, he let go of my hair in disgust. "Worthless."

Worthless? my wolf chuffed. *But he had to cheat, didn't he?*

My wolf was right—they'd used a stun gun to take me down. My dad hadn't even wielded it himself. As far as my wolf was concerned, my dad was showing his fear. His weakness. He hadn't come at us directly. He *had* cheated. But if I said anything, my dad would only say he was delegating because I wasn't worth his attention. It would also antagonize him, which I didn't want to do yet, so I held my tongue.

My wolf was watching now, though. We'd seen weakness once. Maybe we'd catch it again.

"And yet he caused you a lot of trouble." Eva's voice was sultry, the humor lending a false warmth to it. She had always enjoyed tweaking Angus's tail.

Angus grunted. "Caused you trouble, too."

Eva lifted one shoulder and let it drop, as if she didn't care, but I knew the affectation was false. She wanted to bait my father and pretend indifference, but underneath that burned a very different emotion. Eva would want her pound of flesh, just like Angus. "He surprised me. One time. Won't happen again."

She leaned down like he had and stroked my cheek. Up this close, I could see the fine lines around her eyes and mouth. Minute differences on a face I'd at one time known as well as my own. "A grown man, now."

I didn't like the way she kept petting me, but I held her gaze. Letting her know I wasn't hers. Not anymore. Never again. The wolf was watching, whispering to me. Angus was strong, but we were smarter. Eva was powerful, but we were bigger. They were so much older than the last time I'd seen them. The images in my head shrank down to fit.

I was the one on the ground, the one in the collar, but my wolf told me that if I could get up, get out, we could fight. We had a chance.

I wasn't a child anymore.

"My little wolf." Eva traced her fingers down my chin before digging in hard. "Shall I take you back now, little wolf? Make you mine again?" Her eyes darted over my face. "You look so much like him. All grown up, my little wolf."

She was running her hand down my chest, the act proprietary. Behind her Angus's eyes narrowed, his mouth tightened. My wolf chuckled. *Afraid, old man?* I didn't want his mate, but it looked like maybe she wanted me. The thought made my nausea come back with a vengeance, but that didn't mean I wouldn't play up to Eva if that helped me get free of the collar.

"I can feel the other one in you, did you know that? The usurper. They can't have what's mine." She dug her claws into my chest. "Such an insignificant little mage."

"She's kept you out so far," I said, knowing I should keep my mouth shut but unable to not defend Lou.

Eva's lip curled, a pale imitation of my father's earlier expression. "Far away, when my power was limited by distance. But now?" She walked her fingers up my chest before plunging a hand in my hair, cooing. "Now? I could snap it without even trying."

My wolf tilted his head, considering. We weren't sure we believed Eva, not anymore. Lou had kept her out so far. Then again, our piercings were gone and Lou was nowhere near me. Doubt slithered through me and I ignored it. Maybe if I pushed Eva into action, forcing her to try to snap the bond before she was ready, she'd fail. I'd love to see her fail. I smirked, making my tone as condescending as possible. "Then snap it. Go on."

"Wait," Angus ordered, his words clipped. "We need to wait for the others." His lip curled up, his hands fisted, making his biceps bulge. "I want them to see. They *need* to see." He cracked his neck. There was a desperate edge to his voice I'd never heard before. He hid it well, but my wolf had been watching carefully, pouncing on the detail.

I realized that my dad was *afraid*. Not of me, really, but what I was—a challenge to his authority. To his strength. I'd taken him down before. Not in a fight, but I'd still knocked him from his position of power. He needed to prove he was strong, that he was alpha, and it wouldn't mean a fucking thing if his pack didn't witness it. He really did *need* them to see.

Inside me, my wolf bared his fangs.

Eva's lip pushed out in a pout. "Fine." She took out her phone. "Smile!" After she snapped the picture, she straightened, her fingers flying across the screen. "Technology has changed so much since we've been gone." She waited until her phone chirped. "He got it. Our new friend knows that we're ready to go." Eva put her phone away in her pocket before wrapping her arms around Angus. "What would you like to do now, my love?"

Angus's eyes flashed as he stared down at me. "Maybe it's time for a little reunion while we wait?"

A chill went through me at her words. Who did she have? Zoey and Sid? Lou?

"I'll have Tom bring the others out." She took her phone back out and texted someone, presumably Tom. Then she frowned down at me. "I wish your new little master were here, watching as I tear your bond apart. It would make everything so much better." She sighed wistfully. "Oh well."

Angus wouldn't feel completely in power until he taught me a lesson, and he'd have to do it with an audience. Otherwise, what was the point? But Eva? She'd have been perfectly happy with her revenge alone. Angus needed more. As I watched, he paced, his fingers tapping along his thigh. He was wound up tight, ready to explode.

I wondered what his new pack was like, and I felt a little sorry for them, even if they were partially responsible for what I was going through. A lot of them probably didn't know any better. Alphas were strong, yeah, but it wasn't a power trip, or an empire. A pack was a family. An alpha's strength was in protecting that family, not shoving their noses in the dirt in an act of dominance.

My dad was a shitty alpha. I'd never really understood that until now. Wrong, yes. Depraved, for sure. But when I thought of him, he'd still been this strong, dominant wolf in my mind. My dad wasn't strong. He was *weak*. That was why he'd had to rule as he had.

We are patient hunters, my wolf whispered, his hackles up. *When it's time, we'll take his throat.*

The barn door banged open, and a shifter stomped in, leashes gripped in his fists. One of them connected to a wolf. *Zoey*. The other to a woman. *Sid*. He had them on leashes, like *pets*.

My wolf stilled as rage flooded us both. He was dragging Zoey and Sid. The lantern wasn't throwing off a lot of light, but it was enough for me to look them over. Sid's dark, curly hair was pulled back from her face so I could see the yellowing bruises on her skin. Long rips and streaks of dirt and blood on her clothes told me she'd been wearing them for a while. They'd bound her hands but hadn't done anything else. Sid was human, and therefore not a threat in their minds.

"Hey, Declan. Looking good." Sid's mouth quirked, like she hadn't a care in the world, but I could see her eyes and they shone with anger.

"Thanks," I said. "I've been eating more vegetables."

The man shoved Sid, pushing her down until she sat in the dirt across from me on the other side of the fire pit. Next to her, Zoey padded on silent paws. Without me around, had Eva bonded with Zoey? Was that why Sid was beat up—to make Zoey shift?

It didn't matter why, I decided. It was unforgivable either way. All of it.

"Hey, Zo."

She moved toward me, only to be yanked back. Anger burned through me, a hot flame on dry grass. I had to close my eyes and breathe. They wanted me angry. Angry people made mistakes.

They were succeeding, too. Lou's crash. Her pain. Her screams. Sid's bruised face. My sister on a leash. Rage pulsed in me like a second heartbeat.

I was breathing hard, nostrils flaring. If I hadn't been wearing the collar, I would have shifted.

My father's low chuckle washed over me, and I hated him so much in that moment that I felt the wolf surge forward, only to have the inhibitor collar snap him back into place. He was leashed as surely as my sister and Sid were.

The wolf snapped his jaws, his eyes blazing. He growled, long and low, only to stop abruptly, his head snapping up. His body language changed completely, going from rage to joy, his tongue lolling out in laughter as a cool wave flooded my mind. Before I could wonder what was going on, Lou was there, using our bond to take my anger. Lou had our back, letting us know that no matter how awful Angus and Eva got, I wasn't alone.

Lou was here for me.

Oh shit, Lou was really here for me. She was close. I could feel her. *Fuck.*

I tried to tell her to go, to make her run, but she wasn't listening. Lou was going to save me whether I wanted her to or not. A shiver of fear ran through me, and I knew that Angus could smell it. He wouldn't know what actually caused it, though. Eva would, if she'd been paying attention, but she was too busy gloating over Zoey and Sid.

I had to keep her from examining me too closely. I didn't want her anywhere near Lou. If I could draw Eva and Angus's attention, keep their attacks focused on me, my pack could stay safe.

We are going to have a long talk about how unattractive martyrdom is to me as soon as I've saved your wolfy butt.

Lou, I said, my inner voice desperate, *I need you safe.*

I need you safe, too. The best way to do that is to work together. Distract, but don't let them hurt you.

Okay. I love you.

I felt a rush of love from Lou before our bond went quiet. She was there, but hiding, not wanting to draw Eva's attention. But I knew the truth. Lou was there. I wasn't alone anymore.

I grinned at Angus, showing all of my teeth. A threat. My dad glared back at me, his shoulders bunched like he wanted to pounce.

"Are we doing this anytime tonight?" I sounded downright gleeful.

"In such a rush to die, whelp?" His voice was a deep growl, his wolf close to the surface. He moved around me, still pacing.

"Unlike you, I've got shit to do," I said. "I can't wait all night for you to get your sad excuse of a pack together."

"Light the fire," Angus spat.

Eva started to argue.

He spun on her. "I said light the fucking fire. We've waited long enough."

Eva hesitated. Was she waiting for something besides the pack? She didn't care about that like my father did. Which begged the question—why was she dragging her heels?

A low growl rumbled out of my father's chest, his muscles twitching and straining. Whatever Eva was waiting for, it wasn't as important as keeping Angus happy. "I'll get the matches."

I heard the low rumble of several engines coming closer and my father smiled. "Seems our audience is here, anyway. Your wait's over, pup. Hope you're ready."

CHAPTER THIRTY

Lou

After I confirmed that Declan and the ferrets were all at Whittaker Farms, Luis pulled up a map on his phone and directed my mom to an access road alongside that part of the property. From aerial photos, it looked like there were some trees, but not a lot. Places to stash the van would be limited.

My mom navigated the van down a rutted dirt road, looking for the best area to pull over. We needed to get close to where Declan was being held while staying hidden for as long as possible. There was no way we'd be able to sneak up on a barn full of shapeshifters. All we could manage was delaying our discovery.

As soon as we parked, I peered out through the tinted windows. Because of the windows, the trees, and the low level of light outside, the landscape was mostly a series of blobs. I would have to ask the pigeons for intel. They were strangely invested—partially out of fear that we'd unleash Dammit on them again, but mostly because they felt they were part of our mission now.

So when I asked what they could see, I was flooded with information. There was a beat-up truck and a handful of other vehicles pulled up around the barn. They couldn't see very well into the barn itself—the thin glass was old and dirty, the windows closed. After a good look at one of the windows, I was able to explain to them how to open it. The pigeons were thrilled to discover this new trick and to try their hand at a little breaking and entering.

Glad someone was having a good time. I felt like any second now my heart was going to crawl out of my chest.

I passed on everything the pigeons had told me to our group.

"Vanessa, can you get an accurate head count from the ferrets?" Mama Ami asked, her expression solemn. "We don't want Lou to keep contacting Declan. Eva will be paying attention to him, but so far she hasn't scanned the barn for other creatures." Mama Ami shook her head, disgusted. "Careless, if you ask me."

Van's eyes took on a distant cast as she did as she'd been asked. "About twenty shapeshifters in human form, plus Angus. The ferrets don't have very nice things to say about him. I'm trying to convince them to not bite his delicate bits." Van wrinkled her nose. "Kodo also says there's some kind of nasty spell attached to the fire pit, but it's not one he's seen before."

"Avoid the fire pit," Will said. "Got it."

Vanessa leaned forward in her seat, like she was trying to peer at something far away. "Eva's lighting the fire pit. They're starting some kind of ritual." She tilted her head, like she was listening to a far-off voice. "Angus's pack is clearing a spot for him to fight Declan." She paused. "There's a human, too—a woman. Kodo says she's banged up, but seems okay otherwise. She's clinging to a wolf."

"Sid and Zoey." I'd gotten that much from Declan.

"Will they be on our side?" Trick asked. "Or has Eva done something to Declan's sister?"

"I'll peek." Mama Ami closed her eyes, her hands folded neatly in her lap. Her magic brushed past me, uninterested, subtle like the faintest puff of air against my skin and then gone.

"Right," Bay said. "While my mom does her thing, it's time for me to get to work." He pulled a Sharpie out of his pocket. "It won't be as good as an actual tattoo, but it will help." He started drawing on Trick's face, his movements quick, his lines sharp.

"If you draw a dick, I'm going to be pissed," Trick said, trying to not move his lips.

Bay snorted. "Please. This is serious. We're being serious. But if you don't stop moving, I'll draw a dick on you later."

"I recognize that sigil," Will said helpfully. "It will help you focus and boost your power. So stop wiggling so he can get it right."

I carefully checked my end of the bond, relieved that it was still strong. I suspected Eva would wait until severing it would hurt Declan most—probably mid-dominance fight. She seemed like the type to fight dirty.

Mama Ami's soft chuckle filled the air. "Oh, very clever, little wolf. Eva won't be able to get Declan's sister. She's firmly out of reach." She opened her eyes, a question in them. "Unless you think she might side with her father?"

"No," I said without hesitation. "She's on Declan's side. Are you sure she's safe?"

"Unless they kill the human—which I'm not discounting, from what I know of them."

"Sidney," I repeated. "Her name is Sidney." An unexpected wave of relief hit me, hearing they were okay and out from under Eva's magical influence. Declan had been so worried. Even though the situation was a nightmare, at least they were there, alive and whole. We could fix anything else. We just had to free them first.

No pressure or anything.

Bay had finished drawing on Trick and moved on to Vanessa. The delay made me fidget—Declan was *right there*. He was in danger. It was hard, keeping my anxiety in check. But running in there without every advantage we could scrape up would be beyond careless. We were already outnumbered.

The wait bit at me, but I also knew it was worth it. "Why would they need to kill Sidney?"

"She's mated to the wolf," Mama Ami said, watching Bay as he moved on to Will. "Interesting choice of sigil."

"Are you drawing a dick on *me*?" Will asked. "You should be drawing on the others, anyway. My magic isn't much."

Vanessa reached out to punch his arm, but stopped herself just in time, giving him a gentle pat instead. "I don't want to hear that."

"It's the truth," Will said, trying to not move the muscles in his face. "Mine is more study than innate skill."

"I'm giving you luck," Bay said. "We could all use a little bit of that, couldn't we?"

"Focus, people," I said, exasperated. "Go back, Mama Ami. Zoey and Sid are mated?"

Mama Ami nodded. "I checked. Good, healthy bond, too. I bet Eva is furious." She rubbed her hands in glee, an evil look on her face. I loved her so much.

It was my turn now, and I held still while Bay drew on my cheeks. He moved with a practiced ease, the symbol done in seconds. After me, he drew on his mom and then himself. The second he was done, he licked his palm and smacked it against the sigil on Trick's face. The symbol flared an incandescent purple before the magic settled into the skin, looking like a Sharpie drawing once again.

"Did you have to smack quite so hard?" Trick asked.

Bay grinned. "I can have a little fun, can't I?"

I ignored my brother. Mama Ami's report about Zoey and Sid had given me an idea. Could Declan and I do what they'd done? We hadn't discussed it. It was such a big decision and everything with us had happened so fast. I think we both thought we'd have time for bigger discussions later. But all of a sudden *later* had become *now*.

Would Declan want to? Did *I* want to?

I thought of Declan then. The way he threw himself into everything he did. The care he took with the people around him, especially those smaller and more vulnerable. The way he held me.

And I realized I'd already made this decision. This was the mountain I needed to move for him, and it wouldn't even be a hardship. I'd go at it with a smile on my face and a freaking song in my heart.

I would move the *fuck* out of this mountain.

"I have an idea," I said to our group. "But to do it, we're going to need a distraction—Dammit, how do you feel about working with the pigeons?"

The phoenix chirped low, ruffling his feathers. The pigeons were still on his shit list, but he'd work with them. Excellent. "Here's what I need you to do…"

Declan

My father's pack surrounded us in a rough oval, edgy with anticipation. Growls punctuated the air, every eye on me. They stopped paying attention to Zoey and Sid as soon as they were shunted off to the side, left to huddle close to the fire pit. Eva watched them as she tended the flames, nasty magic pouring off it in a sickening flow.

Tom, the shifter who'd held Zoey and Sid's leashes, leaned into the oval across from me. He drew back and spit, the saliva arcing across several feet to land in the dirt by my head. Nice. Several in the pack laughed, the sound almost as nasty as the magic from Eva's fire.

They were here, and they wanted blood. *My* blood. And they weren't alone in that.

My father bounced on his heels in the middle, warming up. Eager to fight. Buoyant from the adulation of his pack.

Angus stretched out the muscles on his neck. Now that his pack was here, his movements had gone from edgy and desperate to confident. He'd stripped off his shirt as he waited for Tom to free me.

I very carefully did not look over at Sid or Zoey or the two ferrets currently helping them out of their restraints.

The crowd parted, letting Tom into the oval. He strode over to me, his chest puffed out, ready to undo my collar and get this party started. Tom approached me with little care, his attention more on the crowd than me. Either he was cocky or he hadn't noticed that my other restraints were gone yet.

As soon as Tom was close enough, I surged to my feet, grabbing him by the neck. Using his own momentum against him, I tossed Tom against a few of my father's pack, knocking them over. The pack growled, angry, surging forward, but I ignored them, my focus on Angus as I took off my inhibitor collar.

Angus snapped at them to get back, his eyes aglow with anticipation, ready to pound me into the floor. He didn't want them interfering, just witnessing.

I dropped the collar in the dirt where it belonged. "This is your shindig," I said, taking off my shirt. "Human or wolf?"

"Human." He bared his teeth. "I want to hold your heart in my hands, whelp."

I snorted, tossing my shirt away from the crowd. If I had kept it on, he could have used it as a handhold. If I'd left it on the ground, he could have used it as a weapon. I didn't particularly want to be choked by my own shirt. "I didn't know you cared, Dad. You been practicing that line in prison?"

He growled and I gave him an air kiss and a saucy wink, because fuck that guy.

He snarled, leaping forward, fists swinging.

I ducked, dancing out of the way. We circled each other, wary. I'd kept in shape, and before I left Portland, I'd regularly worked out with a reinforced shifter-grade heavy bag at my gym. I hadn't got around to finding one to use in Seattle yet. That wasn't the same as sparring, though. My dad had probably been practicing in prison all he could. When it came to strength and skill, he'd have the edge.

I could fight, but I wasn't a fighter.

Angus rushed me again. I ducked, barely missing a left hook, as his right fist plowed into my ribs. I countered, driving my fist into his gut. He grunted but kept moving. We tussled, and for several heartbeats, we were in a deadlock.

Then he snaked a foot behind me somehow, and I tripped, falling backward.

I hit the ground hard, dust puffing out in a cloud. The taste of blood filled my mouth.

My dad strutted around, amping up the crowd. He was moving easy, his joints liquid. I'd been giving it my all, but my dad had been toying with me so far. It hit me that I could lose this. I could be seconds away from dying in this shitty barn for no good fucking reason. I felt a flare of rage at the absolute pointlessness of this whole thing.

My own father was going to kill me.

And all I wanted to do was hold Lou one more time. Get her to smile for me.

I struggled to breathe, watching as the pack seethed around us. Calling me names. Snarling. Starting to lose control. My father fed their blood lust, finally turning back to me to finish what he'd started. If I wanted to hold Lou again, I'd have to go through Angus first. So fucking be it.

I bared my teeth at him. He mimicked me, shoulders bunched. Ready to strike.

The crowd started murmuring, the mood changing. Faces turning up to the ceiling. As I watched, something white dripped down into the crowd, hitting Tom's face with a splat. He growled, swiping it away with his arm. He looked up at the same moment that more of the white stuff came down, hitting other pack members.

I think Tom and I saw them at the same time—pigeons. The rafters of the barn were full of them. Dozens and dozens of pigeons, and all of them shitting on my father's pack.

I wheezed, trying to breathe and laugh at the same time.

"What the fuck?" Angus hollered, his face red. He was *pissed*. He glared at his pack. They stared at the pigeons.

"Well?" my father said, disgusted. "Do something!"

The pack quieted, for a minute perplexed. Then a few enterprising souls started climbing the support beams. I used the distraction to roll to my feet.

A noise cut through the clamor then, the high, trilling song of a phoenix. Dammit burst through one of the windows, a fireball come to earth. He screeched, pulling up in the air, wings out. Flames licked his sides, his wings. He screamed again, unleashing his pigeon army upon my father's pack.

As one, the birds took flight, dive-bombing the crowd. Harassing the few that tried to climb up to the rafters. I watched, a feeling of joy filling my aching chest.

The barn doors burst open then, the rest of my pack running in, coming to my rescue. I laughed when I suddenly realized there wasn't a single shifter among them. My pack was a motley bunch of mages, elementists, ferrets, and even a baby bird. And that was okay.

They didn't need to be shifters.

They just needed to be mine. Like I needed to be theirs.

I didn't have a chance to bask in the warmth of it all. Angus decided he'd had enough interruptions. He came at me swinging, his face twisted in rage.

I cut away from another punch, but not quite fast enough. His fist clipped my side, sending me spinning. I moved with the motion, ducking down and sweeping out with my leg. He hit the ground, but rolled into the fall, springing to his feet smoothly. Angus brought his arms up, ready to block, but he was eyeing me a little more cautiously now. I must have surprised him.

As we circled each other carefully, chaos reigned, spilling out of the barn. Trick grabbed handfuls of Dammit's flame, arcing it around him like a whip. Sidney, her former leash wrapped around a man's throat as she clung to his back. He shifted to wolf, losing her only to get a face full of Zoey's snarling maw.

Mama Ami, arms wide, sent a flock of pigeons surging toward Eva. They battered her with their wings, scratching her face as she screamed. Bay stood behind his mom, protecting her back, a rusty pitchfork in hand. I couldn't see Lou, Vanessa, or Will, though I knew they were around somewhere.

Again my dad came at me. I dropped down, barely avoiding a right cross that would have hurt, but didn't miss my father's knee. Pain flared as he connected with my ribs. I ignored the pain as I pushed forward, knocking him off me.

Angus circled again, laughing, his stance loose and ready. Confident. He was the stronger wolf here.

Physically. My wolf chuffed. *We are faster. Smarter. Better hunters.*

He had a pack of actual shifters. I had … ferrets.

We can do a lot with ferrets, my wolf reminded me, his voice filled with pride. *Our pack is strong* and *wise. Look how they fight.*

Behind Angus, I watched his pack, half of them shifted to wolf, try to take on mine. It was a full-fledged brawl, but my pack was holding their own, even outnumbered.

I wasn't sure if I could out-punch Angus Campbell, but I was absolutely positive that my pack could outthink him.

Dec?

Relief swamped me at the sound of her voice in my head. *Yeah, sweetheart?*

I don't want to interrupt, Lou said, *but this can't wait.*

I had to split my attention between my father and Lou as she sketched out her plan. I wiped at my forehead, keeping Angus in front of me. My hand came back smeared with blood. I hadn't felt the cut.

What do you think?

I didn't know what I thought. I knew what I felt. Humbled, and a bit in awe. What Lou wanted to do—I wasn't sure I deserved it. But I sure as hell wanted it.

Angus switched directions, circling back toward me. I stalked him, fists up. *Lou—are you sure about this?*

Yes.

Her answer came so fast. Too fast? I wasn't sure she'd thought this through. *There's no backsies on this, Lou.* I danced away as Angus feinted in my direction, playing with me. Tired of the game, I rushed him and we collided, taking the fight back to the ground. *If you're doing this just to save me—I don't want regrets, Lou. I won't be able to stand it.*

Angus elbowed me in the face. I grabbed a fistful of his hair and yanked him back, plunging my fist repeatedly in his face until he jerked out of my grip.

Lou must have glimpsed the fear behind my words, because I was hit then with an emotional wave from her so strong it was practically a typhoon.

Love. Lou loved me with a clarity and certainty that would have brought me to my knees if I wasn't already rolling around on the ground with my father. Lou's love was so strong that it filled me, making me feel light enough to fly.

I grinned right into my father's face, my teeth bloody. Angus looked confused for a moment. Unsure. I didn't care. She loved me and for a split second that was all that I gave a shit about.

I sent her my own wave back, making my intentions crystal clear. What I lacked in elegance, I made up for in brevity. *Mine.* Somewhere inside me my wolf howled in agreement.

Get ready. This might hurt.

A light flared above us, Dammit in all his glory. I bucked my dad off me, climbing to my feet just in time to see Trick's phoenix diving at Eva. It was a distraction, because for a split second, I would be unbonded and vulnerable.

Searing pain sliced through me. Lou had severed the bond, and I felt like I was coming apart at the ligaments. Cold then, freezing, like being dropped into an ice-covered lake, the water so glacial it hurts. Everything in me seized. I staggered from the shock of it, barely able to move away from my father as he rushed me. I swung my fist at the side of his head, connecting. Sharp pain flared through my knuckles. It hurt, but I'd hit his ear, and that would hurt him more.

He wavered, moving unsteadily to the side. I'd rung his bell good.

I took a second to catch my breath, wiping more blood off my forehead before it dripped into my eyes. I felt it then—Lou reaching back out to me, to my wolf. *Mine.* Her voice rang through my head, sweet and true. Pure music.

Yours. Even in my head I sounded smug. Why wouldn't I? Lou was mine and she was glorious.

Ours, my wolf growled, and he sounded pretty fucking smug, too. The magic snapped between us, a new bond forming in the place of the old. Heat chased away the cold, everything inside me reforming in an instant.

Mate. My wolf howled, triumph ringing through his voice. We were safe, now. Eva couldn't touch us. Across from me, Angus gave his head a final shake. I may have rung his bell, but he was back online now.

I'll handle Eva, Lou assured me. *Go kick your dad's ass.*

I tuned everything out then, concentrating only on Angus. My pack was strong. They would give everything to this fight, not because they feared me, like Angus's pack, but because they loved me. And I refused to let them down. They were mine to take care of. That was my privilege and I would honor it.

I threw myself at my father, going on the offensive. Letting my rage power me but not cloud my mind. Because I had to win.

We collided again, hammering at each other with fists, elbows, knees. It wasn't tidy—the kind of fight with a ref and timed rounds. This was a no-holds-barred out-and-out brawl.

My father attempted to put me in a headlock, but I dipped my chin, blocking him from my neck. Before he could try again, I bit down on his arm, tasting blood. He pinched my nose with his free hand, trying to block my airway to make me let go, but I stubbornly held on. It was then that I felt the brush of Eva's mind as she tried to take me, make me hers. Her magic slid right over it, like she was struggling to hold on to a bar of soap in the shower. I felt her wrath and it was sweet.

I spit out Angus's arm, flinging my elbow back until it connected with his face. I heard the crunch of bone. He stumbled, his grip on me loosening. I shoved myself backward, slamming him into one of the wooden support pillars.

I spun, keeping my body low and ready to rush. My father's face and chest were smeared with blood. I didn't think I looked any better. I could still taste the tang of iron from his blood in my mouth.

"We could call this done," I said, my voice a low rumble. "You don't have to die today."

Angus growled, his eyes burning bright with fury. "Pathetic."

At least I'd tried. We tore back into each other. My vision tunneled to the fight. We hit the ground again, and for a second, I had him pinned. I slammed my fist into his face. Again. And again. He was dazed, body limp. My fist was raised for the killing blow. It would be so easy to tear out his throat. Snap his neck. He'd killed, I knew he had. He'd made my life hell.

But still I hesitated. I hated him. I wanted him gone. But I didn't want his blood on my hands. To carry that with me into my future. He'd already taken so much.

My hesitation cost me. My father knocked me off him, into the dirt. He grabbed a handful of dirt, throwing it into my face. My eyes stung. I blinked, trying to get my vision back.

By the time I could see again, Angus had regrouped. He grabbed me by the throat, hauled me off my feet, and slammed me up against the barn door. Somehow, we'd fought away from the original circle. Wood bit into my back as he slammed me again. And again. The back of my skull cracked against the wood. Sparks filled my vision. He got both hands around my throat. I couldn't breathe.

His face was mostly in shadow, the fire pit lighting him from behind. Everything hurt. I clawed at him, trying to get pressure off my throat. He had me pressed tight against the door. I couldn't get the leverage to throw him off me.

"You had me, pup." His lip curled in a sneer. "That's the difference between you and me. It's what makes me an alpha and you a piece of shit. I have the guts to finish it." His teeth flashed white in the darkness, his grin feral.

That would be my last sight. My father would kill me.

He wasn't even hesitating now, he was *savoring*.

I clawed harder, digging at pressure points. He grunted, and his chokehold loosened enough for me to suck in a breath.

"I thought about this a lot in prison, you know." He leaned in so close to whisper it, we were almost touching. "Years of visualization about to come true."

I ignored him. What was he to me? Nothing. But Lou? My pack? They deserved my final thoughts. I sent them love, joy, everything I had in me to tell them how much they meant to me.

My father pulled back his fist.

And then the world exploded as a pickup truck barreled through the barn doors. They splintered, shattering around me, and I flew through the air. I soared toward the fire pit, and there wasn't a damn thing I could do about it. A weight crashed into me from the side and we rolled into a pile of hay. I looked up to discover I was being held by Will. He'd tackled me out of the air and then curled to take the blow. Behind me something crashed.

He smiled. "Lucky catch."

"You really do give the best hugs," I wheezed.

"I do," Will said. "You look like shit, and you're bleeding all over my favorite shirt." Will gently patted my cheek. "But I forgive you."

My father started screaming. Vanessa and Bay appeared above me, hands out to help us up. Once I was on my feet, I saw what would have happened if not for Will's lucky catch. He'd saved me from the bonfire.

No one had saved my father.

He'd hit it square on. Whatever spell Eva had set, it was eating my father alive. The fire turned purple, then a bright, neon blue before a shockwave blew out and knocked us all down like bowling pins.

CHAPTER THIRTY-ONE

Lou

Prisha eventually arrived, tribunal enforcers and medics in tow. There were a lot of flashing lights and yelling, and it took them a while to sort everything out. Someone called my mom and she came out from the van with Luis, bossing everyone about. I really loved my mom. She had absolutely no authority here, but not a single person was arguing with her. Several of us had been wrapped in blankets before being separated so we could be examined by the medics and questioned by Prisha.

I was sitting on the front porch, wrapped in my weird space blanket, drinking water and being lectured extensively by Prisha. It was hard to pay attention to her. I was really tired, and probably a little in shock.

I could also see Declan, Sidney, and Zoey. His sister had shifted back to her human form, and someone had found sweats for her. Declan was a fright—what wasn't covered in dirt was covered in blood, or both. His father's blood streaked down his chin and chest, but he'd waved off the medic in favor of being with his sister and her mate. All three of them were crying, hugging, and laughing. He looked tired, but happy.

Prisha snapped her fingers in front of my face. "You're in so much trouble you're practically drowning, but are you paying attention to me? No." She folded her arms, glaring.

I blinked, bringing my focus back to her. "I'm sorry. I'm not trying to be a jerk. I know I'm in trouble." I decided to be honest with her. It couldn't hurt at this point, could it? I was already fucked. "It's just, look." My hands were full, so I jerked my chin at the mini-reunion.

She turned to see what I was talking about. Her posture loosened.

I took in a deep breath. "When Declan first got here, he could barely talk to his sister. He couldn't talk at all to Sidney. They were trying to fix it, but everything was so broken. I know we fucked up. I know I broke the rules. I'm sure I'll wake up tomorrow and freak out. But it's been a really shitty day, everything hurts, and watching a family come back together like that is making it all worth it."

We quietly watched them for a few minutes. Declan had his arms wrapped around Sidney and Zoey, his eyes closed. He may have looked like an escapee from a post-apocalyptic movie set, but the bone-deep contentment on his face made my heart want to explode.

Prisha pursed her lips at me, then took a look around the rest of the chaos. The tribunal enforcers were gathering up what was left of Angus's new pack, loading them into a van. They weren't fighting. With Angus gone, there didn't seem to be much purpose to it.

Prisha crossed her arms and sighed. "You're so lucky, you know? I've never seen anything like the entrapment spell Eva made. I didn't think I'd ever feel bad for Angus, but what an awful way to go."

"What did the spell do?" I didn't feel any sympathy for Angus, but I was also very aware that spell had almost been Declan's fate.

"As far as we can tell, it took his magic." She shuddered. "Drained every drop. Eva got all of it. That level of magic, she probably didn't even feel her mating bond sever." She scowled. "I'm actually surprised she got away. Someone must have helped her escape. If I'd had that dose, I wouldn't have been able to walk."

"She might have built up a tolerance," I said, internally shuddering at the thought. How many people had Eva tortured in the name of magic over the years?

"Probably." Prisha wrinkled her nose. "Arcanist Woodbridge is beside himself. You should have heard him over the phone. How can someone be so happy over something so awful?"

"It's his super power, I guess."

She snorted. "I'm actually surprised he's not here."

My mom came over then, wrapping her arm around me. "Mage Bhatt, can we finish this tomorrow? My daughter is exhausted."

Prisha rubbed a hand over her eyes, suddenly looking as tired as I felt. "I should lock all of you up for ignoring my orders."

Luis, looking fresh as a daisy compared to the rest of the crowd, came over, his smile wide. He was having a blast. "Mage Bhatt." He held a hand out to her and she shook it. "It's good to see you again."

She lit up, her grin genuine. "Mr. Velasquez, always a pleasure. What are you doing here?"

He flashed her his million-dollar smile. The man was so handsome it should be illegal. Go, Mom. "A date gone slightly haywire." He slipped an arm around my mom's shoulders.

Prisha dropped her hands to her hips. "They got to you." She shook her head. "And you were so reasonable, too. I've seen how this family works, Luis. Good luck."

"Thanks," he said. "Think I could take them all off your hands?"

Prisha sighed. "Fine." She pointed a finger in my face. "Tomorrow. Three o'clock. Uncanny Tribunal Commission. You and this whole sorry lot will be there, or you will not like the consequences."

"We will be there," I said. "Promise."

She walked off, muttering to herself about mages, shifters, and well-earned vacations.

"How do you know Mage Bhatt?" I asked.

Luis's grin turned decidedly sly. "Fundraisers. My company has donated to some of Prisha's pet projects over the years."

"She seems nice," my mom said.

"If she'd said I couldn't leave, you would have put her head on a pike," I said.

"Well, yes, but she didn't, so she gets to be nice."

Luis laughed and kissed her temple. My mom actually blushed. She didn't stand a chance against Luis. He held out a hand and pulled me up. "Gather your troops and let's get you home."

We all piled into the van—including a sleeping Dammit and two very elated ferrets. Luis volunteered to drive so Mom could talk without having to pay attention to the road. I made my way to the back of the van, Declan trailing behind. Zoey and Sid naturally followed Declan, both of them looking ready to collapse.

The rest of the van was noisy—everyone telling my mom their part of the story, but back where we were sitting was quiet, like it had its own little bubble. It didn't take long before Sid flopped over in the seat, her head in Zoey's lap, dead asleep. Zoey was stroking her hair, a soft smile on her face.

Zoey glanced up, catching me watching her. "I didn't have a chance to thank you." Her words were pitched low to not wake Sid. "I'm not sure what would have happened if you hadn't shown up."

"I'm just going to imagine that you would have managed fine without us." I didn't want to think about it otherwise—how close I'd come to losing Declan.

"I still want to thank you," Zoey said, yawning. "Not just for tonight." She brushed another hand through Sid's hair. "I was worried when Declan left for Seattle. He was so hurt." Her fingers hit a tangle, and she began to carefully undo it. "And we hurt, because we knew that we'd caused it, even if we didn't mean to. But now?" Her grin was soft and a little sad. "We'll miss him in Portland, but it won't be as painful. He has all of you. He's not alone."

I reached out, touching her knee. "You and Sidney aren't alone either, you know. And you haven't lost him." I shrugged. "You gained us. Which you may or may not regret in time."

She laughed quietly as she finally pulled the knot apart, tucking that lock back in with the rest of Sid's hair.

"You're always welcome to visit," I offered, and I meant it. Zoey and Sid were vital to Declan, and I wanted to do everything I could to keep that branch intact. They weren't his in the way that me and my roommates were, but they were his nonetheless, and that was important. "And we'll come down there, but you're right. He's family now. We're like one of those mafia families—once you're in, there's no getting out."

I'd spoken the last part loudly enough, and during a lull in the chatter, that Luis heard me. "Should I be worried?" He glanced back at me using the rear-view mirror.

"Yes," I said, "but on the upside, we'll always feed you, and my mom is worth it."

He nodded. "Can't argue with you there."

Once we were home, Mama Ami and my mom checked us over one last time to make sure everyone was fine—and reminded me to take my medicine that the akesoite had prescribed—they finally went home to their own beds and the rest of us were left to sort ourselves out. Showers were embraced. Declan tried to take over the kitchen, but Juliet quite firmly made him grab a seat at the table while she heated up food that Bay's cousins had brought over from the food truck. It was like our battle with Angus and Eva had been catered.

I dug around in our pantry until I found some sunflower seeds, which I sprinkled on the sidewalk for the pigeons. They'd earned it.

I got Sidney and Zoey settled in Declan's room. It wasn't like he was going to sleep there—he hadn't slept in there for weeks. He had the forethought to warn them about early morning ferret visits. Though said ferrets were currently snuggled up to Will, who had passed out on Vanessa's bed.

Bay took the couch after drinking his magic-hangover cocktail. He'd expended a lot of magic on everyone tonight, but I was so grateful he had. Without that extra luck, Will might not have caught Declan and he could have triggered Eva's spell. I brought my brother an extra blanket and tucked him in, kissing him on the forehead. "Love you."

He snorted. "Of course you do." He pulled the blanket up to his cheeks. "Love you too, Sister." His eyes snapped open, and he pulled the blanket down to reveal an evil grin. "Hey, I've got a new brother now."

I heard Declan clear his throat behind me. "I hope that's okay."

"Just treat her right." Bay's grin remained evil. "I won't give you the possible consequences if you don't. I'm just going to let you imagine it."

I snorted. "Be nice."

"I am being nice," Bay offered. "I'm warning him, aren't I?" He laughed at the expression on my face. "Fine, fine. I'll stop. Good night, Lou. Good night, my brother."

"Good night, Bay." I grabbed Declan and dragged him back to the bedroom.

Once we were in there, I shoved him toward the bed, closing the door behind me. He sat down, looking up at me through his lashes. My wolf, playing at submissive. He'd showered, wearing only a pair of pajama pants. He appeared almost...wary. He hadn't reached for me, either.

I walked over, giving in to the need to touch him. He wrapped his arms around me as soon as I climbed into his lap, making me think he'd wanted me there, but he'd been afraid to initiate it. "Have you checked the new bond yet?"

He shook his head, eyes still downcast.

I gently tipped his chin up, needing to see his eyes. "Why not?"

He grimaced, turning away.

Deciding he'd had a tough night, I didn't push him to say it. "You're worried you'll see regrets?"

That got him looking at me again. He dipped his chin down, a barely there nod.

Words would take too long to sink in on this one, so I gently gave a mental tap on our new bond. It felt a lot like our old one, only more. Like we'd been held together by dental floss before and now we had the kind of rope they use on big ships. Sturdy, and made for all weather.

Declan carefully let his mental walls drop. As soon as he did, his shoulders relaxed, and his face lit up. His wolf was there, expression patient. He'd had no doubts in me, at least.

I cupped Declan's face in my hands, letting all of my fears and worries from today rush through me, exorcising them like demons. "I could have lost you."

He tightened his grip on me, pulling me even closer. "But you didn't." He looked up at me, his whole heart in his eyes. "Thank you for coming for me, for fighting for me."

I grinned. "Any time. You know, as long as I don't have other plans."

He growled, tossing me on the bed. I was laughing as he crawled over me, kissing his way up to my face. He kissed me breathless. "I love you."

"That's probably good," I said. "Considering you're stuck with me now."

He pulled something out of the pocket in his sweatpants, and I was surprised to see a tight roll of blue terrycloth washcloth. "But I figured words are easy, so I better show you."

And he did.

Several times.

Declan

This time, when the tribunal met, my family was there. This now included all of Lou's family, Zoey, Sid, and my housemates. My pack. My heart felt full, complete in a way that it never had. They all knew me for who I had been, and who I now was.

But I was still afraid. Not for me, but for Lou. For Mama Ami. For my new pack and what they had to shoulder because of the people I brought into their lives.

Because of me.

Burdens we have chosen to help carry, Lou reminded me, *because we love you. Because many hands can make moving mountains manageable. Because you are worth it. You have never been the burden. Now, please hold my hand so I don't take this opportunity to punch Woodbridge in the eye. I'm having cat thoughts.*

I held her hand. It was my privilege to comfort her. Lou was using humor to mask her own anxiety over the tribunal findings, which I understood. Underneath all that I could feel her firm resolve—even if she lost her license, even if she lost her dream, she'd find a new one.

She squeezed my hand. *I won't lose my dream. Life happens and sometimes we must adapt. I won't pretend that I will be the same happy I might have been if I got it, but I will find a different happy. I promise.*

I kissed her hand. *I love you.*

She smirked at me. *Good.*

I coughed to hide my laugh. Wouldn't want to give the Tribunal the wrong idea, that we weren't taking this seriously.

Once Patrice, Woodbridge, and Prisha were settled into their seats, the tribunal hearing was called into session.

We all gave our testimony. Zoey, halting, her voice cracking, told her side. Mama Ami, her shoulders back, confident, told them about her experiences with us, with our bond. Dr. Kobayashi-Jones and Juliet took the stand and answered the questions I'd given them permission to answer.

Juliet and her father treated each other as strangers.

I expected Woodbridge to be antagonistic as usual, but he was oddly removed from the whole thing. Composed. Before, he'd practically salivated during these meetings, and I definitely thought he'd freak out over Zoey, but he didn't. It was odd, but then, he was a strange man.

When I took the stand, I kept my answers short, clear, and stated in no uncertain terms that I was fine and didn't consider myself a "victim of an unprincipled, unethical animal mage." Their words, not mine.

I might have growled. Okay, I definitely growled. Prisha hid it well, but I saw her lean back before she could stop herself. Though it was her job and she meant well, she was still threatening my mate. My wolf didn't like it and neither did I. Until yesterday, Prisha had only seen the caretaker side of me being an alpha. Once you see a man half naked and covered in blood, it's a little hard to shake the image. I wasn't mad about it, either. I wanted them to remember that side of me. To remember both sides of the alpha.

"I thought you were going to bite her," Lou whispered as I slid back into the seat next to her.

"Naw," I said, putting my hand on her thigh. *Mine.* "Woodbridge, though…" The ferrets had wanted to TP his car. They were very unhappy with him, not only for how he'd treated me, but how he'd treated Van and Juliet. I probably wouldn't do it. I would wait a few weeks. Consider my options. I could be a patient hunter.

Lou held my hand through the proceedings. She kept her chin up, her eyes clear. Only I knew she was shaking inside, fearing the worst. I couldn't control whether the council would take away the possibility of her certification. All I could do was be here to support her no matter what happened.

Our mate is strong, my wolf reminded me. *And when she is not strong, we will be strong for her.*

Sometimes the wolf had a very simple way of looking at things. He never borrowed trouble. But then, simple didn't mean wrong. In this case, he was right.

After hearing all the testimony, the Tribunal left the room to confer.

It was a long forty-five minutes.

And there was nothing I could do except hold Lou's hand. It felt inadequate.

It also felt like a lot.

Finally, the Tribunal filed back in, taking their seats. Prisha took a long sip of water before she addressed the room. "Thank you to everyone who spoke today, for giving us your expertise and opinion. This was a difficult case, and you helped us come to a decision." Prisha didn't look thrilled with the decision, but she wasn't angry. Patrice smiled, which made me relax some. Woodbridge looked like he was irritated that we were all still here, taking up his time.

Maybe instead of TP, I could get the ferrets to hide a dead fish in his office.

Cat thoughts, Lou said, *are so seductive, aren't they?*

I put my arm around her. *Maybe cats are on to something.*

Prisha folded her hands in front of her. "After much discussion, we've decided that Louise Matthews didn't act in a malicious manner. The bond was created as an act of empathy."

I felt relief through our bond as Lou relaxed.

"However." Prisha paused, glaring at the sudden muttering in the room. No one liked a "however." Prisha cleared her throat and spoke louder. "The tribunal feels that, despite good intentions, we must set an example. In no uncertain terms should this type of bonding be encouraged or condoned. With that in mind, the Tribunal has decided that Louise Matthews will undergo three years of probation."

She looked at Lou. "That means I—and other licensed, vetted animal mages—will be routinely assessing your work, checking in, and staying in contact with Dr. Larsen. We will not block you from becoming licensed, but you will have some oversight during your probationary period. Do you understand?"

Lou nodded, squeezing my leg when I wanted to argue. It wasn't fair that she had to do any of this.

Life isn't fair. She's right. They can't let me go without any sort of consequences. Oversight won't hurt me.

That doesn't mean I have to like it.

"Furthermore," Prisha said, "in lieu of a fine, we will accept community service of no less than one hundred hours to be completed within a year from this date." She looked pointedly at Lou. "The place we chose is one that specifically helps injured or damaged familiars and offers resources to their mages who otherwise might not be able to afford it. If you have another place in mind, we can discuss it, but I think you could do some really good work there."

Lou agreed to Prisha's conditions without hesitation. *Just because it's court ordered doesn't change the fact that she's right, I can do a lot of good there.*

Then I will go with you. I wasn't an animal mage, but I'd been a familiar. I knew what it felt like. I could help, too.

Prisha turned her attention to me. "Declan, we would encourage you to continue your meetings with Dr. Kobayashi-Jones and Juliet Woodbridge if you are able to do so. If you want to continue but the sessions are a financial burden, I'm sure Juliet Woodbridge can point you in the direction of additional funding."

I glanced at Juliet and she gave me a thumbs up.

"I will be giving you my card as well," Prisha added. "And the Tribunal encourages you to reach out at any time if you feel the need." She examined the room. "Are there any questions?"

Lou's hand was tight in mine. "Just to be clear—I'm not banned? I can still work with familiars?"

"You're not banned," Patrice said, her smile wide and friendly.

"Yet," Prisha added, but her lips were curled in a faint smile as she said it. "We will be watching you closely. You cannot afford any other infractions."

Lou gave a little salute. "Got it."

Prisha's eyes narrowed.

Lou gave her a cheeky grin.

The animal mage gave up and smiled back. "If there are no other questions, we will call this meeting of the Uncanny Tribunal Commission to a close."

The room erupted. We were overwhelmed then, friends and family laughing, hugging us both. There was so much noise, one of the guards tried to tell us to keep it down. No one listened and he finally gave up. Patrice and Prisha both came out to shake hands and congratulate us. When I tried to find Woodbridge, he was gone, slipping out when no one noticed.

Mama Ami and Jory finally took pity on the guard and corralled us all out of the courtroom, inviting everyone over to a celebration dinner.

Lou and I extricated ourselves quickly, heading to the car—we were ready to say goodbye to the UTC building. We hit traffic, of course, because Seattle breeds traffic even worse than Portland, which was saying something.

Lou huffed a breath. "Get out of my way, you time-wasting bastards."

I popped open Lou's glovebox, pulling out a granola bar and handing it to her.

She blinked at it. "How did you know? One of those mating bond things?"

I unwrapped it for her and held it out so she could take a bite. "I don't need the bond to tell me you're hungry. You barely ate breakfast because you were worried. The traffic delay has made you irritated, which makes it worse."

She took a bite. "When did you sneak snacks into my glovebox?"

"Does it matter?"

"It does not," she mumbled around a mouthful of granola bar. "Sneaky wolf."

Twenty minutes later, Lou managed to find street parking about a block from Mama Ami's house. I unbuckled my seatbelt, moving to grab the door handle, but paused when I noticed Lou hadn't done the same. I sat back, turning to face her. She was looking out at the street, her eyes unfocused.

"What is it?" I brushed a hand along her jaw, giving in and following up the touch with a soft kiss. "Upset about today?"

"No." She leaned into my touch. "I don't like being on probation, but I understand why. I might have been acting in your best interests, but they can't take a soft line with binding shifters. They shouldn't."

"Then what is it?" I nuzzled her neck. She smelled good, and I smiled when I caught my own scent on her skin.

She turned then so we could look at each other. "So much has happened in so little time. A lot of change. It feels like I just brought you here, and now look at us."

"You're worried that with everything happening so fast, one of us will have regrets later."

Her nose scrunched up. "It's going to be really hard to hide things from you, isn't it?"

I nodded slowly, keeping our gazes locked. "But you're welcome to try. The wolf is learning to play. Hide and seek is about his speed."

I checked her through the bond, my touch light. She was uncertain. It made my heart ache. Lou hid it, often behind bluster, but she had a layer of sweetness that reached to her core. I took her chin in my hand. "You have doubts, and if I was doing my job as your mate properly, you'd feel secure. That will take time, because you're stubborn."

She started to argue, but I put my thumb over her mouth. She glared.

"Don't interrupt. It's my turn." I removed my thumb and kissed her, making sure she knew I'd been teasing. She glared again, but I kept going. "I like stubborn and the wolf is patient. We will slowly, thoroughly overwhelm you with so much love that you won't doubt. You're mine, Lou. I'm yours."

I kissed her again, because I could. "And as far as I'm concerned, that's the end of it. We'll fight, we'll argue, and there will be days where you probably want to hex me. But at the end of the day, every day, every week, until months pile into years, you will know that I will never, ever regret choosing you."

Lou sniffed, her eyes full. "Pretty hard to argue when you say stuff like that."

"You can argue if you want to." I brushed a kiss across her cheek. "We have time now, Lou. That's all I'm saying. We'll figure everything else out together as we go."

She kept her eyes wide, trying to not let the tears fall.

"It's okay to cry," I said gently. "I won't tell anyone and ruin your badass image."

"Badasses can cry," she said, sniffing again.

"Yes, they can."

She gave in and closed her eyes, tears going down her cheeks so slowly that I easily caught them with my thumbs and brushed them away. "Your secret is safe with me."

Lou laughed, kissing me because she could, and I let her, trying to hold it all in my mind. It was a memory I'd want to keep for a long time. When life was hard, trying to break me down, I'd want to remember this moment when I felt whole, happy, and loved. I had enough bad memories. I was looking forward to building more good ones with the people I loved most.

EPILOGUE
SIX MONTHS LATER

Lou

The trees outside Wulver Craft Brewery were a riot of color—fall in all of her glory. The day was cold, the sky clear, blue and bright. The kind of day that made you think of hayrides and hot apple cider. I couldn't keep the smile off my face.

My wolf, however, was currently having a minor meltdown.

"What if they changed their mind?" Declan fidgeted. He'd been a ball of fidgets all day. Right now he was shifting his weight back and forth between his feet, and he kept looking up and down the street. "I should have picked them up from the airport."

Tomorrow would be Zoey and Sid's big prewedding dinner, but tonight was family only. Since Declan's fussing had been driving everyone else crazy, I'd dragged him outside to wait, giving the brides-to-be a moment to themselves. Zoey was excited to see the twins, too, but she'd seized some alone time with Sidney with both hands. They wouldn't get much of it until they were off on their honeymoon.

Though the formal dinner wasn't until tomorrow, we'd both dressed up a little. And I have to say, my wolf cleaned up nice. His jeans were new, as was the thin black sweater that hugged his frame. He'd even shaved. It was the first time I'd ever seen all of his face without the beard. He'd told me that he thought it would be easier on the twins—they'd never seen him with a beard, and he wanted to make himself as familiar to them as possible.

I slid my arms around him from behind. "Declan, did you really want your family reunion to happen in the busy airport pickup area?" We'd been emailing the twins for several weeks, setting up their visit, even traded a few phone calls, but this would be the first time he'd seen them in years. He wouldn't want to have that moment in a pickup zone, cars honking at him to move.

"No," he grumbled.

My poor, anxious wolf. "Give them a little space to get their bearings between the flight and now. You can reimburse them for their Uber or whatever if that makes you feel better."

He huffed. "I would give them space."

He would try, but he hadn't seen the twins in a long time. If I wasn't careful, Declan would be glued to them every second of the day.

"Let them ease into things," I said. "Shit like this is awkward."

"I know." He rubbed a hand over mine before turning so he could pull me into his arms.

I touched his face, silky smooth where his beard normally would be.

"You don't like it?"

I dropped my hand, curling it on his chest. "I like your beard. It's soft. But I like this, too." He was handsome with the beard. Without it? He was *devastating*.

A bachelorette party was gathering outside before going into the brewery, all of them glancing over at him covertly, even the bride. I couldn't blame them, really. He was ridiculously handsome. I mumbled a few words, letting go of the spell with a flick of my fingers. Hexing certainly wasn't my specialty, but I could manage it.

I chanced a glance over at the women. One looked over, her cheeks pinked, but she grinned and gave me a thumbs up.

Declan put his face against my neck, laughing. "What did you do?"

"Nothing," I said.

He sighed. "It's on my back, isn't it?"

"I promise that it's not bad."

He pushed us over to a window so he could turn and look at his back. The word "taken" danced along his shoulders, bright as a neon sign. He threw back his head and laughed. "Was that necessary?"

"Yes," I grumbled into his chest. "I'm not proud of myself."

He tipped my chin up. "If I kiss you in front of all of those nice ladies, will you take the hex off?"

I sighed, and cancelled the hex. "No, it's fine. You're not property."

He kissed me anyway and I heard a collective sigh from the bridesmaids. "I don't mind being property," he mumbled into my mouth. "As long as I'm yours."

"Declan…" With his history, I wasn't sure I was comfortable with him labeling himself as property.

He bumped his forehead against mine. "It's not like that. I'm yours, like you're mine. It's like…joint property." He gave me a smug grin. "Give up, Lou. You're mine."

I turned away with a sniff, my nose in the air. "Well, I hope you appreciate what you got. I'm a pretty good catch for someone with a probation officer."

He buried his face in my neck again, his body quaking with laughter. "Well, I'm a hot mess, but I'm your hot mess. So I don't care if you put 'taken' on my back or not."

"You're reinforcing bad behavior," I said. "Specifically mine."

He dropped his hands to my waist. "You're smart. I trust you to make good decisions, even if I reward bad ones."

A silver Toyota pulled into the parking lot, an Uber sticker on the window.

Declan straightened, his face suddenly serious. "I think that's them." He dropped his arms, taking one of my hands so we could stand side by side as we waited to see if this was the right car.

After a few seconds, two people emerged. The boy had the lean, unbalanced look of someone about to hit a growth spurt and fill out. He shoved his hands in his pockets, focused on the driver as he got their bags out of the back of the car. The girl was a few inches shorter, her long auburn hair pulled back in a ponytail. She scanned the front of the building, searching for something.

The girl held out a hand to her brother to get his attention. "Rory. Look." He looked up, both of them staring at Declan. I felt him still, his body stiff. He wanted nothing more than to scoop both of them up, but he was letting them take the lead. True to form, Declan wanted them to be happy so much that he put their needs before his own.

Noise continued around us—people talking, cars going by—but between the four of us, the moment was frozen and quiet.

Rory smiled, the expression as familiar to me as my own. Rory had Declan's smile. Declan returned it, though his was tentative. Then, slowly, like they were skittish creatures who might bolt at any sudden movement, he dropped my hand and raised his arms out.

Tamsin let out a whoop, and then the twins ran forward, colliding with their brother. They didn't say anything for a long time, just held each other while I collected their luggage and gave them a moment to themselves.

When Declan loosened his hold, all of them were a little teary-eyed. He pressed palms to their hair, their cheeks, like he was afraid if he stopped touching them, they'd disappear. "Look at you two. So grown up." He pulled them both back into a hug, quicker this time. "I missed you both so much. Tell me everything. What have you been up to?"

I grabbed his arm. "Probably starving if you keep them out here."

He pulled a face and sighed. "Right, we have all week."

Tamsin held up her phone. "Don't worry, Rory and I made an itinerary. After the wedding, we're going to fit in as many sibling activities as we can."

Rory rolled his eyes, but on him the expression was affectionate. "Tam is convinced we can fit years of bonding into seven days."

She held her phone to her chest, affronted. "Not all of it." She tipped up her chin. "But we can make a good start."

Declan beamed at her. "A good start sounds perfect."

"He doesn't want to admit it, but he's also made a list, so you'll have to do some negotiating." I hugged the twins, kissing them both on the cheek before handing over their bags. "Think of it as good training for when you visit us in Seattle."

"Good to meet you in real life," Tamsin said, slipping an arm through mine. "Email, while a great invention, leaves much to be desired." We walked through the front door, quickly losing the twins to their curiosity of the brewery itself. Wulver Craft had a tasting room and a restaurant, but to get to either, you walked past photos of the brewery's founding.

Long windows also let you look in on the giant metal tanks where the beer was made. Rory and Tamsin were trying to see everything at once.

Declan grabbed my hand, pulling me back. "Thank you."

"For what?"

"If I hadn't gone to Seattle, met you, none of this would have happened."

I shook my head. "You fought to get here, Declan. This is all on you."

"No," he said. "Without you, I wouldn't have been able to fight. Eva would have captured me that first night. You gave me the space to do what needed to be done."

"We make a pretty good team, then," I said.

We reached the double doors that led to a private dining room. Declan and I held back—giving the twins time to greet Zoey and Sid without us.

I used the time to take a better look at the photos. There were so many—from opening day to behind the scene shots of the brewing process. In a few of them, Declan had his arm around Sid.

"Does it bother you?" he murmured. "I know how possessive you are."

I elbowed him, almost dismissing the question as a joke until I realized there was a small part of him really asking, a thread of tension I'd missed.

"Of course not. It's not like I expected you to come fresh out of the box." I tapped one of the photos. "This is your history. Seeing this helps me know you. You're not going back to her, or vice versa, I know that." I examined the next photo, all three of them together, goofy party hats above their equally goofy faces as they celebrated the first anniversary of the brewery. "Really, I'm just kind of grateful. Proud that now I'm part of the story."

That little thread of tension in him dissolved. Declan reached out, rubbing his fingers along the crepe paper framing Zoey and Sid's wedding announcement. "I know we're in no rush, but when the time comes, is this the kind of thing you want? Big wedding, all the bells and whistles?"

"Fuck no," I said, making him laugh at how quickly I'd answered. "Let's elope. I'll take the ring, and definitely the honeymoon. The rest can go hang."

He kissed me. "Your family would be so mad."

I shrugged. "Got to keep them on their toes. What about you?"

He tipped his head. "I've never really thought about it, but as long as I get you out of the deal, I don't really care. Far as I'm concerned, we've said our vows."

"Your vows consisted of 'mine,' if I remember correctly."

"I like to keep it simple. 'Mine' pretty much sums up most vows."

I went to argue, then stopped. "You're right."

"I'll make sure to mark the momentous occasion down on the calendar," he said. He peered at the double doors. "You think they're ready for us?"

"Ready or not, here we come," I said, grabbing his hand, both of us stepping through the doors like we did most things—together.

ACKNOWLEDGMENTS

Every single time I write a book I think about keeping a list going from the start so that I can keep track of all the people who helped me, as I live in constant fear of leaving someone off the list. I get so much help and I'm so grateful, but my memory is a wonky thing made of strainers and duct tape. So if I forgot you, friend, I am truly sorry.

With that in mind, here are all of the people who helped make this story book-shaped.

Many thanks to Rose Lerner for edits that made the book eleventy million times better, and to Kim Runciman, the most patient copy editor on the planet. To Vlad Verano for formatting, design, and general book skull duggery, as well as to Jennifer Zemanek at Seedlings Design Studio for the most adorable cover ever.

Many thanks to the following writer friends for support, suggestions, and so forth: Christina Lauren, Olivia Waite, Molly Harper, Jeanette Battista, Chelsea Mueller, Kristen Simmons, Melissa Marr, Rachel Vincent, Jaye Wells, Ann Aguirre, Kendare Blake, Martha Brockenbrough, Marissa Meyer, Sajni Patel, Gwenda Bond and Ryfie Schafer.

I also want to thank my beta readers who answered various research-y questions: Alethea Allarey, Juliet Swann, Mel Barnes, Jasmine & Mariah from Movies, Shows & Books, as well as Megon Shore and Adam Aman. All mistakes are ultimately mine—they tried their best. Finally, thanks to my family, friends, booksellers, book reviewers, librarians, Team Bog Witch, and everyone on the internet that helps me keep my head up on the bad days. My deepest, squishiest, thanks. (I know, I made it weird.)

LISH McBRIDE is a writer, former bookseller, and amateur goblin living in the PNW. In the crime of the century, she tricked not one but two universities into giving her degrees, ending up with an MFA from the University of New Orleans. (They cannot have it back, either, as she has invoked the ancient law of "no backsies.") When she is not writing or reading, she's usually hanging out with her family and friends…and talking about writing or reading. Her ultimate dream is to have her own castle and one of the libraries with the wheely ladder. You can find her online in all of the usual places under the handle @lishmcbride, usually posting pictures of her dogs.

CPSIA information can be obtained
at www.ICGtesting.com
Printed in the USA
LVHW110339130123
737042LV00001B/171